DRIVEN

DRIVEN

KERENA SWAN

This edition produced in Great Britain in 2022

by Hobeck Books Limited, Unit 14, Sugnall Business Centre, Sugnall, Stafford, Staffordshire, ST21 6NF

www.hobeck.net

Copyright © Kerena Swan 2022

This book is entirely a work of fiction. The names, characters and incidents portrayed in this novel are the work of the author's imagination. Any resemblance to actual persons (living or dead), events or localities is entirely coincidental.

Kerena Swan has asserted her right under the Copyright, Design and Patents Act 1988 to be identified as the author of this work.

All rights reserved. No parts of this book may be used or reproduced by any means, graphic, electronic, or mechanical, including photocopying, recording, taping or by any information storage retrieval system without the written permission of the copyright holder.

A CIP catalogue for this book is available from the British Library.

ISBN 978-1-913-793-95-1 (pbk)

ISBN 978-1-913-793-94-4 (ebook)

Cover design by Jayne Mapp Design

Printed and bound in Great Britain

❀ Created with Vellum

To Mum & Dad,
with all my love
Kerry
(Kerena Swan)

This novel is dedicated to my dad who has recently been diagnosed with Alzheimer's Disease. Thank you, Dad, for fixing my car, decorating my bedroom, laying the carpet and cooking the Christmas dinner. Thank you, Dad, for the wonderful school holidays spent driving around while you sold sliding door gears and I sat in the car with a book waiting for our riverside picnic. Thank you, Dad (and Mum), for encouraging me to buy a house, start a business, take risks and try my best. Thank you for showing me that kindness to others and selflessness are so important. I wouldn't be who or where I am without you both. Dad, I dread the day you don't know who I am but I hope you realise that I will always love you and will do my utmost to bring you happiness. Thank you for my wonderful childhood. no one could wish for better parents.

To Mum + Dad
with all my love
Kerry
(Kerrie Sian)

Are you a thriller seeker?

Hobeck Books is an independent publisher of crime, thrillers and suspense fiction and we have one aim – to bring you the books you want to read.

For more details about our books, our authors and our plans, plus the chance to download free novellas, sign up for our newsletter at **www.hobeck.net**.

You can also find us on Twitter **@hobeckbooks** or on Facebook **www.facebook.com/hobeckbooks10**.

Praise for Driven

'Wow! Really hooked me.'
Lucy Honey

'Another great page turning conundrum from Kerena Swan featuring DI Paton.'
Graham Rolf

'Holy cannoli and swirly macaroni! I cannot believe how much I absolutely adored and loved this book!'
Courtney (Caffeine Read and Repeat)

'A book of multiple threads that tie together in a very satisfying way. It will have you thinking "what if" the whole way through.'
Angela Paull

Chapter 1
9.10AM

Child missing - 10 minutes

Woody and Roach

Woody clutched the car door handle, every muscle tensed as he pressed his foot onto an invisible brake pedal.

Roach looked over at him and grinned. 'What's the matter, Bell-end? I've driven plenty of cars before.'

'Doesn't mean you're any good.' Woody nodded towards the windscreen. 'There's a bend coming up.' *Watch the bloody road, muppet,* he yelled in his head. This countryside was as familiar to him as Dundee and Perth and it had been his suggestion to go this way. Next time he'd insist on driving. He was sure he'd be better than Roach. He knew the basics. After all, he'd driven Grandad's tractor without crashing. He was confident he'd pass his driving test first time when he reached seventeen next year. If he lived that long.

Roach accelerated, laughing as Woody swore, but slowing

the car in time to make the corner. Woody let out a breath. Roach was hyper today. A high from what they'd just done? Or a high from something else?

'I can't believe how easy this was,' Woody said. Perhaps if he got Roach talking, he'd calm down.

'Yeah, silly bitch. Who leaves keys in the ignition?' Roach shook his head.

'Good spot though, mate. How much do you think we'll get for this one?' Woody asked.

'Fiestas are bread and butter. Soon we'll get ourselves some proper jam.'

'I fancy driving a Porsche,' Woody said.

'Not many of those around here. We'll need a few more like this before we get promoted to the good stuff. Left or right?'

'Left here. Don't want to get caught on a main road by one of those cameras that remembers your number plates.'

'I'm not brain-dead.' Roach rolled his eyes and hit the pedal to pull out of another bend.

He might not be brain-dead, but he was hardly Brain of Britain either. The more time Woody spent with him the less respect he had for him. It had been fun to start with. A diversion from the mind-numbing boredom of a life with no purpose. A group of mates he could have a laugh with. An escape from his mum's nagging. It was escalating rapidly out of his control though, and Woody wasn't sure if this was the direction he planned for his life. Not that he had any plans. Or other options really.

He was beginning to relax now they'd left the villages behind and Roach seemed to be handling the car okay so he let his mind drift to thoughts of what he'd spend the money on. He'd bought himself these Nike Run Swift trainers last time, mainly because he liked the name. They looked cool too.

Maybe he'd order some new clothes to impress Courtney or even...

'Where's Mummy?' A small voice from behind froze his heart with horror. He spun around and looked behind him.

'Shit! There's a bloody bairn in the car.'

'Fuck! Didn't you check the back when you got in?'

'Didn't you?' Woody glared at Roach then again at the sleepy child appearing from under his fleece blanket decorated with teddies.

'Mummy's busy,' Roach told the kid.

Busy looking for her car, Woody thought with a pang of guilt. He wasn't cut out for this.

'I want Mummy.'

Woody stared as the small boy's bottom lip quivered, his chubby little hands clutched his blanket and his eyes pooled with tears.

'What do we do now?' Woody asked Roach.

'We'll have to dump him.'

'What? Where?' His mind raced. A shop? A park? No, they couldn't do that. 'He'll be missed soon and reported. It won't be long before the Old Bill is crawling everywhere.' Woody felt sweat prickling in his armpits as the toddler began to wail. 'He looks even younger than my cousin's kid. Two, maybe three.' Woody had to shout to be heard against the racket that filled the car like an air-raid siren. How would he feel if this happened to Tyler?

'Shut that bloody noise up!' Roach yelled, then, setting his jaw tight, he slammed hard on the brakes and swerved onto a patch of grass in front of a five-bar gate. He jumped out of the car and ran around to the rear passenger door. Woody swivelled in his seat and gasped as Roach unclipped the small boy's harness and pulled him from his car seat.

'What are you doing? You can't leave him here.' He looked

around wildly at the hedges and empty fields. This was insane. They were taking enough risks stealing cars but kidnapping a kid and leaving it in the middle of nowhere? Fucking hell. The time they'd serve for this didn't bear thinking about, especially if the kid wandered into the road and got splattered. Woody shuddered and reached for his door handle, but Roach was already coming back.

'Wait there for Mummy,' he yelled over the car roof then he got in and accelerated away.

Woody, already halfway out of the car, scrabbled back in and slammed his door shut. He stared at Roach who was laughing manically. Who was this person? Not the kind he wanted to be mates with after all.

'You shouldn't have done that,' he said. 'We should go back.'

'Yeah,' Roach said. 'He'd fetch a lot more money than the car. Just a shame we don't know anyone who deals in stolen kids.'

'He's so little,' Woody said, 'and it's bloody freezing out there.'

Chapter 2
9.10AM

Child missing – 10 minutes

D I Paton

Detective Inspector Paton rubbed his arms and shivered as he leaned forward to peer through the glass in the front door. A ridged pattern distorted the view of the hall but he could tell there was no movement inside. Damn. Who could he get to look after his son now? Tommy wasn't safe to leave on his own. What a time for Tommy's school to discover asbestos and close for a week. How could he possibly plan for that at such short notice?

Paton looked along the street of neat, white, semi-detached houses in the hope of seeing his neighbours' car, but it wasn't parked nearby so they must have left for work. Was Kirsten home though, and ignoring the door? He knew she'd recently given up her college course, much to the disappointment of her mum and dad. He tried again then, driven more by the cold than a desire to give up, hurried back to his own front door and shut it firmly behind him.

Paton stood for a moment soaking up the warmth and wondering what to do. If he didn't want to irritate his DCI further, then he really must follow up on a lead he'd had. He grabbed his coat from the hooks by the door. 'Tommy, get your coat on, we're going out.'

A scuffle sounded from the lounge then the door flew open. 'Am I going to work with you, Dad?' Tommy's up-tilted almond eyes and flat face, typical of a boy with Down's syndrome, shone with hope.

'Sort of. You'll need to wait in the car while I talk to someone.'

'Is he a suspect? Are you going to arrest him? Wait!' He ran out of the lounge and scampered up the stairs then came down wearing his police helmet and clutching his notebook.

'Got your handcuffs, son?' Paton said with a smile. He knew he shouldn't encourage the lad, should treat him more like the adult that, at sixteen years old, he nearly was, but it was difficult not to take pleasure in Tommy's excitement at his dad's chosen career.

They drove for fifteen minutes along frosted lanes with Tommy chatting constantly, barely pausing for breath as he relayed the car chase and arrest, he'd just watched on television. 'Am I going to Auntie Ursula's today?' he asked.

'She's got toothache. Had to rush to the dentist.'

'I bet she ate too many toffees.'

'Or broke it on her pastry,' Paton said.

Tommy laughed. It was a standing joke in the family that Ursula was a terrible cook. Even Ursula admitted she was no *MasterChef* contestant. Tommy continued to chatter, this time doing his best to describe the plot of the *Death in Paradise* episode he'd seen the day before. Paton felt exhausted by the time they arrived at the breaker's yard on the edge of Crieff. With his wife Wendy being called away to her sick mother in Weymouth, it was going to be a long week. He thought about the rules he was breaking, but surely leaving Tommy in the car for five minutes wouldn't be a problem? He was only going to collect something and ask a few innocuous questions.

As he parked the car a short distance from the breaker's yard, Paton could see a river through the trees and he marvelled for a moment at the beauty of the Scottish countryside.

'Look at that view, Tommy. I never get tired of scenery like this,' he said. It was lovely where they'd lived in Weymouth, England, but not on this scale and even after being in Perthshire for eighteen months it was still a source of wonder.

'Is the burglar's house down there?' Tommy asked, his attention focused instead on the rutted lane to the left.

'It's an office and he's not a burglar.' Paton glanced at his son whose face had fallen with disappointment. 'He's a goodie,' Paton tried to explain. 'I'm just going to ask a few questions because he might help us catch the baddie.' *Or he might be part of an organised crime ring*, Paton thought, *but Tommy doesn't need to know that.*

'Aah. Okay.' Tommy opened his car door.

'I'm sorry, son. You have to wait here. I'll get into trouble if I take you with me. Look. I've brought the iPad so you can watch *Line of Duty*.'

Tommy adjusted his police helmet, took the iPad reluctantly then leaned back in his seat. Paton got out of the car then poked his head in again. 'Don't touch anything. I won't be long.'

He set off along the lane, glancing back to check Tommy was still in the car before turning the bend and scrutinising the yard ahead. Twisted metal and carcasses of what were once someone's pride and joy were stacked haphazardly in teetering towers. A crane was lifting an old blue Nissan into the compactor. A large DO NOT ENTER sign hung on an unlatched gate. Paton paused to watch the car being lowered and crushed then he followed another sign directing him to the office. Tommy would love watching that but safer for him in the car. Paton was glad he was a good boy, well mostly. He could be stubborn with Wendy at times but he wouldn't disobey his dad.

Paton knocked on the rickety office door of the 1970's prefab building and waited. A stout man in his fifties, with a pitted complexion and a poorly fitting tweed jacket, opened the door, an overweight black Labrador at his side. Warm air from the gas heater and the smell of strong coffee drifted out. The man pulled a pack of cigarettes from his pocket, lit one and exhaled. Paton resisted the urge to step away from the stinking smoke expelling through the man's nostrils.

'I called earlier about the electric window motor.'

'BMW Series 4?'

'That's the one,' Paton said.

'Wait here.' The man shuffled off towards the yard followed by the waddling dog then returned shortly afterwards with a lump of something wrapped in newspaper. He unfurled it and showed Paton the small car part. Paton nodded and pulled his wallet from his pocket.

'Got any other spares from this vehicle?' He glanced around at the tumbledown sheds nearby and overgrown hedges bordered with brown weeds, tempted to look around the corner of the prefab at the cars parked in the yard behind. 'Was it involved in an accident?'

'Why do you ask?' The man tensed and narrowed his eyes.

'I need a new tail-light. Women, eh?' Paton grinned but

sent a silent apology to Wendy who was a careful, or if anything, an over-anxious driver.

'Left or right?'

'Left. The gatepost jumped out at her, apparently.' He laughed but the man didn't even smile and Paton sensed tension in the air.

'You'll have to come back later. We haven't finished stripping it down.' The man shifted his gaze sideways and Paton felt his instincts kicking in. He didn't trust this man.

Paton was about to leave when the dog emitted a low growl. The man shoved its rump hard with his knee and the dog stopped but stared fixedly at the side of the building.

'Quiet, Diesel.'

'Do you need my taser, Dad?' Paton flinched as Tommy appeared at his side, holding out an old pricing gun that Muriel in the general stores had given him.

'Tommy, I told you to wait in the car.' Bloody hell, not now.

'Is this your son? Hello, Tommy, nice to meet you. Are you a policeman?' He looked pointedly at Tommy's police helmet.

Tommy gave him an unfriendly stare. 'It's not nice to hurt your dog, is it, Dad? You can get arrested for that.'

'Tommy's passionate about detective TV dramas,' Paton explained, warming to the man a little now that he'd shown Tommy a measure of respect and kindness.

'Not *The Sweeney*, I hope. That always gives us breakers a bad press.'

'That's his favourite,' Paton said, hoping Tommy wouldn't say something inappropriate. 'Come on, Tommy.' He turned towards the lane.

'Do you know any other policemen, Tommy, or are you the only one around here?' The man asked.

Paton stiffened. 'Time to go, Tommy.' Paton silently willed him not to say anything.

'My Dad arrested someone once because they hurt their cat.' Tommy looked with pride at his father then glared at the man.

Paton's heart dropped like a bungee jumper. Now his cover was blown.

'And is Dad on duty now?' the man asked.

'Yes. I'm helping him with his enquiries.' Tommy puffed up his chest, put his thumbs in his non-existent braces and stood tall.

The man looked at Paton. 'I didn't realise you police officers were allowed to take your bairns to work with you.' The man's mouth moved into a smile but his eyes remained hard. 'Funny, I can't imagine your chief inspector allowing you to have the lad out with you.'

Paton refused to acknowledge the threat. He took Tommy's arm and pulled him back to the car.

'I didn't like that man, Dad. I think you're wrong. He's got a baddie face.'

'You could be right, Tommy.' Paton would call in the information and would have to admit to his boss about taking Tommy with him on the visit. The DCI wouldn't be pleased, but if he found out about Tommy from someone else it could make the situation much worse. The man Paton had just met seemed the type to use the situation to his advantage. As they drove away, he suddenly felt overwhelmed with the weight of his responsibilities and sighed deeply.

'You should have stayed in the car like I told you. It's dangerous there.'

'Why? Has he got a gun?'

'I meant the cars piled on top of each other.'

'Did you sell my Spiderman rucksack?'

'No. What made you think of that?' Paton marvelled at his son's ability to change the subject.

'I saw it in one of the car windows when I was looking for you. It was on the floor in the back.'

Paton felt a twinge of excitement. At the first opportunity he pulled into a layby and called DC Cheryl Campbell.

'Cheryl, the stolen BMW. What belongings were in the car again?'

Chapter 3
9.12AM

Child missing - 12 minutes

Melanie Cameron

Melanie fiddled with her earring, waiting for a break in Jemma's monologue to shoehorn a word in. She opened her mouth to speak but one sentence segued into another, with Jemma barely drawing breath. Yes, Melanie was interested in the nursery Christmas party arrangements but now was not the time.

'So, I thought we could do a little nativity scene and—'

'Look, I have to go,' Melanie finally interrupted. 'Louie might have woken up. He's outside. He had a bad night so it was a shame to wake him and bring him in.'

'Outside?' Jemma looked startled. 'You should have said.'

Melanie pressed her lips together then hurried towards the door. 'I'll catch up with you later,' she called over her shoulder.

She looked quickly at her older son Noah who was happily playing with the Lego. Thankfully, he hadn't noticed her heading towards the exit. She left the village hall through the kitchen and out towards the car park at the rear then stopped abruptly on the doorstep, unable to comprehend what she was seeing. Or rather, not seeing. Her new blue Fiesta wasn't where she'd left it. Admittedly she'd parked it in an inconvenient place, a couple of metres from the kitchen door, but she'd only planned to be away for a minute or two. Maybe someone had moved it. She'd left the keys in it after all.

Melanie scurried around the small car park, looking behind a huge 4x4, her fear building like a migraine. Her car wasn't there. Ice crystallised in her veins and the backs of her hands prickled as realisation broke through the denial playing in her head. *No, no. Surely not.* This was a safe neighbourhood. There weren't robberies in Burrelton. Everyone knew each other here. She turned back to the village hall and stumbled into the kitchen where one of the mums was pouring orange squash into small plastic beakers.

'My car...' She couldn't get her words out properly. 'Louie.'

It was as though she were retreating into a dark tunnel. The room became a pinprick of light, and she felt miles away. The woman turned to stare at her.

'Are you okay, Mel? You've gone a funny colour.'

Melanie grabbed a chair and sat down. 'Please, ask everyone if they've moved my car. Oh, God! What if it's been stolen with Louie inside?'

'Louie? Good grief! I'm sure there's a simple explanation. Wait there while I ask the others. Put your head between your knees. You look like you might faint.'

Melanie hung her head down low, willing strength back into her limbs so she could find her boy. Within a minute several women had crowded into the kitchen and two ran through to the car park. Melanie looked from one face to another, hoping for a smile and an explanation but all she saw was fear. Raw, naked fear.

'Call the police,' she whispered as the blood left her brain and she slipped off her chair.

Chapter 4
9.50 AM

Child missing - 50 minutes

DI Paton

'Can we go bowling soon, Dad?' Tommy hung his coat on the hook by the door and went through to the kitchen.

'I'm sorry, lad. I need to work today. I'm waiting for Auntie Ursula to get back so she can look after you.' Paton needed to speak to his DCI to see if there was enough evidence of car theft at the breaker's yard to justify a search warrant.

'Can we have a snack first?'

'It's a bit early. Surely Auntie Ursula can make a decent sandwich?' Paton said.

'I'm hungry now.'

Tommy was always hungry. Paton would need to find something that didn't contain too many calories as Tommy was already verging on overweight. He opened the fridge and peered inside.

'You only had breakfast two hours ago. How about a ham salad?'

'How about cheese on toast?' Tommy grinned, knowing full well this was his dad's favourite.

'I don't—'

Paton's phone rang.

'Boss, you need to get to Burrelton village hall.' Cheryl's voice was tight with tension. 'Another stolen car.'

'I might not get there straightaway...'

'You don't understand, Boss. This time there's a small kid in the back. They've taken the bairn.'

Paton's stomach churned with horror. 'I'll be there soon,' he said. He ended the call and rang his sister. Hopefully, she'd be back from the dentist by now.

'Sorry, Dave. I've got a puncture. I'm waiting for the breakdown service. I'll be another hour or two at least.' Ursula's voice was sincere with apology.

Paton said he'd call her later then rushed out of the front door as he called to Tommy to wait in the house. He knocked heavily on the neighbour's door and moved from foot to foot with impatience. *Open the bloody door!*

Kirsten answered on his second knock and leaned against the frame while he explained his situation.

'I'm busy today,' she said, barely looking up from her phone. She didn't look busy. In fact, he was almost certain she was playing Candy Crush – he recognised the annoying music.

He was about to say more when his phone rang again. The screen showed it was the DCI calling. 'Can you give me a sec?' Paton asked Kirsten.

She nodded but said she didn't want the house to get cold so closed the door on him. Relieved to see that she was waiting behind it, Paton accepted the call. 'Sir?'

Are you on your way, Dave?'

'Be there soon, sir.' If he persuaded Kirsten to change her mind, that was. He knocked again and she opened the door still looking at her phone. 'I'll pay you ten pounds an hour,' he offered in desperation.

Attention caught, she put her phone in her pocket and smiled.

'I'm seeing Blake today but I could do the rest of the week. Would that help?'

It would, though it didn't solve today's problem. 'Great. You need to be at our place for 8am. I'll call round later to speak to your parents and give you a key.'

Her eyes widened at the early start but all she said was, 'Cool', as she closed the door.

Ten pounds an hour was going to put a hole in the family budget but Paton couldn't see any alternative. As for today he'd throw a snack together then he'd have to leave Tommy on his own for an hour or so until Ursula was back. Surely he'd be safe in front of the television?

Chapter 5
9.50AM

Child missing - 50 minutes

Louie

Rubbing blankie on his nose felt nice and soft and it smelled of home. Louie stared along the road to where Mummy's car had disappeared and wondered when she would fetch him. The grass was bumpy under his yellow dinosaur wellies and he wobbled as he tried to move so he stood still. He shivered and was surprised how cold blankie felt. Maybe he should keep it warm inside his jacket. He pushed it down the neck of his bright blue coat, until he had a fat lump of fleece over his chest, and felt a bit better.

Mummy was taking a very, very long time. Louie turned on the spot to look about him. He usually liked fields, especially when Mummy, Daddy and Noah were with him on long walks. He wished they were here now. He didn't like being on his own. Why had those big boys left him here and where was

Mummy? The wind bit his nose and his hands hurt. Louie struggled to put them in his pockets and began to cry. Big fat tears rolled down his cheeks then dripped off his chin. He cried noisily for what felt like ages but no one came to ask what the matter was so he cried even louder.

All this effort was making Louie feel tired so he tried to stop, but it was hard because his body shook every time he breathed. Then a big black bird squawked in the tree above his head and he ducked. What if it pecked his eyes out? Noah had told him a scary Hallowe'en story about birds that flew at little children. Louie felt his face scrunch up and his chest jump as he started to cry again. He didn't want to be eaten by birds.

Maybe he should get away from the tree. Louie wiped his wet face on his sleeve then stumbled across the patch of long grass towards a big metal gate. Could he climb over it? He didn't think so but he needed to get away from the nasty bird. The gate was higher than his climbing frame at home and his legs weren't long enough to reach from one bar to the next. He stood wondering what to do when he spotted a huge puddle in the field beyond. It was white and crusty around the edges but the middle was shiny and wet.

Maybe he could climb through the bars and play in the puddle while he waited for Mummy. She wouldn't mind. After all, he did have his dinosaur wellies on and this was the best puddle he'd ever seen.

He bent forward, put his head through the gap then lifted the rest of him over the bar. The ice made a lovely cracking sound when he walked on it so he stomped around the edge of the huge puddle until it was all broken. Next, he took careful steps into the middle, making sure it wasn't too deep like Daddy had shown him. The muddy water covered his feet and halfway up his wellies, making his toes cold. His hands were hurting again too. He pushed them back into his pockets and trudged up and down, watching the swirls of mud that looked like Mummy's chocolate cake mix.

Wait until he told Noah. He'd be sad he'd missed such a big puddle. Louie was glad. Noah was always doing more fun things than him – going to playgroup, playing round friends' houses, and going to lots of parties. When Louie was three, he'd go to playgroup too. Mummy said his birthday was soon. Thinking about his party made him happy – the bright balloons and colourful presents, friends to play with and games. He stamped a foot and grinned as a spray of water flew up in the air and left mud spots on his coat. Stamp! Stamp! Stamp!

A car sounded in the distance and Louie stood still, listening hard. Was that Mummy coming for him? Those scary boys had her car but perhaps she'd borrowed someone else's. The sound got nearer so he ran towards the gate to wave to her. As he hurried along, his feet slipped and he fell hard onto the ground, one cheek on the pointy, sharp ice and his nose and mouth in the muddy water.

Chapter 6
10AM

Child missing - 1 hour

Woody and Roach

'I told you it was that turning. I know this area.' Why wouldn't Roach bloody listen, arrogant twat? Woody was desperate to arrive at the meeting point. Not only had Roach refused to go back for the kid but his driving had worsened to the point that Woody just wanted out. Out of the car, out of this nightmare and out of this crazy friendship. He clutched the door handle as the car bounced down another pothole. 'You need to turn around. The barn's a mile back.'

'Shut up, you dick.' Roach wrenched the wheel to the right and the car jerked violently, causing Woody to bash his head on the window. 'Think you're so bloody clever. Too far up your own arse. You won't last five minutes in this trade if you don't shut that fat mouth of yours.'

Woody stared out of the window, anger building in his

chest as he bounced around in his seat. The car would be knackered before they delivered it at this rate. He wanted to snatch the wheel out of Roach's hands but knew that would be too risky. The track they'd turned onto was getting narrower and soon Roach was forced to slow down. When it ended at a gate leading to fields full of sheep Woody wanted to laugh out loud. Not a good idea though as Roach was gripping the wheel and swearing profusely. He'd likely punch Woody in the head if he said anything.

Woody stared at the sheep and the land stretching ahead of them. He'd checked the location on Street View on the Google Maps app before he left home. Grandad's farm was only a couple of miles away and he knew the area fairly well from long summer holidays spent roaming the woods and fields and cycling along country lanes. Would it be worth jumping out here and setting off across the fields on foot? He might get to the barns first as Roach may not find the track on his own and it would serve Roach right.

Perhaps it was best to go along with the plan until he got home though, and could call the police. But could he do that? His life on the estate would be hell if he dobbed on Roach because they'd all know it was Woody. Roach would set The Dogs on him. Woody shuddered as he remembered the state of a local guy after the two heavies in the gang had 'taught him a lesson'.

Woody's stomach churned. He wished he could go back in a time machine. This time he'd walk past the boys in the park who were laughing, drinking from cans and smoking joints. This time he'd refuse their offer to join them, say he had to be somewhere, and choose a different route home. He'd been pissed off at his mum though, constantly whingeing about his dad not paying any maintenance, what long hours she worked to keep her son in clothes and food. It wasn't his fault he was always bloody hungry and the clothes she bought were shit anyway. He hadn't asked to be born into his useless family.

The boys in the park hadn't taken much notice of him to start with but when he'd thrown their football back over the fence, they'd invited him to play. He liked a kick-around and was pleased when they'd asked him to make up a side. Moving to Perth and leaving his old friends behind had been tough. Woody had no say in where he lived and it made him angry that his dad could piss off with his new fancy bint. Woody hadn't known what his new mates did for money. Not straight away.

Roach was turning the car around now, but it wasn't easy in the narrow lane. The hedges scraped the bonnet then the bumper as he inched it back and forth. Woody knew he needed to jump out now if he was going but something held him back. If Roach delivered the car to Spanner, he'd get the full reward and all Woody would be left with was a guilty conscience. Spanner wouldn't care about the kid. He was a ruthless bastard and Woody couldn't risk getting on the wrong side of him. Woody's mum was irritating as hell, but he didn't want Spanner threatening her safety.

Once they were back on the road Roach put his foot down. 'The turning is half a mile on the right,' Woody said. 'Slow down or you'll miss it.'

Roach scowled but did as Woody said and soon they were pulling up outside an old hay barn surrounded by smaller sheds. A huge man with a short neck as wide as his head, wearing loose clothes and bright, white trainers approached them, carefully avoiding patches of mud. They climbed out of the car.

'Nice little run-around, lads, and nearly new. Well done. Any problems? Anyone spot you?'

A sharp pain shot up the back of Woody's arm. He bit

down on a yelp and stepped away from Roach. It didn't do to show weakness. It was one hell of a pinch though, and Woody knew he'd have a bruise tomorrow.

'Definitely not, Spanner. There was no one around.' Roach said.

Woody wanted to wipe the smug smile from his face. *No, just a poor bairn who we've dumped by the roadside.* He looked at his watch trying to work out how long the child had been out in the cold. He needed to get away from these two so he could decide what to do.

'Need to be somewhere?' Spanner looked at Woody with one eyebrow raised.

'Just getting hungry. I missed breakfast.'

Spanner walked slowly around the car then peered in the back window. 'A car seat? I hope there isn't a kid in the boot.' He threw his head back and laughed showing a gob full of fillings. 'Right then. Let's switch these plates and get it in the barn. I'll deliver it to the chop shop next week when the dust settles. Want a lift back to Perth?'

Of course we fucking do, thought Woody. *We're in the middle of nowhere and it's cold enough to freeze your nuts off.* Was the kid all right? Was he still waiting by the road shivering in his little blue coat, or had someone found him?

Woody was distracted from his worry by Spanner reaching into his back pocket, pulling a fat wad of notes out and peeling some off. 'Before I forget, £300 each, boys. Not bad for a morning's work, eh?'

Woody stuffed the notes into the front of his jeans feeling a thrill at what he could buy with the money. He'd get Courtney that gold-plated bracelet she'd admired in the Argos catalogue and he'd treat himself to a warmer jacket and a new pair of jeans. He ought to get his mum something for Christmas too. She'd ask where he got the money from – she always did – but he'd tell her he'd been doing odd jobs for people on the estate. It wasn't exactly a lie, after all, and she'd be relieved she didn't have to find the money to buy his new clothes.

Spanner checked the boot but only found re-usable shopping bags. He changed the plates on the car and reversed it into a smaller barn as the two boys stood watching, rubbing their arms in the cold, then he closed and padlocked the door.

'We'll try the other side of Perth on Friday. We don't want to over-fish the area, do we?'

Chapter 7
10.10AM

Child missing - 1 hour 10 minutes

DI Paton

It was clear from the white faces and the fact that everyone was speaking at once that emotions were running high in Burrelton village hall. Paton looked around the sparsely-furnished kitchen, noticing a woman huddled on a chair with a circle of friends around her.

He turned to his DC, Cheryl Campbell. 'We need to give the mother some space. Can you get these women back to what they're supposed to be doing?' He looked through the open doorway to the room full of noisy children running around and squealing as they grabbed at each other's clothing.

Cheryl had a knack when it came to dealing with distressed people, especially families, and was often called upon to be the Family Liaison Officer. She approached the nearest pair of women and nodded towards the children. They hurried away to restore order in the hall. Within a minute the kitchen was clear apart from the distraught mother and a friend who was perched next to her, ineffectually holding her hand.

Paton pulled up a chair. 'We need to ask you some questions, Mrs Cameron.'

'Please just call me Melanie. I can't deal with any formality. It makes everything so much scarier.'

'I think it'll be best if we take you home, Melanie. It'll be quieter.' As he said it, Paton cursed himself. What a bloody stupid thing to say. It certainly would be quiet without a small child tearing around.

Melanie frowned at him. 'I need to stay here though. They might bring him back soon.' She looked searchingly into Paton's face for reassurance.

'Some of the team will stay here so they'll let us know if there's news.'

'What about Noah?' Melanie asked, glancing towards the hall full of children.

'I can take Noah back to my place for a while after playgroup,' the friend said. 'I'm sure he'll be happy enough with Poppy for the afternoon. As long as he doesn't mind dressing up as a princess!' The woman holding Melanie's hand gave a forced laugh and was rewarded with a faltering smile.

'I'm Jemma,' she said, looking up at Paton. 'It's all my fault. I kept Mel talking when she wanted to check on Louie.'

Melanie pulled her hand away. 'It's not your fault, Jemma,' she said. She stood on shaky legs and followed Cheryl towards Paton's vehicle parked on the road.

'I'll catch you up in a minute,' Paton called to Cheryl then addressed the DCs standing by the door.

'Tony, I want you to take witness statements here then knock on some doors along possible exit routes from the village. There are several houses so I'll see if I can get someone to help you. A local may have seen the car being driven erratically or at speed. You know the registration, don't you? Maybe bring up a photo of a car of that age and colour on your phone to jog their memories. The Scenes of Crime Officers are on their way to check for any footprints and look for any other evidence in the area. Colin, you need to tape off the car park and approach road. We don't want anyone spoiling potential evidence.'

'Do we need a crime scene log, Boss?'

'This is a potential crime scene, Colin, so yes please.' Paton nodded his thanks then strode out to his car with his phone to his ear.

'I need a check on the ANPR cameras within a twenty-mile vicinity of Burrelton,' he told DC Douglas Jackson at the station. 'I'm not sure if there are any cameras on these A-roads but the vehicle might be detected at the main junctions. I just hope whoever took the car isn't clever enough to stick to B-roads only.' He glanced around at the scattering of houses with fields all around the village perimeter. 'And there are a lot of those around here.' He thanked Douglas then got into the driver's seat.

'Have you contacted your son's father?' he asked Melanie as he put the car into gear.

'I've tried calling but he hasn't picked up yet. He might be out of signal range. It dips in and out around here.'

Paton saw her pinched face in the rear-view mirror. Melanie's hand shook as she wiped hair from her wet eyes. She dried her face roughly with the back of her hand and took a deep breath. 'It's all my fault. He's going to be so angry.'

'I should think blaming you will be the last thing on his mind,' Cheryl said. 'Let's get you home then you can tell us exactly what happened. We'll keep calling your husband. Is there any chance he might have taken your car?'

'He's got a company car. He's in Perth today visiting the

pharmacies. He's an account manager for a pharmaceutical company.'

Paton followed Melanie's directions and parked on her driveway. Once they were inside the neat, detached house, Cheryl went to the kitchen to make everyone tea and Paton tried calling the husband again. Melanie sat staring at him, her eyes dark hollows in her white face.

'Will you find Louie soon?' she whispered. 'He'll wonder where I am.'

'We're doing everything possible, Melanie. Now tell me from the beginning exactly what happened.'

'I... I think I'm going to be sick.' Melanie ran to the downstairs cloakroom and returned, pale-faced, a few minutes later. She perched on the edge of the sofa and clasped her hands tightly in her lap as she told him in detail what had happened.

Paton did his best not to judge Melanie when she revealed she'd left the keys in the ignition. Was the thief an opportunist who decided on the spur of the moment to take the vehicle? Or was it the little boy he or she wanted? A chill ran across Paton's skin. He'd heard of child trafficking but not around here. And traffickers were far less likely to be opportunists. Car theft then. Probably a teenager fancying a spin.

Cheryl joined them and placed a tray on the coffee table. 'Can you manage a cup of tea with sugar in? It might help with the shock.'

Melanie nodded and Cheryl spooned a heaped sugar in and handed her a mug.

Paton pressed on with the questioning. 'You say Louie was asleep when you arrived at—'

A key turned in the front door and a voice called from the hallway. 'I left my laptop charger behind and no one else's fitted. Had to come all the way back from Perth. Bloody nuisance.' A tall, smartly dressed man appeared in the hall doorway. He looked from his wife to the strangers in the room. 'I've just seen missed calls from you.' His eyes grew wary. 'Is something up?'

As Paton explained that Melanie's car had been stolen with Louie inside it, Mr. Cameron swayed slightly.

'Please, sit down,' Paton urged.

'I'd prefer to stand, thanks.'

Paton was surprised that Mr. Cameron didn't go to his wife to offer comfort, as she was clearly in distress. Was it because the shock was too much for him or was there little love and affection between them? Paton answered the man's quick-fire questions and tried to reassure both parents that the police were doing all they could to find Louie. 'We think there might have been an opportunistic car thief.'

'Why do you say that?' Mr. Cameron demanded.

'I'm so sorry, Simon.' Melanie put her face in her hands and spoke through her tears to explain about leaving Louie alone.

'You did what?' His voice rose to a shout and he began to pace the room, hands balled into his hair. 'You stupid woman! You might as well have put a neon sign on the roof saying, 'Take me, I'm yours.'

'Getting angry and blaming your wife won't help anything,' Cheryl said in a quiet but firm voice. 'You'd be surprised how many people leave their keys in the car when they think they'll only be a minute.'

One family left their car on the drive with the engine running to de-ice it and thieves took it with their two sons inside, Paton wanted to add, but this would be insensitive so he kept quiet.

'I don't give a damn what other people do. It doesn't make it any less moronic.' He looked wildly around the room then stared at a wicker basket full of bright plastic toys. 'I just want my son back.' He headed towards the hall. 'I'm going to look for him.'

'Wait!' Melanie leapt from her chair and rushed over to grab his arm. 'Don't go. I need you here.'

He shook her off and strode to the front door.

'Mr. Cameron,' Paton was in the hall with him now. 'There's nothing to be achieved by driving around and we'll struggle to contact you. As you know, the mobile signal around this area can be hit and miss. We've also alerted patrol cars in the area so they'll be looking for him.'

'I can't stay here.' He turned abruptly to face Paton, his eyes glistening with tears. 'You don't understand. Louie has epilepsy and needs medication and a special diet. He has most of his seizures at night and may need his rescue meds. We have to find him before bedtime or it could be fatal.'

Chapter 8
10.10AM

Child missing - 1 hour 10 minutes

Tommy

Tommy sat glued to the telly as Detective Inspector Jack Regan picked himself up from the dirt and pointed a gun at the criminal in the getaway van.

'Switch off or they'll collect your head in a bucket,' Tommy said, through gritted teeth in time with the actor.

He jumped up and tucked his feet under his bottom, bouncing with excitement. The doorbell rang but he ignored it. He didn't want to miss his favourite moment where one of the baddies shot Regan's friend.

A sharp rap on the window jolted him out of the drama and back into the living room. There was a face peering in, but the sun was behind the head so Tommy couldn't work out who it was. He wasn't sure what to do. Would Dad be cross if he answered? He grabbed the remote, paused *The Sweeney* then made his way to the front door. He opened it a little bit and peered out.

'Hello Tommy, is your dad in?'

It was the man from the scrap yard. Tommy gripped the door tightly. He didn't like this man. He definitely had a baddie face. 'What do you want?'

'I need to talk to him.'

'He's not here.'

'Your Mum?'

'She's in Weymouth.'

'On your own then?'

Tommy tried to close the door but the man grinned and stuck his big boot in the way.

'You can't come in,' Tommy said. 'Dad says I mustn't talk to strangers.'

'But we've met before,' the man said. 'I'm Nigel and you're Tommy so there you have it. Not strangers at all. In fact, to show we're friends you can make me a nice cup of tea.' He pushed the door and Tommy had to step back. 'You don't want your dad thinking you've got no manners,' the man said. 'Get the kettle on, there's a good lad.'

Tommy didn't know what else to do so he led the way along the hall towards the kitchen. Looking back, he saw Nigel's eyes moving from side to side at the photos on the walls.

'This your mum?' Nigel asked, pointing to a photo of her on the day she and Dad got married.

'Dad will be back soon,' Tommy said. He didn't add that Dad had called ten minutes ago to say sorry, but he'd be another hour. Nigel followed Tommy into the kitchen.

'My lad tells me you were snooping around my yard this

morning,' Nigel said, 'and I thought you'd just come to find your dad.'

Tommy licked his lips and looked at the floor. 'I wasn't snooping. I was looking at the cars,' Tommy told him. 'I wanted to see one go in the crusher like on *The Sweeney*.' He looked up at Nigel who was slowly shaking his head like he didn't believe him.

'Do you want tea or coffee?' Tommy filled the kettle and fetched two mugs from the cupboard. He wouldn't give horrible Nigel a biscuit.

'Tea, two sugars and not too much—'

Nigel's phone interrupted him and he pulled it from his pocket. Tommy couldn't hear exactly what the person who was calling said but it was a man and he didn't sound happy. 'I'm sorting it,' Nigel said. 'No worries. All under control.' He shoved the phone back into his pocket.

Tommy watched him, feeling surprised. Nigel was rubbing his chin and frowning as he stared out of the window. Was he scared of the man on the phone?

'I need to go,' Nigel said to Tommy. 'Give your dad a message from me. Tell him... tell him that the little fish get eaten by the big fish. Got that?'

'Little fish get eaten by big fish.'

'Good lad.' Nigel patted Tommy on the shoulder and walked back to the front door. 'And we're nothing but sprats caught in the net,' he muttered as he left.

Tommy was relieved to see Nigel leave and he made sure the front door was properly closed. 'Little fish get eaten by big fish.' Tommy kept saying to himself. He'd need to remember that. He pulled a piece of paper from the drawer and drew a big fish with sharp teeth then a small fish near its wide-open mouth.

He didn't understand what Nigel had said about sprats. Whatever they were.

Chapter 9
10.10AM

Child missing - 1 hour 10 minutes

Mabel Grimstone

Everywhere seemed grey today. Mabel looked at the bare trees and thin hedges surrounding the empty fields on either side of the road. She missed the golden browns of autumn and the green of spring. This time of year was just bloody cold, colourless and depressing. Christmas was nothing to look forward to either. Not when it was the usual dinner for one and no presents to give or receive.

Loneliness clawed at her gut as she thought about her empty cottage and the garden full of buried memories. She could feel the weight of the season and all its expectations pushing her down into a deeper state of misery. Going to the farm shop with her delivery of eggs hadn't helped either. Seeing the mistletoe, rows of Christmas trees and mince pies had only deepened her sense of isolation. Mabel had sat at a small table in the coffee shop desperately trying to gather up enough courage to speak to a lone woman on the next table but then another woman had arrived, they'd hugged and, after fetching a large cappuccino, spent the next ten minutes chattering and laughing.

Mabel drove on towards her empty cottage with mixed emotions. Part of her wanted to curl up in her armchair by the fire and escape from the world but another part of her wanted to be around other people. People who would notice her. Even the woman who she sold eggs to had barely wished her a good morning and thanks before turning to serve customers.

As Mabel carefully negotiated a bend, she caught a flash of deep summer blue to her left. *What was that?* Nothing in nature was that colour, not in late November. She replayed the image she'd seen. If it wasn't such a ludicrous notion, she'd imagined it had looked like a small child. Surely not. She slowed the car and debated whether to reverse and take a proper look. The lane was narrow though, so it was too risky. She drove on a little further then pulled off the road into a gateway. Reluctant to face oncoming cars in the dangerously twisty lane, she carefully put her foot on the bottom rail of the gate and leaned over. She could faintly hear crying. Was it a child? Out here?

She might only be sixty-two and still relatively agile but climbing the slippery, icy gate wasn't easy. Mabel took her time and was relieved when she was standing on the edge of a grassy field. Skirting some old sheep droppings, she kept close to the hedge and made her way towards what was now clearly the plaintive wailing of a small child in distress. Her heart squeezed with concern. Maybe a family was out for a walk and the child was injured. She hoped she could help. A bit strange to hike right out here though, especially at this time of year. There were no houses for miles, and she hadn't seen a car parked anywhere. She'd have noticed.

Mabel rounded a bend and gasped. A small boy was sitting in the mud, his mouth a wide cavern of anguish. She rushed forward, her heart leaping in her chest.

'What's the matter, you poor wee thing? Where's your mummy?'

The boy stopped abruptly and looked at her in surprise.

She bent over him. 'Have ye hurt yoursel'?'

He nodded and rubbed his cheek which was smeared with mud then began to cry again. Mabel put a hand gently under his elbow.

'Come on. Let's find Mummy.' Mabel looked all around the empty field then through a nearby gate to the road. The place was deserted. How had he got here? 'What's your name?' she asked the small boy.

His crying had subsided into sobbing now, big hiccupping sobs that lifted his little chest and distorted his face. Mabel waited while he communicated his distress. 'Louie,' he said eventually, with a sniff.

Mabel took a tissue from her pocket and wiped the tears and snot from his face. 'How did you get here, Louie?'

'In the car.'

'Where's the car now?' she asked.

'Gone. That way.' He began to cry again. 'I want Mummy.'

An abandoned child? Mabel felt herself tighten with anger. How could anyone leave a child alone in such a desolate place? 'Come on,' she said.

She leaned down and picked him up, savouring the weight of him in her arms until she felt cold dampness from his bottom seeping through the sleeve of her coat. Had he wet himself with fright, the poor wee lamb, or was it from the puddle?

'How about I take you home for a nice hot chocolate,' she said. She'd bring a smile to his little face. She'd take proper care of him. 'It's too cold to stay here, Louie. You'll be safe with me.'

Chapter 10
10.45AM

Child missing - 1 hour 45 minutes

DI Paton

The sound of gunshots and shouting assaulted Paton's ears as he entered his hallway. That television was far too loud. He really should encourage Tommy to do something else to fill his time. A walk perhaps or a board game. If Paton had known Wendy would be away caring for her mum and the school would be closed, he'd have booked annual leave to look after Tommy. He couldn't take time off now though. Not with a small child missing. He put his head around the lounge door and had to raise his voice to be heard.

'Turn that off now, Tommy. Are you ready? Auntie Ursula is making you some lunch.' He waited for a complaint about her cooking.

Tommy pressed the remote. 'I've got something to tell you, Dad.'

'Tell me on the way. I need to get back to work.' Paton didn't have time to hear about whatever TV programme Tommy had been watching.

Throwing Tommy's coat onto the sofa for him, Paton went through to the kitchen for a glass of milk and a handful of biscuits. Not the healthiest of lunches but still. He pushed the fridge door shut and noticed a sketch Tommy must have drawn. At least he was doing something other than watching TV. Paton smiled briefly at the picture then hurried to the front door where Tommy was pulling on his trainers.

'Nice drawing of fish,' Paton said. 'Would you like me to get you some new colouring pencils or paints so you can do more?'

'Yes, please. Can I tell you what the man said yet?'

'What man?' Had Tommy been watching an art programme? 'Come on. Tell me in the car.'

They got in and Paton lost no time in setting off.

'It was the bad man. The man from the broken car shop.'

'Eh?' Paton bit down his frustration as the traffic light ahead turned red and he was forced to stop. He glanced at the clock on the dashboard.

'You're not listening, Dad,' Tommy folded his arms and glared out of the side window.

'I'm listening now. Sorry.'

'The baddie came in, but I didn't give him a biscuit, then he didn't drink his tea, and he said to give you a message.' Tommy spoke without drawing a breath.

Paton felt as though he'd been punched in the gut. He swerved to the side of the road, cut the engine then turned to face Tommy. 'The man from the wrecking yard came into our house?'

'That's what I'm trying to tell you.' Tommy nodded to emphasise his point.

'And you let him in?' Paton's voice had risen, something he regretted when he realised he was frightening Tommy. Was the man using Tommy to threaten Paton? He tried not to let the panic show on his face.

'He said we were friends because he's called Nigel and I'm called Tommy. He put his big boot in the door too so I couldn't close it.'

Paton took a deep breath to calm himself. 'It's all right, son. Just tell me the message.'

'Little fish get eaten by the big fish. And we're all in a net. I drew you a picture, so I'd remember...'

Was it a threat? Was Nigel a big fish or was he afraid of being eaten by someone higher up the food chain? Paton dragged his thoughts away from his investigation and back to Tommy. 'Good lad for telling me but don't *ever* let anyone in who you don't know again. Why did he leave before he drank his tea?'

'Someone told him off on the phone.'

Tommy was still looking upset so Paton forced a smile. 'All sounds a bit fishy to me,' he said, and was relieved when Tommy giggled.

'I can't leave him on his own again.' Paton stood on Ursula's doorstep having explained what had happened to Tommy. She pulled the door closed behind her and shook her head.

'I feel terrible. I'm so sorry I wasn't here for you both.'

'It wasn't your fault. I shouldn't have left him alone. I can't understand how the man found out where we live.'

'Do you want me to book time off for the rest of the week? I'm sure Jeannie will be able to cover me. She's always after more hours.'

Paton thought of the ten pounds an hour he'd promised Kirsten. It was probably similar to what Ursula earned as a shop assistant. He'd rather have paid her. She'd probably refuse the money though and then he'd feel guilty that she was using up her holiday allocation.

'I've arranged for Kirsten to sit for the rest of the week. We'll be fine. I've got a difficult case on so I need to put more hours in.'

'How's Wendy's mum?'

'Not great.' Paton glanced towards his car. 'The fall really shook her up and she's badly bruised. She's lost her confidence so Wendy is organising grab rails and such like. She says she'll be back in time for work on Monday.'

'At least she'll know what she's dealing with.'

'Being a carer for the elderly does have some advantages, I suppose.'

'How is Wendy in herself?'

'Coping.' Paton was aware of the minutes passing and Ursula was fully in the picture about Wendy's anxiety and depression anyway. Wendy had suffered for years and often spent a week in bed unable to cope with the world.

'Does she know you're struggling with Tommy this week? Perhaps she can come home earlier.'

'She's got enough to worry about with her mum. We'll be fine. Tommy loves spending time with Kirsten.' Paton kissed his sister's cheek, waved to Tommy who was watching from the window and got into his car. He desperately wanted to visit the breaker's yard again to confront Nigel, but he had a small child to find first.

Chapter 11
10.45AM

Child missing - 1 hour 45 minutes

Mabel

Mabel looked in the rear-view mirror at the child as her small car bounced up the rutted track. Even with three cushions wedged under his damp bottom Mabel could barely see his little face. She swivelled her head briefly to smile at him and marvelled at the fact she had a child in her car. Happiness bubbled up inside her and she fought the urge to sing out loud. Time for that later. 'Are you okay, Poppet? We'll be home in a minute.'

'Home?' he gripped the edge of the window then pressed his nose to the glass. 'Me Louie, not Poppet.'

'My home. We'll get you into some dry clothes and make you a scrummy hot drink. Do you like shortbread?'

'Is Mummy and Daddy there?'

'We'll find Mummy and Daddy later. Let's get you clean

and dry first.' Mabel turned the car between two rough wooden gateposts and for once was glad to be home. Chickens flapped and scurried away with squawks and cackles as she pulled up outside a small white cottage in need of a layer of paint.

'Will they peck me?' Louie's face was pinched with worry as he looked out of the window at the ruffled birds.

'Not at all. They're very friendly and lay lovely brown eggs for breakfast. You can help me find some later. Come on. I've got someone who would love to meet you.'

Louie slid out of the car and tottered along beside Mabel. She took his plump little hand in her rough, bony one and led him to the back door where they slipped off their muddy footwear. Once inside, she stood him in front of the bright red Aga and put some milk in a pan to warm. 'We'll make you the chocolate drink then pop you in the bath to warm you up. You can wear an old T-shirt and jumper of mine while I rinse your clothes out.' What a dear little soul he was, with his blond hair and soft cheeks. Even the mud on him added to his charm. She wanted to scoop him into her arms again and squeeze him.

Louie looked around the kitchen in consternation. 'Will Mummy get me?'

'Plenty of time for that. You don't want to be wet and smelly when she comes for you, do you? She might be cross that you've got yourself all dirty.'

Louie bit his lip and slowly shook his head. 'No,' he said in a small voice.

'And you want a nice warm drink and biscuit, don't you?' Mabel bent her face close to his and smiled.

Louie took a step back but nodded. Mabel could see his fear building again, so she said, 'Oh, I forgot to introduce you to Humbug. I bet she's hiding through here. Humbug? Where are you?' she said in a sing-song voice. She walked through to the cosy lounge, with its colourful rugs and squashy sofa, making kissing noises. Louie followed her, wide eyed. Curled up on a velvet cushion was a huge, grey and black stripy cat. Mabel watched Louie's face and was delighted when he smiled for what was probably the first time that day.

'Walk over to her slowly so you don't frighten her, there's a good boy.'

Louie sidled up to the cat who watched his every move intently, muscles tensed ready for flight.

'Don't be scared, Humbug,' Mabel said. 'Louie won't hurt you, will you Louie?'

The little boy solemnly shook his head. Mabel took his small, dimpled hand in hers and gently placed it on the cat's back. He ran his flat palm along the soft fur and the cat visibly relaxed.

'How about you sit here on this old cushion next to Humbug while I bring your chocolate in.'

Louie sat upright on the sofa, his short legs sticking straight forward, and his hands clasped in his lap. He looked up at Mabel.

'You can stroke her again. Just move slowly so you don't frighten her.' Mabel hurried through to the kitchen and returned with a small cup of chocolate and a piece of shortbread. Louie gulped his warm drink, leaving a brown tidemark on his upper lip. He crammed the biscuit in his mouth, dropping crumbs into his lap then spoke before he'd finished his mouthful, spraying crumbs everywhere.

'Me go home now?'

Mabel's heart sank. 'Not yet, Louie. You need a bath first and then it's probably time for a little nap.'

Chapter 12
11AM

Child missing - 2 hours

Woody

The cheap plastic front door stuck in the warped frame as Woody tried to push it open and he nearly butted his nose on it. He cursed and shoved it harder then stepped into the narrow hallway, kicking aside a pile of pizza and Indian takeaway flyers. He stood for a moment rubbing the tops of his arms through his thin jacket. The cold had seeped into his clothes and sadly it wasn't much warmer indoors.

'Mum?' Bloody hell, he was starving. He walked to the kitchen and yanked open the fridge. *Please, please let there be some bacon.* The shelves were bare apart from a tub of margarine, a packet of suet and some shrivelled carrots. He pulled a carton of milk from the door and took a deep swig. It took two swallows before the taste registered. It was rank. He spat the last mouthful into the sink and checked the date. Four days past it's sell-by date.

'Mum!' He yelled again but the house was silent. She must be at work doing overtime again. Woody grabbed a packet of Cheerios from the cupboard and shoved handfuls into his mouth before checking his phone. He retrieved his mum's number and rang her.

'I'm not supposed to take calls while I'm working,' she whispered. 'What's wrong?'

Woody wanted to tell her that everything was wrong. He hated the house, the empty fridge, the people he hung around with, but mostly he hated himself for what he'd done. His mind raced trying to work out how to unburden himself about the child.

'Did you get the shopping?' she asked.

'What shopping?'

'I left you a note. The milk's off.'

'Why the fuck didn't you throw it away then?' *Stupid cow*. 'It tastes disgusting.' He glanced around the kitchen for the note then saw an envelope propped up against the kettle. All thoughts of the abandoned child were forgotten in his irritation.

'Don't swear at me, Darren Woodrow.' His mum always used his full name when she was mad with him. 'Just go to the shops and stop calling me at work. Can't talk now. Bye.'

The phone went dead and Woody slung it onto the counter. He grabbed the envelope and peered inside at the five-pound note and scrap of paper. He'd go to the shops for some milk, bread and bacon then call the police once he'd eaten, otherwise he might not get a chance for hours. There was no way he could give a witness statement on an empty stomach and he needed to decide how to tell them without dropping himself in the shit.

The row of shops was quiet and the wind viciously cold. A woman, hunched in a thick coat and headscarf, cut in front of Woody and he stumbled as he avoided her shopping bag on wheels. A laugh rang out to his left and he turned to see two of the gang leaning against a wall nearby. Roughhouse nudged Spliff and pointed in Woody's direction. He gave them a small nod then hurried into the Co-op. He didn't want to speak to them.

'Brought your own bag? What a good boy you are,' Roughhouse whined in his ear a few minutes later. 'Here. Some extra shopping for you.' He pulled Woody's canvas bag open and slipped in a pack of fillet steaks.

'Fuck off. I'm not lifting that for you,' Woody hissed looking around in alarm. 'I'm already on a caution.' Was there CCTV in here? It was one thing to nick an unattended car in a village with no cameras but the staff in here were extra vigilant and he had to be on his best behaviour. He needed to keep a low profile.

'I'm sure Mummy won't want to hear about where you've been this morning then.' Roughhouse's mouth twitched but didn't quite manage a smile. 'Don't take too long. I'm hungry.' He strolled out of the shop again.

Woody stood, undecided. He could put the steak back on the shelf but Roughhouse would be waiting for him outside and his anger would be instant. Woody shuddered to think what Roughhouse might do. Woody grabbed the items he'd come in for then went to the till, taking the steak from the bag and putting it onto the conveyor belt as a member of staff hovered behind him. He tugged a ten-pound note from his pocket and reluctantly handed it over to the cashier then left the shop.

'Wicked. Cheers mate!' Roughhouse snatched the steak

and ran across to where Spliff stood waiting. 'Lunch time!' he said, waving the meat in the air.

Woody headed for home, a buzz of anger in his gut at having to part with his own money. He'd have liked a fillet steak but he didn't want to spend his money too fast. Even rump was a rare treat at home. If he shopped again, he'd have to get here early while the local boys were still in bed. Once word got out, they'd all be using him as their personal shoppers.

A siren sounded a few streets away, turning Woody's mind back to the abandoned child. He needed to hurry. He'd scoff his sandwich and then call the police. He broke into a jog but as he turned a corner he slowed to a walk. Ahead of him were two police cars and an ambulance. Maybe he should say something now. Get it over with.

A dog walker hurried past. The huge, fluffy teddy bear of a dog lunged towards him with its tail rotating like a wind turbine. 'Here, Branston!' The owner pulled at the lead. 'You can't say hello to everyone.'

She looked worried to death, thought Woody, momentarily distracted. 'It's okay,' he said. 'I like dogs.'

As he walked along, he tried to work out his story for the police. How could he explain about the abandoned child without confessing to stealing the car with Roach? Would they arrest him? Would he get off any charges for telling on the gang? Woody's stomach growled and churned with hunger, or was it nerves? The scene ahead dipped and swayed. He was starting to feel lightheaded.

He was only yards away from the vehicles now and he could see the still form of a figure lying on the pavement – a pool of blood around the head and a face unrecognisable from the beating it had taken. He paused. It was a boy of around fourteen or fifteen, judging by the clothes and size. The figure wasn't recognisable until he saw the trainers. Hell, was it Gus?

Or Gusset as the gang cruelly called him. Woody had overheard him being threatened with a beating from The Dogs for not bringing his fit sister to the park for their entertainment. He must have decided her safety was more important than his own. Poor bastard.

'Did you see what happened here?' A police officer asked.

'No. I just got here. I've been to the shop.' Woody's voice was high-pitched with shock.

'On your way then, laddie. You've seen enough for now. Get yourself home.' The uniformed police officer stepped across his path, arms wide, as though to shield him from the gruesome sight.

Woody looked again at the red pulp of flesh that was Gus and felt bile rise in his throat. He turned away, swallowing hard, his appetite gone. As he walked, he glanced back at the police officer. If he told him about the kid, it would be him lying on the pavement next. Or even worse, it could be a firework through the letterbox in the middle of the night. Woody might find his mum annoying at times but he'd rather take the beating than they get burned to death in their beds or any harm come to her.

He needed time to think. Perhaps he should go home and cook his bacon sandwich while he decided what to do.

Chapter 13
11AM

Child missing - 2 hours

DI Paton

'What have we got so far?' Paton pulled a chair over and sat next to Douglas, the team analyst, to peer at the screen where ANPR data was displayed.

'Nothing, Boss. There are no ANPR cameras in the vicinity. Here's the closest one, look.' He pointed at the screen. 'On the outskirts of Perth.'

Paton sighed and sat back.

'You could look elsewhere for evidence though,' Douglas said. 'Loads of people have video cameras on their doorbells these days that link to their mobile phones – particularly if they have a lot of deliveries and are not home to receive them – and some people like to see who's at their front door when they're out. My auntie worries about someone stealing her dogs so she constantly checks her phone when she's at work. The data is stored for a month on the iCloud so can be retrieved as evidence.'

Paton slowly shook his head feeling old. It was difficult to keep up with technology these days and sometimes he yearned for the simple life before mobile phones and the internet.

'Thanks Douglas. I'll radio through to Tony and tell him to ask around Burrelton. They'll still be carrying out the door-to-door enquiries. Someone must have seen something.'

'Not many people out in this weather,' Douglas said.

'They are if they've got a job to do. Check the local council website to see when bin collection day is. Find out the post office delivery routes and check who the postman was today. Are there any industrial units in the area where lorries or vans visit? They may have dash-cams.'

Douglas nodded and turned back to his screen.

Paton radioed through to Tony and told him to ask local residents about doorstep cameras and whether anyone had seen anything unusual. It was a small village so strangers might be noticed. He was acutely aware of time passing and knew the first 24 hours was critical. Strange that it was called the golden hour when it was actually a whole day and night. The period when witnesses had fresh memories, evidence was still present and uncontaminated by time and weather and villains had less time to cover their tracks. It was already two long hours since the incident and now there was the added worry of Louie's epilepsy.

Maybe he should initiate a Child Rescue Alert, or CRA as it was often called, as it would pull in resources from the media and get the public involved in the search. It may also yield some dashcam evidence. The triggers were fully met, he thought. Louie was under 18 and he could be in imminent danger of serious harm. Especially if he wasn't discovered before bedtime as there was the risk of him having major seizures and going into status where he didn't come out of them. He might sustain brain damage. He wasn't sure if the third criterion was met. Was there sufficient information for the public to be able to help with the police investigation? He didn't know yet. All they had was the car model and number plate to go on and Louie's description. He could see the advantages of public exposure but they had to be weighed up with the serious disadvantages of involving the press at this early stage.

The thought of over-eager photographers trampling over potential evidence and journalists doorstepping Melanie and her family made him shudder. They'd want to know where the child had gone missing from and the circumstances surrounding his disappearance. If they found out he'd been left alone in a car with the keys in the ignition they'd rip Melanie to pieces and the trolls on social media would have a field day. She'd be slated and hated. Also, the real cost in time for officers answering calls from a well-meaning public was enormous. A separate incident room would need to be set up and manned by several officers to take the hundreds of calls that would likely ensue. Each call would need to be carefully assessed and followed up if it was likely to be a lead to finding Louie. The whole country would be full of little boys matching his description and some callers would even create scenarios just to be involved in the drama.

He wanted to give the investigation a few more hours before triggering the CRA. There were still lines of enquiry to explore and this approach would be a better use of the team resources. He'd discuss it with the DCI. Paton rose from his chair and thanked Douglas before crossing the room to Ian's desk.

'I need details of all car thefts within a fifty-mile radius of Burrelton, please, Ian. Let's see if we can decipher any pattern.

Find out the locations, times, whether the vehicles were recovered, any witnesses etc. Also check if any arrests have been made for car theft and joy riding.'

'How far back shall I look, Boss?'

Paton thought for a moment. 'Start with the past month then work backwards. I'll speak to the DCI to see if we can call in some extra help with this.' He looked at the young DC nearby. Mitchell Tomkins had joined the team at around the same time as Paton and they'd both been keen to prove themselves as worthy colleagues. Paton couldn't deny he had a soft spot for the hard-working lad but he kept it well hidden. It wouldn't do to show any favouritism.

'Mitchell, can you work alongside Ian here and look at all the hotspots where stolen vehicles have been dumped over the past three months then check them out to see if a blue Fiesta has been spotted? If they're in remote places you'll need to drive out to investigate. Also, speak to the fire brigade to see if any vehicles have been set alight and tell them to alert us if they see anything.'

'Isn't it a nearly new car, Boss?' Mitchell asked and Paton nodded. 'Would they torch it?'

'Unlikely, but if we're dealing with a joy rider or two, they may have their bit of fun then dispose of any evidence.'

'Do you think there might be a link with the breaker's yard we're investigating?'

Bright lad, thought Paton. Mitchell would go far. Paton smiled at him.

'You could be right. It's certainly worth keeping an open mind. Let's gather as much information as we can then we'll look at that possibility.'

Paton stood and went to his own desk then called Cheryl for an update. He couldn't begin to conceive the torment the parents must be going through. He'd go to pieces if anything happened to Tommy.

'Hang on, I'm just going outside,' Cheryl said when she answered. The phone rustled and Paton could hear the murmur of voices and doors opening and closing.

'How's Melanie?'

'Totally distraught. Crying, rocking, almost physically beating herself up for leaving Louie in the car. It's horrible to watch.'

Paton rubbed his hand across his eyes. 'I can imagine. Have you been able to get any information from her? Is there any motive for Louie being kidnapped?'

'I don't think so. From what I've gleaned so far, the family is relatively comfortable and able to live a decent standard of life, but I wouldn't describe them as loaded. I've broached the subject of wealth in the extended family but again there's nothing out of the ordinary.' Cheryl sighed.

'Has the father returned?'

'Not yet. He's called a couple of times to see if we've found him. Says he's driven around the area and seen nothing. He thinks we're not doing enough and is threatening to go to the press to get everyone looking.'

Paton groaned. 'I'll try calling him but if I don't succeed then please tell him to call me next time he makes contact. Have you found out more about the boy's medical condition?'

'I've got the name of his community nurse. Do you want to call her or shall I? She's the one who writes and updates his epilepsy intervention plan.'

'We'll do it here. Send her details over. I need you to focus on supporting Melanie and seeing what else you can find out. How's the relationship with her husband? There didn't appear to be much warmth between them.'

'I haven't asked any direct questions but from the things

she's said I wouldn't say tolerance and charm were his strongest assets. Any news of the car, Boss?'

'Not yet. Have you got your Mobile Data Terminal? You can check the investigation progress sheet on there.'

'I've been looking. Just wishful thinking that there would be more news.'

'I understand. We need to find the car to find the child. It's out there somewhere and someone must have seen it.'

Chapter 14
11.15AM

Child missing - 2 hours 15 minutes

Mabel

Louie stood quietly as Mabel peeled off his wet clothes and he shivered, despite the warmth emanating from the radiator. Mabel put her hands under his little armpits and swept him up, resisting the urge to clutch him to her chest. She swung him over the edge of the bathtub and gently lowered him into the warm, bubbly water. He sat upright, patting his hands on the mounds of bubbles then looked up at her, a small smile flitting across his face.

Mabel's heart flipped. He was such a cutie and it seemed as though he was beginning to trust her.

'Would you like something to play with?' she asked and he gave a small nod. She reached sideways and picked up a plastic cup and colander, a wooden spoon and balloon whisk she'd collected from the kitchen.

'Let's make ice cream,' she said with enthusiasm. She dipped the colander into the water and lifted it high so that water poured through the many holes.

Louie's smile widened and he clapped his hands with excitement.

'Again!' he said, so Mabel lifted the colander over and over until a sizable tower of bubbles wobbled underneath.

'What flavour ice cream would you like?' Mabel asked, scooping up bubbles and spooning them into the cup.

'Drawberry,' Louie said. 'Drawberry is my bestest.' He took the proffered cup and pretended to eat the foam. 'Yum.'

'Nice? Can you make me one now?'

As the game progressed to whisking, adding pretend cherries and chocolate flakes, Louie became more animated, all thoughts of his mother seemingly forgotten. He slapped his hand into the water, splashing Mabel with droplets and bubbles. A clump slid down her nose and she widened her eyes in fake surprise. Louie's laugh rang out and filled the room and Mabel with happiness. It was incredible that such a little being could bring so much joy. This was everything she'd ever wanted. Everything she should have had.

A sudden chill descended, raising goosebumps on her wet arms and her thoughts pulled away from the happy domestic scene in front of her. All those wasted years of emptiness. The familiar aches of loss and longing were back like unwelcome relatives paying yet another visit. Mabel had long ago accepted that they would be with her forever.

'What your name, lady?'

Mabel jolted in surprise. For a moment she'd forgotten the small, slippery child shyly gazing at her, a sponge clasped in his chubby fists and pressed against his cheek. Her mind raced with possibilities.

'Grandma,' she said. 'Call me Grandma.'

She didn't want him calling her Mabel. Not only did she detest the old-fashioned name she'd inherited from her grandmother but she wanted him to feel a sense of security.

'Grandma, can I get out now?'

'Of course.'

Mabel pulled a towel from the cooling radiator. She'd need to chop some more wood for the Aga to keep the little mite warm. She held the towel up and he stood, bubbles sliding off his shiny limbs as she wrapped the towel around his little body and lifted him from the bath. He felt so good in her arms that she couldn't bear to put him down so she gathered him to her chest and sat in the old chair, rocking gently. It was all she could do to resist dropping kisses onto his damp hair. Instead, she lowered her face and breathed in the wonderful fragrance of him.

Louie wriggled impatiently. 'Is Mummy coming soon? We need to get Noah.'

'Noah?' Mabel tried desperately to distract Louie. She couldn't bear to part with him yet.

'My brother. He this big.' Louie struggled to unwrap his arm and held it up towards the ceiling.

'Wow! That is big.'

'He can ride a bike. Daddy said I can when I'm four.'

'Are you three?' Mabel watched his animated face, enjoying every fleeting expression.

'Me two but it my birthday soon. Mummy said I can have dinosaur cake.'

Maybe Louie wasn't as neglected as Mabel first thought. 'Why were you on your own when I found you?'

'Mummy put me in the car and went for a long time. The scary boys didn't like me. I cried loud.'

Hmm, not such a loving family after all.

'Let's find you something to wear while I wash and dry

your clothes. They're all wet and muddy so you can't put them back on yet.'

'Me want to go home.' Louie's mouth turned down and his bottom lip trembled.

'How about you cuddle Humbug while I wash your clothes and we make puppets and do a puppet show while we wait for them to dry?'

'Okay.' Louie slid off Mabel's lap trailing the wet towel, and headed for the stairs.

'Let's find you something to wear first.'

Mabel steered him towards her bedroom and pulled open a drawer. 'Put this tee-shirt on and this warm, fluffy jumper.'

She tugged the items over his head and they fell down past his knees. She rolled the sleeves up then found a pair of soft woollen socks that were long enough to meet the jumper.

Louie spotted his reflection in the mirror and paused. 'Me not like these clothes,' he said.

'Listen, is that Humbug calling you?' Mabel said, desperate to keep Louie from sinking into misery.

He looked towards the stairs then set off, clutching the banister and putting two feet on every stair, his inappropriate outfit forgotten. Mabel scooped his clothes up from the bathroom floor, thrust her hand into the cooling bath water to pull out the plug and hurried after him. Thank goodness for Humbug.

Chapter 15
12 NOON

Child missing - 3 hours

Woody

For once the bacon sandwich didn't taste delicious. If anything, it seemed dry and difficult to swallow. Woody took another gulp of sweet, milky tea to wash it down and stared out of the window at the scrubby patch of grass and concrete slabs outside. Maybe some ketchup would help. Woody grabbed the plastic bottle from the cupboard and squirted a generous dollop onto his bacon. Instantly, an image of Gus's mashed face rose before him and he almost gagged. He pushed the sandwich away and put his head in his hands.

If only he had someone to talk to. Someone to ask advice. He couldn't face the shame of telling his mum about the small boy they'd abandoned and Dad was a waste of space. The last time they'd spoken had been six weeks ago when his dad had called to invite him to visit at his new flat. As if Woody wanted to see Dad mooning over that home-wrecking bitch. Woody couldn't even bring himself to think of her by name.

What to do? What to do? Woody curled his fists into his thick brown hair and pulled hard, making his eyes water. Okay. Think. He could make an anonymous phone call but the police were smart and had all sorts of clever technology. They might track him down. If he reported stealing the car and dumping the kid to the police he'd be charged with theft and probably abduction. He hadn't wanted to dump the kid though. That had been Roach's doing. Would the police be any easier on him if he grassed up Roach and the gang? More importantly, could they protect him?

Woody hadn't a clue about how big the gang was. He'd only met the boys from the park, and Spanner at the drop-off point, but he knew there were people higher up the chain. How far did it go? If he split on them, would they smash him to a pulp like they had Gus or would they come after his mum? The sudden ringing of his phone broke the silence in the room, the sound made louder by it vibrating against the tabletop at the same time. Shit. That made him jump.

The display said withheld number.

'Yeah?'

'Yo, Woody. Got another job for you tomorrow morning. I'll pick you up at eight outside the chippy.' Spanner didn't even ask if Woody was free. Woody knew he wasn't being given a choice.

Woody's mind raced. He wanted out now. This was getting dangerous and as his stomach churned, he realised he was actually scared. 'I can't tomorrow,' he said. 'I've got an appointment.'

'Are you kidding me? "*I've got an appointment.*"' Spanner's tone was full of mocking sarcasm. 'You'll be there,' he said, 'if you know what's good for you.'

The line went dead.

The pressure was building in Woody's gut. Throwing the phone onto the table he rushed upstairs to the bathroom and slammed the door. A few minutes later he was washing his hands and splashing water onto his face when he heard his phone ring again.

'Hello love. Sorry about earlier but you know how strict Mr. Pearson is about taking private calls during work hours. I'm on a break now. Did you get the shopping?'

The warmth in his mum's voice was nearly enough to undo Woody. He blinked hard against the tears that threatened, and swallowed the lump in his throat. He didn't deserve her love. He was a wasteman, a useless piece of humanity, a shit-for-brains.

'I got milk, bread and bacon,' he said. *And fillet bloody steak.*

Woody suddenly felt exhausted. He didn't want this life anymore. He didn't want to be Darren Woodrow, beholden to a vicious, heartless gang, living in a crummy rental with a mum who had to work constant overtime to make ends meet. Perhaps he should try and get a job. But really, what was the point in breaking his balls for a measly minimum wage? He could earn more than a week's wages in one morning stealing cars.

'What have you been doing today?'

'Nothing much.'

Mum sighed. 'Have you done the washing up?'

'Don't start nagging.'

'You could tidy your bedroom.'

'I'm busy.'

Woody's mind raced. He needed to think of a reason for having the money to buy new clothes. 'Someone wants me to help move a shed and hold the ladder while he cleans the gutters. Says he'll pay me.'

'Who? Do you know him well?'

'He's not a nonce if that's what you're worried about. I got chatting to him the other day. He lives on the estate.' The lies were flowing now, his dilemma almost forgotten. 'He said his friend wants help laying a patio too. It'll be like a workout at the gym and I'll be able to buy some new clothes.'

'Don't forget Megan is bringing Tyler for tea. They'll be here at four.'

Woody was brought back to reality with a jolt as his small cousin reminded him of the little kid they'd dumped. How could he forget even for a moment? Was he that heartless? Should he tell his mum? Woody couldn't begin to guess what her reaction might be. Horror and disbelief probably, then she'd march him down to the police station.

'Darren? Are you still there?'

'Yeah. Just working out what time I'll be back.'

'Oh, and don't forget you also promised to look after Tyler tomorrow morning. Megan has a doctor's appointment and I'm working.'

Woody's heart sank. Bloody hell. If he weren't at the chip shop for eight, he'd end up like Gus or worse. How much did the gang know about his family? Would he be putting Mum, Megan and Tyler in danger?

'I can't, Mum. I've promised to help the guy down the road.' Woody braced himself for a lecture. 'He's paying me,' he added. This wasn't a lie.

'Oh Darren.'

The disappointment in Mum's voice added to the weight of guilt he was carrying and he snapped.

'She'll have to change her appointment. Not my problem.'

'Why are you like this, love? You were always so keen to help Megan when she first had Tyler on her own. You've changed so much I hardly recognise you.'

It's this place, he wanted to say. This dump of a house and the shit he'd got himself into. He wished he were back in his old house with Mum and Dad where the biggest worry was whether he'd get his favourite chicken curry for dinner. He wanted to leave here, hide away.

'Can I go and stay at Grandad's for a few weeks?'

'And leave me on my own?'

Bloody hell. It wasn't his job to keep her company.

'You're always working anyway,' he said.

'It'll be Christmas soon. Perhaps you can visit for a week after that. Any luck with the jobs you applied for?'

'Not heard,' he said. Not likely to either, given that he hadn't even sent the forms off. 'I'm sure Grandad could find me some stuff to do.'

It would get him out of the gang's clutches too and right now a boring farm where nothing happened was just what he needed.

Chapter 16
12.15PM

DI Paton

Child missing – 3 hours 15 minutes

'Any possible sightings of the bairn yet, Dave? What name has the operation got?'

The detective chief inspector looked up in anticipation as Paton entered his office and sat down.

'Operation Oakwood, sir. No sighting yet, I'm afraid. We've got Tony and other officers doing house-to-house calls in Burrelton and the SOCOs should be there now. Cheryl is with the mother and the father is out looking, despite us asking him to stay home with his wife in case there's news.'

The DCI nodded. 'Understandable. What else?'

'Douglas is looking at ANPR data and tracking down the postman for potential sightings in the area, and Ian and Mitchell are investigating other car thefts to look for any links.'

'It sounds like you've got it organised.' The DCI smiled at Paton and he allowed himself a small measure of satisfaction.

It had taken several months to earn this level of respect and confidence in his work. Finding the Tay Killer had been a huge achievement, especially after they'd almost given up hope. It had only been Paton's tenacity and determination that had finally resulted in an arrest and subsequent imprisonment. However, Paton still couldn't help noticing a flicker of irritation passing across the DCI's face at times, when Paton had to prioritise his family's needs above his duties.

'We have a major concern for the boy, sir.' Paton's tone had become grave and the DCI gave him his full attention. 'We've been told the child has epilepsy and needs twice daily medication. Without it, and even with it sometimes, he may have night-time seizures that lead to stasis.'

The DCI frowned. 'Remind me what that means.'

'Where one seizure runs into another and they don't regain consciousness. His community nurse tells us Louie needs buccal midazolam rubbed into his gums to bring him out of the seizure and may even need to be hospitalised. He's also on a Ketogenic diet where he eats high levels of fat and has to avoid carbohydrates. Without this diet his seizures will worsen.'

The DCI opened his mouth wide and rubbed both cheeks as though deep in thought. 'How often does he have these seizures?' he asked.

'He has frequent absences, where he goes into a daze and doesn't respond, but also tonic clonic seizures that make his limbs twitch. These can be once a month or so, but sometimes two or three times a week. His mother told Cheryl that excitement or worry can trigger them, especially if he's not sleeping properly.'

'What does a three-year-old usually worry about?'

'That's what I wondered but apparently his seizures

increased when his brother started playgroup and from reading between the lines Cheryl is picking up some marital tension in the family.'

'Sounds like I need to call in some extra resources,' the DCI said.

Paton nodded, his lips pressed together, but inside he could feel his excitement mounting. This could turn into a high-profile case and a complex enquiry. He'd only been the senior investigating officer for routine enquiries before – rape, robbery, assault. Were all his years of hard work and commitment about to reap the reward of being the leading officer on a major investigation? After all, finding the Tay killer had proved he was good at tracking people. He'd love to be given the opportunity to organise the search for Louie. He held his breath and waited.

'I'd like you to be the SIO for this one, Dave. I'm about to attend a three-day course and this will need the full focus of a competent officer. Can I rely on you?'

Paton wanted to leap out of his chair in delight but he controlled himself. He couldn't stop the wide grin splitting his face.

'Most definitely, sir. One hundred percent.'

'I know I shouldn't discriminate and ask you this, but is everything stable at home with Wendy and Tommy? I'm aware it's extra pressure sometimes.'

'Everything's fine, sir.' Paton's smile weakened.

'I heard Tommy's school has been closed for a week.'

'I have support arranged.'

Paton could feel his frustration building. He would have to emphasise to Kirsten how important her supervision of Tommy was. His career prospects depended on it. If he could prove himself capable on this case and reunite the missing boy with his family, then he was sure he'd be SIO for major investigations in the future. He knew it was probably too late in his career to become Detective Chief Inspector. Twenty years of marital demands and being the parent of a boy with Down's syndrome had seen to that. But this was enough for him. To lead prominent investigations and organise the team without all the headaches brought on by budget constraints and policy decisions was enough.

'Good. Have you had any thoughts about activating a Child Rescue Alert, Dave?'

'I'd like another day, sir, if I can. I don't want the press getting in the way and hindering evidence gathering, and the impact on the family could be catastrophic.'

'Why do you say that?'

'Mrs Cameron left her child in the car with the keys in the ignition. Can you imagine how the press would portray that and what stance the public would take?'

'True,' the DCI said, with a frown.

'And we'd need a lot more resources if the public were made aware. We had a similar case in Weymouth and received hundreds of calls to the team, all of which had to be analysed and investigated. I think our resources would be best used looking for him first.'

'Agreed. Call and update me in the morning and then we'll decide.'

Paton exhaled and stood.

'Before you go, Dave, isn't there something else you want to talk about?'

Oh no. He must have heard about Tommy visiting the breaker's yard with him. But how? Had the dealer grassed him up? Unlikely, really, given that the man had visited Paton's house and left a threatening message. Should Paton confess? He hesitated in the doorway. The DCI liked Tommy – ever since he'd been on work experience in the staff canteen and delivered hot pies to the DCI's desk – but he wouldn't be pleased about Paton taking Tommy out with him in work time. Paton didn't want to jeopardise his new position. Besides, he wouldn't do it again.

'Not that I can think of, Sir.'

'When we agreed to meet you said something about a Spiderman backpack.'

Damn! Paton had forgotten about that. He was going to check with his boss whether there was enough evidence to get a search warrant for the breaker's yard. The stolen BMW had a Spiderman backpack in it. His mind raced. Should he lie and say he'd seen the same bag in the rear footwell of the car or should he confess that Tommy had been there and seen it? Paton didn't want to lie in court if it was usable evidence but he didn't want to lose the DCI's trust by confessing to taking Tommy on the visit. *What to do? What to do?*

'I went to the breaker's yard in Crieff on the pretext of getting a car part. I had a wander and peered through a car window.'

No point in bringing Tommy into this. It would only create more problems and right now he needed to crack on with looking for Louie. There was also the danger that Tommy wouldn't be called to give evidence in court given his learning disability.

'There was a backpack in the car exactly like the one mentioned in the stolen BMW owner's statement. I wonder if we have enough evidence to apply for a search warrant. There may be a link somewhere with Louie's disappearance.'

'What other evidence do you have?'

'Despite the plates being different, the BMW was the same model as the one stolen in Perth two weeks ago so it would be useful to check the vehicle identification number on the chassis and so on. Also, there's been a spate of car thefts in the area.

We think there may be more to this breaker's yard than is presented outwardly. A chop shop maybe?'

'Not exactly evidence then. Find more links and then we'll apply for a warrant.'

The DCI stood and tucked his chair under the desk. Clearly the meeting was over. It was all very well to say *find more links*, thought Paton, but how hard was that going to be?

'What course are you doing, sir?' Paton asked to hide his frustration. He wondered if it was something he might be able to do one day. He was always keen to learn.

'The MAGIC course.'

'Doing a bit of moonlighting at kids' parties?' Paton teased, then regretted it. Was he pushing a boundary here? They'd never engaged in banter before.

The DCI smiled and Paton relaxed. 'I thought you'd have been aware of the Multi-Agency Gold Incident Command training, Dave.'

'I am sir. It will be good to have a Gold Commander on the team.'

He left the office and after a brief nod to the team, he exited the building and headed for his car. A chill wind was gathering strength so he drew the lapels of his jacket together and tucked his chin into his chest. He hoped the poor little mite wasn't out in this weather. He'd get hypothermia.

Chapter 17
1PM

Louie

Child missing - 4 hours

Louie was sad. This bed smelled funny. Like the old biscuits Mummy found in Noah's bag. Mummy didn't let Noah eat them. There was no puffy duvet here either. Only scratchy blankets and a sheet. He wanted his cover with the red and green dinosaurs. He wanted his bedroom with his best toys, the red curtains, and blankie. He couldn't sleep without blankie. He lay still thinking about it. Where might blankie be? He pushed it down his jacket to keep it warm, didn't he? Yes. The nice lady must have it. Grandma she said. Call her Grandma. He never knew he had three Grandmas.

He pulled the covers off and stood on the floor. His feet were cold so he stayed on the rug all the way to the door.

'Grandma?'

He called down the stairs and listened. She wasn't coming.

He called again then walked to the stairs. The long jumper got stuck round his legs. *Oh no!* He might fall. He clung to the wooden pole and went one step at a time. When he got to the bottom, he looked in all the rooms but she wasn't there. Where was she? Was he all on his own again? In the kitchen he saw his clothes going round and round in the washing machine. He bent and peered through the little window. There! There was blankie.

He tried to open the door but the handle didn't work. He pushed it. The machine went click then whizzed round really fast. He couldn't see blankie now. It was just lines and colours and was making him dizzy. If Mummy was here, she'd get it for him. Where was Mummy? She should fetch him. He'd been here a very long time. His tummy felt funny. Like it was hungry but didn't want food.

'Louie! What are you doing out of bed?'

Grandma was at the door in her coat. She wasn't cross though. She was smiling.

'I want blankie.' Louie pointed to the washing machine.

'It'll be ready soon. How about I find you something else that's soft and cuddly?'

He shook his head and stared at the floor. Blankie wouldn't smell right now it had been washed. He bit his lip with worry. Something else wouldn't have a shiny label to rub on his nose either. The floor went all blurry.

'Is Mummy coming soon?' he said in a small voice. He looked up at Grandma. Her smile fell off her face.

'The phone isn't working at the moment,' she said. 'We don't get much signal here.'

Louie wasn't sure what that meant but Daddy always moaned about the signal. Grandma must be right.

'Let's get you back to bed for a little nap then when you wake up the phone might be working again.'

Grandma put her hand on his back. He twisted away.

'I don't want to.'

He wanted to go home. He pressed his feet hard on the floor and kept his legs stiff.

Grandma sighed, just like Mummy when she got cross.

'I'll make you a little bed on the sofa with Humbug, just this once.'

She held out her hand. Louie thought for a minute then took it and went with her. A sudden ringing made them both jump. Louie looked up at her. Was the phone working now? Was it Mummy?

Chapter 18
1.30PM

Child missing - 4 hours 30 minutes

Mabel

A fist of fear clenched around Mabel's heart as she lifted the mobile to her ear. Who would be calling? Her brain screamed through the possibilities as she imagined a policeman saying, 'You're under arrest for abduction,' or a distraught mother sobbing, 'You've stolen my child. How could you?'

Mabel watched Louie's face as she tentatively answered. He'd stopped in the lounge doorway and was staring up at her, eyes wide with hope.

'Hello?'

'Miss Grimstone?'

'Yes.' Mabel's stomach clenched at the unfamiliar voice.

'I was wondering if you had any more eggs you could bring over. I know you've only just delivered to us but Julie has been in and bought most of the stock. She's got two big wedding cakes to make.'

Mabel let out a long breath as her mind raced ahead. She'd need to collect more eggs and take Louie with her. Someone might see him and report her to the police. What could she say? That she'd just been looking after him briefly before taking him to the police station? Surely getting him warm, dry and fed would be essential first? She imagined Louie looking small and lost in the back of a police car. Louie being re-united with a family who had barely noticed his absence. Then she'd come home to an empty sofa, a vacant bed and a kitchen where only one plate and mug was needed again. A sharp pang of loss took her breath from her. She couldn't give him back yet. Just a few more hours, then she'd call the police. She could say she found him later. No one had seen her pick him up as the lane had been deserted.

'Is it Mummy?' Louie was hopping from one foot to the other and reaching for the phone.

Mabel put her phone behind her back and shook her head. Louie's face dulled and he bit his bottom lip.

'Hello?' The woman sounded puzzled at Mabel's lengthy silence. 'Sorry, have you got company?'

Mabel thought quickly. 'Just my cousin's little granddaughter. She's staying with me.'

'I can always ask Glenda if you're busy.'

Mabel stiffened. She couldn't afford to lose a good customer such as the farm shop owner to her rival, Glenda Blackthorn. Mabel's eggs were bigger, cheaper, and fresher but even so it might be risky to let the farm shop down even once.

'Can I call you back in five minutes? I need to see how many eggs I've got.'

'Of course.'

Mabel ended the call and held the phone to her chest. She

could leave Louie in the car while she ran in with the eggs, but what if he tried to get out or cried and someone saw him? She stood imagining scenarios of him being taken from her, his tear-stained face pressed against a car window, of him being reunited with his impassive mother who chastised him for going astray and yanked his arm to drag him into her car. Who was Mabel kidding though? The mother was probably frantic.

Mabel delved deep into her conscience but it was no match for the longing she felt when she looked at Louie. Her whole adult life had been defined by yearning for a child to hold in her arms. For a small face to burrow into her neck and grace her with butterfly wing kisses. *Just a day*, she thought. *I'll keep him for one more day.*

Mabel gave in to her desire and squatted down until her face was level with the little boy.

'Louie, how would you like your very own pet rabbit?'

'A real one?' Louie's eyes were huge and his mouth a perfect O.

'A warm, cuddly one with a wiggly nose and hoppity feet. Come and see.'

Mabel scooped him up into her arms and wrapped her long jacket around him, relishing his solid warmth. She stepped out of the back door and followed a terracotta tiled path that wound like a stream through the untidy lawn. Flowerbeds lay dormant with the winter cold but showed the skeletal promise of abundant colour and fragrance in the summer. She paused at a tangled rose bush and mouthed a small kiss then moved on. A collection of outbuildings stood at the end of the cottage garden, with tiled or corrugated iron roofs, higgledy piggledy blue-framed windows and crooked red doors, giving the appearance of a fairy story village. As they approached, a chorus of clucking and cooing could be heard and Louie craned his head around to see where they were going.

'I'll show you all the chickens later,' Mabel said. 'First I want you to meet Flump.' She turned the corner and crossed a small courtyard to a wooden hutch and wire run. She hunkered down so Louie could see through the mesh at the front of the cage. A large grey and white rabbit stared at them both as it chewed a dandelion leaf before turning its back and hopping out of sight. Louie squirmed to get closer.

'Oh dear. I think Flump likes girls better,' Mabel said, struggling to balance Louie on her knee. 'Maybe I should give him to a little girl.'

'No! I want him.' Louie was unable to keep still and Mabel was in danger of dropping him. She grabbed the top of the hutch and hauled herself up.

'I've got an idea,' she said. 'Let's go back inside.'

Back indoors, Mabel led Louie up the stairs and into the small bedroom he'd lain in earlier. She crossed the room to an old stripped-pine wardrobe with ornately carved flowers and a long mirror in the door. She tugged on a metal teardrop handle and breathed deeply. The smell of roses drifted out from the reed diffuser in the corner. *The best smell in the world*, she thought. Louie stood next to her and peered inside. Above his head was a row of outfits graduating from baby size to adult. Mabel lifted her hand to stroke fabrics of soft cotton and velvet in delicate shades of pink, mauve and lemon then moved garments to left and right, her head slightly tilted as she assessed their sizes. After glancing down at Louie, she plucked a pink cotton jersey dress with detailed smocking across the front. She held it against him and he backed away, a look of horror on his face.

'I not wear that,' he said. 'I not a girl.'

'If you just wear it for today, I'll give you Flump then when you go home to Mummy you can take her with you.' Mabel watched the conflicting emotions flit across his small face.

'We can make your hair look pretty too.' Mabel scooped up two handfuls of his curls and pinched them into a pineapple top knot on his head. The transformation was immediate. Louie's brow furrowed.

'We need to deliver some eggs then you can sit and cuddle Flump in this pretty dress.'

'Will Flump like me then?'

'Definitely. We'll tell her your name is Louise. Can you say that?'

'Louise,' Louie said after a pause.

'Perfect. If anyone asks your name at the farm shop you can tell them it's Louise. It'll be practice for when you cuddle Flump.'

Louie nodded and stood patiently while Mabel peeled off the T-shirt and jumper then pulled the dress over his head and fastened the buttons. She opened a small wooden box on the chest of drawers and pulled out a pale pink ribbon. 'For your hair,' she said. 'There! Don't you look lovely?'

Louie stared at his reflection. A little girl with a curly topknot and pretty dress stared back at him.

Chapter 19
2PM

Child missing - 5 hours

Woody

There were nine cracks in the ceiling, three cobwebs in the corners and a dead fly on the windowsill. Woody lay on his bed and studied his surroundings with an air of disgust. He pictured his dad and new girlfriend – or was she as new as he made out? – relaxing in the neat two-bed flat they'd moved into. Woody had only been there once but that was enough. Everything looked shiny and fresh and... Oh, how to describe it?

Cared for. That was it. Woody's new home looked anything but, and it made him miserable. Gone was the comfy sofa to sprawl on, the curtains that met in the middle, and the warmth. Gone was the steaming beef casserole on the table and family to share it with. Now, he was lucky to get a biscuit pizza and half-cooked oven chips, that he ate while Mum rushed to get ready for her evening job.

Woody reached for the remote and switched on his FIFA game, but somehow he couldn't get up enough enthusiasm to pick a team. His brain kept nagging him about the kid. It was bad enough that they'd stolen his mum's car then dumped him, but how would Woody feel if he heard on the news that the boy was found frozen to death? Guilt gnawed at his gut but he felt weak and useless. Trying to make a decision was too exhausting and he lay back on the pillow again. The sudden ringing of his phone jarred him and he sat up, his mood sinking lower when he saw the caller was Roach.

'Yo, Woody. Spanner tells me you're on the Dundee job with me tomorrow.'

'Dundee?'

'Didn't he say? We're being promoted to the team in the city.' Roach sounded excited but Woody's mind was in a tailspin. Dundee? Fuck! He couldn't go there. He knew too many people. Someone might recognise him. And there would be cameras everywhere. The bacon sandwich threatened to reappear and he gulped down air to stop it.

Roach hadn't noticed Woody's silence, it seemed. He sounded too hyped-up by the news.

'We can learn new skills from that team – like how to get cars off driveways using computer stuff so you don't need a key. Isn't that sick? We can nick the BMWs, Mercedes, Range Rovers and Audis.'

Woody didn't reply. This was all getting too serious for him. He wanted out. Roach finally slowed down and paused.

'Still there? I hope you're not backing out. Hey, you haven't reported that bairn, have you?'

'No, course not. I—'

Driven

'Did you hear about Gus?'

Woody flinched. It was clear why Roach mentioned Gus straight after talking about reporting the kid. Woody wasn't stupid.

'I saw him lying on the pavement.'

'See much claret?'

Sick bastard. 'He looked pretty bad.'

'I heard he didn't look pretty afterwards.' Roach laughed. 'Unlike his sister. She's peng.'

Woody had heard enough.

'I've got to go. I'll see you in the morning.'

'Half past eight outside the chippy.'

Woody ended the call and looked around the room again. What the hell had he got himself into? He felt trapped. And scared. Shit scared. The image of Gus's body sprawled across the pavement rose uninvited, and he swallowed then swung his legs off the bed and switched off the TV.

Calling the police might be a no-no but Woody could go and look for the bairn. He stood and straightened his clothes and laced up his trainers. He needed to get away from here anyway. Today. Now. Before Mum got home and before it got dark mid-afternoon.

As he squeezed into the over-stuffed shed, he noticed his tatty old trainers in a box of gear from the old house. He looked down at his shiny new Run Swift trainers bought on a trip to Dundee and thought of the muddy fields he was going to. Best not to wear these. He pulled off his new trainers and shoved them in the box then put the comfy old ones on.

It wasn't easy disentangling his old bike from the lawnmower handle, rake and rusty sunchair, but eventually Woody managed to haul the front wheel over the doorframe of the shed and onto the cracked concrete path. He brushed a cobweb off the saddle and rubbed his sleeve along the handlebars to remove a layer of dust. Bloody hell. He was almost sweating despite the cold and suddenly he was totally pissed off. He couldn't help comparing the cluttered, sorry excuse for a garden shed with the large, organised one they'd left behind in Dundee.

Woody pressed the tyres with his thumb then detached the pump to add some air. He checked them again then leaned the bike against the wall while he went indoors to pack his rucksack. A quick glance at his phone showed he had another hour before Mum arrived home but he didn't want to hang about in case she was early and tried to stop him leaving. It would also take over an hour to cycle to the place where they'd dumped the kid and the daylight already seemed to be leaking away. He didn't feel safe with no lights on his bike.

Grabbing hoodies, jeans, joggers and underwear, he crammed them into his backpack and pulled the strings tight. Wait a minute though. It was always freezing in Grandad's old farmhouse and the log fires only warmed small areas. Woody yanked a drawer open and pulled out extra T-shirts, a thick jumper he barely wore and his old pyjamas. The pyjamas were too short for him now but they'd be better than nothing. As he reached the door he paused and looked around the room. Dashing over to his bed he lifted his pillow and snatched up Fred Bear, the small, almost bald bear he'd hidden underneath. He pushed him to the bottom of his rucksack. There. No one would know.

As Woody fetched his toothbrush from the bathroom his phone rang again. It sounded loud, the ringtone bouncing off the tiled walls. Mum.

'Sorry, Darren, I'll be a bit late home. My boss has asked me to stay on and process the invoices because Mary is off sick. I've rung Megan and cancelled tea. She said she's trying to get a new doctor's appointment. I'll grab us something for dinner on my way back. Fancy fish and chips?'

'Nah, I'll get something out of the freezer.'

He felt bad enough leaving her and couldn't cope with the added guilt of her wasting money. Fish and chips weren't cheap.

'I'll tell Megan I'll sit for her next time.'

'You're a good boy, Darren.'

No, I'm not, he thought. *I'm a shit.*

Woody cycled out of Perth as fast as he could. If anyone from the gang saw him, he'd say he was on his way to see Courtney but that might not stop them giving him new tasks. Personal shopping being one of them. As he cycled, he wondered what Spanner's reaction would be when he didn't turn up in the morning. Would he go to Woody's house? Woody hoped not. At least Mum was starting work early tomorrow so wouldn't be around if he did and Woody had switched his phone off so they couldn't contact him.

As soon as Woody reached the fields he slowed down. His thighs burned and his breath was ragged. He pressed on, revelling in the downward hills and cursing the upward ones. It was another hour and the sky was darkening before he reached the spot where they'd dumped the boy.

Woody pushed his bike into the undergrowth and laid it down so that no one in a passing car would see it. Not that many cars were about. He climbed the gate and jumped down into a field with a long puddle. He looked from right to left, eyes narrowed as he scanned the distant horizons, but there was no sign of a small boy. At least he wasn't lying here freezing to death. Someone must have found him. He was probably back at home having his tea, watching cartoons on the telly. Still, Woody would check the news later just to be sure no kid had been reported missing.

Feeling lighter than he had all day, Woody pulled his bike from the long grass and brown weeds and set off for Grandad's house. Before he'd pedalled ten metres the sky split open and a torrent of rain, like the contents of a bucket, fell on his bare head. Woody stopped to pull his hoody up but it was already soaking wet. Water ran down his neck and dripped off his nose. Before long, his clothes weighed a tonne, and trying to pedal uphill was impossible. He got off the bike and pushed it in the gloom, his wet hands slipping on the handlebars, before turning up the muddy track to the farm.

By the time he got to the main entrance he was wet through to his underwear, muddy, starving and miserable. The old wooden front door creaked open and Grandad peered out into the murky afternoon. The light from the hallway clearly did little to help him work out who was standing bedraggled and shivering on the doorstep but Cassie, Grandad's sheep dog, didn't need to see. As soon as she smelt Woody she bounded outside and danced around his legs, her body wiggling with excitement.

'Darren?'

'Hi Grandad.'

'Good God, boy. Look at the state of you.' He looked over Woody's shoulder as though expecting to see his daughter. 'Here on your own?'

'Can I stay for a bit?'

Woody looked down as Cassie dashed back into the house then reappeared with a ball in her mouth. She dropped it at his feet and stared up at him, her mouth a wide grin and her tongue hanging out. Without thinking, Woody bent to pick up the ball then tossed it back into the house. She skittered after it.

'Get yourself inside, laddie. You're wet through. Does your mum know you're here? I'll only let you stay if she agrees.'

Chapter 20
2.30PM

Child missing - 5 hours 30 minutes

DI Paton

Driving along the lanes to Burrelton again, Paton constantly scanned the verges for any sign of a small boy in a blue coat. He knew it was probably pointless because the child was hardly likely to be wandering around the countryside, but Paton looked anyway. He ran through the possibilities in his head. If it had been car thieves, what would they have done when they realised there was a kid in the back? Would they have hidden him somewhere safe until they could think where to drop him off without being spotted? Would they have dumped him somewhere? Would they have sold him to other criminals who might...? Paton's guts churned and he felt a fresh wave of empathy for Louie's parents. They must be torturing themselves with worry and going through hell.

The side road approaching the village hall was cordoned

off with blue police tape that vibrated in the wind. A handful of people stood huddled together and Paton hoped none of them were reporters. He parked a short distance away and walked briskly over to Colin who was recording the crime scene log. He stopped to put on white coveralls and shoe covers then Colin lifted the tape and Paton ducked under. He headed over to the CSI team within the next cordon of red and white police tape. A short woman with serious brown eyes straightened up and watched him approach.

'Yvonne. Good to see you.'

Her smile was warm. 'Come to destroy the evidence?' she teased.

Paton knew he'd never live down the incident where he'd knocked Cheryl off a step plate onto blood spatter evidence, but his honesty in owning up to it later in a meeting with the SIO had earned him the respect of this CSI officer.

'Found anything?' he asked.

'Possibly,' she said. 'It's not easy to gather skin, clothing and hair samples in a car park where its damp and windy but we did stumble across one potential little treasure.'

Paton raised his eyebrows. This sounded hopeful.

'A lump of freshly chewed gum near where the car was parked. We alerted Tony who checked with all the mums in the hall.' She paused for effect. 'None of them chew gum.'

Paton's heart gave a lurch of hope. If the car thief had spat the gum out, and if he had a criminal record, they might be able to link him to this place by his DNA. Paton nodded slowly but the grin on his face must have given away his optimism.

'Could be something,' Yvonne said. 'We also found a used tissue, a partial footprint, a pen lid, an elastic hair band and an old receipt for a Co-op in Perth for the purchase of a white sliced loaf and chocolate. We'll get DNA from the tissue and might get a partial fingerprint on the pen lid but the receipt is quite soggy so it's unlikely to yield much.'

'Does it have a date and time on it? We might be able to check the in-store cameras.'

'Sadly not. That part of the receipt was mashed up and unreadable. The customer didn't use a card either.'

Paton sighed. 'Shame it wasn't for a packet of gum.'

He thanked Yvonne then went to find Tony, who was halfway up the street, calling door-to-door. Tony hurried back down a front garden path when he spotted his boss.

'How's it going? Anything to report?' Paton asked.

'I've spoken to the postman who saw two teenagers entering the village on foot as it was getting light this morning. He thought it odd as they weren't jogging or anything and he didn't recognise them. He wondered where they'd come from that early. He's given a full statement. In his words one lad looked 'decidedly shifty, glancing around and over his shoulder a lot with his hood up. The postman lost sight of them when he turned down a different street.'

This was promising. 'Anyone else see them?'

'No one so far. I'd already spoken to the mothers but we've got all their contact details so Sandra at the station is calling them to check if anyone spotted them.'

'Any doorstep cameras?'

'Apparently Mrs. Smythe around the corner has one. I was about to knock on her door.'

'I'd like to take this one if it's okay with you.'

Paton should really let his team do the house-to-house calls but he was heading to Louie's parents' place next and he felt he needed to do something that might yield positive news.

'Be my guest,' Tony said. 'Any help is appreciated.'

The house stood on the main road leading to the village hall, and Paton noticed a small white box next to the front door as he waited for it to open. Mrs Smythe was almost as wide as she was tall, with an unhealthy sheen of sweat on her rounded pink cheeks.

'Sorry to keep you waiting,' she panted. 'I was at the back of the house.'

Her hands restlessly smoothed her flowered dress and Paton marvelled at the heat billowing out of the front door. She stared at him expectantly.

Paton introduced himself and showed his warrant card then pointed at the box.

'Is this a camera?'

'Such a clever wee thing. My son installed three cameras for me so that I can look out for my dear old mum when I'm at the shops or at the whist drive. You wouldn't believe what a difference they've made to my life. I couldn't go anywhere before without the worry of her falling or taking ill. This one tells me if anyone comes to the door, which is handy when I have a parcel or I'm at the back of the house with Mum and don't hear people knocking.'

Paton waited for her to draw breath.

'Is it triggered by motion and do you have footage stored anywhere?'

'Aye, it stores it in the sky for a month. It starts recording when someone comes to the door. It's a tad sensitive, though. Comes up on my new phone every time someone walks down the street. Good job we don't live on Piccadilly Circus!'

She gave a deep belly laugh and slapped him lightly on the arm.

Paton grinned, warming to this gregarious woman.

'When you say the sky do you mean the iCloud?'

Paton was grateful for the quick lesson Douglas had given him in doorstep camera technology.

'That'll be it. Probably that one over there.'

She pointed at a dark cumulus cloud in the distance and laughed again.

'Why do you want to know? Has someone been dropping sweetie wrappers in the street or letting their dog poo on the pavement?'

Paton was relieved to realise that Mrs Smythe hadn't heard of the events in the village. The other mothers must have heeded the advice not to discuss the car theft and Louie's disappearance too widely, or put it on social media. They had been warned about the problems that might ensue if the press got wind of it.

'We're investigating a car theft and believe the thieves may have come this way.'

Mrs Smythe's eyes widened slightly.

'You'd best come in,' she said.

Paton followed her down a narrow hallway into a front room papered in an explosive flower pattern. He sat on a red leather sofa and slid backwards involuntarily. Crikey, the house smelled deliciously of buttery baking but it was hot in here. He ran a finger around his collar. He'd have to take his jacket off. It was a good job he'd ironed his shirt sleeves and not just the collar and front as he'd been tempted to do.

'Would you like a drop of tea? I've made shortbread.'

Paton's mouth watered, but time was precious so he politely declined.

'I'll fetch my iPad and tell Mum I'll be a short while.'

Mrs Smythe bustled from the room and was back within minutes. She placed a tin-foil wrapped parcel in Paton's hand.

'Thought you might fancy a bit of shortbread for later. I've made plenty.'

Paton took it gratefully.

'Thanks! I'll enjoy that with a mug of tea back at the station.' He looked at the iPad. 'I don't have much time now.'

Mrs Smythe understood.

'I'll just log in and bring up the footage. What time frame do you want to look at?'

'Between 8am and 9.15am. Can you scroll through?'

Mrs Smythe touched the screen and dragged a bar slowly across. The view of the road and pavement outside her front door remained unchanged until a figure with a small dog flitted across.

'That's Susan with Sammy the sausage dog,' she said and reversed the film clip briefly to show Paton.

He nodded and made a note of the time in his pocket-sized notebook. The image fast-forwarded again and Paton thought he saw the postman. He definitely had a big bag over his shoulder.

They repeated the process several times.

'Wait!' Paton said. 'Go back.'

At least this camera was at face level, unlike other security cameras that only captured the tops of heads, which meant hats or hoods could prevent identification. They both watched the image of two figures ambling by. It was difficult to judge their age, but from their outfits of hoodies and trainers and their lolloping walks and slouching posture, they appeared to be teenagers or young adults. *Turn your head. Look this way*, Paton willed them silently, but they continued to look ahead or at each other until they were out of range.

Paton bit back an expletive and sighed.

'We'll need this footage at the police station. Can you email it to us or give us your log-in details?'

'I'll give you my log in to the iCloud.'

'Do any of your neighbours have doorstep cameras?'

'Not as far as I know. I tell Susan to get one every time she misses a delivery but she's not as good with technology as me.' She spoke with a hint of pride in her voice.

Paton thanked Mrs Smythe for her help, and the welcome shortbread, then stepped back outside. The sky over the houses opposite was black and full of the promise of rain. Paton hurried to find Tony who was on a doorstep a few yards away. He thought about the image he'd seen of the two lads. If it was them at least he had an idea of what they were wearing. The postman might be able to verify whether it was the same two he'd seen entering the village earlier. What would two young lads be doing at that time of the morning? How did they get there? Had someone dropped them off to steal cars? If this was the case then the car theft was part of something far more sophisticated and organised than a couple of lads taking a car for a joy ride. Was Louie just in the wrong place at the wrong time or was he a target?

Chapter 21
2.30PM

Child missing - 5 hours 30 minutes

Mabel

Louie lifted his foot obligingly as Mabel pushed his yellow dinosaur wellies on. The boots worried her as they were so recognisable but for now they'd be perfect for egg collecting. Louie wriggled with excitement and hopped off the chair as soon as his boots were secure.

'Let me fetch the basket first,' Mabel said, as he rushed to the back door.

His enthusiasm at seeing the animals warmed her heart. Clearly this was something he lacked in his normal life. Something she could provide.

With the wicker basket over one arm, and Louie's warm hand tucked in hers, Mabel felt happier than she had in decades. This is what she'd been missing all her adult life. The void in her soul was Louie-shaped and he filled it perfectly. She swung Louie's arm and burst into song. 'Five little ducks went swimming one day...'

Louie looked up and smiled. 'Me cuddle Flump now?'

'We need to collect the eggs first for the lady at the farm shop. You can be a big boy and help.'

She led him through the gap in the outhouses and over to the chicken shed. Inside, the warm and comforting aroma of straw, feed and chicken crap clung to their clothes and tickled their nostrils.

'Pooh! It stinky in here.' Louie wrinkled his nose in disgust.

Mabel hurried him forward and lifted a hinged wooden lid. Underneath lay four large brown eggs. He stared in awe.

'Milly, Molly and Mandy have laid these.' Mabel said with pride.

Her eggs were far superior to Glenda's. Her yolks were a dark orange – full of Omega 3 – from the marigold petal powder she bought online. Mabel was an expert in online shopping.

'You pick them up and put them in the basket,' she said to Louie.

'They warm,' he said, as he gently put them on the heap of straw in the basket.

They moved along the hut, naming the chickens as they went, until the basket was almost full.

'Let's hope they lay a few more before we get back then we can have omelettes for tea.'

Keeping an infrared lamp on for warmth and low lighting to encourage winter production was paying off, and Mabel was gratified to find such a good yield. The eggs were an essential part of her income, along with the patchwork quilts and oven mitts she made and sold online. Life had been tough since her parents passed away but she'd coped. The small inheritance from her mother's will had been a surprise and had given her enough to manage on and set up various income streams.

Mabel lived far more comfortably now – compared to the frugal years after Dad died. Who'd have thought Mum had a secret stash in the bank? Mabel felt a fresh ripple of irritation as memories of gristly meat, darned jumpers and cold, empty grates resurfaced. A far cry from the comfortable farmhouse she'd grown up in across the fields. Although that had been cold too. At least they'd eaten well, though. She pictured the long, scrubbed wooden table in the huge kitchen, laden with homemade chicken pies, big bowls of creamy mash and newly-picked vegetables from the plot behind the house. She could still see her parents and the farmhands ladling stew onto their plates, see Andrew holding eye contact with her a fraction too long.

A slight tug on her hand brought her back to the present and she smiled down at Louie.

'I think we've got enough now, don't you? Let's go and put them in the trays. You'll be good at that.'

While Louie carefully placed eggs into the cardboard wells, Mabel dashed upstairs to rummage through the spare wardrobe again. When she'd initially collected outfits, she'd included footwear – tiny, knitted booties, small leather shoes and even a pair of miniature sheepskin slippers. She wished she hadn't stopped now. Pulling shoe boxes from the back of the wardrobe, Mabel rummaged through tissue paper to expose the petite footwear. The biggest pair she could find were traditional T-bar Clarks sandals in a delicate shade of pink. She pulled them from the box and rushed back downstairs.

'Pretty little girls don't wear wellies with their dresses,' she told Louie gravely. 'We need to see if these will fit you.'

Louie stared at the shoes, a look of disdain on his face.

'I not wear girl shoes,' he said, frowning.

'Just try them on,' Mabel pleaded. 'Look, they match your dress.'

Louie clearly didn't give a fig if they matched. He turned away and picked up his wellies by the door.

Mabel thought fast.

'You can wear your wellies in the car but just wear these in the shop. If you do, we'll buy some juicy carrots and you can bring them back for Flump. They're her favourites,' she added.

Louie allowed himself to be led to a chair to try them on and the shoes were squeezed onto his plump feet.

'Ow,' he said. 'Too tight.'

'They'll do for five minutes. Just long enough to drop off the eggs and buy the carrots. We'll put your wellies back on for the journey.'

Mabel parked a short distance from the main entrance to the farm shop and quickly changed Louie's footwear and removed his distinctive blue coat. It was cold, but they wouldn't be outside long. She picked him up and snuggled him into her side then balanced the trays of eggs in her other hand. Pushing the car door shut with her bottom she glanced about. An elderly couple was getting into a vehicle nearby but took no notice of them.

Inside the shop, Mabel slid the eggs onto the counter and waited, quickly scanning the aisles to see who was in there. Thankfully, the shop seemed quiet. Louie looked around with interest and wriggled to get down. Mabel held him tighter.

'Wait,' she said.

'Ah, Miss Grimstone. Thank you so much for bringing these.'

A woman with short brown curly hair, a round face and eyes magnified by thick glasses, leaned forward and peered at Louie who hid his face in Mabel's neck.

'Who's this then? I didn't know you had grandchildren.'

Mabel cursed silently. Why couldn't the bloody woman just take the eggs and hand her the money like she always did? She never usually bothered to strike up a conversation. Before Mabel could answer, the woman said, 'What's your name? Would you like a lollipop?'

Louie's head snapped round to face her.

'Louie,' he said, holding his hand out for the round purple lolly.

Mabel tensed but plastered a fake smile on her face.

'This is Louise,' she said. 'My cousin's granddaughter. I'm just looking after her for the day.'

'Oh, yes. You said on the phone.'

Mabel quickly unwrapped the lolly and gave it back to Louie who immediately popped it into his mouth. At least it would stop him saying anything else. She took the money offered and hurried over to grab a bunch of carrots – their green fronds tied with string. Her arm and hip were aching from the weight of the small boy, but she didn't dare put him down for fear he'd run off or complain that the shoes hurt his feet. Dropping the money on the counter she muttered her thanks and left.

The sky to the east was charcoal black, and the first few spots of rain dotted her jacket and Louie's dress. Mabel moved as fast as she was able, mindful that Louie had no coat on. Back in the car and along the lane, Mabel let out a long breath. That had been scary. She'd need to be better prepared if they went out again. Clearly it was time for some more online shopping. A suitable coat and shoes being top of the list.

Chapter 22
3PM

Child missing - 6 hours

Melanie

As soon as she heard the hum of the engine outside, Melanie was at the door, holding it wide open, paying no heed to the frigid air coiling around her ankles. She stared at DI Paton's face as he climbed out of the car, trying to read his expression. The tightness of his lips and puckered brow told her all she needed to know, and she grasped the doorframe for strength. Dear God, where was her darling Louie? Was he cold? Was he hungry? Was he frightened and crying for her? She couldn't bear this. Her chest was a giant void of nothingness. As empty as a sinkhole that threatened to swallow her whole world. Everything seemed insignificant, invisible, pointless. Everything apart from finding Louie.

'No news, then?' she asked Paton as he approached her.

'May I come in?'

He glanced sideways at the neighbour's front window, and Melanie glimpsed the curtain moving slightly.

She stepped aside, resisting the urge to clutch his arm and beg him to find her son. She followed him into the lounge where Cheryl stood waiting, then perched on the edge of a chair clasping her hands in her lap to hold herself together.

'Is your husband back yet?' he asked.

Surely someone had spotted a little boy in a bright blue coat? Surely it couldn't be that difficult to find him? Melanie stared blankly at Paton, unable to take in his question.

Cheryl filled the void.

'He came back momentarily. He asked for an update, grabbed a coffee, and went out looking for Louie again. He's driven around Perth and said he was off to try Dundee.'

'We've put out an alert to all the squad cars within a 200-mile radius for any sightings of a small boy fitting his description,' Paton said, 'and we've contacted the airports and ferries. We've interviewed other mothers from the playgroup for any new information. We're currently doing house-to-house calls in Burrelton and asking for footage from any cameras.'

Melanie tried to concentrate on what the detective was saying but her focus kept slipping like sand through her fingers. What were the other parents saying? That she was a terrible mother? But who cared what they thought? Nothing mattered apart from finding Louie. She pictured again the last time she'd seen his wee face. Head turned into his car seat, dark eyelashes curled onto his smooth cheeks like tiny feathers and his plump fingers rubbing the silky label of his blanket on his nose. She heard the echo of the DI's last word and dragged herself back into the room.

'Cameras? What cameras?'

'I'd like to show you something.'

Paton pulled an iPad from his bag and opened it. He

touched the screen a few times, explaining that someone near the village hall had a doorstep camera.

'Have you seen these lads before?'

Melanie leaned forward and peered at the screen.

'Are these the boys who took Louie? Who are they? Can't you find them by their clothes? By their walk?'

She knew she was clutching at straws but when you're sinking you'll grab at anything.

'We have people analysing the images now. We're studying the clothing for anything identifiable. This one, for example, has writing on it. Another interesting feature is this lad's back pocket. It's ripped away at the top corner. See?' Paton pointed out the boy's baggy jeans then said, 'you're right, though. There are specialists who can analyse body size, shape, posture and movement. They've been known to pick out suspects in a football crowd or busy underground station. If it comes to it, I'll see if we can call them in to help. We'd need something to compare it to though, such as CCTV footage.'

'What else?'

Melanie was alert now. The thought of people who could identify villains in this way gave her a small measure of hope.

'We're examining details of recent car thefts locally, and other emergency services are on the lookout for abandoned vehicles. We've got the CSI team scanning the vicinity of the village hall for any evidence and they've given us a couple of leads to follow.'

'What leads?'

'They found some used chewing gum so will run DNA tests on it to see if it matches any known criminals on our database.'

'How long will that take?'

'It depends how busy the lab is, but we're asking for this to be a priority so we should get the results within a couple of days.'

'A couple of days! That's too long.'

Melanie thought of her child alone and abandoned somewhere, or imprisoned in a grotty house in a rough area, while the thieves decided what to do with him. He must be so frightened.

'If he gets anxious, it can trigger his nighttime seizures. You have to find him soon. He's in danger.'

Melanie could hear her voice rising in pitch and volume but was powerless to calm herself. Her self-control was slipping away to be replaced by hysteria. She put her face in her hands and rocked back and forth.

'Oh God. Oh God. What if he needs to go to hospital? What if no one knows what to do?'

Melanie felt a gentle hand rubbing across her shoulder and the soft voice of Cheryl trying to soothe her. She took a deep breath and sat upright. She couldn't turn into a gibbering wreck. She had to stay strong for Louie.

'How often are his seizures?' DI Paton asked.

'He usually has them once or twice a month, but when he gets upset they're worse. He wets the bed too which upsets him. He had more when Noah started playgroup without him and... and...'

Melanie had said enough. She could feel heat building in her cheeks. They didn't need to know about the bitter arguments she and Simon had. It wouldn't help them find Louie.

'How often has he been to hospital in an emergency?' the DI asked.

He was looking at her intently and it made her feel uncomfortable. It was as though he could see straight into her mind and knew about the friction in her marriage. Her hands went to her stomach and his eyes followed them. She lifted them quickly to the arms of the chair.

'Twice this year. They kept him in for two days last—'

A loud ringing interrupted her. Paton apologised then stood and put his phone to his ear, listening intently. Melanie watched his reactions but couldn't work out what was being said. The inspector told the caller that he'd be back soon.

'One more question before I go,' he said. 'How much petrol was in the car?'

Melanie thought hard. 'I filled it up a few days ago and haven't been anywhere much. Probably three quarters of a tank left.'

Paton pinched his lips together and nodded slowly.

'They could get a long way on that,' Melanie said. 'It's an economical little car.'

She shuddered at the thought of Louie being whizzed down the motorway, the distance between them tearing open like a wound.

Chapter 23
3.30PM

Child missing - 6 hours 30 minutes

Woody

The sky was darkening into dusk as Grandad knelt to put more firewood in the stove then slowly stood upright to pull the curtains shut. Woody settled back into the old sofa that fitted his body like a pair of favourite slippers and sipped his mug of Horlicks. Funny how he wouldn't normally touch this stuff, but then it didn't taste the same anywhere else. Horlicks was only delicious at Grandad's house. He stared at the flickering flames as the kindling caught. For the first time in ages, he felt safe and relaxed.

'We need to phone your mum now,' Grandad said.

Woody's mood plummeted. She wouldn't be happy. He sat forward and jiggled his knee up and down as Grandad held the phone to his ear. Woody's mum answered immediately.

'Don't worry, he's safe with me,' Grandad said. 'Why don't

we let him stay the night then we can decide what to do in the morning? It's dark now and to be honest I don't feel like turning out in this weather.'

Woody sat back and let out a long breath as Grandad chatted to mum about the farm, the dog, and his aching knees. Their conversation then turned to Woody's cousin and her doctor's appointment and Grandad stared at Woody, his eyes narrowing. He cupped his hand over the old-fashioned phone receiver and said, 'What's this about you letting Megan down after you promised to look after Tyler tomorrow?'

'I thought I was busy,' Woody muttered, staring at the floor. He didn't want to see the disappointment on Grandad's face.

'Talk to Megan and we'll see what we can sort out,' Grandad said into the phone. 'If she hasn't cancelled her appointment maybe Darren could look after him here. I'm sure I can find them some chores to do.'

'Time we had a little chat,' Grandad said, after the call ended. 'What's going on? I can tell something's not right in your world, and your mum said your phone was switched off. I may be old and stupid but isn't that unheard of with kids your age?'

Woody wasn't surprised. Grandad always knew when Woody was stressing over something and he usually listened without judging him – apart from letting Megan down tomorrow. He clearly wasn't happy about that. Grandad had been there for him when his parents' marriage fell apart and Woody had often stayed over to get away from the bickering and tension in his home. Grandad always fought his corner but he'd be shocked and angry if Woody told him what he'd done. Stealing the cars would be bad enough, but dumping a little kid by the road would be too much. Woody didn't like himself at the moment, but he couldn't bear to lose the respect and love of his Grandad who was the only solid thing in his life. Grandad reached over and put his hand on Woody's shoulder. To his shame Woody's eyes filled with tears.

'Come on Darren, you can tell your old grandad. I promise not to shout at you.'

Woody's mind raced as he worked out what to say. It would be so good to unburden himself. He took a deep breath then began to explain what had happened to bring him here. The loneliness and boredom, the pressure to keep up with the other kids at school, the lack of decent food and clothes, how he felt abandoned by his father, and the boys in the park who had invited him to play football.

Grandad nodded encouragingly when Woody faltered, and urged him to go on.

'The older boys asked me to do a job for them. Moving something from one place to another, they said. I wanted the money, but I swear I didn't know they meant steal a car until it was too late to back out.'

'Steal a car?'

Grandad sat upright in shock then rubbed at the back of his neck. 'Carry on,' he said, when Woody stopped talking.

'They threatened to dob me in to Mum if I didn't do it again. But that wasn't the worst thing, because then they said I knew what would happen to me if I didn't help. And after Gus got mashed up and...'

'Mashed up?'

'I saw him this morning. Lying on the pavement. The police were there and everything. I'm supposed to be outside the chip shop in the morning. They're going to pick me up and take me to Dundee, but I... Grandad, I don't know what to do.'

'We should call the police.'

Grandad picked up the phone again but Woody lunged forward to knock the receiver from his hand.

'No!'

Seeing the surprised look on Grandad's face, Woody sat back down and mumbled an apology.

'Sorry, Grandad, but they know where I live. I'm worried about Mum,' he said, 'and I don't want to be beaten up like Gus. The police won't protect me.'

Grandad frowned as the phone began to wail from being off the hook. He picked it up and put it back on the base.

'How many are in this gang?'

'I don't know. I've only been out with them a few times and I haven't met the ones in charge. Surely it's better if I just disappear for a while? They don't know about you so they won't find me here. If they go to my house, we can ask Mum to tell them I've gone back to Dad's. Please?'

Grandad put his elbows on his knees and his head in his hands. His voice was muffled when he next spoke.

'It sounds like you've got yourself mixed up with some serious shit here.'

Woody was shocked. Grandad must be upset to use a swear word. He was always really strict with Woody about his language.

'I had to get away, Grandad. I'm scared.'

Grandad sat still, deep in thought, then put his hands on the arms of the chair and pushed himself up.

'I'll phone Megan and arrange for her to drop Tyler here. We'll decide what to do in a day or two. You'll need to get up early tomorrow and pull your weight if you're going to stay for a while. Lord knows I could do with some help.' He rubbed his knees to prove his point. 'I'll wake you up at six.'

Woody's eyes widened and Grandad chuckled.

'Okay, you can have a lie-in. I'll wake you at seven.'

Chapter 24
4PM

Child missing - 7 hours

DI Paton

The incident room was a hive of activity when Paton hurried past it to the DCI's office. He wondered whether he should call a late briefing meeting then decided to wait until morning. If he let people crack on with their actions, they'd have more to report. He knocked on the DCI's door and waited as his boss finished his phone call.

'Come in, Dave. Sit down. I'll get straight to the point as I have to leave soon. There's been a serious assault in Perth today on a teenage boy. The SIO allocated to the case has had to leave suddenly as his wife is giving birth prematurely to twins.'

Paton knew what was coming but couldn't decide if he was pleased or not.

'I'd like you cover the case as SIO for a couple of days, just to ensure that everything proceeds as it should. From what I've heard this could be attempted murder, given the vicious beating the lad took. Who knows what they might do to the next victim? This investigation could so easily turn into a murder inquiry.'

Paton opened his mouth to speak but the DCI silenced him with his raised hand.

'I know what you're thinking, Dave. *What about finding the bairn?* As I said, it's only for a couple of days maximum and your main focus can still be on Operation Oakwood. You and I both know being a detective isn't like the television dramas where you only get to work on one case at a time. Resources are seriously stretched here at present. I don't just mean financially. Finding good replacements for officers that retire is getting harder.'

'I understand,' Paton said.

He could hardly believe this. He'd waited his whole career to be the SIO on prominent cases involving murder, abduction or terrorism and now he'd been given two in one day. Part of him was flattered, but how would this impact on his personal life? He wanted to visit the breakers' yard again and speak to the greasy owner who had invaded his property and threatened his son. He doubted he'd have time now, and it wasn't a task he could delegate.

The DCI stood and put his jacket on. 'Sorry to leave you with all this, Dave. I can't get out of this training, otherwise I'd take more responsibility myself. Will you manage?'

Paton knew his boss was really asking if Tommy would be an issue.

'I'll get right on it, sir, you can rely on me.'

'If you feel out of your depth at any point, you can text me and I'll call you when I can.'

The DCI turned towards the door then hesitated and stepped back over to Paton. In a rare gesture of intimacy, he patted Paton's shoulder and said gruffly, 'Thanks, Dave. I really do appreciate this.'

'I'll do my absolute best for you, sir,' Paton said. He just hoped Kirsten didn't let him down with minding Tommy.

'Before you go, sir, I just need to check that I'm still on the right track with not initiating a Child Rescue Alert.'

'Has anything changed since you made that decision?'

'I think we're close to finding the thieves who took the car. Two suspicious youths were seen walking through the village early in the morning and we've got them on video. They're wearing distinctive clothing and we found chewing gum at the scene.'

'I'm undecided. I'll leave it to you, Dave, but keep me updated.'

Paton was undecided, too, and had hoped for more guidance. Still, he couldn't take on additional responsibility if he couldn't make decisions.

'I'll give it until tomorrow lunchtime,' he said. If we don't have a strong lead by then, I'll contact the press officer.'

Knowing it was below his paygrade, but needing to get a feel for the serious assault case, Paton decided to accompany the DC to the hospital to see the injured lad for himself. Getting to the nucleus of the crime usually gave him the focus and direction he needed.

The first things Paton noticed when he reached the hospital ward were the brightness of the lights and the constant noise. Trolleys clattered, cupboard doors banged, machinery bleeped and footwear squeaked on the shiny floors. He imagined the night times weren't much quieter. No wonder people always said they found it difficult to rest or sleep in hospital.

He approached the nurses' station and asked for the whereabouts of Gus Chambers. He was relieved when a cheerful nurse directed him to a side room and grateful that the medical team had considered the need for privacy, knowing the police would want to interview Gus.

As Paton entered the room, he was struck by the contrasting hush and stillness within. A form lay motionless on the bed whilst a woman sat alongside holding his hand. Paton took a sharp intake of breath when he saw Gus. The poor lad had taken a thorough beating. Even though the bruises had yet to emerge properly his eyes were puffed up like two overripe plums ready to split, a cut ran down his left cheek and his bottom lip resembled a shiny, wet slug. Blood crusted his nostrils and his breathing was shallow.

Paton nodded to the DC then introduced himself to the woman by the bed. She was petite and neatly dressed, her delicate features framed by thick auburn hair. Paton had to hide his surprise when she said she was Elaine Chambers, Gus's mother. He'd thought she might have been his older sister. She must have been young when she had him. A younger version of her sat in the far corner, her heels up on the edge of the wooden chair and her arms wrapped around her knees. Her long hair swept across her face but her eyes burned through and remained fixed on the boy in the bed. Gus's sister maybe?

'Have you caught them yet?' she asked.

Crikey. People had such high expectations of the police.

'I need to ask Gus a few questions if he's able to talk,' Paton said.

'I'll wait outside,' the young DC said. 'Give you some space.'

'Go and grab yourself a coffee then come back here. I won't be too long.'

The DC looked grateful.

'Anyone else want a drink?' he asked politely.

The family declined, clearly too upset to think about beverages, and Paton shook his head.

As the DC left, a nurse bustled into the room.

'You can have ten minutes but then he needs to rest,' she said to Paton.

She lifted Gus's wrist and took his pulse then put a cuff around his arm to take his blood pressure. Gus moved slightly and Paton could just see his eyes opening a fraction and scanning the room. He winced and closed them again.

'We've got Detective Inspector Paton here,' the nurse said. 'He wants to ask you a few questions.'

'I didn't see who it was,' Gus muttered through his swollen lips. 'I can't tell you anything.'

'How many people attacked you?' Paton asked.

'I don't know. Two, maybe three. They sprang on me from behind.'

'Could you describe them?'

'It all happened too fast.'

Gus's breaths were getting shorter. He fell silent, his eyes remaining tight shut.

His mum stroked the back of his hand.

'Are you sure you can't tell the policeman anything, Gus? He wants to help.' She looked at Paton. 'He's got two broken ribs,' she said. 'It hurts him to breathe.'

'We've done a full body scan,' the nurse added. 'He's got a fractured collar bone, too, and will have multiple bruises but, thankfully, there's no visible head trauma.' She looked up at the clock. 'I'll be back in eight minutes to see you out.'

'It's a terrible shock for you all,' Paton said. 'We'll do our utmost to catch the offenders.'

Elaine's eyes filled with fresh tears as she gazed at her battered son.

'It could have been so much worse,' she said quietly. 'My poor boy.'

A tear slid from the corner of Gus's right eye and rolled into his ear. His mother leaned forward and dried it gently with a tissue then kissed him tenderly on his forehead.

'Ask the lady with the massive red poodle,' he murmured, his voice barely audible. Paton leaned closer. 'She was there. I think his name was Pickle or something. She must have seen them.'

And then you won't be punished for snitching on them, thought Paton. What sort of person doesn't report a beating like this, though? Surely she'd have called the police. Unless the gang threatened her too. He looked at the clock and stood up as the nurse bustled in again. He wanted to visit the breakers' yard before picking Tommy up but it might be closed soon and he had another team to meet, share updates with and allocate actions to. The first of which would be to question local kids in the park and ask around for witnesses.

Chapter 25
5PM

Child missing - 8 hours

Tommy

'Can you show me how to draw cats?' Tommy asked Auntie Ursula. 'Mine are rubbish. I want to paint a black and white one for Dad. He likes cats. I'm going to get one when I have my own flat. I'll call it Oreo.'

'Such a shame your mum is allergic to them,' Auntie said. 'When are you getting your own flat?'

She glanced up at him then pulled another sheet of paper off the pile.

'Start with the head.'

She drew a circle and Tommy copied her. He loved Auntie Ursula, but it was a bit boring at her house. Fancy not having Netflix or Prime TV. She didn't even have many channels on her telly. He'd rather be watching detective dramas but drawing was okay. Auntie was good at drawing. And painting. She painted people's dogs and they gave money to charity.

Tommy dipped a soft brush in black paint and swiped it down the cat's back.

'One day I'll get a flat. Will Dad be back soon? Do you think he'll get fish and chips?'

'You need to watch your weight, Tommy. You don't want to put too much pressure on your heart, and besides, you had a good lunch.'

Tommy's heart was like his favourite old jumper. It had a hole in it. He could still wear the jumper though and he could still run about. A little bit. He got puffed out quickly so he liked his exercise machine better.

'I'm going on my boat machine in the shed when I get home,' he said. He also wanted to add that it wasn't a good lunch, as none of Auntie Ursula's cooking was good, but he kept quiet. He wished she'd buy soup instead of trying to make it. The vegetables were as hard as toenails and it tasted of old socks.

The painting was finished and dry and Dad still hadn't arrived. Tommy was bored and hungry but he mustn't show it. His dad had an important job to do, and Tommy had to be patient.

'Your Dad is going to be another hour, I'm afraid,' Auntie said.

Tommy sighed and took another sheet of paper. He'd paint a ginger cat this time.

Chapter 26
6PM

Child missing - 9 hours

DI Paton

The journey to the breakers' yard gave Paton the opportunity to reflect on his meeting with the new team. He'd been relieved to discover they were a cheerful, welcoming bunch. They'd run through all the information they had about Gus's assault so far, though it wasn't much. It was surprising how no one had witnessed the beating, despite it being in a public place in broad daylight. House-to-house calls were continuing, and checks were being made on local cameras. The lady with the giant red poodle could be a vital witness. Paton had set them actions for the next morning, then said he'd catch up with them once he finished his own team briefing.

The yard was only a mile or so ahead now. Paton tried to work out what to say to the owner. In all his years with the police, his family had never been threatened before. He could kick himself for bringing Tommy into this situation and fervently hoped he could sort it out without Wendy hearing of it.

Paton wondered how Nigel had found out where he and Tommy lived. Nigel could have approached the special needs school Tommy attended but that was closed and they wouldn't divulge such information anyway. He could have looked on the electoral rolls for Patons within commuting distance, but it would take a while to go through them all, and there might be several Patons to rule out before finding the right one.

Lights illuminated the road ahead, and Paton caught flashes of a large vehicle approaching through the trees as he negotiated the bends. He slowed as it neared but wasn't prepared for it to be taking up the majority of the road. It powered towards him like a menacing mythical beast.

'Watch out!' Paton yelled as he yanked on the steering wheel to avoid collision. His left wheel hit the bank of earth and the car tilted. The huge lorry maintained its speed and clipped Paton's wing mirror as it thundered past.

'You absolute... basket case,' Paton roared. He'd promised himself he wouldn't ever swear for fear of Tommy picking up bad language, but at times like this it was really difficult. What the hell was a huge lorry carrying scrap doing in this quiet lane? Paton approached the breakers' yard but before he drove into the muddy lane he parked and got out of his car. Switching on the torch on his phone, he examined the scratched wing mirror, that had luckily folded against the car, then swept the beam over the damp earth. Deep double tyre tracks were clearly visible. This was more than a typical breakdown truck towing or transporting a smashed-up car. What had it been carrying?

Paton took photos then got back into his car and drove along the track. Before he could reach the terrapin hut, he saw

Nigel swinging a huge metal gate across, his black Labrador at his heels. Paton stopped, got out of his vehicle and approached.

'We're closed.' Nigel said abruptly, as he hooked a large padlock through a thick metal loop.

'Why did you visit my house today?' Paton didn't have time for niceties and Nigel was unlikely to appreciate them anyway.

'I was doing you a favour, mate. Stay away from here and keep your minions away too or you'll regret it.' He twisted the numbers on the padlock while Diesel, the dog, stood rigid and eyed Paton with suspicion.

'Why are you threatening me? What are you hiding?'

'Not me. If you love your kid you'll do as I say. This really isn't worth it and he's a nice lad.'

'How did you find my house?'

'Easy. My niece goes on the same bus as Tommy so knows where you live.' Nigel started to walk away, Diesel following close behind.

'Wait!' Paton's mind was racing. Nigel almost sounded decent. What was he hiding? Who was he working for and why?'

Nigel paused then turned around.

'Please don't ask me for more information. I love my family too and this is bigger than both of us.' He turned back towards his office.

'We can help you,' Paton said. 'You can't let criminals run your life.' He didn't want them ruining his either. It would be so easy to ignore all this, with its implied threats of violence and harm to his family, but it wasn't in Paton's nature. He had a strong sense of what was right and wrong, and a society without strong justice was unthinkable.

'If you do the honest thing and tell us what's going on, we can protect you,' Paton called after the man's retreating back.

'You can't, and if you've any sense you'll protect your son,' he called back.

Paton's jaw clenched and he grabbed the gate and shook it in frustration. Diesel paused, turned his head and emitted a low growl.

'Come, Diesel,' Nigel said, still heading for his office, then he raised his hand in a final gesture of farewell and disappeared inside.

Chapter 27
7PM

Child missing - 10 hours

Tommy

As soon as he heard footsteps in the porch Tommy rushed to open the front door. Dad smiled but his shoulders were droopy. He rubbed his eyes with his thumb and fingers.

'Are you tired, Dad? Have you been chasing the baddies?'

'I have indeed. Let's get you home then you can make me a nice cup of tea. I've bought us a couple of pizzas from Tesco.'

'Cool.'

Tommy would have preferred fish and chips or even one of Mum's stews, but never mind.

'You look stressed out, Dave,' Auntie said. 'Are you sure you're not taking on too much?'

Tommy waited while Dad told Ursula about his day. It sounded like he was doing two jobs now. His dad must be good if he'd been given so much to sort out.

'Know anyone around here with a giant red poodle called Pickle?' Dad asked her.

'I don't think so. Was it definitely a standard poodle? My neighbour had one years ago but you don't see many these days. Most are crossed with another breed.'

Tommy listened carefully. He liked dogs. Maybe he could help Dad look for it.

'The lad was quite sure,' Dad said. 'Apparently his uncle has one.'

'I suppose you might spot it around the local parks or you could look on CCTV,' Auntie suggested.

'We don't have the resources for that, I'm afraid.'

'Try looking on Facebook for a standard poodle group. You may come across a red called Pickle on there. My friend has a pedigree Vizsla and she belongs to a group for owners of Vizslas. She's always showing me pictures and funny stories on there.'

'Shall we go and look for it, Dad?' Tommy asked.

'I'll ask one of the team to check out Facebook. We need to get home now, lad. I need that cup of tea.'

Tommy made the tea and enjoyed his pizza but as soon as Dad sat down with a cold beer, he took the torch out of the drawer and went to the shed. He put the light on and looked around. A pile of stuff covered half the shed, but he could still use the rowing machine. It was cold, but Tommy wore his thick jacket, hat and gloves. He'd get hot soon then he'd take them off.

As he settled onto the seat, he heard a rustling sound behind some boxes. His heart went mad in his chest. *Was it a rat?* He sat very still and held his breath. A small squeak had him ready to run away but then he heard a sad meow. Wow, a cat! Tommy wanted to jump up and drag the boxes out but that might scare it. He made a kissy noise instead and waited.

It wasn't a long wait. A small ginger, black and white face appeared and Tommy stared. *A real kitten, in his shed.* He wanted to jump up and do a happy dance but it cried again. It must be hungry. He reached out slowly and the kitten came out and nuzzled his hand. It was so soft. It stared up at Tommy and let out another wail.

'I'll go and get you some food,' he said. 'Wait there.'

Tommy rushed back to the kitchen and grabbed slices of ham and a lump of cheese. He'd have to ask Kirsten if they could go to the shops tomorrow to buy cat food.

'Still hungry?' Dad was standing in the doorway.

Tommy was about to tell him what he'd found in the shed then stopped. Dad would say he couldn't keep it because of Mum. He'd say they had to find the owners or a new home for it. Perhaps Tommy could keep it for a few days first.

'I'll put it back,' Tommy said, moving towards the fridge.

'You can eat it,' Dad said. 'I expect you didn't eat much at Auntie's house.'

Tommy pulled a face and Dad laughed.

'Can I have a glass of milk too?'

'Of course. Here.' Dad poured him some and Tommy took it then headed to the back door.

'Going out again?' Dad asked.

'I'm growing my muscles on my boat machine.'

'Ah, that's good. You won't get fat from all that cheese and ham then.'

Tommy opened the shed door a tiny bit and squeezed in. The kitten was hiding again.

'Here Puss Puss,' he said.

He put the ham on the floor and waited, hardly able to stay still and quiet, as the kitten crept forward and sniffed the ham.

It was soon gobbling it up and looking around for more. Tommy giggled then broke off small lumps of cheese. He found a flowerpot saucer and poured some milk in. The poor thing was starving.

It was cold in the shed. Tommy looked around then saw the fruit box mum used for the apples off the tree. He took out the last few apples wrapped in newspaper and carefully set them in a row on a shelf. Next he took off his jacket, pulled his fleece jumper over his head and put it in the box. It made a nice cat bed. What about a tray for its toilet though? He looked around again, making sure he didn't frighten the kitten. A paint tray would do. Tommy found a bag of compost and tipped some in. There. The little cat had everything it needed now. He'd visit every day and bring it food. He'd think of a name and it would be his pet.

It would be his secret.

Chapter 28
7PM

Child missing - 10 hours

Mabel

'How about a story?' Mabel asked.

Louie sniffed and gave a slight nod. He'd kicked up a fuss when Mabel had told him it was bedtime, throwing himself on the floor, slithering out of her grasp when she tried to pick him up and curling into a ball. She didn't know much about children but she'd once read somewhere that routine was important. Did he have a proper routine at home? She'd asked him what time he usually went to bed but he just carried on crying.

She had to promise he'd see Mummy tomorrow just to get him up the stairs. She knew she would have to hand him over soon, but she couldn't bear the thought of giving him up yet. Just one more day should be enough. Just one more day of pure happiness and lasting memories to see her through the rest of her lonely life.

She wondered if his parents were even looking for him. There had been nothing on the TV news. Odd really. You'd think a missing child would make national headlines. She'd sat with the remote in her hand ready to switch it off at the first hint of a mention of Louie. She'd checked the BBC News app regularly on her phone too.

'I've got just the book for you,' Mabel said.

She took the old dining chair from the corner of the room and placed it in front of the wardrobe. Louie stopped snivelling and watched as she teetered unsteadily on the chair and reached to the back of the top shelf.

'Here we are!' Mabel fanned out the small pile of children's books like a dealer in a casino. 'I bought these a long time ago,' she said. *I was keeping them for my future children,* she wanted to add.

'This one's my favourite, *The Tiger Who Came to Tea.*' She showed Louie the cover and his eyes widened.

'Look at this big, furry, stripy tiger. Isn't he handsome?'

Louie put his thumb in his mouth and waited while Mabel climbed carefully down off the chair and sat next to him on the bed.

As she spoke the old familiar words her mind began to drift. Her mother used to read *Norgy in Littleland* to her when she could spare the time. Life on the farm was always an endless list of chores that left very little time for the pleasurable things in life. Having a story read to her, and her mother's undivided attention, was one of the best memories of her childhood and it was probably why she loved books so much.

Louie was leaning against her now, taking in every detail, his warmth seeping through her clothes to warm her soul.

'More,' he said.

'How about this one?'

Mabel drew *Mog and the V.E.T* from the pile and began to

read. When she was a child, her books had been her whole world, her friends. Being an only child and living on a remote farm had been a solitary existence. She lived for her school days, when she could be with other children and more books, and had promised herself that she'd have lots of children when she grew up so they'd never be lonely. She rarely visited friends' houses or had friends back to her place. Her parents were always too busy to ferry her around and the few friends she had outside of school soon dwindled away when their parents realised their invites weren't reciprocated.

It was no wonder, really, that she'd fallen so hard for Andrew when he'd started at the farm during the summer she turned fifteen. A flirtatious comment from Andrew and she was a giggling, quivering wreck. The gap between them seemed so much more than two years. She was the naive schoolgirl and he was almost a man. Seeing his little red mini, with the union jack roof, turning into the farm gate lifted her spirits and made her heart race.

It didn't take long for him to sneak her into the barn for a secret kiss and a clumsy fumble inside her bra. She was flattered by his compliments and unable to say no when he took further advantage of her.

The long, hot summer was so exciting she was oblivious to the problems within her family. When she missed her period for the second time and began feeling nauseous she knew she would have to tell Andrew about their predicament. It would be fine though. Andrew could move into the farmhouse and they could have their own set of rooms. It was big enough.

Mabel could barely suppress the joy she felt at the growing baby inside her. She planned to tell Andrew the next day so they could face her parents together.

'What this one?'

Mabel was jerked from her memories like a dog about to

step into the road. Louie had picked up another book and was staring at the cover. She must have read the whole *Mog* story on autopilot. How amazing that the brain could perform such a task whilst being immersed in another time and place.

'That's Winnie the Pooh and that's Tigger.'

'I like tigers.' Louie said.

He took the label on his blanket and rubbed it on his nose.

As Mabel watched him, totally entranced, his eyes glazed then began to roll back in his head. That was a bit weird but maybe it was something he did when he was tired. Mabel gently laid him down and crept out of the room.

Chapter 29
8AM

Child missing - 23 hours

DI Paton

Tommy reached the front door first, his excitement at hearing Kirsten's knock reassuring Paton that he'd done the right thing by arranging for the young girl next door to sit with Tommy.

'Can we go to the shops?' Tommy asked, before Kirsten had even crossed the threshold.

'Let the poor girl in before you start planning your day,' Paton said. 'What do you need at the shops? There's plenty of food in the house.'

Tommy looked away and didn't answer.

'No chocolate or cakes, Tommy. Remember what the school dietician said?'

'How about a game of pairs?' Kirsten said, unsuccessfully suppressing a yawn. 'If you want to be a good detective you need a good memory.'

Tommy's face brightened.

'Can we do the remembering game too?'

Paton smiled. He'd done this with Tommy many times, gradually adding random items to a tray then covering it with a tea towel to see how many Tommy could recall. He was up to seven objects now.

'Go and find the tray and a tea towel while I have a word with Kirsten,' Paton said.

He'd had a restless night worrying about Tommy and had vivid nightmares of him being snatched and Paton searching for him in crowded places. The feelings the dreams evoked lingered and fear still tainted the day.

'Don't leave Tommy on his own, Kirsten. He's not capable of looking after himself yet.'

She looked at him in surprise.

'You left him on his own yesterday, though.'

Paton opened his mouth to tell her about the visit from Nigel but closed it again. It was best not to frighten the girl.

'I had no choice then. I've got you to help now and Tommy has almost caused a fire in the kitchen before so please keep a close eye on him.'

He wanted to tell her not to open the door to strangers, but that would sound odd. He doubted whether whoever was issuing the threats would do anything today. Surely they'd wait to see if he'd heeded their warning first?

'We'll be fine. Don't worry.' Kirsten smiled.

As Paton drove to work he called Wendy to see how she and her mother were and to update her about Tommy.

'He's happy to see Kirsten,' he said.

'Are you sure she's sensible enough to look after him all day? Perhaps I should come home sooner.'

'Your mother needs you more, and you have to get all the

grab rails installed before you come back, otherwise her next fall could be worse.'

'I suppose so, but I feel bad leaving everything to you, especially when you've a big case on.'

Paton refrained from saying that he now had two big cases and was used to coping without her. Depression was tough for the person suffering from it, but it was also difficult for loved ones trying to help them through it.

'What day and time will you be back? I'll see if I can pick you up from the station.'

'I'll get the early train on Saturday. Dave, I wanted...' Wendy paused.

'Go on,' he said gently, sensing she was struggling to say something.

'I'm late this time. Maybe this is it.'

He heard the excitement in her voice and his heart sank. Each month Paton dreaded the hope in Wendy's eyes if she was even a day late getting her period. They'd been trying for another baby for years and time had all but run out. Wendy might be eight years younger than Paton but forty was too old in his opinion, and forty-eight definitely was. Crikey, he'd be approaching his seventies by the time the child reached adulthood.

The risk of another Down's baby was high, too, and even though Paton would give his life for Tommy, he knew Wendy wouldn't cope with the trauma of bearing another child with a disability. He wouldn't cope either. There was no way he could juggle his career and the extra demands a baby would make on their family unit. Maybe his reluctance to father another child subconsciously affected his fertility. Who knew?

He guiltily recalled the sense of relief each time Wendy emerged from the bathroom and took to her bed, red-eyed and devastated. The later her period the longer the depression lasted. It was time to bring the situation to a close. He'd discuss it with her when she returned and tell her he wanted a vasectomy. He cringed inwardly at the thought, but her longing wasn't healthy for either of them.

'Let's talk about it when you get home, love,' Paton said. 'Look after yourself.'

He ended the call as he pulled into the police station car park. He had to drag his thoughts away from his personal problems and onto the missing child. If the investigation didn't make significant progress soon he'd have to initiate a Child Rescue Alert and all that it would entail. With the DCI on his course for three days, would the press officer suggest Paton make the media announcement? Would he have to appear on television? He smiled at the thought of Tommy's excitement if he did, but the sobering image of Louie's parents sitting in front of cameras to make a public appeal was enough to replace it with a grim tightening of his jaw.

There was the assaulted teenager to think about, too, but the priority had to be finding Louie. Some officers on his team would have worked through the night, so Paton would get a quick update and see if there were fresh leads to follow.

The incident room filled quickly with officers, all keen to find the missing boy. Paton noticed the lack of banter about whose turn it was to provide the cakes or make the coffee. Instead, everyone focused on Paton as he asked people to present their findings.

Mitchell was the first to speak.

'We've trawled through all the data and spoken to adjoining areas and it seems the incidences of car theft are rising significantly.'

Paton processed this information even as he listened.

'I also visited local hotspots yesterday, where vehicles are more often dumped, but saw no evidence of stolen cars,'

Mitchell continued. 'The Fire and Rescue Service hasn't been called out to any car fires and no joyriders have been arrested in this vicinity.'

Paton already had a theory, especially after his meeting with Nigel last night, but he wanted to hear what his team thought.

'Anyone want to speculate on this data?' he asked.

Mitchell spoke again.

'If the cars aren't being dumped or incinerated they're either being driven right out of the area or they're being sold.'

'And if the number of thefts has risen significantly, are we looking at something on a larger scale than the usual opportunistic theft or joyriders?' added Tony.

'An organised crime ring,' muttered Ian. 'Great.'

Paton's body shot through with adrenaline at hearing his thoughts validated, and the mood in the room shifted. The Perth police had been fortunate, so far, in avoiding crime on a larger scale but it was happening in the neighbouring towns and cities so it was only a matter of time. They'd all been trained to spot county lines activities, and the use of vulnerable kids and adults to distribute drugs, but they hadn't foreseen car thefts being such a threat to their community.

The image of the huge lorry descending on his small car loomed in Paton's mind. Should he mention the lorry leaving the breaker's yard or would it put Tommy at risk? Was it carrying parts of stolen vehicles? He had to decide quickly. It could be vital to this case.

'What does this mean for little Louie, boss?' one of the DCs asked.

Everyone stared at the cute photo of the small boy pinned to the board at the front of the room.

For a fleeting moment, Paton, crushed by the weight of his responsibilities, felt envious of people in simple jobs. Sitting behind a checkout in Tesco, sliding shopping past a scanner, seemed attractive right now. He gave himself a mental shake. This was no time to be a wimp, and hadn't he always wanted to be the SIO on a high-profile case? He had a job to do and people were depending on him. He also had to protect his own family.

'We need to investigate anything even remotely linked to the car thefts. I'm certain there's something dodgy happening at the breaker's yard. Last night my car was scraped by a heavy goods vehicle on the narrow approach road. Why would a huge lorry have been there? I saw the owner but he refused to engage in any questioning.' Paton omitted to say that he'd been threatened. He needed to think everything through then discuss it with the DCI on his return.

'What else have we got on the missing boy?'

Cheryl, back in the station for the team briefing before heading back to Louie's family, spoke next.

'I've talked with Louie's parents and there's nothing to indicate this could be a kidnapping. No significant wealth to speak of and no rich or famous relatives. Mr Cameron is blaming his wife, and you can almost taste the tension in the home. I hear it in their tones, see it on their faces and feel it in my gut.'

'Very poetic, Cheryl. You should write a book,' Tony quipped and everyone laughed.

Cheryl pulled a face at him and carried on. 'In my opinion this was a strained marriage before Louie went missing. Mrs Cameron wanted Noah to stay at his friend's house last night, but Mr Cameron insisted on fetching him home. The little boy was extremely distressed. I hope they've allowed him to go to his playgroup today because he's better off out of the house and in his usual routine given, that he's too young to understand what's going on. Mr. Cameron is planning to drive around the local area again, convinced he'll find Louie.'

There were murmurings amongst the team as they considered the trauma the family must be going through.

'I've checked the background of the parents through various means,' Douglas said. 'It all stacks up with what they've told us. I also looked at businesses in the Burrelton area to see if there might have been any vans with dashcams. There's a coach hire company on the outskirts, so Tony visited early this morning before the coaches left for the school runs. We've obtained the footage from a couple of vehicles that were on the road around the time the two lads were seen by the postman and Mrs Smythe's doorstep camera. We're about to go through it.'

Paton looked at Tony.

'Anything to add?' he asked.

Tony looked at his notes.

'I visited Mrs Smythe's friend Susan, the one on the footage with the sausage dog. She hadn't seen anything of any significance. There's also a car showroom along the main road from the village hall. We looked at their CCTV but there's no sign of the two lads or a blue Fiesta which tells us the driver took another route out of the village.'

'Okay, everyone, thanks for your hard work. Those of you who burned the midnight oil, go and get some sleep. Douglas, let me know of any findings from the dashcam straight away. If we don't make progress this morning then we're going to initiate a Child Rescue Alert. Cheryl, I might need you to talk to Louie's parents about doing a public appeal. I'll speak to the press officer as soon as I've spoken to the team dealing with the assault on Gus Chambers.'

'I've checked out the standard poodle Facebook page as you requested,' a young officer said, rising from his chair to head home. He'd been there all night so it had made sense to Paton to ask him to check out Facebook rather than wait for the other team to be in the station.

'Getting yourself a fancy dog, Boss? I thought you'd be more of a Labrador man.' Tony grinned and the team tittered.

'I was thinking of a Chihuahua actually,' Paton retorted.

Everyone laughed then headed off to their respective actions. He turned to the young DC.

'Did you find Pickle?'

'Not exactly, but there is a large red on the group called Branston. I checked the owner's Facebook page and she lives in Perth.'

'Brilliant. That's a huge coincidence if they're not linked. Can you find me the address before you go home? If it's not listed on Facebook, ask Tony to call local vets. As soon as we've got a lead, I'll get someone over there.'

Paton felt the exhilaration of the chase before the gravity of the situation hit him again. He'd ask a DC on the other team to phone the hospital to check on Gus too.

Chapter 30
8.30AM

Child missing - 23 hours 30 minutes

Melanie

A flush of heat and a sudden wave of nausea sent Melanie scrambling to the bathroom to lean over the toilet. She recalled a friend saying morning sickness was a sign of a healthy pregnancy, and for the first time in twenty-two hours, Louie wasn't the only thing on her mind. She didn't recall feeling this sick with the boys. Maybe she was carrying a girl this time. She heard Simon in the doorway and swung her head around, instantly regretting the sharp movement as the room tilted and she felt sick again.

He was staring at her dispassionately and she fought back the tears that were never far away.

'Noah needs to clean his teeth then he's ready. I'll drop him at play group,' he said.

Melanie felt a surge of relief. She wanted to keep Noah

close, but the little boy had been so distressed when no one knew where Louie was that it would be good for him to have some normality to his day. Melanie had wanted to accept Jemma's offer to let him stay at Poppy's house last night but Simon wouldn't hear of it.

'Will you come back afterwards?' Melanie asked.

'I'm going to drive around again. I'll call in at lunchtime. I can either fetch Noah or you can ask your friend to have him for the afternoon.'

Melanie stood and brushed strands of hair off her clammy face.

'I need you here, Simon,' she said.

She moved towards him, desperate to feel the comfort of his arms around her, but he side-stepped and turned away.

'Wash your face,' he said. 'That policewoman will be here soon.'

Melanie gripped the edge of the washbasin. How could he be so cold and distant? Surely they should pull together to help them through this nightmare. Melanie was so tired she felt weightless. She'd lain flat on her back most of the night, staring at the lamplight shining through the crack in the curtains and constantly checking her phone for updates. Thoughts about Louie, where he might be and what he might be suffering, had threatened to overwhelm her. She'd physically clamped her teeth onto her tongue to stop herself wailing with fear and grief. She'd stretched a hand across the bed to rest it on Simon's arm but he'd turned over and her hand had fallen into the empty space between them.

Melanie could understand Simon's anger and would probably resent him if he'd been the one to leave Louie in the car with the keys in the ignition, but his bitterness went deeper than that. She wondered if their relationship could survive this.

But without Louie what did it matter? What did anything matter?

Noah. He mattered. And this small being growing inside her. Simon had made it very clear that he didn't want this baby. Yes, it was unplanned, but she really hadn't missed her pills on purpose, despite what Simon thought. And yes, she had been overjoyed at the positive result on the pregnancy test but the sun had disappeared behind his cloud of negativity when he'd told her to get an abortion. She didn't care that they could barely afford their mortgage now, and he was expecting her to return to work. They'd manage. People always did. They had another two weeks to decide then it would be too late for the abortion. Perhaps, given the situation, it would slip from Simon's mind.

Melanie called Noah upstairs and helped him clean his teeth.

'Will Louie come home today?' he asked, spattering toothpaste dots onto the shiny chrome taps.

'The nice policeman will find him. He'll have been out all night looking, so don't worry about it.'

'What if Louie gets the wobblies? Will someone look after him?'

The image of Louie in the throes of a tonic-clonic seizure with no one to talk him through it, make sure he didn't bang his head, or administer his meds if his seizure was prolonged, filled her anew with horror. She tried hard to keep her expression neutral and her voice light.

'Have fun at playgroup and go to Poppy's house, then when you come home Louie will be back. You'll see.'

Melanie wanted desperately to believe her own assurances. The alternative was unthinkable.

Chapter 31
8.45AM

Child missing - 23 hours 30 minutes

Louie

Louie was very cold. And wet. The naughty elf must have been in the night. The one who threw water over him in bed and made his pyjamas and the sheet soggy. Not that he had proper pyjamas on now. Just Grandma's leggings and T-shirt. Naughty elf! Mummy would wag her finger and tell him off but she wouldn't be cross with Louie. The little elf would sit on the shelf in his red suit, watching.

The elf wasn't here though. Louie lay still, thinking. Perhaps Elf ran through the night and found Louie then ran back to Louie's real bedroom. Perhaps he was doing naughty things at home. Noah said Elf broke the vase with the football. Noah said Elf put shampoo down the toilet. Louie saw Noah do it. They'd laughed when the toilet filled with bubbles.

Louie rubbed his head. It hurt lots today and he was still very tired. If he wasn't so cold and wet, he could go back to sleep. The door squeaked and Grandma came in. She opened the curtains. Ow. That hurt his eyes too. Had he had a wobbly in the night?

'Morning Louie,' she said.

Louie didn't answer. He didn't like her today. He wanted Mummy. Mummy would wash him with the tickly shower. She'd make him clean and warm. Grandma might say he'd wet the bed even though it wasn't him. He was a big boy now. He didn't do that. She walked over and he slid under the covers.

'Time to get up,' she said. 'We can have some nice dippy eggs for breakfast.'

He didn't want dippy eggs. He wanted Coco Pops so he could make the milk chocolatey. He wanted to sit next to Noah. Noah pulled funny faces and made him giggle.

Grandma tugged the covers back. 'Oh dear,' she said. She reached for his hand. 'Let's get you out of your wet things and put you in the bath.'

'Elf did it,' Louie said.

Grandma's eyebrows went up but she didn't tell him off.

Louie shivered as she peeled off the wet clothes. She put a towel around him and he waited while the bath filled.

'It was naughty Elf,' he said again. 'I'm a big boy.'

She shook her head. She thought he was fibbing. The bath took ages but it was nice and warm. She went to the warm cupboard. Yay! She had his own clothes. She pulled them on him. They were stiff and scratchy. Mummy made them nice and soft when she washed them but he was still pleased. He didn't like Grandma's rolled up things.

'Is Mummy coming soon?' Louie's head felt funny. Like it was full of sloshy water. And his eyes hurt when he moved them. Mummy would say he'd had a wobbly turn and let him go back to bed. He wanted his own bed.

'Maybe see Mummy later,' Grandma said.

Louie didn't want to see her later. He wanted her now. He needed to look at her face. He couldn't remember it properly. He sat on the bathmat and thought about it. He looked up at Grandma.

'I want Mummy,' he said.

There was lots more to say but he didn't know the words. His chest was too full. All the words he couldn't say were stuck there and it hurt. He began to cry.

'Come on, Louie,' Grandma said.

She took his hands and pulled. He tugged them away and cried louder.

'I've got a nice surprise for you,' she said. 'Come and see.'

Louie hiccupped, then stopped crying and wiped his nose on his hand. Was Mummy here? Grandma went downstairs and after a minute he followed. She pointed to a box in front of the big, red, hot thing that cooked the dinner and warmed the kitchen. He lifted the lid and moved the straw. Underneath was a big fat, white rabbit.

'Flump!' he said.

Grandma lifted the rabbit out of the box. It hopped under the table and Louie laughed. A rabbit indoors. How funny! He giggled and ran after it as it jumped into the lounge. Grandma followed.

'Don't let him chew any wires,' she said. 'And tell me if he does a wee wee or poo poo.'

Poo poo! Louie laughed. Fancy Grandma saying a rude word.

'Poo poo,' he repeated. 'Poo poo.'

Louie sat on the floor and patted his knee. Flump hopped behind the sofa. Louie lay on the floor to look underneath.

'Get up! Now.'

Grandma sounded cross. Or scared? What had he done wrong?

Chapter 32
9AM

Child missing - 24 hours

Mabel

The sight of Louie's body lying between the coffee table and the sofa sent Mabel's brain into turmoil. She put her hands to her cheeks and squeezed her eyes shut. no one had lain there since.... since...

She couldn't let the memory frame itself in her mind. She snapped at Louie to get up then shoved the sofa aside to retrieve the daft rabbit before it could chew the telephone wire. Tucking it under her arm she carried it back to the kitchen with Louie trotting at her heels. She shut the door firmly and put the rabbit down.

'I want Coco Pops,' Louie said.

'We don't have any of those. I told you, we're having dippy eggs.'

Mabel watched in consternation as Louie's face distorted

then his mouth turned into a grimace as he began to howl. His words were garbled but the meaning was clear. He didn't want eggs for breakfast.

Mabel was exhausted. She'd had a terrible night's sleep. When she'd finally drifted off she'd awoken to a knocking sound. Was there someone at the door? Had the police traced Louie to her cottage? She lay still, trying to replay the sound in her now conscious state. It had been knocking but where from?

Mabel had climbed out of bed and pulled on her dressing gown. She'd tiptoed to Louie's door and peeped in. He was lying flat on his back, his arms and legs flung wide and the duvet hanging half off the bed. He must be a restless sleeper too. Maybe he'd had a nightmare and had been running in his sleep like the old dog used to. She examined the wall behind and found a mark where the headboard had scraped it. Poor little lamb. It must have been some dream. She pulled the cover over him again and crept out of the room.

It had taken her ages to get back to sleep. Guilt had gnawed at her insides like a rat in the wainscotting of her old farm bedroom. She couldn't keep the boy from his family any longer. She had to hand him in. What would happen to her though? Would she go to prison for abduction? Most likely. Hell. If she was going to sacrifice her freedom for him then why end everything now? Why not keep him for a week before giving him back? A week to cherish forever. His parents might be distraught but she'd suffered for years. They would get over it once they had him back and she'd take good care of him until then. He wouldn't even remember this episode of his life and perhaps his family would look after him better in future.

A week. Yes. That would be enough to sustain her for the rest of her life. She'd keep a diary too, so she didn't forget the small details. Maybe she could even find a way to leave him somewhere safe. Somewhere that wouldn't link him to Mabel Grimstone.

Louie's cries grew louder and were starting to give her a headache.

'Let's have a look in the larder,' she said in desperation. 'See if there's anything else you fancy?'

Five minutes later she sat with her hands wrapped around a fresh cup of tea while Louie munched on toast and strawberry jam. She'd have preferred him to eat a healthier breakfast but she couldn't face a battle today. Maybe he always had sweet breakfasts. Mabel would have raised her child differently. A diet rich in sugar and salt hadn't done her family any favours, but people didn't know much about diabetes and blood pressure in those days.

The image of her father lying between the coffee table and sofa rose unbidden into her mind. Mabel had watched as her father's face had altered like a candle too close to the fire. The melting flesh sliding down one side, the staggering gait that had caused him to crash to the floor and his slurring words – were they all signs of a stroke like Nan had died of a few years before? Mabel should have called for help straight away. She remembered her dad saying how they might have saved Nan if help had arrived sooner but they'd had no telephone back then.

Her mother was out visiting a friend and wasn't due home for hours so Mabel was the only other person for miles. She stood in the hallway of the cottage, staring at the green telephone before picking it up and holding the receiver to her ear to hear the purr of the dialling tone. Her forefinger hovered over the number nine in the dial, her mind strangely calm when really she should have felt fear and panic. She turned the dial and released it, watching it hum back to the starting point. She put her finger in the slot to dial another nine but this time she couldn't bring herself to do it. Didn't the bastard deserve to die after what he'd put her through? She replaced the receiver and returned to the lounge.

Mabel sat on the chair opposite her father and watched in morbid fascination. He stared at her, desperation adding to his distorted expression, imploring her with his eyes to help him. He garbled nonsense as Mabel got up and left the room. She'd go and hunt for eggs in the hedges and come back in an hour.

By the time she finally summoned help, her father was unconscious and he died before he reached the hospital. Her mother had looked her straight in the eye.

'Where were you?' she'd asked, her accusation clear in her tone.

'I was out egg collecting,' Mabel said. 'I found him on the floor when I came in. I called the ambulance straight away.'

Her mother's eyes had narrowed at Mabel's lack of emotion but she said no more. Mabel knew her mother was fully aware of the animosity between her husband and daughter but was powerless to do or say anything else. What would have been the point anyway? Her husband had gone and nothing would bring him back.

'Shall we play treasure hunts?' Mabel said now to Louie. 'Milly, Molly and Mandy are outside today and they like to hide their eggs in the hedges. I'll make some toffee and you can have a piece for every egg you find.'

Sod the healthy eating idea. A week of goodies would do no harm.

Louie slid off his chair and ran to put his wellies on.

'Come on, then,' he said.

Chapter 33
9AM

Child missing - 24 hours

Woody

It was a struggle to leave the warmth of his bed and stumble to the fridge-like bathroom. There was no point in refusing though. If he didn't earn his keep, Grandad might send him back home, and that was the last place he wanted to be. He exhaled heavily to see if his breath left a cloud of steam and was disappointed when it didn't. It certainly felt chilly enough in here. He turned on the tap and waited for what seemed ages for the clonking pipes to spit out lukewarm water. He washed hurriedly, dragged on cold clothing then made his way to the kitchen.

The Aga had been banked up for the night and needed bringing up to temperature so Grandad set him to work. He carried in two baskets of logs, chopped up some kindling and filled the coal bucket. And all before breakfast.

At least the Aga was warming up nicely now, and the smell of eggs and bacon made his stomach growl. Cassie, the sheepdog, lifted her head from her paws and looked at him in astonishment. Woody laughed.

'Don't worry, Cassie, it's only my guts needing breakfast.'

'I bet you're not used to physical labour before you eat. In fact, I bet you're not used to physical labour.' Grandad laughed at his own joke and Woody gave him a faint smile. 'The food will taste better for it. You'll see.'

Grandad was right. Eggs and bacon had never tasted so good. Woody wondered briefly what the small boy was having for breakfast. Was he at home tucking into a sugary cereal or was he lying in a ditch somewhere? Woody shuddered.

'Still cold?' Grandad asked. 'It'll warm up in here soon. I've got plenty for you to do today so you won't be still long enough to feel the cold.'

Cassie lifted her head and stared towards the hall a second before a knock sounded on the front door. Woody's heart kicked inside his ribcage and his breath stalled in his throat. Thoughts raced through his head. Had the police caught up with him? Had the gang found him? Was Mum okay?

Cassie leapt up and ran into the hall before changing her mind and dashing back for her beloved ball. She pranced and twirled at Grandad's heels as he heaved himself out of his chair.

'I'll get it, shall I?' he said, looking at Woody with a tut and flick of his chin.

Woody sat welded to his chair as the front door opened.

'Can I ride on the tractor, Great Grandad?'

The excited voice of Tyler bounced off the walls, then the door slammed open and a whirlwind of woolly hat, scarf and padded coat burst into the kitchen.

Woody grinned with relief.

'Is Tyler in there somewhere under all that clothing?' he asked. He plucked the hat off the small boy's head to release a cloud of soft blond hair. 'Ta da! Here he is.'

Tyler laughed then began to chase Cassie around the table to get the ball. Megan dumped a bag on the floor then sat down opposite Woody. He lowered his head, looked up at her and braced himself.

'So, Darren Woodrow, what have you got to say for yourself?' Her face was serious, her blue eyes like lasers scoring a direct hit on his guilt button.

'Sorry,' he mumbled. 'I thought I'd be busy.'

'Tea?' Grandad said. 'Or have you got to rush off?'

Woody was grateful for the interruption.

'I'll make it,' he said, springing out of his chair.

Megan glanced at her watch then her voice softened.

'Just a quick one,' she said. 'And is there any bacon left? It smells divine.'

As she ate, Grandad listed jobs for Woody and Tyler to do.

'When you've washed up and made your bed, I'd like you both to sweep the barn and bag up all the loose hay. If you do it well you can feed the sheep later.'

Woody was just wondering why this was a reward when Grandad added, 'On my new quad bike.'

'Quad bike? Yay! When did you get that?'

Woody was delighted.

'Is it safe?' Megan asked.

'I bought it because my poor knees were suffering walking around the fields. They can be dangerous so it might be best if I take Tyler out for a gentle ride then Woody can check on the sheep.' He looked at Woody. 'I'm trusting you to take it steady,' he said. 'You'll have the trailer of hay on the back so you'll need to be sensible.'

'I will be,' Woody nodded, his mouth set in a straight line to hide the thrill of excitement he felt.

As soon as Megan left for her appointment Woody and Tyler tackled the washing and drying up. Tyler struggled to reach so Woody had to hand the items to him.

'Here, wear this. You'll freeze in your thin coat.' Grandad handed Woody an old Parka jacket. 'You'll need these as well.'

'Thanks,' Woody said as he pulled on the wellies and thick coat. 'Thanks for not letting Megan nag me.'

'I wanted us to start the day on a positive note and you'd already apologised. I'm sure you won't do it again.'

Tyler danced around with Cassie bounding after him, jumping up to get her ball from his raised hand.

'That's enough,' Woody said. 'She'll have you over in a minute.'

They crossed the muddy yard then pushed through the old wooden gate to the meadow. Cassie followed them. The barn stood to their left, it's corrugated metal walls creaking in the weak sunshine.

The ground floor housed the old tractor and other farming machinery while the upper floor stored bales of hay. Woody's eyes fell on something new in the corner hidden under a tarpaulin. He lifted a corner to reveal a gleaming red quad bike. He let out a low whistle.

'Cool!' Tyler said, and Woody laughed.

Cool indeed. Perhaps life on the farm wouldn't be so boring after all. It was strange not looking at his phone constantly but he had to admit that life was easier and less worrying when it was switched off and in his bedside drawer. At least Roach and Spanner couldn't reach him. He had a sudden urge to run and leap into the air.

'Come on. Let's sweep the hay up. I'll race you to the ladder.'

Woody guided Tyler carefully up the wooden ladder onto the platform above.

'Don't go near the edge,' he said. 'We don't want any accidents.'

He made his way to the window on the far side.

'Look, we can see for miles up here.' He lifted Tyler to show him the rolling land spread out below like a duvet.

'Can you see the sheep?'

Tyler narrowed his eyes as he gazed into the distance.

'There's some,' he said, pointing. 'And there's a blue one.'

'A blue one?'

Woody stared in the direction of Tyler's outstretched finger.

'That's not a sheep. That's a little boy in a blue coat.'

As the words left his mouth his heart plummeted into the borrowed wellies. Shit. Was it...? No, it couldn't be. His breath caught in his throat as he watched the figure moving slowly along the hedgerow. It was only a couple of miles from where Roach had dumped the boy so it was possible. But how had he survived the cold night? Was he alone? Woody would have to go and see. He'd have to go now, before the boy disappeared again.

Chapter 34
9.30AM

Child missing - 24 hours 30 minutes

DI Paton

The three officers sat close together and peered at the screen, all of them uncomfortably aware that the 'golden hour' for finding Louie had already passed. The dashcam footage from the coach was playing out before them and they watched intently as the village streets rolled by. There was very little to see until two figures, initially pinpricks in the distance, grew close enough for details of clothing, build and gait to emerge.

'Pause it there,' Paton said.

Douglas froze the image then enlarged it. Two young males, dressed in jeans and hooded sweatshirts, were captured. One had his head turned slightly, revealing the end of his nose in profile, but the other had his head forward and down so all they could see was his hood. Douglas zoomed in further.

'Wait,' Paton said. 'What's that in his right hand?'

He pointed to the screen. The image was grainy but the item hanging from his grasp was clearly visible, the splash of a red label giving it away.

'A Coke bottle!'

Paton couldn't curb his excitement.

'We'll need to get Colin back out there to search the hedges and bins. With any luck we'll get some fingerprints and DNA from it.'

Paton checked for landmarks. The boys were outside a large, white detached house with wrought iron gates.

'Won't the heavy rain have washed the prints off?' Mitchell asked.

'I'm not sure,' Paton said, 'but it's worth a look and DNA from saliva might still be on it if the lid is on.'

He called to Colin across the office and beckoned him over.

'Check the footage from Mrs Smythe's doorstep camera again, please,' Paton said, 'and see if one of the lads is carrying a Coke bottle. If he isn't, I want you to search along the street, bins and hedgerows back to this white house. If the bottle is on Mrs Smythe's footage then search between there and the village hall.'

Colin nodded and went back to his desk to open the file Douglas was sending him. Paton turned his attention back to the screen.

'Look.' Douglas said as he pulled up the dashcam footage again. He pointed to the backside of the lad on the right. 'See this? His pocket is torn from the top left corner, and his hoody has something printed on the back.'

They all leaned in closer, then Paton pulled away.

'Sorry, I can't read that. It's too blurry.' He rubbed at the outer corners of his eyes with a thumb and finger. 'Your eyes are younger than mine,' he said to Mitchell.

Mitchell stared.

'Do Not Subverge,' he read.

'Subverge? What the heck does that mean? It's not even a real word.' Paton said.

Both Mitchell and Douglas shrugged then Douglas swivelled his chair and tapped his keyboard.

'There's a website.'

He turned his screen to face them. A range of quality hoodies and sweatshirts was displayed, all with slogans and writing on and modelled by young men with chiselled features. Douglas clicked on the Facebook link.

'Looks like Ben Chilwell wears it too.'

'Who?' Paton asked.

'The England player,' Douglas replied. 'You should know, being a Sassenach.'

'I don't get time to watch football, and besides, Tommy's always watching crime dramas. Get onto the company and see how many they've sold. If it's a young business they may have a manageable list of postal customers for us to check.'

A fingerprint to place the lad in the village, and an unusual item of clothing to yield a name and address, would be excellent. Paton gave a grim smile and nodded his head with satisfaction. They were getting somewhere now. If they could track the youth down and bring him in, he might tell them where Louie was or at least say where they'd taken him. If they had strong leads to follow they might not need to initiate the Child Rescue Alert after all. Their limited resources wouldn't be wasted fielding useless calls.

'Boss,' Tony approached Paton. 'I've spoken to three local vets this morning. Only one has a standard poodle on its books and it's the red called Branston. Here's the owner's name and address.'

He handed Paton a slip of paper.

'Thanks.'

Paton was pleased to see the address was on his route home. 'I'll visit this one,' he said.

He'd call on the woman after his next team briefing then nip home to check on Tommy and Kirsten, to put his mind at ease. He should really delegate the interview to a more junior officer, but if the woman had witnessed a brutal attack and failed to report it, then the situation would need careful handling. He couldn't risk a less experienced officer asking insensitive questions and causing the woman to clam up even further. He'd compromise and take a DC along with him though. It was a shame Cheryl wasn't available, because her gentle interview techniques were legendary. She could charm the wildlife from their burrows, but she was part of a different team and she was needed to support Louie's family.

Before he left the office, Paton checked his emails. The CSI team had been unable to obtain a partial fingerprint from the pen lid – too small and the wrong shape – but Paton wasn't too disappointed. It was unlikely to have been dropped by the car thief anyway. He was more interested in the DNA from the chewing gum, but that result could take another day or so. The footprint was interesting though. The National Footwear Reference Collection had shown a match with a *Nike Run Swift* and Paton couldn't suppress a wry grin. Equipped for a quick getaway, eh? Huh, not if he had anything to do with it. He had a reputation for tenacity and determination to maintain and he'd like nothing more than to see Louie's abductors locked up. Whoever had taken that little lad had better make the most of their last days of freedom. Paton was on the trail and he wasn't giving up.

Chapter 35
10AM

Child missing - 25 hours

Mabel

A bitter wind swept across the open field and cheated its way through even the smallest gaps in her winter clothing. Mabel adjusted her scarf and tugged her hat down over her ear lobes. She scanned the empty horizon towards her childhood home then looked down at Louie who was squatting on his haunches peering under the hedge.

'Are you warm enough?' she asked him.

He was wearing his blue coat and had insisted on tucking blankie down the front *'to keep his tummy warm'*.

He didn't reply. Instead, he tilted his head sideways to avoid a twig and reached forward. He plucked something from the ground then backed out, his little face beaming with triumph and his pink nose and cheeks glowing in the pale light.

'Got one!' he exclaimed.

He clutched it to his chest.

'Careful. Don't squeeze it too hard.'

Mabel held out the basket and he reluctantly placed the brown egg on the pile of straw. She reached down and adjusted the old woollen scarf she'd wound around his head and neck.

'We need to keep your ears covered,' she said.

She'd been relieved when she'd discovered fleecy mittens in his coat pockets and wondered why he hadn't been wearing them when she found him. Surely, if he'd been out for a walk with his family, he'd have had them on. Mabel couldn't comprehend why Louie had been abandoned in the middle of nowhere. Had he been in a car? Had he opened the door and fallen out and no one had noticed? It just didn't make sense. Why wasn't anyone looking for him? Why was there nothing on the news or local Facebook groups? She'd checked both regularly so doubted she'd have missed a story as high profile as a missing child.

'Can I have a toffee now?'

Mabel handed him his reward of sticky toffee wrapped in greaseproof paper. A fat brown hen, probably Molly, waddled from a bush further along the field and Louie rushed off to see if she'd laid another egg. Mabel's chest swelled with affection for the little boy. She was shocked at how deep an imprint he'd already left on her heart and she knew she'd be devastated when she had to return him. Another six days before her life shattered into a million shards of misery. She shook herself. *Don't waste the moment,* she thought, *store it in your memory bank.* She watched as Louie rested his buttocks on his heels again, with the agility only small children could achieve, and parted the grass to seek his treasure.

Mabel could still recall the excitement of finding golden eggs in the hedges with her mother. It was good, Mum said, for the hens to scrabble in the dirt, eating insects, seeds and green roots. It helped make the shells stronger too. Mum was so clever and wise. Mabel had idolised her then. Such a shame it hadn't lasted.

Looking back, Mabel guessed she must have been thirteen before she noticed how insular and restricting her upbringing really was. Rules and routines that had once offered security and comfort suddenly became claustrophobic and restrictive. The end-of-year school disco didn't compare to the extravagances of modern-day prom nights with their stretched limos and ball gowns, but had been the event everyone talked about for weeks and had also been the catalyst for her unhappiness. Mabel could no longer deny the growing divide between her and her friends. Whilst they compared outfits of the latest fashion and giggled about dancing with the boys, Mabel was dismayed to be told by her parents that there was no money for new clothes, especially something she might not wear again, and to make do with what she had. She'd feigned a tummy bug in the end and hadn't gone.

It wasn't just the financial hardships, geographical isolation and pace of farm life that marred her teenage years and alienated her from her friends. It was her parents' strict moral code too. Their idea of fun was helping at the local village fête, inviting children from the primary school to feed the lambs, and singing in the church choir. Mabel, discouraged from spending too much time with boys, was instead taught how to raise chickens and lambs and to sew and bake. Skills she valued now, but which, at the time, held no interest for her.

When the young farmhand, Andrew, had arrived during her fifteenth summer at the farm he had knocked her humdrum existence completely off its axis. Her parents, too preoccupied with their escalating debts, had failed to notice the growing relationship between their daughter and the boy.

Mabel, oblivious to anything but this new and passionate relationship, had naively believed her future was gilded.

Then Andrew disappeared.

Mabel shivered as the echo of raw misery resonated across her skin. She thrust her hands deeper into her pockets. It was time to go home for a warm drink.

'Come on, Louie. We can look for more eggs later.'

'In a minute,' he said, trotting further along the hedgerow in the direction Molly had taken.

Didn't the child feel the cold? She hunched into her coat. She'd give him a couple more minutes, then insist they return to thaw out.

As she searched under the hedges with Louie, Mabel's mind again churned up events from nearly fifty years ago. It didn't matter how many times she picked over the unhealed wound, she would never find the answer. Had Andrew guessed she was pregnant before she got a chance to tell him? Had he baulked at the idea of being such a young father, and fled the area? Mabel tried to recall whether she'd displayed any symptoms. She'd winced slightly when he'd squeezed her tender breasts, and she'd been sick a couple of times, but if she hadn't even considered pregnancy then how had he? Had her parents guessed? Had they got rid of Andrew?

Her unexpected teenage pregnancy was Mum and Dad's worst nightmare and their united front had been a formidable force. Without Andrew to stand by her, Mabel had to battle alone to keep her baby. In the late 1970s it just wasn't acceptable to be a single parent. Life for young people today was so much easier, Mabel thought, with a pang of envy.

So many young parents didn't appreciate their children either. Mabel read plenty of autobiographies about children who'd been neglected and abused. She watched documentaries about it and read news articles frequently. It was everywhere and it was shocking. Louie was probably one of them. Would she be returning him to a life of misery if she gave him back? Should she keep him longer?

The sound of a small engine spun her around. What the blazes was that? A vehicle was coming across the field. Mabel darted to Louie and dragged him up. He started to protest but she pulled him back along the edge of the field and through the gap in the hedge. She swept him up into her arms and ran unsteadily around the chicken huts and through the garden back to the cottage, her heart kicking in her chest.

Chapter 36
10AM

Child missing - 25 hours

Tommy

'A teaspoon, the salt pot, a stock cube, er... a pen, an elastic band,' Tommy paused and stared at the tea towel covering the tray. Something big was under there. 'A mug!' he shouted.

'Well done. Two more items to guess,' Kirsten said.

Tommy scratched his head.

'A comb!'

He was jiggling in his chair now. One more thing and he'd score his bestest ever. What was it? He looked around the kitchen hoping for clues. He couldn't think. He'd need to remember better than this if he wanted to be a detective like Dad. Wait... wait. He nearly had it.

'Dad's tie!'

Tommy was off his chair now and jumping around the room pumping his fist into the air.

'I did it!'

'Brilliant. You're very clever.'

Kirsten whipped the tea towel off the tray to check the items.

'Shall we add one more?'

Tommy was about to say 'Yes' when he remembered something far more important. His new cat, who he'd decided to call Pringle, would be getting hungry again. Tommy had already sneaked the last of the ham to her (he thought it was a her, anyway) but she had still meowed with hunger. Tommy had searched for a tin of tuna but there was none left.

'Can we go to the shops?' Tommy asked.

Kirsten looked out of the window at the cold, damp garden.

'What for? We've got everything we need here.'

Tommy thought fast. What could he say to make Kirsten go?

'Can we make pancakes?'

He knew they needed eggs to do that and there weren't any in the fridge.

'Okay.'

Kirsten got up and began to gather the ingredients. 'Where's the flour?'

Tommy told her which cupboard to look in. She placed it on the worktop then put her head in the fridge.

'Oh, no eggs.'

'Let's go to the shops.' Tommy said again, trying not to grin.

'I'll get one from home.' Kirsten pulled on her coat and headed to the door. 'I won't be long.'

Tommy wasted no time. He grabbed some money from the pot on the shelf and put on his coat and shoes. He shut the front door with a quiet click and went down the path. He hoped Kirsten wouldn't see him. He'd run to the shops and buy two cans of cat food then run back.

It was stupid having Kirsten round. He didn't need looking after. He wasn't a baby. He was sixteen now and he'd had a job at the police station helping in the canteen. He was nearly a man! It wasn't his fault that the tea towel had fallen into the gas flame. If Dad hadn't grabbed it and thrown it in the sink, Tommy might have done that anyway. Okay, he'd run out of the room when he saw the flames but he'd have gone back in.

Tommy hurried along the street towards the mini supermarket, a plastic carrier bag in one hand and some pound coins in the other. A white van was parked a few doors down and he jumped when the engine started and loud music blasted through the open window. As he walked it crawled next to him. He looked across at the driver but he had a scarf around his neck and chin and a baseball cap down to his eyes.

The van pulled ahead then stopped and the back doors opened. Another man jumped out, also with a scarf over his mouth, and stood on the path. Tommy slowed down. The man was in his way and he was staring at Tommy. He looked like a baddie.

'Tommy! Wait.' Kirsten called from behind and he heard her feet smacking on the pavement. The man in front of him looked at her then climbed back in the van. He banged the doors shut and it drove away. That was odd.

'Tommy! Where are you going?'

Kirsten was out of puff and she sounded cross.

'The shops,' he said in a dull voice.

He was cross too. Now he'd either have to tell her about the cat or try to sneak out again. If he told her, she was bound to tell Dad. Poor Pringle would be starving. Tommy would have to wait until Kirsten was busy doing something else then he'd try again.

'Your dad said you weren't to be on your own and he said you don't need anything at the shops.'

'Forget it,' he mumbled and turned towards home. He didn't want to talk to her.

'I found us an egg,' Kirsten said, holding it out to show him. 'We can make pancakes now.'

Tommy's heart lifted. He loved pancakes. Maybe Pringle would like them too.

Chapter 37
11AM

Child missing – 26 hours

DI Paton

As soon as Paton knocked on the smartly-painted front door, a volley of deep barks could be heard from the centre of the house. With a fierce-sounding dog like that to protect her, why had the woman felt the need to scurry away from the scene of Gus's attack? Paton glanced at Becki Lewis the young DC standing next to him. She smiled with nervous apprehension.

'His bark is probably worse than his bite,' Paton said. 'I think poodles are usually friendly.'

The door opened to reveal a small-framed woman with one child-sized hand clutching the collar of a huge shaggy dog. She didn't look as if she had the strength to hold him back as he was rearing and bouncing with excitement. In the end she wrapped her arms around his chest and hugged him to her. Up on his back legs, his head was as high as her shoulder. He quietened and stared at Paton and the DC with shining brown eyes. Was this a poodle? It didn't look like one to him.

'Mrs Roberts?'

She nodded and Paton showed her his warrant card. 'Is this Branston?' He gestured at the copper-coloured dog.

'Yes. Is there a problem?'

Alarm flashed across her face.

'We need to ask you a few questions. Can we come in?'

Mrs Roberts reluctantly opened the door wider then shut it firmly behind them. She lowered Branston's front paws to the floor and let him go. Immediately, he ran and picked up a toy fox then danced around the two visitors, his bum wiggling with ecstasy at this unexpected treat.

'He'll calm down soon,' Mrs Roberts said. 'He just loves people.'

She led the way to a small lounge diner and sat on the edge of a chair, hugging her dog to her, one hand tickling his chest and the other fiddling with the neck of her blouse. He calmed immediately and shut his eyes with pleasure but she looked quite agitated.

'He's a handsome boy,' Paton said, trying to ease the tension in the room.

He took in his surroundings as he spoke. It was comfortably furnished but cluttered due to a sewing machine in one corner and a pair of half-made curtains spread across the dining table.

'Do you have to walk him much?'

'I take him out three times a day to get rid of his energy. He's still a puppy.'

Becki's eyes widened in surprise.

'But he's huge! Will he get any bigger?'

'Maybe.'

'Where do you walk him?' Paton asked.

'I take him in the car to try out different parks. It gets

boring just walking around the local streets. Look, I know why you're here. It's about that boy, isn't it?'

Paton nodded but waited for her to continue. It was better to let her speak freely to see what information she gave rather than constraining her answers with specific questions.

'I'd just left the park and they were ahead of me along the street. I thought they were typical boys playing a bit rough at first.'

Paton wanted to ask how many boys there were but held back for the moment.

Mrs. Roberts continued.

'One of them started pushing the other and didn't stop when he stumbled. He went down hard onto the pavement and then they started kicking him. I shouted at them to stop but one turned and flashed a knife at me.'

Her voice began to tremble.

'It was horrible. I haven't been able to sleep for thinking about it.'

Branston looked at her and whined.

'It's okay, boy,' she said. 'I didn't know what to do. I froze. Then one of the boys left the group and ran over to me. He said if I called for help, he'd track me down and kill my dog. He could have done, couldn't he? I mean, you've found me.'

She buried her face in the dog's curly fur.

'Can you tell us how many boys there were?' Paton asked, after a pause.

'Three. No, four if you count the one that fell over. I crossed the road and hurried away. I walked around for a bit to calm myself then went back again to see if they'd gone but the police were there by then.'

'Can you describe the boys?'

'Not really. They all had hats on and big hooded jumpers. I

remember they were all tall. Children seem to get taller with each generation, don't they?'

She looked at Paton with a fleeting smile.

'They had white skin if that helps.'

'What about their clothing?' Paton asked.

'I think one had a blue top and another was grey. I'm not sure about the third. Wait, there was something. The boy in the blue top had a ripped back pocket on his jeans. I notice things like that because I'm a seamstress.'

Paton could feel his pulse quicken but he kept his expression neutral.

'It might be a weird fashion like the ripped knees but it makes me want to repair them.'

She gave a hollow laugh.

'Did you notice any writing on the clothing? Slogans, labels, that sort of thing?'

'Sorry, no. Only that the jeans needed repairing. Is the boy all right? I can't stop thinking about him. I should never have walked away.'

'He's in hospital but he's stable. Don't be too hard on yourself. You were in a frightening situation and you've done a brave thing today by helping us. You're a valuable witness to a vicious crime and it must have been terribly upsetting.'

Paton reached into the inside pocket of his jacket.

'If you need support with this or just want someone to talk to, you can call Victim Support Scotland. They offer a live chat or you can go online. Here.'

He handed her a leaflet that he'd picked up from the station.

'We'll get this statement written up then we'll need you to come to the station to sign the witness statement.'

Mrs. Roberts took the leaflet and turned it over.

'What if they come looking for me?'

'I think it was most likely an empty threat, but if you're worried, please call us straight away.'

As they left the house Paton's phone rang.

'Boss?'

It was Jeanette, a young DC from the new team.

'You asked me to call the hospital to check on Gus Chambers. I've just heard back from the ward matron. He's got a massive bleed on the brain and he's been rushed into theatre.'

Chapter 38
11AM

Child missing - 26 hours

Woody

A quad bike was so much more fun than driving a car or tractor. Woody guessed he probably wasn't going as fast as it seemed, but with each tussock of grass bouncing him out of his seat and the closeness of the ground rushing under his wheels, it felt like eighty miles an hour. It was awesome.

As he concentrated on steering around dips and troughs in the land, he took his eye off the small boy in the blue coat and was surprised when he lifted his gaze and saw the field was empty. Damn. Where did he go? He slowed the quad bike then stopped. The boy must have slipped through the hedge.

Woody tried to remember what was beyond this field. He didn't usually come over this side of the farm. The sheep were on the other side and the winter crops were to the left where they'd catch the best of the sparse sunlight. This part of the farm had been left to do its own thing in the winter. There were too many ditches for the sheep to tumble and land on their backs – potentially fatal for them in heavy snow or when they were lambing – according to Grandad. Woody recalled him saying the farm was getting too big to manage, and he regretted buying more land off his neighbour. Uncle Chester was supposed to take over when Grandad got too old, but he'd buggered off to live in Aberdeen. Said he couldn't bear to look at another empty, silent field. He managed a nightclub now, so had plenty of people and noise to satisfy him.

Woody quite liked all this space and quiet. At least he felt safe here away from Spliff, Roughhouse and the others. He revved the bike again. He should head back to Tyler. Woody had told him to stay in the barn and play ball with Cassie. Grandad would be pissed off if he found out Woody had left Tyler alone and gone off on the bike. Maybe Woody should just cruise along the hedgerow quickly to see if he could spot the bairn before he went back. Could it be the same kid? It was hard to tell from a distance but the coat had looked the same colour. Woody supposed it was possible as it was only two or three miles from where Roach had dumped him. Could the boy walk that far? What would he eat out here? Had he slept under a hedge last night? The poor sod must be crapping himself.

The hedge was thinner in places so Woody was able to peer through to the next field. It was rough grass, much the same as this one, but as he cruised along further and came to a gap in the spiky hawthorn, he saw a muddy path leading towards a huddle of low outbuildings surrounded by trees. Was there a house as well or were they just old farm storage barns? Woody was tempted to follow the path and take a look but he was worried about Tyler. He'd have to sneak back later. Or should he raise the alarm so the kid could be rescued? If

Woody told Grandad, he'd have to confess to everything and he wasn't brave enough for that.

As he drove back to the hay barn Woody plotted what to do. He'd try and find the bairn then report him as lost and found. Yes, that would work. Woody would be the hero instead of the villain. The boy must be sheltering in those sheds. Woody would bring food in case the kid was hungry then take him back to the farm.

Woody drove slowly as he neared the farm to reduce the noise of the engine so Grandad, who was fixing a fence two large fields away, wouldn't hear it. As he entered the barn and crossed the dirt floor he looked around for Tyler but there was no sign of him. Shit. Where was the little beggar? He'd been told to stay put. Woody parked the quad bike, pulled the tarpaulin over it and slipped the key onto the hook on an old beam in the corner. It had been easy to find as this was where the key to the tractor always hung.

'Tyler,' Woody called.

Cassie rushed over, her tail wagging furiously, but Tyler was nowhere to be seen. Woody crossed the barn, the dog at his heels.

'Tyler? Where are you?'

He looked out of the door to the yard and his heart stuttered in his chest as he saw Grandad coming across the field. Tyler wasn't with him. Now Woody was for it.

Perhaps he should hide then look for Tyler when Grandad left again. Maybe the little devil was back in the house. Woody ducked behind a pile of bales to wait.

'Raargh!'

Tyler leapt on Woody who sprang away in shock. Cassie barked and span around in delight as though she was part of the game.

'You little shit!'

The swear word was out before he could stop himself.

'Ooh, you said a bad word.'

'Only because you gave me a fright.'

Woody tickled Tyler and he squirmed away, giggling.

'Best keep it a secret about me riding the quad bike and you playing hide-and-seek. Grandad would tell us off if he knew. We're supposed to be working. Here, sweep the hay up and be quick about it.'

He grabbed a brush and dustpan and thrust it at Tyler.

'He's on his way over.'

Tyler did his best to sweep, with Cassie constantly dropping her ball at his feet. Woody shoved handfuls of hay into sacks.

Grandad hurried in but didn't seem to notice that they hadn't cleared much floor.

'Good work lads,' he said, distractedly.

He went straight over to his store of materials on the far side of the barn and started pulling stuff about.

'Now that's annoying,' he muttered. 'I was sure I had another roll of wire here.'

He rubbed his chin and stared at the mess he'd made.

'I'll have to go into town and get some more. The fence is worse than I thought and the sheep aren't secure.'

He looked at Woody as though trying to make a decision.

'Perhaps we can all go.'

'I can look after Tyler, Grandad. You'll be quicker on your own.'

'True. I don't want you doing anything silly though.'

Woody's mind was racing. If Grandad went out, Woody could go and look for the boy in the sheds. It would be easier without Tyler in tow.

'If you take Tyler I can finish up here and make us some sandwiches for when you get back.'

Grandad hesitated then walked over to the beam. He picked up the tractor and quad bike keys and slipped them into his pocket.

'Aw, don't you trust me, Grandad?'

He smiled and patted Woody's shoulder.

'It's easier to trust someone when temptation is out of reach. Behave yourself, lad. We'll be back in an hour or so.'

He took Tyler's hand and led him from the barn then called back.

'And not too much pickle in my cheese sandwich.'

Chapter 39
11.30AM

DI Paton

Child missing - 26 hours 30 minutes

Events were happening so fast that Paton didn't have enough time to analyse all the information he'd received, in order to work out how it all fitted together, before something else occurred. He wanted to process what Mrs Roberts had said but his immediate concern was for Gus and his family.

'Becki, I'm going to drop you at the hospital so you can call me straight away with any news and be on hand if the family needs support.'

He glanced at her and she nodded, her eyes fixed on her lap. He couldn't decide if she was anxious about the responsibility or if her serious demeanour was normal. She appeared to lack confidence but maybe she had hidden strengths. As her senior officer, even a temporary one, he felt responsible for her so perhaps he should ask her direct supervisor for his opinion.

She'd passed all her training, though, so she must have some level of competence. He decided to probe further.

'What did you think about the interview with Mrs. Roberts?' he asked.

She looked straight at him.

'That it's going to take a lot for her to forgive herself,' she said.

'She'll look at her dog and try to decide whether his welfare should have taken priority over the boy's.'

Paton looked at her with new respect.

'I agree,' he said. 'Guilt might prove the motivator we need to keep her on board with the investigation. Let's hope the poor lad survives or we'll have a murder case on our hands. Even as it is, we may need her to identify the offenders in an ID procedure and possibly give evidence in court.'

'Let's also hope the gang don't find out where she lives and try to scare her off. She'll need a lot more courage if they do. I hope we'll have the resources to support her if that happens.'

Becki was clearly a bright young woman and not the timid side-line spectator he'd first assumed her to be. Her silences were probably due more to her brain analysing information than trying to avoid interactions. Paton liked this trait and decided he'd ask her to accompany him again if needed. She'd be a useful partner to have. He should remember not to judge people too quickly next time. He was always telling his team not to make assumptions and now he'd done exactly that.

He dropped her outside the hospital, after making general chit-chat, telling her he needed to head home briefly to check if his son and sitter were okay. He'd had a brief text from Kirsten saying they were having a great time, but he still heard the echo of Nigel's warning in his head and Paton was sure the breakers yard had something to do with the stolen cars. '*Stay away,*'

Nigel had said. '*I love my family too and this is bigger than both of us.*'

Paton was somewhat reassured by Kirsten's text but he needed to see Tommy to put his mind at ease. He parked outside his neat house and scanned the street before he walked up his path. Everything seemed quiet. A van was parked further down the street but it could be a delivery driver or a local workman and probably nothing to worry about. Still, Paton would check it again on his way out.

He let himself into the hall, his nose twitching at the aroma of something tasty cooking. He poked his head around the lounge door, gratified to see it empty and the television switched off, then made his way to the kitchen. For a brief moment he wished he hadn't come back yet. The room looked like a crime scene after the CSI team had been in. White powder, probably flour, dusted surfaces, the floor and door handles. Spatters of red – was it ketchup or strawberry sauce? – sat in shining splotches on plates, worktops and... Paton looked at his son, Tommy's face.

Tommy was standing with a frying pan held in two fists. Kirsten was behind him and reaching around, her hands covering his.

'Ready, steady... flip!' They both moved in unison and a disc of part-cooked batter flew towards the ceiling with ominous intent. Just before it reached the whitewashed plaster it turned lazily to make its descent. Tommy and Kirsten dived sideways but the pancake eluded them and landed with a faint splat onto the tiled floor.

'Doh.' Tommy's face creased with laughter. 'Not again!'

Kirsten giggled then noticed Paton in the doorway. Her laughter died away and her face became a picture of worry.

'Dad! We're making pancakes. Want one?' Tommy put the pan back on the cooker.

'We'll tidy up soon,' Kirsten said, bending to pick up the soggy heap of batter.

'I'm not sure I fancy one right now but it looks like you're having fun.'

Paton smiled at his son then turned to Kirsten.

'Tommy's good at washing up so make sure he helps. I don't think he's capable of cleaning the ceiling though, so maybe not so high next time.'

He looked up to check there were no greasy stains to contend with.

'I can't stop for lunch, I'm afraid,' he said to Tommy. 'I just wanted to make sure you're okay.'

Paton took a banana from the fruit bowl and a handful of chocolate digestives. He'd try and cook a decent meal tonight. He was starting to miss Wendy's cooking. When she was well she'd always create tasty pies and casseroles, roasts and Italian dishes, not to mention delicious cakes and desserts. In fact, Paton missed her company too. Tommy was lovely, but sometimes Paton needed another adult to share thoughts and ideas with. A few more days and she'd be back. He should be grateful that she wasn't here to see the desecration of her beloved kitchen.

'I need to get back to the station,' Paton said. 'Make sure you help tidy up, Tommy. No police dramas or detective games until it's done.'

'Have we got any tuna fish, Dad?'

'I thought you'd be eating pancakes for lunch. I don't think tuna really goes as a topping.'

'I wanted a sandwich.'

'We're out of tuna. Have ham instead.'

'It's all gone.'

Tommy's eyes swivelled to the left, a sign that he was lying or feeling guilty about something.

'The whole packet?'

Paton didn't have time for this. He needed to see if Colin had found the Coke bottle and whether the DNA results were in from the chewing gum.

'I'll try and get a few supplies on the way home,' he said.

'We could go to the shops, couldn't we Kirsten?' Tommy looked hopeful.

'We can make do with the things we've got here. It's starting to rain.'

'Kirsten's right. We can do a supermarket shop tomorrow. I need to go. See you later.'

Paton hurried out and scanned the street for the van. It was still there. Not a delivery driver then. Perhaps a workman? He checked his watch and saw that he didn't have time to walk along to the vehicle now. Louie had to be his priority. He'd see if there was writing on the side as he drove past.

Paton slowed his car as he passed the van and looked in the window. A man was lying back in the seat, his feet on the dashboard and a baseball cap pulled down over his face. Probably just someone taking a power nap on their break.

As Paton climbed out of his vehicle back at the station, he saw Colin walking across the car park.

'I found the Coke bottle,' Colin said, clearly pleased with himself. 'It was in the corner of the bus shelter so was nice and dry. I also found a Fanta bottle so I've asked the SOCO to check them both against IDENT1 and he's sent the bottles to the lab to see if there's any DNA from saliva around the rims.'

'The youths were only spotted with a Coke bottle, though,' Paton pointed out.

'I know Boss. I thought there might only be a partial print on the Coke bottle but they might be able to match it to a whole print on the other bottle. We might also see a Fanta bottle on other footage if more comes to light. The boys might have handled both bottles.'

'Good thinking, Colin.' Paton was impressed by his colleagues for the second time that day. He was privileged to work with such capable officers.

'Let's find out if the team has anything else then I'll contact them for the results.'

When he reached the office, he asked everyone to gather around.

'I visited a witness to the assault on the lad in Perth this morning and she said something of great interest that could possibly link that crime with Louie's disappearance. One of the youths was wearing jeans with a torn pocket but, sadly, she didn't notice any slogans, labels or writing on the clothing.'

A murmur of comments broke the silence.

'She's a seamstress,' he pointed out to Tony, who was muttering about the witness's selective observation.

Then he addressed the room.

'It's possible that one of the youths who stole the car was also at the scene when Gus Chambers was attacked. Douglas, have you got any further with the company that sells the DO NOT SUBVERGE clothing range?'

Douglas nodded. 'We've spoken to one of the directors and he's going to email us a list of all their online customers in Scotland. About thirty-five or so, he reckons. They've got around 350 customers across the UK.'

Lynn, the office manager, appeared at the door, her face split with a grin.

'Boss, we've got the results of the fingerprints on the Coke bottle and they match someone on the Police National Computer. He was cautioned two years ago for possessing cannabis and arrested last year following a fight in a nightclub in Dundee but there was no further—'

'What's his name?'

Paton interrupted her. Was this the lead to finding Louie? Could he now delay the Child Rescue Alert and spare the family untold grief?

'Jayson Roachford,' she said. 'Known as Roach to his friends. Last known address in Dundee.'

Chapter 40
11.30AM

Mabel

Child missing - 26 hours 30 minutes

Mabel's hands were still shaking as she filled the kettle to make tea. That had been close. Too close. Mabel had watched through a gap inside the chicken shed as the young lad had driven his bike thing along the boundary. Thankfully, Louie had grasped his arms around her neck and stayed quiet – probably because he'd picked up on her fear.

Who was it? Patrick Harcourt's grandson? It couldn't have been. He was still a child, wasn't he, barely into double figures? This boy had looked to be in his mid to late teens. But if not him, then who? Maybe Mr. Harcourt had taken on paid help. It seemed strange, though, that the bike had been heading straight for Louie and then driven along the hedge as though looking for him.

Fear itched anew across her skin. Maybe it had been a

policeman. People always say you know you're getting old when the police look too young. Would they drive around in a field like that though? She didn't think so. Mabel put a tea bag in her favourite bone-china mug then made warm blackcurrant cordial for Louie. He took it and smiled at her, and her heart melted. Gosh, it was worth this stress and worry.

'Me not like big boys,' he said. 'I like biscuits. Me hungry.'

Mabel gave him some Rich Tea biscuits and mulled over what he'd said. He turned a biscuit over as though looking for chocolate then took a big bite.

'Why don't you like big boys?' she asked, taking a seat opposite him.

Louie shrugged and crammed more biscuit into his already full mouth.

'Where Humbug?' he asked, spraying a shower of crumbs across the table.

'Don't speak with food in your mouth, there's a good boy.'

Clearly he'd not been taught proper table manners. And why the dislike of older boys?

'Have you got any brothers, Louie?'

He nodded vigorously.

'Noah,' he said. 'He a naughty boy.'

Probably an older sibling in trouble with the police, thought Mabel. She'd love to be a fly on the wall in Louie's home, love to see how his delicate young mind was being shaped for the future. Mis-shaped more likely. She was sure she could do so much better than his own family. She'd teach him to love and care for animals, respect the countryside and value nature. She'd teach him self-worth and confidence and all the qualities she lacked herself. Why, she could educate him at home and keep him safe! They'd cook and bake and tend the garden and they'd be happy together. He'd quickly forget his family. She'd be all the family he needed.

Louie slid off his chair and trotted to the hallway. Mabel jumped up and followed him.

'Me go now.' He said simply. 'Me find Mummy and Daddy.'

He tried to reach the door latch but, realising it was too high, he stared up at Mabel expectantly.

Her fantasy of their happy life together dissipated like a summer morning mist.

'Let's find Humbug,' she said, hearing a note of desperation in her voice.

'Me want Noah.'

When it became clear to Louie that Mabel wasn't going to open the door, he stamped his little foot on the wooden floor and yelled at the top of his voice, 'Me go now!'

Mabel was momentarily stunned by this display of rebellion but then sprang into action. She couldn't risk the boy on the four-wheeler motorbike hearing Louie. He might be snooping around right now. Mabel scooped Louie up and headed for the staircase but Louie was strong and as slippery as a raw chicken breast. As she reached for the banister to haul them both up the stairs he wriggled and slithered down her leg. She had no choice but to lower him to the floor, whereby he used the palms of his small hands to give a surprisingly strong shove.

Mabel stumbled over her own feet and fell backwards, landing heavily on her bottom and biting her tongue. She let out a gasp of surprise and pain then put her hand to her mouth. She touched her tongue and pulled her fingers away. It was bleeding.

Louie stood in front of her, his eyes huge with shock and filling with tears.

'Sorry,' he said in a high-pitched voice.

Mabel clambered to her feet and stood unsteadily. Her

back twinged as she straightened and she winced with pain. She felt like crying herself. Why was everything so hard? All she wanted was to love and be loved. Surely that wasn't too much to ask for? She'd spent her whole adult life trying to fill the huge crater of loss her own child had left when she slipped away from her. She'd even taken desperate measures at times. For a moment she was back in the bed of a stranger who called himself Pete, although she doubted that was his real name. He'd returned to the room from visiting the toilet along the corridor and stood over her.

'Come on, get up. You can't stay here all night.'

Mabel had propped herself up on one elbow and tried to look alluring. She couldn't arrive home in the middle of the night. Her elderly mum would ask her why she'd left her friend Tanya's house at such a time.

'Can't you come back to bed?' she'd asked.

She lifted the sheet and blankets aside but as he looked down his lip curled as though he'd trodden in cow dung. She covered herself over again, suddenly conscious of the soft cushion of stomach fat that hung slightly to one side and breasts that no longer defied gravity. She felt heat rise in her cheeks and she shrank into herself with humiliation.

'I start work at six and my landlord won't be happy if he finds out I've got a lodger,' Pete said.

He picked her dress up off the floor and tossed it onto the bed.

Hardly a lodger, she thought bitterly, and a few hours ago he'd been keen for her to stay. She leaned out of the bed, her modesty secured under the tightly wrapped bedsheet, and grabbed her underwear. She felt dirty and cheap. She was the dented tin of value beans sold for a few pennies then discarded, half-eaten.

As she wriggled and writhed into her clothing under the

covers, she tried to think instead of the seeds that had hopefully been sown inside her. Of them drifting upriver to settle and grow in her fertile pasture. This was what she'd bought the dress for, visited the nightclub for, drunk too many vodkas and danced with wanton abandon for. Any humiliation was worth it if she managed to conceive a baby. She couldn't bear to think about failure.

A tug on her long wool skirt dragged her back to the present and she looked down to see a small face staring intently at her.

'Sorry, Grandma,' Louie said, and tried valiantly to smile at her.

Mabel sat down on the bottom stair and pulled him to her. She wrapped her arms around him and breathed in the aromas of baby shampoo and fresh air on his hair. For the first time, he snuggled in and let her hold him. She rocked him gently and let the tears slide silently down her cheeks.

'It's okay,' she said. 'Everything will be okay.'

When Louie began to squirm in her arms, she released him and stood, roughly rubbing her cheeks dry. She needed to go back outside and see if that boy was back. She couldn't risk taking Louie with her, though.

'Come on, Let's find you something to do.'

Mabel took Louie's hand and led him back into the kitchen. She fetched a large tea tray, a bag of rice and some food colouring. She tipped rice into two bowls then added a few drops of red and green.

'Here, stir these'.

She handed Louie a large metal spoon and he scrambled up onto a dining chair. As he stirred vigorously, Mabel pulled on her boots and jacket again.

She tipped coloured rice onto the tray and showed him how to draw pictures in it with his finger.

'I'll be back in a minute,' she told him and hurried out of the door.

He barely looked at her as he was soon engrossed in swirling the rice into patterns.

Mabel scurried along the garden path towards the sheds and field beyond, peeping around corners for any sign of the teenager and taking care to stay out of sight until she was sure it was clear. She reached the hedge and peered through the twigs, straining her ears for the noise of a small engine. *Oh, Lordie!* Her heart faltered as she realised the boy was coming back over the brow of the hill, on foot this time, and heading straight at her. What did he want? She couldn't risk him seeing Louie.

Mabel stumbled back to the cottage and burst into the kitchen. Louie looked up at her, his brow pleated with worry.

'Sorry, Grandma,' he said for the third time.

The tray had fallen to the floor and coloured rice was scattered across the room, Mabel hurried over, slipping precariously on the loose grains against the hard tiles. She took her car keys from a bowl then grabbed Louie's coat and wellies.

'Let's go for a drive,' she said.

Louie's face brightened and he climbed down from the chair.

'We look for Mummy and Daddy?'

'We'll drive around and see if we can find them.'

Louie needed no prompting. He tugged on his boots and coat and ran to the front door. Mabel poked her head back into the kitchen and scanned the scene. Apart from the rice there was nothing out of place or any indication that a child was staying there.

The car bounced precariously along the track to the gate. Mabel peeked at Louie in the rear-view mirror, propped up on his cushions and doing his best to see over the sill of the window.

She was pulling out into the lane when he wailed.

'My blankie! Where's blankie?'

Mabel glanced back to scan the rear seat. A sudden blast of a car horn made her jump and she braked hard as a large black saloon car almost collided with her. She swore softly under her breath as the driver slowed enough to glare at her then sped away. *Good grief!* That was close. She looked back at Louie. He was white-faced but thankfully the seat belt had held him in place although a red mark was appearing on his neck.

'Are you okay, Louie?' Mabel studied his face.

Louie didn't reply. He was staring at the back of the headrest in front of him, his expression empty of any emotion. How odd! Maybe it was the shock. Mabel reached behind and patted his knee but he didn't respond. A flame of worry ignited in Mabel's chest. Surely this wasn't normal behaviour for a small boy. She shook his knee and still got no response. She was about to get out of the car to get in the back with him when he seemed to shake himself and the light inside him switched back on.

He looked at Mabel expectantly.

'Come on,' he said. 'Let's find Mummy and Daddy.'

Chapter 41
12 NOON

Child missing – 27 hours

Melanie

The front door banged shut and Melanie's eyes sprang open. She must have dropped off, she thought, and instantly felt guilty. How could she sleep when her precious boy was missing? It was no excuse that she hadn't slept all night. She sat up and straightened the sofa cushions. She brushed hair off her face and was adjusting her crumpled blouse when Simon walked into the lounge. One look at his face told her he hadn't found their son.

He stared at her for a moment then walked towards the kitchen.

'Tea?' he asked.

Melanie scrambled to her feet, relieved that he hadn't had a go at her.

'I'll make it,' she said.

'Where's the tea lady?' Simon asked. 'I thought she was staying all day.'

'Cheryl's a highly trained officer, Simon,' Melanie's tone was reproachful. 'She went to the team briefing then she's coming back.'

Melanie was desperate to ask Simon where he'd been searching today and whether he'd seen anything, but she couldn't bear to hear his answer heavily laden with blame. She pictured him driving up and down roads, scouring hedgerows and peering into crowds on busy streets, desperation mounting when there was no sign of him. It was unbearable.

Would they ever see their beautiful son again? Her knees weakened so she grasped the kitchen worktop and took steadying breaths. She couldn't fall to pieces now. Simon wouldn't cope. He wasn't great at dealing with emotions at the best of times so this would tip him over the edge.

Simon pulled two mugs from the cupboard and filled the kettle.

'She might be highly trained and so might the rest of them but I've seen no progress whatsoever. It feels like I'm the only one doing anything around here. Driving around all day with ignorant bastards overtaking me on blind bends as I look in the fields and batty old ladies pulling out in front of me while they talk to their dog on the back seat.'

He paused then put the teaspoon down and turned to her, his face distorted with pain.

'Where is he, Mel? Who's got our son?'

He stumbled towards her and wrapped his arms tightly around her. Melanie felt her own face crumple. She clung to him as his body tightened then began to convulse. He was sobbing. This strong, detached and self-contained man, who she loved dearly despite his aloofness, was actually sobbing into her shoulder, his tears trickling over her skin and soaking into her top.

They clung together for several minutes, sharing this flotsam of support in their river of grief, mouths contorted in anguish as the pain of loss wracked their bodies. Eventually the tears slowed and they pulled away from each other.

'I'm sorry,' they both said in unison then laughed softly, almost embarrassed at this raw display of emotion.

'It's all my fault,' Melanie said. 'I hate myself. I just never thought anything like that could happen in Burrelton. I thought we were safe from criminals around here.'

'Sadly, nowhere is safe these days. I've driven around numerous streets looking for Louie and I confess it's been an eye-opener. We forget how lucky we are living here. Some of the poorer areas in Dundee are downright depressing, especially their high streets. It seems the only businesses that thrive there are the pound shops, the bookies and off-licences.'

Simon turned back to the mugs and squeezed the teabags with a spoon.

'There are beautiful parts, don't get me wrong, but I think we need to check the underbelly of society for the parasites who would steal a three-year-old boy.'

'But surely you're not going to find him by driving around? He's hardly going to be wandering the streets or lanes, is he?'

'I know,' he sighed, sitting heavily on a kitchen chair. He put his head in his hands. 'I don't know what else to do though. I feel so helpless.'

Melanie stroked his hair gently and wondered what she could do or say to ease their pain.

Simon sat up and took a deep breath.

'The police need to appeal to the public. I don't understand why nothing is on the news. Someone must have seen something or know where he is.'

The doorbell rang.

'That's probably Cheryl,' Melanie said. 'You can ask her yourself.' She hurried from the room. 'Or maybe there's news.'

Melanie led Cheryl to the kitchen and invited her to sit opposite Simon while she finished making drinks.

'We want to go public with this,' Simon said. 'If you don't arrange a press conference this afternoon, I'm going to call the local news team. They'd be on it like ants on a dropped lolly.'

'We need to avoid that if we can. There would be hundreds of calls from people wanting to be part of the drama and it would take all our resources to work through them for any real information,' Cheryl said. 'Our time is better spent on investigating and following leads.'

'I can see that a public appeal would have its downside but it might have an upside too. It might give you vital information.'

Melanie heard the belligerent tone in Simon's voice and she hoped he wasn't going to get awkward and confrontational.

'I agree, but I've come to tell you we're making good progress.'

Melanie paused on her way to the fridge, her heart racing.

'Progress?' Simon's tone lightened. 'Tell us everything,' he said. 'We need to know every detail, good or bad.'

He looked across at Melanie and she nodded. She held her breath, determined to be strong if it helped find Louie.

'We've checked doorstep cameras, and dashcam from a local coach hire company, and identified two youths walking through the village. One was carrying a Coke bottle and we found one discarded in the bus shelter. We took fingerprints from it and they match someone on our Police National Computer.'

'I fail to see how this could link him to the car theft. It might not be the same bottle.'

'We also have a sample of chewing gum from where the car

was parked and are expecting the DNA result back very soon. If it matches the Coke bottle, we can put this lad at the scene of the crime.'

'Still doesn't prove anything though.'

'It's enough to arrest him and bring him in for questioning. Two of the team are on their way to pick him up now. Let's hope he can tell us where Louie is and who else was in the car.'

Simon stood.

'We must get to the station. I want to be on hand when they bring him in.'

'We need to stay here, Simon.' Cheryl put a hand on his arm. 'I'll be contacted as soon as there's any news and I'll be right here beside you.'

Chapter 42
1PM

DI Paton

Child missing - 28 hours

The front door opened a crack and a boy of similar age to Tommy peered out. He stood with his hand on the latch as though ready to slam it shut again.

'Jayson Roachford?' Paton asked.

He was pretty certain this was the lad they were looking for. The company DO NOT SUBVERGE had given them a handful of addresses in Scotland and this had been the nearest by several miles.

The boy was silent but eventually nodded. Paton felt a wave of relief and held up his warrant card to introduce himself and DC Mitchell.

'What do you want?' The boy asked sullenly. 'I'm cooking my lunch.'

'Can we come in?' Paton asked.

'No, you can't. I need to turn the pan off.'

He began to close the door but Paton put his hand against it and pushed it open again.

'We can do this on the doorstep if you want everyone to see, or we can go inside.'

Roachford looked over Paton's shoulder at whoever Paton could hear walking along the pavement then pulled the door open.

'I s'pose.' He shrugged and stepped aside. 'That way,' he gestured along the cluttered hallway.

As Paton and Mitchell stepped over several pairs of trainers and junk mail before negotiating their way around a basketful of dirty washing, Paton tried to scan the trainers on the floor for a pair of Run Swifts but couldn't differentiate between them all. Still, there would be a thorough search after they arrested Jayson Roachford.

The smell of scorched meat assailed Paton's nostrils as he entered the small kitchen. Roach rushed forward and turned off the gas.

'Sod it,' he muttered as he speared a piece of steak with a fork and dropped it onto a plate heaped with oven chips. 'Best fillet, that was.'

Mitchell raised his eyebrows at Paton, who acknowledged the unspoken judgement with a slight raising of his own. Fillet steak didn't come cheap and, looking at the poorly equipped and grubby kitchen, it seemed a luxury that could be ill-afforded.

Roachford took a fat chip from the plate, bit it and leaned against the worktop, chewing with his mouth open.

'Well?'

'We're arresting you on suspicion of stealing a car.'

Paton watched the boy carefully as he recited the usual script about the right to remain silent. He needed to gauge his reaction and be alert to any sign that the boy might try to make a run for it.

Roachford stopped chewing and jutted out his chin.

'I haven't stolen any car.' he said as Paton finished speaking.

He waved the chip in the air as though to push away the accusation.

'I don't know anything about stolen cars. You've got the wrong person.'

'We can discuss this at the station. We'll need to handcuff you.'

'Cuff me?' The cockiness wasn't so evident now. 'I haven't done anything. This is harassment.'

'Do you have a parent who can come with you?'

'Mum's gone to visit Nan and I haven't seen Dad in four years.'

Roachford straightened his back in a clear attempt to look taller and braver.

'Is your mother nearby? You'll need an appropriate adult with you.'

'She's gone to Aberdeen. Won't be back until this evening.' As he spoke, the front door banged and a female voice called out.

'Jayson? I thought I told you to put your washing on. You really are a lazy little—'

She stopped abruptly as she walked into the kitchen and saw the two men standing there. Her eyes narrowed and her long, thin face hardened. 'I hope you two aren't dragging him into no good. You should be ashamed of yourselves, using children to line your pockets. Go on, bugger off!'

She dumped a Tesco bag onto the worktop pushing dirty dishes aside.

'Mum!' Roachford's voice was high with panic. 'These are

policemen. They want me to go to the police station,' he looked at Paton, 'to help them with their enquiries. Can you come with us?'

Paton read the pleading look the boy had given him and stepped forward. He introduced himself and Mitchell and explained that they were arresting her son on suspicion of stealing a car.

'Can't you just interview him here?'

'We need to question Jayson under caution at the station, Mrs...?'

'Ms. Eden.'

Paton looked pointedly at his watch, aware that valuable time was being lost from the search for Louie.

'Can you accompany your son to the station or do we need to find an alternative appropriate adult? We have to leave now.'

'Don't suppose I have much choice, do I?'

She went back into the hall then threw a coat at Jayson and dropped a pair of trainers at his feet.

'Put these on before they slap the handcuffs on you.'

'You'll need to bring your son an extra set of clothes to change into because we'll need these for testing.'

'What! Hey, you can't have my clothes.' Jayson's voice was high pitched with indignation. 'These are new. When will I get them back?'

'It's unlikely you will get them back, I'm afraid. Can you turn around please?'

Jayson reluctantly turned around and Paton was disappointed to see there was nothing written on the back. He'd been sure the lad would be wearing his *DO NOT SUBVERGE* hoodie. He hoped they'd find it when they searched the house because so far the evidence was slim. Fingerprints on a Coke bottle found in the bus stop, and taking delivery of a hoodie worn by someone on CCTV in the area, was hardly enough to reasonably suspect him of stealing the car. He'd watch the interview on live streaming at the Perth station and hope more came to light.

Jayson slid past his mother to pick the shoes up and flinched as she lifted her hand to brush a long strand of black hair out of her eyes. Mitchell snapped the handcuffs on and they led Jayson to the car.

They drove to the station in near silence until Ms. Eden said, 'I want a solicitor present. I know how you lot can twist what's said or bully kids into saying the wrong thing.'

Paton's hackles rose at these unfair accusations but he stayed outwardly calm.

'Jayson is entitled to representation,' he confirmed. 'The custody officer will explain everything to you.'

Paton handed the lad over at the custody centre, explaining why they'd brought him in and asking to be called when all due processes had been carried out. It would probably be a couple of hours by the time they'd taken Roachford's fingerprints, DNA and the clothes he was wearing for testing.

They'd also have to wait for a solicitor to be appointed and allow time for Roachford to meet with him before the interview. If they wanted evidence to use in court, then everything had to be done properly, though it was frustrating when the clock was ticking away. How many doses of medication would Louie have missed now? Three probably. And what effect would that have on his epilepsy?

Chapter 43
1PM

Child missing - 28 hours

Woody

As he squeezed through a gap in the hedge further along the field and crept across the grass, Woody puzzled over the sheds in the distance. From this angle he could see a brightly-painted red door and blue window frames. They looked so familiar that he felt as though he'd been here before, but, at the same time, he was totally surprised by their existence. Perhaps it was that weird déjà vu stuff or maybe they reminded him of pictures he'd seen in an old fairy story book.

He'd been coming to his Grandad's farm all his life but couldn't remember visiting this place. Most of his childhood had been spent in meadows and woodland the other side of the farm. Because building dens, damming streams to create rock pools, and rolling down hills provided far more entertainment than the boring fields and hedges on this east side of the farm.

He checked the time on his phone. He needed to scout around quickly as Grandad would be back in forty-five minutes or so, and Woody had sandwiches to make.

He reached the first of the sheds and peered through a dusty window for any sign of the child. To his surprise the sheds were occupied. Racks of wooden ledges covered in straw were home to puffed up hens that cooed and clucked softly in the half-light. As he watched, an egg rolled slowly to the front of the shelf and wedged into a gully ready to be collected later. He had a childish urge to fetch it and put it in his pocket.

He walked on to the next shed and followed the quarry-tiled path with his eyes. It wound through an archway into a garden, and beyond the trees and shrubs he could just make out a whitewashed cottage with small-paned windows. Chimneys were visible above the treetops and a wisp of blue smoke drifted away with the breeze.

The feeling of familiarity was stronger now. A loose welly boot, a bumpy path and falling. Falling onto hands that held warm brown eggs and the sudden transformation into crunchy, slimy mess. He brushed aside the memory and continued to follow the path.

Was the bairn in the house? It was more likely than in the sheds. Woody quickly looked into the other huts then circled the edge of the property until he was at the front of the house. There was no car but fresh tracks in the mud showed one had been there recently.

Woody ducked under a side window then took a swift look into the room. A cosy lounge, with a glowing stove and huge cat sprawled on the sofa. Nice. He crept around the back of the house and took a peek into what was clearly the kitchen. There was no one about so he cupped his hands around his eyes to see better.

Cream cupboards, lots of red jugs and bowls on a dresser,

and a pine table in the middle of the room. It appeared neat and clean apart from a tray on the floor and loads of bits – he wasn't sure what they were. He looked for the small blue coat but guessed if the owner of the cottage had taken the boy out in the car the boy would probably have been wearing his coat. As Woody was turning away, he noticed a piece of fabric on the floor behind the door. It was in shadow so he couldn't see it clearly. A tea-towel perhaps.

He moved to the back door and tried the handle. To his surprise the door was unlocked, but then places often were in the countryside. He opened it slowly then slunk into the room. Warmth caressed his cheeks and the delicious smell of vanilla and melted butter made his stomach growl. Yum. He bet whoever lived here made loads of cakes and biscuits. For a moment he felt a pang of longing. How he wished he lived in a snug place like this with a mother who made him delicious home-baked goodies.

Maybe he could nip through to the lounge to stroke the cat. Yeah, why not? There was clearly no one here. He glanced around the room again, realising the bits on the floor were coloured grains of rice, and headed for what he assumed was the lounge door. He'd momentarily forgotten about the piece of fabric near the doorway, but as he went to sweep it aside with his foot he froze. Oh my God. It was the kid's blanket covered in teddies. The bairn had definitely been here.

Woody stood still, his thoughts racing. Maybe the boy's grandma lived here and she was looking after him while the mum worked or something. Perhaps Woody had been worrying for nothing. After all, when he and Grandad had watched the news last night there had been no mention of a missing kid. Woody decided he'd take a quick look around the rest of the house before he could be totally reassured. He went through to the hall and jogged up the steep stairs. Two bedrooms and a bathroom. The second bedroom had a single bed with a flowery duvet on it. There were no clothes around but the bedding had been recently changed judging by the pile of washing on the floor. Woody crossed the room and opened the wardrobe. A row of pretty dresses in various sizes hung neatly on miniature coat hangers. Maybe the woman had a granddaughter too.

Woody headed for the door and paused at the pile of story books by the bed. *Mog and the V.E.T.* His old favourite. He picked it up and flicked through the pages. If the little boy was staying here then he was being well-cared for. Woody felt the weight of guilt lift from his shoulders. He could put the boy from his mind now.

Bloody hell. Look at the time. Woody needed to get back. Grandad would be home soon and ask what he'd been doing. He scurried down the stairs, through the kitchen and out of the back door. He put on a spurt of speed and tore past the chicken sheds to the grassy field beyond. He ran until he was through the hedge and halfway across the field. Once he was over the brow of the hill he stopped and doubled over. God, he was unfit. His heart was pounding and he could barely breathe.

He walked the rest of the way to the farmhouse and quickly gathered the stuff to make lunch. Cassie was too well-mannered to beg for food and lay feigning sleep in her basket, eyebrows dancing as she opened one eye then the other to watch him intently. He was just cutting the sandwiches in half and putting the kettle on when Grandad returned. Tyler rushed in and waved a bag at Woody.

'Look what I've got!' Tyler dumped the bag on the table and pulled out a miniature trowel and fork and several packets of seeds. 'Grandad said we can grow our own beans and carrots. Can you help me?'

Woody looked at Grandad who was ruffling Cassie's soft head and nodding encouragingly.

'There's plenty of old pots in your nan's greenhouse. She would have enjoyed growing things with little Tyler. Always grew our own veg and flowers.'

'I'm going to be a farmer when I grow up. I'm going to grow lots of things and have sheep like Grandad. What are you going to be?' Tyler studied Woody's face expectantly.

'I... er, I'm not sure yet.' Woody suddenly felt pathetic compared to his four-year-old nephew. He wished he knew what he wanted to do with his life instead of drifting aimlessly through each day, mixing with people who didn't give a toss about others and causing misery with his petty crimes. 'I might be a rocket man or a brain surgeon,' he said. 'Or maybe a racing driver.'

Tyler's eyes widened then he looked across the room.

'You said I could go on the fast bike, Grandad.'

Woody's heart fluttered. Bloody hell, why had he said racing driver? Tyler might blab in a minute and tell Grandad Woody had already ridden the quad bike. 'We need to eat lunch first,' he said quickly. 'Look, you can have some of these crisps with your sandwich. You must be hungry.'

Tyler took the bait and climbed up on a chair. That was close. Woody desperately tried to think of some way to distract Tyler and, needing to find out who lived in the cottage, he said, 'How about we draw a map of the farm so you can work out where to put your plants and look at what you could do if you were the farmer?'

Woody lifted his head towards Grandad who was smiling at him.

'I can see why Megan likes you looking after the boy. You're good with him.'

Woody felt a warm glow at this unexpected praise, but it

was swiftly cut short by the memory of what he and Roach had done with the toddler. He'd love Grandad to be proud of him, to feel he was doing something good. He had to find out more about the little kid and the cottage.

'Have you got a big piece of paper?' he asked Grandad. 'And some thick pens?'

Grandad rubbed his chin.

'There's a roll of old wallpaper you can draw on. Not sure about pens though.' He rummaged through a drawer full of odds and sods. 'Here, you can have the one your Nan used to label freezer stuff if it hasn't dried out.'

Tyler watched avidly as Woody and Grandad mapped out the layout of the farm. They roughly sketched the house and barn, fields and fences then let Tyler draw puffy circles for sheep.

'What's the other side of this fence?' Woody was at last able to ask. 'I thought I could see smoke in the distance.'

'That'll be Mabel Grimstone's place,' Grandad said. 'I rent the cottage to her and she supplies me and the local area with eggs. Don't you remember? You went there once or twice as a wee nipper.'

Woody opened his mouth to say it had looked familiar then stopped just in time. 'I don't think so,' he replied slowly. 'How long has she lived there?'

'Must be forty years or more.'

'Did I go there to play with her children?'

'She never had kids. Don't ask me why. Never got married either. Proper spinster of this parish. She let you collect the eggs once but you fell over and smashed them. Cried your eyes out. You wouldn't go back there, which was sad because she was kind to you and she clearly liked kids. Although rumour has it—'

Grandad stopped abruptly and shook his head, clearly regretting saying too much.

'Rumour has what?' Woody asked, intrigued.

'Nothing. Finish your lunch. We've got planting to do.'

Chapter 44
2PM

Child missing - 29 hours

Tommy

Tommy was worried. Pringle hadn't had any lunch and she'd be getting hungry. Tommy had sneaked out to see her when Kirsten went to the bathroom. He'd hidden a bit of pancake in his pocket, but Pringle just sniffed it then turned away. Tommy ate it instead, but it was cold and bits of fluff had stuck to it. He wasn't surprised the kitten didn't like it. But it was annoying because now his pocket was greasy.

Pringle gazed up at him with big eyes and let out a long, high miaow. Tommy didn't know what to do. He couldn't wait until tomorrow for Dad to buy more food and he didn't want to let the cat leave the shed. It might not come back. He'd have to get to the shop somehow. Maybe he could wait until Kirsten was on her phone. She spent ages on her phone – looking at it or texting her friends. Sometimes she forgot all about Tommy.

After giving the cat a fuss Tommy carefully closed the shed door behind him and went back to the house.

'Where have you been?' Kirsten stood in the kitchen frowning.

'On my boat machine. I'm growing my muscles.'

'A rowing machine? Is it in the shed?'

She looked over his shoulder and down the path.

Tommy nodded reluctantly.

'Can I have a go?' she asked.

'No.'

Tommy closed the back door firmly behind him. He didn't want her finding the cat. She'd tell Dad and he'd get rid of it.

'Oh.'

Kirsten looked sad and Tommy felt his tummy go funny. He didn't want to upset her. He really liked Kirsten.

'It's broken,' he lied. He hated telling fibs but he didn't want to lose Pringle. 'Dad's going to mend it.'

Kirsten opened her mouth to say something then closed it again. She gave a small shrug.

'What do you fancy doing then?'

'I'm tired. I need a sleep.' Tommy went towards the hallway and put a foot on the bottom stair. 'Can we watch *The Sweeney* later?'

'Of course. I suppose your heart trouble makes you tired, doesn't it. I'll sit in the lounge until you come back downstairs.' She pulled her phone from her pocket and Tommy smiled.

Good. He'd wait until she was busy chatting to her friends, then he'd sneak out. Tommy sat on his bed and waited until he could hear her voice. She must be talking about boys again. He checked he still had the pound coins in his pocket from earlier then walked slowly down the stairs.

'Yeah. He sent the text by mistake. She was livid! He

managed to convince her it was meant for her in the end though. It was hilarious!'

Kirsten sounded like the man on the telly when he talked about football and someone nearly scored a goal. Too loud and too fast. Tommy took his coat and a bag from the hooks in the hall and quietly let himself out of the front door.

It wasn't until he was halfway down the street that he remembered the white van with the loud music and the men who'd stood in his way. He hoped they didn't come back. They hadn't looked friendly. He crossed the road carefully like Dad had taught him then hurried towards the shop.

Tommy stared at the shelves. So many different cat foods. He chose a box with a picture of a black and white cat on it. He hoped he had enough money. It was £3.50. He frowned as he tried to remember what he'd learned at school. It was important to understand money. He wandered to the till and put four coins on the counter feeling pleased with himself. See, he didn't need looking after. He wasn't daft like some local kids called him.

The lady took his money and gave him 50p back.

'If I had a black and white cat like that,' Tommy said, pointing to the box, 'I'd call it Oreo.'

'Great name,' the lady smiled at him.

He put the box in his bag, said thank you and left the shop. Waiting by the kerb was a white van. Tommy felt a shiver down his spine. Was it the same one with the baddies in? Tommy wouldn't wait to find out. He rushed along the pavement towards the zebra crossing. The van's engine started up and it pulled into the road.

Tommy hurried over the crossing and began to run. The van slowed as it drew alongside then pulled ahead and waited. Tommy's heart was beating too fast and he was beginning to feel dizzy. He looked around for someone to help but there was only an old lady across the street pulling her shopping trolley and a boy on a scooter that moved without being pushed.

'Hello!' Tommy called.

The boy looked across the road but kept going. The old lady had her head down and didn't hear him.

Tommy leaned against a wall to wait for the dizzy spell to go and watched the van.

It didn't move.

What should Tommy do now? He could go back to the shop and tell the lady behind the counter or he could keep going and try to get home. The lady at the shop might think he was being silly. Kirsten would be at home and she'd look after him. She'd phone Dad if the men went to the house. But wait a minute. Tommy had a mobile phone now. He felt in his pocket for it then thought again. Dad would take ages to get here and he'd ask why Tommy had gone to the shop and he'd see the cat food. No. Tommy would go home. But then he'd have to get past the van and it looked scary. He was about to turn back to the shop when a man jumped out of the van and ran up a front path with a parcel.

Phew! Just a delivery man. Tommy began walking but slower now so his heart could stop going crazy. As he got closer the man came back down the path whistling a tune. Without warning he grabbed Tommy's arm and pushed him towards the kerb. The van doors at the back flew open. There was another man inside and between them they hauled Tommy into the back. He gave a yell of surprise then fell heavily onto his knees. The doors slammed shut, the men jumped into the front and the van pulled away.

Too shocked to think straight, he shifted to his bottom, untangled the bag of shopping from his wrist and rubbed grit from his hands. Where were they taking him? Why had they taken him? He was about to shout at the men when a phone rang in the front of the van.

'We've got him. I'll put you on speakerphone so Ronnie can hear you,' a man with no hair said as he tapped his phone.

'Good work,' the voice said. 'Bring him to the barn.'

'Can't say I'm comfortable with this, Spanner. You can see the poor lad isn't the full ticket and he doesn't look that well.'

'Going soft in your old age?' Spanner said. 'We haven't got a choice. His dad has pulled Roach in and it won't be long before they get to Woody. We need to stop him or it'll be the end of the whole operation. By taking Paton's son and him being personally involved they'll pull him off the case. My insider tells me he's SIO for the stolen cars case, and Gusset's beating, so his absence will really screw everything up. Besides, I don't fancy our chances with the boss, do you?'

The bald man was silent.

'Have you tracked Woody down yet?' the voice on the phone said.

'No trace of him, Roach went to his house when he didn't turn up for work. The neighbour said he's gone to stay with his dad in England.'

'Take Paton's boy to the barn then pay the mum another visit and put the pressure on. We need to find Woody before the police do.'

Tommy listened carefully and tried to make sense of it all. This was something to do with Dad. They'd said his name. It must be to do with one of his cases. Tommy recalled the last time he'd helped Dad solve a case. The girl thought Tommy was stupid but it was her that was daft in the end. If people thought he couldn't understand then he'd pretend he didn't. He'd listen and take it all in and try to remember everything like when he and Dad played detective games. 'Remember places, names and faces,' his dad would say. 'House numbers, number plates and car models.' They played memory games with numbers, letters and objects and Tommy was good at them.

'Shouldn't you be careful what you say in front of the boy?' Spanner asked through the phone.

The man holding the phone turned to look at Tommy who, remembering how he'd been teased in the past for his big tongue, let his mouth hang open and his face go as blank as his telly in a power cut.

'Nah, like I said, if brains were taxable, he'd get a refund.'

They'd be sorry. He was smart and one day he'd be a detective like his dad and catch baddies like them. Tommy stared at the men and made notes in his head for his dad. Bald head, bumpy nose and tiny ears. One gold earring. A chain with a long tooth on it. A shark's tooth? A black thumb nail. This was going to be the best memory game ever. He just had to find a way to escape so he could tell Dad all about it.

Chapter 45
2.30PM

Mabel

Child missing - 29 hours 30 minutes

Mabel turned the car into her rutted lane and drove slowly, scanning the hedgerow either side for signs of the teenager. As she approached the cottage, her heart gave a lurch of anxiety. The lad had looked like he was heading straight for the property but was she worrying over nothing? He might have just been checking the boundaries for his grandad and coming back to fix a fence. Yes, that must be it. Why else would he come here?

Mabel looked at Louie in the rear-view mirror. His head lolled to one side and his eyelids fluttered as he dreamed. His cheeks showed the traces of dried tears, and Mabel felt the heavy stone of guilt in her chest. The poor wee boy had been so excited at the prospect of finding his mummy that she'd had to play along with the pretence that they were searching for her.

She'd driven around remote country lanes for nearly two hours, trying to avoid populated areas for fear he'd recognise the streets and houses, or someone might spot him in the back of the car. She'd surmised that he'd been dropped on the route away from the villages to the right of her home, as he was in fields on that side, so she'd focused their meanderings to the left, without touching Perth or Dundee. After staring at the passing countryside with no sightings of his mother, Louie had begun to cry. Mabel stopped the car to give him a hug and some sweeties from the glove box. After he'd had a quick wee behind a hedge and she'd promised to look for Mummy again later, she'd persuaded him to climb back into the car where he'd soon fallen asleep.

Mabel had almost wavered as they'd driven around, nearly turning the vehicle the other way and on towards the police station in Perth. But as she'd slowed the car, her mind had accelerated to the scenes that lay ahead, scenes in which she admitted what she'd done to a desk sergeant, followed by another scene in which she was led to a cell, seeing Louie's face crumple as yet another familiar person was taken from him and he was handed to a stranger from Social Services. Fear and guilt wrestled with each other and, even though Mabel hated seeing Louie upset, and despite trying to label his mother as uncaring and incompetent and finally acknowledging that she must be distraught, the fear of being arrested and incarcerated won.

She needed a plan for how she could give Louie back without implicating herself. Another couple of days to work it out and spend time with her precious boy. She wanted nothing more than to get indoors and shut out the world, desperate for the practical comforts of home – her own toilet and a cup of tea in her favourite mug. She drove steadily back to the cottage and parked. Louie, sensing the car had stopped moving, stirred and pulled himself upright to peer out of the window. He slumped down again, disappointment clouding his face, and Mabel felt her resolve give way. She should start the engine again and drive him straight to the nearest police station. She could say she'd just found him by the roadside. They'd believe her, wouldn't they?

'I want blankie,' Louie said.

She gripped the wheel and hung her head. Now wasn't the right time to hand him in. She needed the bathroom and a drink and he wanted his blankie.

'Come on, let's get some lunch and find blankie before we do anything else.'

She helped Louie out of the car and into the cottage. As she opened the front door, she felt a draught across her cheek and around her ankles. Had she left a window open somewhere? She couldn't remember opening one. She took Louie's hand and led him through to the kitchen. The door caught on something as he pushed it wider.

'Blankie!' he said, and clutched it to his cheek.

Her spirits lifted at seeing him smile again, but soon plunged into dread when she realised the back door was open. Christ! Had she forgotten to close it properly in her haste or had that lad been in here? Surely he wouldn't snoop around. No, she was being ridiculous. She closed the door firmly and looked around the room. Nothing was out of place. She'd ensure she locked the doors in future for peace of mind. She put the kettle on the Aga, settled Louie at the table with a big slice of chocolate cake she'd made a couple of days ago – goodness, that seemed a lifetime away – and, realising she'd forgotten to put the washing on, dashed upstairs to fetch Louie's damp bedding.

As she carried the armful of sheets and clothing down the stairs, her foot caught on a trailing corner and she lurched forward. She dropped the washing and managed to grab the handrail to steady herself but her mind was still falling, spinning and falling to that fateful day in the farmhouse forty-five years ago.

She'd landed heavily and at awkward angles, the hall table leg digging into the soft flesh of her stomach and the precious life within. As she lay there stunned, she'd tried to work out what had happened. One second she'd been standing at the top of the stairs arguing with her father, the next she was in a crumpled heap at the bottom. A sharp pain shot from her back to her gut and she whimpered, the heavy tread of her father's footsteps behind her doing nothing to reassure her.

He stepped over her then held out his hand. 'Come on, lass, get up,' he said brusquely. 'You're fine. I'm sure nothing's broken.'

Mabel looked away from him and curled into a ball. How would he know nothing was broken? What did he care? The echo of his words rang through her head.

'You can't bloody well keep it! I told you, we're not supporting you and a kid for the next eighteen years. We can barely afford to feed ourselves.'

'It's too late, Dad. I can't get rid of it now. It's too late!' Mabel yelled at him then leaned in and said in a low voice. 'I am keeping it. It's my baby and I love it.' She cradled her small bump in her hands and he looked down with disgust.

'You'll bring shame on all of us. How will your mother be able to hold her head up in church?'

'How would you be able to hold your head up knowing you'd made me kill my baby? But like I said, it's too late. I'm fifteen weeks pregnant now and you have to terminate by twelve.'

'You'll find yourself on the street then, girl. I won't have that little bastard in my house.'

'Then I'll tell all your precious church-going acquaintances what a heartless man you are. Mum will stand by me.'

'She'll do as I say.'

Mabel was unprepared for Dad roughly pushing her aside to get past her on the stairs. Her hands flailed at empty air and she toppled like a pin in a bowling alley, hitting the treads heavily as she fell.

As she lay there dazed and in pain, trying to summon the strength to stand, her father had gone to fetch Mum. She'd rushed over to Mabel and gently helped her up. After being settled on the sofa with a cup of sweet tea, Mabel had started to feel better until a wave of pain rippled through her. She groaned.

'Call the doctor, Mum, I'm worried about the baby.'

Her mum had shot a concerned look at her dad.

'I'm sure you're fine, Mabel. You're over-reacting. It's late and the doctor will be packing up for the day. We'll call tomorrow if you're still worried,' she said.

More concerned about bringing shame on the family, Mabel thought, *than her and the baby's well-being*.

It was too late by the morning. Despite her cries in the night, her parents had let nature follow its path and Mabel's precious baby had been lost in a riptide of pain and blood. Her father didn't even give her the opportunity to say goodbye.

'Was it a girl or a boy?' she'd whispered. Her father hadn't answered. He'd taken the bloodied towel with the tiny baby wrapped inside and left the room.

Her mother had taken pity on her and eventually told her she'd had a girl. In the months that followed, her grief had dragged her to such deep despair that even the loss of the family farm through bankruptcy, and the subsequent move to the empty rental cottage, had barely touched her. Life was happening around her but not to her. She was as remote from the world as the spacemen that had conquered the moon.

The only emotion left in her was hate. Hatred for her bullying, controlling father and hatred for her weak, insipid mother. There was enough left, too, for all those Christian worshippers whose condemnation of unmarried mothers and bastard babies had stolen hers from her. She knew she would still have her baby if she hadn't been clashing with Dad at the top of the stairs. If he hadn't been so ashamed of her teenage pregnancy. Mabel hadn't crossed the threshold of a church since. God was as dead to her as her baby.

Gathering up the washing from the staircase now, Mabel made her way carefully down to the kitchen and the small parcel of joy waiting for her at her kitchen table. She deserved this oasis of happiness in her barren, cold life and she was going to relish every minute of it.

Chapter 46
3PM

DI Paton

Child missing - 30 hours

The lad in the interview room at the Custody Centre leaned back in his chair and stretched, putting his hands behind his head. Jayson Roachford's outward show of confidence and bravado was undermined, however, by his constant fleeting looks at the camera situated in the top left-hand corner of the room. Paton sat in Perth police station and took in every move and sound on the monitor, through live streaming. Roachford's mother perched beside the boy, picking away at her chipped nail varnish and smacking his leg with the back of her hand when he tipped his chair back too far.

The solicitor sat, head down, with lines of weary responsibility creasing his forehead. He opened a file on the table in front of him then gave his attention to DC Tony King who, after introducing himself and his colleague DC Mitchell

Tomkins, was explaining the interview process and Roachford's rights to him.

Paton felt a thrill of anticipation. Would this lead to the discovery of Louie? He'd almost pulled rank and said that he'd interview the teenager, which wasn't common practice these days for a DI, but then decided he might learn more by observing. They'd planned the approach and the questions he wanted them to ask and was confident both officers would have the skills to get as much information as possible, especially Tony, who was a Tier 3 advanced interviewer.

Tony began. 'We're here because we have what we believe to be evidence that you were in Burrelton yesterday morning at 8.30am where a car was stolen with a two-year-old boy inside. Were you there?'

Roachford lowered his arms and sat forward. He opened his mouth to speak but his solicitor cut in.

'I have a signed statement here from Mr. Roachford regarding his whereabouts yesterday.' He picked up a piece of paper, cleared his throat and read. 'I, Jayson Roachford, have no knowledge of a car being stolen and was not in Burrelton yesterday morning. I was at home in bed and didn't get up until 10am. I only knew about the stolen car when the police came to my house and asked me to come in for an interview. I know nothing about a missing child.'

'Thanks for the prepared statement,' Tony said. 'I'm sure your solicitor has advised you that we still need to ask you questions and it's down to you whether you choose to answer those questions or not. Okay?'

Roachford stole a look at his solicitor and smirked. Paton guessed he'd been advised to say, 'No comment' and felt a bite of irritation. Hopefully, Tony would get something out of him.

'Okay?' Tony repeated.

Roachford glanced at Tony then focused his attention on

Mitchell, even though Tony was the one talking. Maybe Mitchell seemed less threatening, being closer in age.

Tony must have noticed this and was quick to use it to his advantage. He gave a slight nod to Mitchell who saw his cue.

'Are you comfortable?' Mitchell asked. 'Were you given something to drink?'

The boy blinked before answering, seemingly surprised by this gesture of hospitality.

'Yeah, but I wouldn't say no to a cold beer,' he said and grinned.

'Jayson, this is serious. Don't be so bloody cheeky,' his mum cut in.

Jayson shrugged and looked down at his empty hand. 'Can I have my phone back soon?'

'Not yet, I'm afraid. We need to get through these questions.'

At least the boy is speaking, thought Paton. *A small step in the right direction.*

'Can you tell me where you were yesterday morning at 8.30?' Mitchell asked.

'That's an easy one,' Roach said. 'In bed of course. Mum will tell you. What sort of person gets up before nine? Only work wankers.' He chuckled at his own joke.

'It's work wankers who pay for the roof over your head and food on the table,' Paton muttered under his breath. Crikey, he hoped they could soon wipe the smugness off the cocky little git's face.

The solicitor pinched his lips together then leaned forward and muttered in Roachford's ear. Roachford flapped a hand at him.

'We understand that Ms. Eden is unable to verify this. If Ms. Eden wishes to change her statement to say she will now be a witness to your whereabouts we will need to pause the interview and find another appropriate adult.' Mitchell turned to Roachford's mother. 'As we explained, you can't be both.'

Roachford looked at his mother, his eyebrows slightly raised as though expecting her to change her story.

Ms. Eden shook her head. 'I'm staying here,' she said.

Interesting, Paton thought. Surely a mother would jump in to defend her son? She'd clearly been reluctant to lie for him and risk crossing a line herself. Maybe she didn't want to draw attention to any past or present misdemeanours of her own. He made a note to check for any records on her later.

Roachford's shoulders dropped then he breathed in deeply and straightened his spine. 'Whatever,' he said. 'You could ask Rachel Chambers. She was there in my dreams. Know what I mean?' He gave a leering smile and thrust his groin a couple of times.

Dirty little sod, Paton thought, but then his heart quickened. Chambers. That was Gus's surname. Was Rachel his sister? The one he met at the hospital? He wracked his brains trying to remember if he'd been properly introduced to her. Did Roachford know them? He'd check out her name as soon as he could.

Tony continued the questioning. 'Have you been to Burrelton recently?'

Roachford's eyes widened slightly but his sardonic smile didn't falter. 'No,' he said. 'Why would I want to go to a dead-end place like that?'

'In that case can you explain how your fingerprints came to be found on a Coke bottle that was retrieved from the bus stop there?'

'Maybe I touched the bottle while it was still in the shop.'

Roach grasped the edge of the table and stretched back, evidently pleased with himself.

The solicitor wasn't though. He leaned in and reminded Roachford that he could say, 'No comment.'

Tony turned to Mitchell. 'Can you show the suspect the photograph taken from the dashcam, please?'

Mitchell opened his folder and slid a photograph across the desk.

'Is this you in the photograph?' he asked Roachford. 'It was extracted from dashcam footage taken inside a coach travelling through Burrelton.'

The boy leaned forward and peered at the picture like a myopic old man. It showed the back view of two young people in hooded tops, one of which had the slogan, DO NOT SUBVERGE.

'No comment,' he said and shot his solicitor a look.

Was it to say he could follow directions after all or was it a look of alarm at the evidence stacking up against him? Paton couldn't quite tell.

'Do you own a hoody with this writing on?' Tony continued.

'No...'

'We have evidence from the company that makes and supplies this clothing that you were in receipt of a hoody, in this colour,' Tony emphasised the last three words to convey a sense of incredulity at Roachford's denial, 'four weeks ago.'

'...Comment.' Roachford added, struggling to contain his mirth at his little game.

'Okay, let's forget about you for a minute. Do you recognise the other young person in the photograph?'

The boy hesitated then inhaled as though about to speak. The solicitor cleared his throat.

'No comment,' Roachford said.

'I think this evidence shows,' Tony said in a clear voice, 'that you were in Burrelton yesterday morning with this other boy and you both stole a blue Fiesta from the village hall car park. You didn't break in because the keys had been left in the ignition so this was an opportunistic theft. Am I correct?'

'What sort of person leaves their keys in the ignition?' Roach scoffed with derision. 'They deserved to have it nicked if that was the case. You can't be too careful around here.' Roachford laughed but his solicitor's face was tight with disapproval.

'I also think that you stole the car then discovered the toddler in the back.'

'No comment,' Roachford said, not bothering to deny it.

Roachford's mother slowly shook her head and looked at him in disbelief. 'You absolute twat,' she muttered under her breath.

It was no surprise the boy acted the way he did with a mother like that, thought Paton, and from the way he'd flinched as he walked past her in their home, he was most likely on the receiving end of a clout or two instead of love and respect. Paton wondered why some people had children when they obviously disliked them so much.

'Where did you take the child?' Tony asked.

Roachford leaned back in his seat and folded his arms. 'No comment,' he repeated.

'Jayson. Can I call you Jayson?' Mitchell asked, folding his hands on the table in front of him and leaning forward to look the boy straight in the eye.

'I s'pose so.'

'I think it's only fair to remind you at this point that if you say "No comment" now, then provide more detail in court in front of the judge and jury, they're less likely to believe you as you could have had time to think about it and make up a story. It's much better for you to tell us now if you were there and where the boy is. Abduction is far more serious than car theft.'

Roachford looked down at his lap and stayed silent. His

mind was probably racing to create a plausible scenario, Paton thought, and wondered what excuse the boy could come up with for being there at that time of the morning when he'd clearly stated he was still in bed. The more Paton watched, the more he was convinced that the kid was guilty of stealing the car and taking Louie. Paton waited quietly although he was dying to shout at the screen to tell the kid to stop pratting about and tell them what he'd done with Louie. These lost minutes and hours could be vital for the child's well-being. He held his breath as the silence lengthened and inwardly praised his officers for not speaking, thus forcing Roachford to give some response.

'No comment,' he said.

Paton felt the acid burn of anger scorch his gut and his legs tensed with the effort of staying seated. He wanted to drive over there, burst into the room and shake the boy's confession out of him. It was probably just as well he wasn't in the interview. He wouldn't be able to continue with professional detachment, not after seeing how much Melanie Cameron was suffering over her missing son.

'Jayson,' Mitchell continued, his voice calm. 'How about you tell us if you recognise the other lad instead. The judge might look more favourably on you if you help us with our enquiries. Give you some brownie points if you know what I mean.'

'Well, I can't see his face, can I? It could be anyone.'

'Sometimes we recognise people by their walk, body shape and clothing,' Tony interjected. 'DC Tomkins, could you please show Jayson Roachford the footage from the dashcam?'

Mitchell opened his laptop and tapped the keys to bring up a video of two people, probably male, facing away from the camera and walking along the pavement. He turned the laptop towards Roachford who put his face nearer the screen and squinted.

'I might know him. Yeah, I reckon I do. I've seen him at the park. That's Woody.'

'Woody?'

'Darren Woodrow. It must be him who nicked the car. I don't recognise the other guy though.'

The solicitor pushed his chair back a few inches and let out a long sigh.

Back at Perth police station Paton stood and went to the incident room to speak to Douglas.

'Roachford clearly knows far more than he's letting on. We need to examine his phone records to see if he's been in touch with a Darren Woodrow, also known as Woody.'

Chapter 47
3PM

Child missing - 30 Hours

Tommy missing - 30 minutes

Tommy

It was uncomfortable in the back of the van and really not safe. There was no chair for a start. Tommy sat on a wheel arch watching tools sliding about in the dirt as they went around corners. It smelled horrible. Like sweaty armpits and the school dining room after lunch. Tommy had nothing to hold onto so he had to sit with his feet wide apart. It was a bit like the twister ride at the fair but not as much fun.

The van pulled up at traffic lights and Tommy thought about banging the sides so people would look. The bald man looked at him again then turned the radio on loud. Maybe he guessed Tommy might make a noise. The music was terrible.

Not real music at all. Just a man talking fast to thumping noises.

Tommy leaned forward and looked out of the front window to see where they were going, trying to remember things to tell Dad. If he was a baddy, he'd put a blindfold on the prisoner like they did on telly. But these men were silly. They didn't think he could say much. They'd soon find out Tommy was clever when Dad arrested them and threw them in a cell.

The houses were only on one side now and then it was just fields and trees. It was hard to remember things as it all looked the same. They'd gone past the Toby carvery where he'd been for roast dinners with Mum and Dad, and the garage where they bought petrol, but he'd seen nothing else. He tried to count how many left and right turns, but the van seemed to go straight mostly. He saw a few more houses, a place where they put bodies in the ground and a little school.

The bag at his feet slid away as they went too fast around another bend. The cat food. Oh no! How could he have forgotten Pringle? She'd be so hungry by now. He had to escape and find his way home to feed her. But they were going such a long way. He'd never be able to walk that far. He got puffed out going to the mini-market. His tummy felt like it was turning itself inside out and suddenly he wanted to cry.

He needed to phone Dad. Tell him to go home and feed Pringle or let her out of the shed. Tommy felt bad now for locking her in. He'd only wanted to look after her and love her but if she was outside, she could have caught mice to eat.

Tommy felt the shape of his phone through his jacket pocket but didn't take it out in case the men saw it and took it off him. He'd need to hide it somewhere better. He was good at hiding things. He'd once hidden a whole plateful of food in his pile of jumpers when Mum put him on a diet.

He waited until the road was straight then carefully

slipped the phone from his pocket. He lifted his trouser leg and put the phone down his sock then put his trouser leg back. There. You couldn't see it now.

It seemed ages before the van slowed down and turned into a lane. Tommy felt like he was on a trampoline as he bounced up and down. The van stopped in front of a big barn made of metal crinkled like his favourite chips. A few small sheds stood nearby. A man with very white trainers stood in the yard. The men hopped out of the van then opened the back door.

'Come on, son. Out you come.'

Tommy climbed carefully from the van making sure the leg with the hidden phone was facing the other way. The man took his arm and helped him down the step then led him to the other man. This guy was bigger than Dad's garden shed and Tommy felt small next to him.

The bald man nodded to him and said, 'Spanner.'

'Okay, Wiggy?'

Wiggy? That was a funny name. Maybe it was because he had no hair.

'Hello. Tommy, isn't it?' Spanner said.

Tommy didn't speak, just stared at the man with his mouth open.

'He'll be no trouble,' Wiggy said.

'Stick him in the big barn then, so he can wander about. There's no windows and only one way in, and we can padlock that door.'

Tommy was taken into the barn. Stripes of light fell from plastic squares and holes in the ceiling onto a blue car. Dusty bits floated in the air and tickled his nose. He sneezed.

'I hope he doesn't get hay fever.' Wiggy tipped his head towards a pile of old hay bales. 'How long are we keeping him here?'

'Long enough for people to notice he's missing and for

Paton to be taken off the case. Then we need to get everything shifted from here, Nigel's yard and the other two locations. It's not like the boy can identify us or the location so once the dust has settled, we'll probably let him go again.'

Tommy was pleased to hear that but how long would it take?

'If he doesn't cause any trouble, that is,' Spanner added.

'You'll be a good boy, won't you.'

Wiggy leant down and peered into Tommy's face. Wiggy's eyes were the colour of toffee. Tommy was going to nod then changed his mind. He didn't want them to know he understood everything.

'What's he got in the bag?' Ronnie asked.

'Not sure.' Wiggy said. He put his hand out and took it then peered inside. 'Cat food.'

'Oh well, at least he won't go hungry.'

Spanner laughed but Wiggy didn't.

'You have got some supplies for him, I hope?' Wiggy asked.

'Course I have.' Spanner went over to a wooden table and pulled open a bag. 'See, bottles of squash, cakes, biscuits and crisps. He can share my takeaway later too if he's lucky. I just hope he likes vindaloo.' He laughed again. 'Only joking,' he said when Wiggy shook his head. 'Don't worry. I won't let him starve. Like I said, you're too bloody soft. You need to toughen up a bit. Hey, Ronnie, fetch my phone from the shed next door, will you? I need to send a photo of Tommy to the boss to prove we've got him.'

'Doesn't he trust us?' Wiggy asked.

'Trust us? Who'd trust a bunch of criminals?'

Spanner's laugh was like water going down the plughole.

Tommy didn't like him. The silly man laughed at his own jokes for one thing. He stared at him. Brown hair cut short over his ears. Wonky bottom teeth, a big mole with hairs growing out of it on his neck. Tommy wished he had pencils and paper so he could draw everything. He was worried he might forget stuff for Dad.

'Stand there, boy, near that ladder. Smile!'

Spanner pointed his camera phone at Tommy.

Tommy let his face go soft and looked down.

'Come on, guys. That's this job done for now. Next task is to find Woody and get the goods from the yard.'

Spanner left the barn and the others followed. The huge door was slid across and Tommy heard the sound of a padlock rattling. As soon as the car drove away, he fished out his phone. He looked at the screen to unlock it then touched the buttons Dad had shown him. He found Dad's photo and pressed the call button. The phone at the other end rang and rang. *Come on, Dad. Answer!* The answerphone woman came on and told him to leave a message. Tommy was about to speak when the padlock rattled again. He ended the call and put the phone on silent like Dad had taught him then hid it in his sock again.

'I forgot to give you this,' Spanner said.

He put a bucket in the corner. Tommy stared at it wondering what it was for.

'It's your bathroom suite,' Spanner said.

Tommy just stared.

'Your toilet. You know, wee wee and poo poo.'

For a moment Tommy let his guard slip and he widened his eyes in horror. How could he be expected to do his business in a bucket?

Luckily, Spanner had turned away and was soon out of the door. Tommy pulled his phone from his sock as soon as the padlock had clicked shut and made his way to the back of the barn. Dad had better answer this time.

Chapter 48
4PM

Child missing - 31 hours

Tommy missing - 1 hour 30 minutes

DI Paton

'Can you all stop what you're doing for five minutes, please?' Paton spoke loudly, so as to be heard across the phones and chatter in the office. 'I need to re-cap on what we've got so far then allocate actions.'

The team gathered around expectantly. Some swivelled their chairs to the front of the room and others perched on desks.

'I've been watching the interview of the suspect Jayson Roachford. As you know, we have a Coke bottle found near the scene with his fingerprints on and dashcam footage of a lad wearing jeans with a ripped pocket and a DO NOT SUBVERGE hoody. Two weeks ago, Roachford took delivery of a garment the same design and colour from a small start-up company, and no one else in the area has ordered one. Jayson denies being in Burrelton yesterday morning and says he was in bed. His mother has so far failed to vouch for him. Jayson did, however, tell us he thought the other lad is Darren Woodrow, someone he recognises from the local park.

'Ian and Kev are currently searching his home for the DO NOT SUBVERGE hoody and a pair of jeans with a torn back pocket. I'm particularly keen to find the jeans, as an eyewitness tells me one of Gus Chambers' attackers was wearing such a garment. We also have a shoe print in the mud at the Burrelton car park and, according to the National Footwear Database, it's a Nike Run Swift.'

'Fat lot of good they did him, eh?' quipped DC Ian Walters. The team tittered in response.

'We're also still waiting for DNA results from the chewing gum found at the scene and the drink bottles we found later. Douglas, I need an address for Darren Woodrow. See if we've got anyone with that name on the Police National Computer. If we can bring him in, he might implicate Roachford.

'Colin, can you check if Ms. Eden has anything on record and find out the name of Gus Chamber's sister. I need to make a couple of calls then I want you, Andy, to come with me to Darren Woodrow's house.'

With Cheryl and Becki supporting families, and Tony and Mitchell interviewing Roachford, Paton was fast running out of officers to delegate actions to. He might soon need to draft in more from another team.

'Are you going to arrest him, Boss, or just bring him in for a voluntary interview?' Andy asked.

'Arrest him. We need to search his home and take DNA samples etc. so this way we won't need his consent.'

Douglas tilted his head and raised his eyebrows. 'Do you

believe Roachford, boss? He might just be trying to set Woodrow up.'

'It's possible but I'm sure we'll find out more in the interview. Right, I need to call Cheryl to see how Louie's family is and Becki at the hospital to see how Gus's surgery has gone.'

Paton was surprised not to have heard from Becki yet. He looked at his watch. It was four hours since the boy had been rushed into theatre. Surely he wouldn't be in there that long?

When Paton returned to his desk and picked up his phone, he saw a missed call from Tommy and was immediately torn. Should he call him back or make these two important phone calls? Tommy was probably ringing to ask for a pizza for tea or to tell him about a drama he was watching. Paton should find out how Gus was first. He was about to contact Becki when he changed his mind. If Tommy was ringing for something minor then he needed to be reminded that this wasn't acceptable. If he was actually ringing for something important then Paton would never forgive himself if he didn't call back. He rang Tommy's mobile but it went straight to voicemail. Paton smiled as he recalled the fun they'd had recording it.

'*Hi, this is Tommy Paton, private investigator. If you need to catch a baddie then I'm your man. No job too small. Leave me a message and I'll call you back.*'

'Hi son. I'm just returning your call. I hope everything's okay. I'll see you later.'

Next, Paton rang Kirsten's number.

'Hi, is everything all right with Tommy? I had a missed call from him but I think he's switched his phone off now.'

'He's upstairs having a rest. He probably rang to ask you to get something from the shops. He keeps pestering me to go. Maybe he's decided to sleep a bit longer. Shall I wake him up?'

'No, don't worry. He likes a little nap now and then. I'll see you soon after six.'

Paton hung up, a furrow creasing his brow. Tommy didn't often sleep during the day. Still, he had been awake early, so maybe the excitement of the day had been too tiring for him. Paton hoped he wasn't coming down with something. He tried calling Becki next but there was no reply so he rang Cheryl.

'How are the parents?' Paton could hear the sound of a car going past and guessed Cheryl must have left the house to answer his call and keep her conversation private.

'I've had to persuade Mr. Cameron to stay put and wait for updates as he's desperate to go to the custody centre to get news first-hand. Personally, I think he wants to get hold of the lad and shake him. I hope you've got something positive I can tell him.'

'I know how he feels. You can say we've now arrested one youth and have the name of the second. We hope to find out what they did with Louie very soon. My guess is they've holed him up with a relative or friend somewhere while they decide what to do with him. If all goes well, we may have the child back in his own bed tonight.'

'And back on his medication,' Cheryl added. 'His parents are really worried about his seizures and whether he's been given carbohydrates. They mess with his ketogenic diet. I hope we have some good news soon. It's really hard watching the parents suffer. I feel so helpless and useless sitting here doing nothing.'

'Don't under-value what you're doing, Cheryl. We need you there. Remember your FLO training.'

'I know, sorry to whinge, Boss. It's been a long day and still only 4pm. Good luck with finding the second lad.'

Paton rang Becki again but still got no reply. That was odd. He called the hospital ward instead and the Ward Sister answered.

'I've just been looking for DC Lewis,' she said, 'but there's no sign of her anywhere. I've terrible news I'm afraid. Gus Chambers didn't make it.'

Paton was too shocked to answer straight away. The boy had looked badly beaten when he'd seen him yesterday, but his injuries hadn't seemed life threatening. His poor family. It was always difficult to take in the death of a child but when he was a similar age to your own it was doubly hard.

Paton dragged his thoughts back to his professional role. 'What happened? Have the parents been informed?'

'The doctor is with them now. It was highly likely to have been the injury to his head. Probably from a kick. The surgeon tried to release the pressure on the brain but the first attempt missed the bleed. By the time he'd made the second incision it was too late. What a tragic waste of life. I hope you get whoever did this, Inspector. They deserve to rot in hell.'

A crushing sense of responsibility overwhelmed Paton. Not only did he have a missing child with a serious illness to find, he now had a murder case on his hands. What was it his mother had always said? *'Be careful what you wish for.'* Maybe the role of SIO on serious cases wasn't all he'd thought it would be. So many people's hopes were laid at his feet that he wasn't sure he had the skills and knowledge to cope. All he wished for now was a hot supper and a comfy evening on the sofa watching a drama with Wendy and Tommy. Fleetingly, his thoughts turned to Wendy and her hopes of being pregnant. He put his elbows on his desk and rested the top of his head in his hands. He had to be careful he didn't overwhelm himself. He needed to concentrate and plan what to do next.

'Boss? Are you okay?' Douglas was standing beside him. 'We've had the DNA results in. The chewing gum and Coke bottle match Jayson Roachford's DNA. We can definitely place him at the scene of the car theft.'

Chapter 49
4PM

Child missing - 31 hours

Tommy missing - 1 hour 30 minutes

Woody

Tyler leaned forward, the chair he was standing on wobbling slightly.

'Stop! You made it all wet now.'

Woody looked down and realised he'd over-filled the plant pots so water was cascading over the edge of the work bench.

'Silly Darren.' Tyler laughed.

'Silly Darren,' Woody agreed.

He took an old rag and swiped water and mud off the bench, stepping sideways to avoid the brown drips landing on his trainers. It was a good job he hadn't worn his new Run Swifts after all. These old ones he'd spotted in the shed at home were far more practical for Grandad's farm.

Tyler started prattling on again about how he was going to have fields and fields of peas, his favourite vegetable. Woody zoned out and just nodded or grunted occasionally. He couldn't stop thinking about the toddler Roach had dumped by the road. Had Mabel Grimstone found him? Why hadn't she taken him to the police? And what did Grandad mean by his comment, 'Rumour has it...' Woody was dying to ask him but it was difficult with Tyler around. Still, Tyler would be going home soon. Megan had called to say she'd finished her shopping and was on her way to collect him.

They lined the plant pots up on the windowsill in the boot room then wrote funny names on lolly sticks.

'Slim Jim will grow biggest,' Tyler said.

'I think Lofty will,' Woody said. 'We'll have a race.'

As Tyler walked to his car holding Megan's hand, he called back, 'Don't forget to water them!'

Woody made Grandad a cup of tea and waited until they were sat at the table, then asked, 'What were you going to say about Mabel Grimstone?'

'Why do you ask?' Grandad stirred his tea and watched the liquid swirling around.

'It sounded like something bad and I wondered if we should keep Tyler away from there.'

'It was just the gossipmongers at church. People can be cruel.'

'What did they say?'

'I don't like to repeat gossip but, since you're asking, they say she miscarried her unborn baby by falling down the stairs aged fifteen. It's rumoured she did it on purpose, then felt so guilty she spent the next twenty years desperate to get pregnant again. I probably shouldn't tell you this, you being little more than a kid yourself, but I remember the time I was out with my friend Pete and she stroked his leg at the bar. He jumped like a scalded cat.' Grandad chuckled. 'She had several short "friendships", for want of a better word, but she never settled down with anyone.'

'Does she live on her own?'

'Since her old mother died a decade ago, yes. Mabel nursed her for years. She had diabetes and heart problems or some such illness and had her foot amputated so Mabel probably couldn't leave to make her own way in the world. If you ask me, she's been dealt a poor hand in life.'

It was starting to make sense now. It had definitely been Louie's blanket in the kitchen and it was too much of a coincidence for there to be two small boys in the area with the same blue coat. So, had Mabel found Louie and decided to keep him? Was her longing so great that she was prepared to risk being arrested for abduction? From what he'd seen, she was taking good care of Louie. Perhaps Woody should pay her a visit. What would he say to her? Tell her he knew the child wasn't hers? He'd think about it on the walk there.

Woody waited until Grandad was busy doing the accounts before traipsing across the field. He was tempted to take the quad bike again, but he couldn't risk either Grandad or Mabel hearing him, and dusk was turning the field into pools of shadows. He slipped through the hedge and past the sheds to peek through Mabel's kitchen window. The room was empty. He skirted the house and took a swift look into the lounge. Mabel lay on the sofa, her head resting on a cushion and her arm around the small boy lying next to her. He certainly looked like the bairn from the car.

Woody hesitated, not knowing what to do. He still hadn't a clue what to say to her. Should he ring the police? How could he explain why he was calling? He'd have to admit to stealing the car. His guts squeezed with worry. He didn't have the courage to do that. Even if he only got a caution and community payback, he couldn't face seeing the disappointment on Mum and Grandad's faces. Besides, how would he ever get a decent job with a police record? He'd be labelled as untrustworthy at best and a criminal at worst. No one would want to employ him. He might not have been motivated to find work before but the thought of limiting his options was scary.

On impulse, Woody went to the front door and knocked, picturing the confusion and panic on Mabel's face. He'd have it out with her. She didn't answer, but he saw the lounge curtain twitch. He knocked again and decided he'd keep knocking until she answered. She must have realised he wasn't going to give up, as the door eventually opened. Mabel Grimstone stood, her cheeks pink and her hair sticking up in different directions. Her clothes were crooked and she had small dents on her face where she must have laid on a patterned cushion. Woody almost felt pity for her. There was no sign of the little boy though. Had she hidden him?

Chapter 50
4.30PM

Child missing - 31 hours 30 minutes

Tommy missing - 2 hours

Tommy

While he waited for Dad to call back, Tommy decided to look around for another way out. It was a very big barn and had another floor halfway up that seemed like it was floating. That looked dangerous. A steep ladder went from where he was standing to all the way up. He couldn't decide if he was brave enough to climb it. He'd stay down here for now and explore. He walked around a blue car parked in the middle of the barn and found two shiny motorbikes behind it. One black and one red. Wow! He'd show Dad when he came to rescue him.

Tommy swung his leg over the seat of the red bike and sat down. It wobbled on its stand but didn't fall over. Tommy grabbed the handlebars and leaned forward. *He was a private detective off to his next case on his work bike. Everyone watched him as he rode past, thinking he looked cool.* He sat a minute longer, but it was boring when it wasn't moving. He climbed off again and carried on searching the barn for a way out or clues to show Dad.

At the back in a wobbly pile were a load of parcels taped up with labels on. Probably waiting to be delivered. Were they stolen goods? Gold and diamonds perhaps or posh watches? His heart thudded. This could be his first clue. He took a small parcel and picked at the tape then pulled a long strip off. Huh. That was disappointing. It was just a dirty, greasy lump of metal with bits of wire sticking out. He put it back and rubbed the oil off his fingers onto the wrapping paper. He undid another parcel. This was a let-down too. It looked like a metal lemonade bottle with a hole at both ends. A bit of exhaust pipe maybe? These must all be bits of cars. Boring!

There were no other doors in the barn. Just a small open square in the wall upstairs which made it very cold. Lucky he had his warm coat on. And his gloves and scarf. He'd check out the picnic in the bag on the table next. That would be more fun. Inside he found orange squash, salt and vinegar crisps and a few other goodies. Shame. He liked chicken crisps best. He ate them anyway but left the pink icing cakes and chocolate biscuits for later.

Dad was taking a long time to call. Tommy looked at his phone. That was weird. The screen was blank. He must have turned it off by mistake. How did he turn it on again? He pressed a button on top and a drawing came up on the screen. It looked like a square mouse with a long tail. Then it went blank again. Oh no!! Was it flat? He badly wanted to speak to Dad. How could Dad rescue him if his phone didn't work? His chest went tight and his armpits prickled. He so wanted to go home. And what about Pringle? Would Kirsten even be wondering where Tommy was?

He pulled the door handle but it wouldn't budge. He wanted to kick it but that would only hurt his toe. He'd have to wait until Spanner came back, then try to escape. He walked back to the ladder and looked up. What if he hid upstairs, then when Spanner came to look for him, he could run out the door? Hmm, maybe not. He'd have to get down the ladder fast and he didn't think he could do that.

He climbed up a little bit at a time, trying not to look down. It seemed much higher at the top. He clung to the wooden sides of the ladder then got off carefully, glad to be standing on a floor again. He looked about. Just piles of hay and old plastic sheets. The wooden boards creaked as he moved and the dust tickled his nose. It smelt like the mouse cage at school. The floor was broken in places and over there he could see the car through it. He went carefully around the edge and climbed behind some piles of hay. He could make a den up here while he waited for someone to come. He pushed big squares of hay around for chairs and spread a piece of plastic sheet out like a tablecloth to cover the nasty hole. What he needed now was the rest of the picnic.

Holding tight to the top of the ladder, he carefully swung his leg around and onto the first step. It was scary but thinking about the chocolate biscuits helped him to keep moving. Once he was in the right place it was easier to go down and soon he was at the bottom again. Phew. He fetched the biscuits and looked at the ladder. Maybe not. It was getting dark and a bit creepy. There were no lights in the barn and the plastic squares in the roof were dark grey now. If only he could go home. He was tired and scared of the shadows and wanted to tell Dad about the baddies.

He peered through the windows of the car and saw a baby

seat in the back and a colouring book and pencils. He opened the door, climbed in and picked up the book. He'd stay in here because it felt safer. He'd eat his biscuits and draw pictures. At least it'd be more comfortable than sitting on straw and he could draw all the clues he'd seen so he could show Dad. He drew the big man, Spanner, with wonky teeth and the mole with hairs sprouting out. He drew a spanner like the one in Dad's tool kit. It wasn't very good but it might help him remember. Next he drew Wiggy with no hair, small ears and a bumpy nose. Lastly, he drew a gold earring, the shark tooth necklace and a black thumb nail but it was getting too dark to see so it was a bit wobbly. He tore the page out and folded it carefully before putting it in his pocket. He leaned his head against the headrest and shut his eyes.

A sudden noise made him jump. He must have nodded off because everywhere was really, really dark. For a moment he couldn't remember where he was until he heard the big metal door slide across. The barn. The backs of his hands prickled and his mouth went dry. He was still there. A torch shone and the huge man entered. He looked scary in the dark. If only Tommy had hidden near the entrance. He could have run out the door but it was too late now. Spanner shone his torch around and called for Tommy. Tommy stayed quiet and slid down the seat, his heart going bumpety bump.

'I've got us a pizza,' Spanner called. 'Come and get it before I eat the lot.'

Pizza? Maybe Spanner wasn't so scary. Tommy instantly felt a bit better. Perhaps he should eat some before he tried to run away. He was very hungry after all. He opened the door and climbed out. Ooh, yum. He could smell the tomato and melted cheese.

'You've got Wiggy to thank for this. He seems to like you.'

Spanner put a large pizza box on the wooden table with a

big bottle of Coke and two plastic cups. He dragged bales of hay over.

'Sit down,' he ordered. 'You make the place look untidy.'

Tommy sat and Spanner handed him a large floppy slice of pizza. It had Pepperoni on, which Tommy didn't like much, but he kept quiet.

'Thank you?' Spanner said with a raised eyebrow.

Tommy nodded, his good manners winning over his wish to pretend he didn't understand.

They ate in silence until there was only one slice of pizza left.

'I'm having that,' Spanner said, watching Tommy carefully. 'You know,' he waved the pizza at Tommy, 'you don't fool me. Wiggy may have a soft spot for you – probably because you remind him of his brother – but I can see you're not as daft as you make out. I'm going to keep a close eye on you and if you try any funny business, I'll lock you in the smaller shed where the rats live.'

Rats? Tommy caught his breath.

Spanner stood and bent the pizza box in half then shoved all the rubbish in a bag.

'Wiggy dropped you off a blanket as well, the soft sod. I'll fetch it.'

He pulled the door open. It was quite dark outside now.

'Can I have a torch?' Tommy asked, his nerves getting the better of him.

'Hah! I knew it. You can speak.' He put his face close to Tommy's, his eyes like ice. 'You're brighter than you let on. But be warned, Tommy Paton – son of the "oh so clever" DI Paton – I'm a lot smarter than you and nowhere near as nice as Wiggy.'

Chapter 51
5PM

Child missing - 32 hours

Tommy missing - 2 hours 30 minutes

Louie

When he was woken by loud knocking on the front door, Louie first thought he was being cuddled by Mummy on the sofa. He wanted to snuggle back in, but Mummy went stiff like when she saw a spider. But no. This wasn't Mummy. She didn't smell right and her clothes weren't as soft. It was Grandma, and now she was moving him out of the way so she could get off the sofa. He looked at her in the light from the lamp. Her eyes were big and her hand scrunched the front of her blouse.

She pushed him behind the door and whispered,' Stay there.'

Louie's legs felt wobbly. Was it a monster come to eat him

up? He peeked through the crack in the door as Grandma went into the hall.

'Who's there?' she said, but she didn't open the door.

'Darren, Can I have a quick word?'

Louie didn't know who Darren was.

'I don't know any Darrens,' Grandma said, 'and it's not a good time right now. Come back some other time.'

'I'm Patrick Harcourt's grandson. You'll want to hear what I have to say.'

Grandma opened the door just a little bit. It was getting dark outside.

'What do you want? I can't talk now. I need to lock the chickens in or the fox will get them.'

'I'll help you. We can talk while we're putting them away.'

'It's too dark out there. You'll trip.'

Darren pushed the door open, came in and wiped his feet.

'I'll be fine. I'm going back that way anyway.'

He closed the door again.

Louie gasped. It was one of the naughty big boys.

The boy must have heard Louie because he put his head around the door. Louie shrank back against the wall.

'Hello, laddie. Don't worry, I won't hurt you.' The big boy smiled but Louie just stared at him.

'Who's this then?' the big boy asked Grandma.

Grandma went pink and her hands flapped about. She rubbed her face.

'My nephew,' she said.

What was a nephew? Why didn't she say his name was Louie?

'I didn't think you had any brothers or sisters. Grandad said you're an only child and you've never been married,' the big boy said.

Louie looked at Grandma who opened her mouth but no words came out for a long time.

'What's it got to do with you? And what's so important that you barged your way into my house? I think you should leave.'

This big boy wasn't nice. Louie hoped the other one wasn't here too. The one that pulled him out of his car seat and put him by the road. He hoped the big boy didn't hurt Grandma.

Louie hid behind Grandma and tugged on her skirt. 'I not like big boys.'

She looked down at him like she wanted to hug him.

'Big boys nasty. Put me on grass. Mummy's car, not big boys' car. Mummy gone. I cry. Scary bird get me.' Louie wanted to tell her more about that morning, but the words tumbling out were all wrong and he couldn't say what he needed to. He took a deep breath and tried again. 'Big boys drive Mummy's car fast. I felled over.'

Grandma stared at Darren. He turned away from her then went and sat on the sofa.

Before she could say anything else he said, 'You found him, didn't you?'

'What do you mean?' Grandma's voice was quiet.

'You found the kid by the road and decided to keep him. He's not your nephew. I should tell the police.'

Grandma just stood there. She forgot to close her mouth.

'You can't keep someone else's kid. If you wanted one so much, why did you throw yourself down the stairs to get rid of yours?'

'Are you insane? Why on earth would I do that? Who would tell you such a hideous lie?'

Grandma's hands were shaky and her eyes started leaking. She wiped her face on her sleeve. Mummy told Louie off when he did that. Sometimes he made his sleeve snotty.

'Grandad said you've been desperate for a child for years.

He said you kept hanging around with different men trying to get pregnant.'

Grandma put her fingers over her mouth but a loud moan got out and her nose ran. Louie spotted a box of tissues and fetched her one so she wouldn't make her sleeve snotty too. She looked down at him and scooped him up in a hug.

'My lovely boy,' she said, putting her face in his neck.

Louie squirmed to get down. He didn't like her being upset and she was making his neck wet. Grown-ups worried him sometimes. Like when Mummy and Daddy shouted then they cried.

Mabel sat on the chair and rocked Louie in her arms. That was better. He sneaked looks at the big boy who was staring at them.

'Wait a minute,' Grandma said. 'What did you say, Louie?' She peered at his face. 'Were the big boys driving Mummy's car?'

Louie nodded.

'Was Mummy in the car?'

Louie shook his head.

'Had you ever seen the big boys before? Does Mummy know them?'

Louie shook his head again.

'Darren, how would you know I found the boy by the road? There wasn't a soul around.'

'I... er... I—'

'You dumped him there, didn't you! What did you and this other boy do? Steal Louie's mum's car?'

Darren was silent.

Grandma put Louie on the floor and stood up. She wasn't crying now. Her voice was getting louder. 'You did! You stole it. Where from? Did you discover Louie afterwards?'

Darren couldn't say because Grandma kept asking more.

'How could you abandon a small child like that?'

'It was Roach. I told him not to but he wouldn't listen. It's not my fault. I went back to look for him.'

The big boy was shouting too and Louie didn't like it.

'How dare you come here, lecturing me for taking the boy in and caring for him when you're nothing more than a common criminal?'

'Me? Isn't abducting a child a bigger crime than stealing a car? His parents must be going nuts. How could you keep a child from his family?'

Louie watched the two grown-ups. His chest felt like it was full of flapping birds. He didn't understand. If he and Noah shouted, they got told off but grown-ups did it lots.

'You won't go to the police because you'd incriminate yourself.' Grandma wasn't shouting now.

'What are you going to do with him? You know you can't keep him for ever.'

'I don't know.'

Grandma sat down hard on the sofa again. She stared at the floor then put her hands in her hair and her elbows on her knees.

'You'll have to hand him in.'

Were they talking about him? Louie wasn't sure. Hand him in? Like the Lost Box at play group where Noah's teddy had been?

'I can't. I'm afraid. You'll have to help me come up with a plan.'

'Why should I help you?'

'Because you're in this as deep as I am.'

Darren gave a big sigh. 'Let's put those chickens away and we can talk about it. What's the boy's name?'

'Louie.'

'Okay, Louie, get your coat and shoes. You can help.'

But Louie couldn't get his coat and shoes. He was starting to feel funny like he did when he was going to have 'the wobblies' as Mummy and Noah called them. He often got the wobblies when he was upset. He had that nasty taste in his mouth and he felt so, so tired. He sat on the sofa and, like the iPad when Mummy switched it off, his mind went to nothing.

Chapter 52
5.30PM

Child missing - 32 hours 30 minutes

Tommy missing - 3 hours

DI Paton

Before going to arrest Darren Woodrow, who it transpired had a previous caution for shoplifting, Paton called his DCI for advice. Now the Gus Chambers case had escalated to murder status, he needed to know whether he should call in the Murder Investigation Team or handle it himself. He'd been part of MIT before, but leading two major cases in tandem, with a minimal number of officers, was nigh on impossible to manage.

'I'll put a call into MIT and bring them on board,' the DCI said. 'In the meantime, get it entered onto HOLMES2 and send another couple of officers to the park to question the local teenagers again. They might be hanging around even though it's dark and cold. Now the lad has died, they might come forward with information. Also, ask someone to call the witness with the poodle to check she's okay and take a photo of Roachford along with others to see if she identifies him. If she does, you can order a line-up.'

'Will do, sir. I'll also ask the family liaison officer from that team to be with Gus's family. We're trying to find CCTV in the area but had no luck so far. Hopefully, the house-to-house enquiries will locate some doorstep cameras or security devices, or bring out more witnesses.'

'How close are you to finding the missing bairn?'

'I'm optimistic that, once we get the other teenager in custody, it won't be long before we find out where they took the child. Roachford is a cocky little git and his solicitor is a pain in the rear but, hopefully, we can orchestrate it so that Roachford catches a glimpse of us bringing Woodrow in. Maybe the fear that Woodrow could implicate him will bring him down a peg or two and loosen his tongue.'

'Let me know how it goes. If you don't get any information by morning, we'll have no choice but to initiate the Child Rescue Alert and get the press and public involved. I'll be going to dinner soon with the other course attendees but then I'll be back in my hotel room if you need to call me.'

'Not going for a few beers?' Paton attempted a friendly note.

'Definitely not. I need a clear head for tomorrow's lectures.'

It wouldn't hurt to make the odd friendly response, Paton mused. It was so tricky trying to build any rapport with this man. The DCI was professional and supportive, but it would be nice if he was a bit more human at times.

As they pulled up outside the modest three-bed semi and saw it was in darkness, Paton's bright optimism at finding Woodrow dimmed and he drummed his fingertips on his knees in frustration. Damn. He looked at the black windows of the house, then across to Andy who was busy looking behind him to manoeuvre the car into a small parking space.

'You knock on Woodrow's door to double-check whether he' s there and I'll try the neighbours.' Paton said. 'They may know where he and his parents are.'

As they stood waiting, on adjacent doorsteps, Paton was relieved to see someone approaching through the glass panel. A middle-aged woman opened the door with a tea-towel in her hand. Paton introduced himself and asked if she knew the neighbours and their possible whereabouts. Andy was having less luck getting an answer at his door.

'Is everything okay?' The woman asked.

'We just need to speak to her and her son.'

'She's a secretary at the Bloomfield Accountancy firm in Perth during the day and does evening shifts cleaning offices,' the woman said. 'She's a grafter, that one, but then I suppose she doesn't have much choice, being a single parent.'

'What about her son? Do you know where he might be?'

'Not at work, that's for sure. He's a lazy little bugger, that one. His poor mother works all hours and he does sod all.'

'Do you know where he might be now?'

The woman gazed into the distance, a small frown knitting her brows. 'I would usually say kicking a ball with his mates at the park but I haven't seen him around lately. Maybe he's gone to stay at his dad's flat or his grandad's farm.'

'Do you know where the flat and farm are?'

'I don't, sorry. I've got Nancy's number if you want to call and ask her.'

'Nancy?'

'Mrs. Woodrow. Hold on.' She disappeared back down the hall and returned with her phone to read out the number. 'I've had others knocking on my door for that boy today. They looked dodgy so I told them Darren was at his dad's in England but I didn't know whereabouts. They weren't happy.

'What did they look like?' Paton asked.

'One was as bald as a baby and the other the size of a double wardrobe. Quite intimidating.'

Paton thanked her for her help, then went back to the car with Andy. Once inside he tried the number she'd given him but it went to voicemail. He clenched his jaw. He didn't have time for this. It was now 5.25pm. Too late to drive to the accountants.

'Andy, look up the number for Bloomfield Accountancy then call and ask if Mrs. Woodrow is still there.' Paton climbed out of the car again. 'I need to make a couple of calls. Back in a few minutes.'

Paton checked there was no one in the vicinity to overhear him then called his second team to give them instructions. Next, he rang Tony to ask if Roachford had given any more information.

'We're taking a short comfort break, and I mean short.'

'We brought him in at 3pm didn't we?'

'Yes, that only leaves us nine hours minus his entitlement to rest.'

'We should qualify for an extension though, as there's a child in jeopardy.' Paton said.

'I agree,' Tony said.

'Let's make sure Roachford sees us bringing Woodrow in. It might unnerve him.'

'Good idea. His arrogance is wearing thin as time goes on.'

Finally, Paton called Kirsten to ask how long Tommy had slept for and to see if she'd stay longer but the phone rang out then went to voicemail. Perhaps they were busy in the kitchen or the television was blaring. He'd try again soon.

Paton returned to the car as Andy was thanking someone and ending a call. That sounded promising.

'Nancy Woodrow left work at 5.15pm and is now probably on the bus to her office cleaning job.'

Paton's disappointment must have shown because Andy grinned.

'Don't worry, Nancy's boss gave me the name of Grandad's farm and a rough idea of its location. He said Darren was staying there, as far as he knew, because Nancy had been able to work a few extra hours.'

'What are we waiting for then?'

Paton grinned back, and his stomach fizzed with the thrill of the chase. Maybe he'd be able to sleep tonight knowing Louie was tucked up in his own bed.

Even with satnav, the track to the farmhouse wasn't easy to spot. The lanes were shrouded in deep darkness and, when the app told them they'd reached their destination, they'd looked around perplexed. They'd had to drive at a crawl for half-a-mile before spotting the turning.

Paton got out of the car and breathed in a deep lungful of fresh night air. He was pleased to note the driveway was gravelled. Black leather shoes and muddy farmyards didn't go well together. His gratitude was short-lived, though, when he stepped into a dip on the path and water leaked into his shoe. Andy knocked on the door and a dog barked. As they stood on the doorstep and waited, Paton couldn't help marvelling at how many stars he could see compared to being in the town.

'Why didn't you come round the back?' a voice called. 'Making me get up to answer.'

The door opened and an older man with thin grey hair, a rough plaid shirt and a grubby body warmer opened the door. He had a quiet, black and white collie at his heels who sat on command.

'Oh!' the man said. 'Sorry, I thought you were my grandson.'

Paton introduced themselves and the man's smile weakened.

'Is Darren Woodrow here?' Paton asked.

'He's around somewhere. Last seen less than an hour ago when I told him to stack some more wood near the porch.'

'Is he staying with you?'

'Aye. Been here a couple of days.'

'When did he arrive?'

'Let me see.' The old man rubbed his bristly jaw. 'The night before last, I reckon, or was it the one before?'

'Were you here when he arrived?'

The man nodded and chuckled. 'He looked like a drowned rat. I could hardly recognise the lad but Cass here could tell it was him straight away.'

Paton's mind was racing. He knew it had rained heavily yesterday evening but he was wracking his brains to remember what the weather was like the night before or the one before that. His life was so busy that one day blurred into the next.

'And has he been here the whole time?'

'Definitely. He's been helping me about the place. It's a lot to manage on my own.'

It must be, thought Paton, noticing for the first time the peeling paint around the doorframe and the broken quarry tiles on the path. Wendy would love a place like this, even in its current state. It was always her dream to have a rambling farmhouse full of noisy children with space to run and play. Her conversation that morning rushed unbidden into his thoughts again. Please God she wasn't pregnant. He doubted he could cope with a baby.

'Can we come in and wait for him please?' Andy interjected when Paton didn't speak.

Paton shook himself. He needed to concentrate.

'Perhaps you can find him. We'd like to ask him a few questions.'

'What about?'

'We can't say right now, but you're welcome to be with him when we ask him.'

The farmer showed them into a large living room with two worn but comfortable sofas and a wood burner he'd recently lit. It was still chilly, but the flicker of the flames lent the room a cosiness not easily achieved in a modern home with no fireplace.

Once the old farmer had left the room Andy spoke up.

'It can't have been Darren Woodrow if his grandad says he's been here the whole time.'

'My instincts are telling me otherwise so let's see what the boy has to say.'

'Shouldn't we have kept the grandad here with us? They could be getting their stories straight.'

Paton was just thinking the same and was annoyed with himself for being distracted by his family problems. 'Wait here and I'll go and investigate. I can always say I need the toilet.' Paton wandered into the dimly lit hall, admiring an old grandfather clock as he passed it, and headed towards a bright doorway where he could hear voices.

'Where've you been, laddie? The police are here to see you.'

Paton moved nearer to hear the response but his personal

phone began ringing in his pocket. He felt a twinge of irritation. Damn. This wasn't a good time for Tommy to call. It took him a moment, as he hurried back along the hallway, to realise that this wasn't Tommy's ring tone, the theme tune from *The Sweeney*, that he'd insisted his dad install. This was the usual old-fashioned bell sound. Paton pulled the phone from his pocket. Kirsten. She'd probably just seen his missed call and wanted to know when he'd be back. He was going to silence the call when he thought better of it. He needed to check she could stay longer.

'Mr Paton,' she began.

'Please, call me D—'

'Dave, it's Tommy.' Her voice was fast and breathless. 'He's not in his room.'

'What do you mean? Where is he then?'

'I don't know,' she said, her pitch rising. 'I can't find him. I was in the bathroom when you rang. I thought I'd wake him up so he could speak to you.'

'Check the shed. I'll stay on the line because it's dark out there. There's an outside light switch behind the dining room curtain and the interior shed light is on a switch at knee height on the left.'

Paton waited, listening to Kirsten's footsteps as she walked down the garden path. He heard the shed door creak then a click.

Kirsten gasped.

'What is it?' Paton asked.

'There's no sign of Tommy but there's a cat. It looks like he's made a bed for it and everything.'

Realisation dawned. No wonder the boy had been so keen to go to the shops, but where had he got a cat from? It was dark now though, and Tommy wouldn't go out in the dark alone. A cold tendril of fear coiled itself around Paton's innards. Had

Tommy gone out for cat food and been taken? Had Nigel's warning actually become a reality? Surely not. He recalled the white van he'd seen earlier that day. He should have recorded the numberplate. The fear squeezed his gut and for a moment he felt light-headed. He leaned against the wall.

'I'm on my way,' he said and ended the call.

'Everything alright, boss?' Andy stood in the lounge doorway.

Paton flinched and straightened up.

'Fine, fine,' he said, ignoring Andy's narrowed eyes. He couldn't tell Andy any of this. He'd have to admit to Tommy being at the breaker's yard with him. He needed to think what to do before he involved the team. 'Sorry, I need to go. Something's come up.'

'But... aren't we going to arrest Darren Woodrow?'

'Not at this moment in time. It seems he has an alibi. We'll come back later.'

'But you said your instincts were telling you otherwise.'

'Supposition.' Paton had to bite his tongue to stop himself snapping at Andy. He just wanted to get out of here and find his son. 'We need more evidence first and Douglas could be right when he said Roachford might be setting Woodrow up.'

Paton returned to the lounge and gathered his coat and notebook.

'You can take me back to the station to get my car. Call Tony for me when you get in and tell him I'll call him at...' his mind was splintering and he was finding it hard to focus. He checked his watch, acutely aware that time was ticking on '... 9pm to review the detention of Roachford.'

Darren Woodrow's grandad appeared in the doorway. 'Darren's back. He's just going to the toilet then he'll be right with us.'

'We'll need to return another time,' Paton said. 'We still have questions, but something else has come up.'

As they drove back to the station, Paton swallowed the panic that was threatening to choke his self-control. Dear God, had Tommy tried to call him to say he was in danger? Paton checked the call log on his phone: 3.55pm. A wave of nausea struck him and he opened the window an inch. Fingers of cold air ruffled his sparse hair. Nearly two hours ago! Dear God. Anything could have happened to his precious son since then.

Chapter 53
6PM

Child missing - 33 hours

Tommy missing - 3 hours 30 minutes

Woody

The police! Fuck. Wiping his mouth on a towel, Woody stood and stared at himself in the speckled bathroom mirror. The handfuls of water hadn't quite washed away the acid taste of sick and he grimaced. A faint sheen of sweat made the spots on his forehead stand out and his eyes looked like Mum's when she'd been cutting onions. He'd been shocked when he'd entered the back door and Grandad had grabbed his arm, but hearing Grandad frantically whispering that the police were there and Woody should say he'd been at the farm two days, not one, had his lunch leaping into his mouth. He'd bolted up the stairs when they went back into the lounge and just made it to the bathroom in time.

He hung the towel up again, hands shaking, and opened the door. He could hear voices down in the hall so he trod carefully along the landing, staying close to the wall to avoid the creaky floorboards. He paused near the top of the stairs and listened. He was trying to work out what the police were saying when the front door opened and he felt the cold night air wafting up the stairs.

Were they leaving? He held his breath and prayed to a God he'd never believed in. *Please God, please God, don't let them arrest me.* The hall was suddenly silent.

'Darren?' Grandad's voice startled him. 'Come down here, lad, they've gone.'

Gone? He could barely believe it. He took the stairs cautiously, half expecting the front door to open again.

'I thought they wanted to question me?'

'The DI said something more important had come up. He said he still wants to interview you so they'll be back. This is about the stolen car, isn't it? Or have you done something else you're not telling me?'

Grandad's mouth tightened and he shook his head as he stared at Woody.

'I haven't done anything else, promise.'

He hadn't, had he? It was Roach who'd dumped Louie, not him.

'Only I've put my neck on the block for you, boy, so if you're keeping something from me, I'll hand you in to the police myself. I've never had to lie to anyone before and it's not a comfortable feeling.'

Grandad rubbed the palm of his hand on the back of his neck then went through to the kitchen.

'What did you say to them?'

Woody trotted behind and tried to suppress the grin of relief that threatened to split his face.

'Just that you'd been here a couple of days and that you were soaked when you arrived.'

Woody stopped abruptly. It seemed like he'd just swallowed a glass of icy water.

'But it didn't rain the night before last, Grandad. I know because I played football. It was only last night that it chucked it down.'

Woody plonked himself on a dining chair and Grandad slumped opposite him.

'Bugger.'

Woody looked up in surprise. His grandad didn't usually swear and now twice in two days.

'What do we do now?' Woody whispered.

His life was like his favourite joggers, falling apart at the seams. It was all his bastard Dad's fault. If he'd kept his dick in his trousers and stayed faithful to Mum, Woody would still be living a near to normal life. Instead, he was a suspect in a car theft and a boy was missing. Well, not exactly missing because Woody knew where he was. The problem was, how to get the boy back to his parents without Woody or Mabel getting into trouble with the police. The bairn had acted weirdly, too, and hadn't looked normal to Woody.

'There's something wrong with him,' he'd said to Mabel as Louie sat staring into space.

'He's just tired,' Mabel said. 'He's probably upset with us shouting and this is his way of coping. I've noticed him do it a few times. It's as though he's shutting the world out for a few minutes.'

'Doesn't look right to me. I think he needs a doctor.'

'He's fine. Look, I'll lay him down for a rest while we sort out the chickens and plan what to do. Humbug will keep him company.'

She picked the huge grey and black stripy cat off the

window seat and plonked him near Louie's feet. She put a cushion under Louie's head and covered him with a knitted blanket. He'd blinked, as though he'd woken from a heavy sleep, then shut his eyes again.

'Come on,' Mabel said, leading the way through the kitchen and out of the back door.

She clicked a switch that lit up the barns ahead and handed him a flashlight. She shone her beam around the edge of the garden and shooed a stray chicken from under a hedge. It fluttered and strutted towards the outbuildings.

'Molly is a bit stupid,' she said, 'but she's Louie's favourite. I'm surprised the fox hasn't got her yet.'

They continued up the garden then Mabel blew a kiss towards the border.

Woody aimed his torch in the direction and it lit up a bare rose bush.

'Why did you do that?' Woody asked.

Mabel stopped abruptly and turned to Woody. 'I planted that in memory of my beloved daughter. It's called *Victoria Rose* which is the name I'd chosen for her.'

'Is she buried under there?'

Woody felt a chill across his skin and shone his torch at Mabel instead. She looked almost as creepy in the torchlight. What was he even doing here? He wanted to go home and chill out with a mug of Grandad's Horlicks.

'I don't know where Dad buried her. He wouldn't tell me. Said I had to move on.'

Mabel's face contorted but she stepped away.

Woody stared after her, appalled.

'Is that even legal?' he called after her.

'Huh. Asks the boy who has no regard for the law. It wasn't, but no one knew about the pregnancy, or so I thought until you told me you'd heard about it. Was that from your Grandad?'

When Woody didn't answer she shook her head. 'It must have been. Maybe Mum blabbed about it in church to absolve her guilt.'

'Did she help him then? Your Dad?'

'She didn't stop him or get me any medical care. And I didn't throw myself down the stairs. My father knocked into me and I fell.'

'Did he do it on purpose?'

Bloody hell. If he did, was it murder? Woody had no idea. Probably not, if the baby wasn't born.

Mabel shrugged. 'I've never been sure if he did it intentionally or not. It doesn't matter now. The result was the same. I lost my baby and have never been able to get pregnant again.'

Mabel rounded up a couple more chickens and ran with lowered hands to guide them into the shed. They flapped up onto their roosts and fluffed up their feathers. She scattered food in their trays then switched the light off. 'Come on. Two more sheds to go.'

Woody suddenly remembered why he was there. 'What are we going to do about Louie? We have to take him somewhere safe where he'll be given to the right people.'

'A police station maybe?' Mabel's laugh was hollow.

'What about a hospital? We could leave him in the corridor or the toilets. Someone would soon find him and call for help.'

'Someone would soon find us, too. We'd be on CCTV.' Mabel glared at Woody then carried on down the path. 'We need a better plan than that. I don't know about you but I'm not ready to go to prison.'

'A children's park then, where there are no cameras.'

Mabel paused. 'It's too dark. It would have to be tomorrow.'

Woody's shoulders slumped. He just wanted this over with. He made a vow to himself that, once Louie was safely back with his family, Woody would make a big effort to turn his life around. He'd keep away from the boys in the park. He'd sign up for a college course and he'd even get a part-time job. He never, ever, wanted to get on the wrong side of the law again. It was a scary and lonely place.

'I'll keep Louie for just one more night. I'll make him a tasty supper, give him a warm bath and read him his favourite story. I'll even let him cuddle Flump, the rabbit, one more time.'

Woody could hear the smile in her voice and for a moment he had a glimpse of understanding. He enjoyed spending time with Tyler, and Woody had his whole future ahead of him. He might even have kids of his own one day. But what had Mabel got? A life of sadness behind her and an empty one ahead.

Mabel stood and faced Woody. 'He won't remember this when he's older, and his parents will soon recover from the trauma when they get him back. I just want one more night with him before I have to say goodbye. Please, Darren.'

'Okay,' he said slowly, thinking it through. 'I'll come back in the morning. We can take him to a park when it's empty – around school-run time. From what I've seen, a few mums usually turn up with toddlers just after that.'

It was the best idea he could come up with.

'Darren? Darren, are you listening?' Grandad's sharp voice cut through Woody's thoughts and dragged him back to the present.

'Sorry! What did you say?'

'When did you and this other boy steal the car? Maybe we can say I got confused and mixed my days up.'

'Yesterday morning. How will that help me, though?'

Perhaps Woody should leave Grandad out of it. It wasn't fair, dragging the poor man into this mess. Woody studied the familiar face, lined and wrinkled through being outside so much, and felt a wave of guilt and affection. Grandad was the last person he wanted to hurt.

'Do you think you were seen, lad? Maybe they have evidence.'

How? Had they found the car? There couldn't have been CCTV in a small village like that, and he'd been careful to direct Roach along roads without cameras. No. It was more likely that someone had dobbed him in. Probably Roach trying to save his own skin.

'I don't think they'd have anything,' Woody said after a pause. 'It's probably someone trying to set me up.'

Revenge, most likely, for not turning up at the job this morning. Woody was so glad he was at Grandad's. The gang's other forms of punishment didn't bear thinking about. He wondered fleetingly how Gus was. He'd looked a bloodied mess on the pavement.

'Did it rain two days before?' Grandad asked.

Woody looked at him blankly.

'We could say you got here on Tuesday night, not Wednesday like I told the police.'

Woody's mind raced. He couldn't remember what the weather had been like on Tuesday. And what if people had seen him in Perth that day? Would using Grandad as an alibi be bullet proof? Woody suddenly felt exhausted. He hadn't felt this knackered since the cross-country run his school had organised through woodland. He'd been way behind everyone else but hadn't got an ounce of energy to catch up, even though he was shit scared of the shadows in the trees. Now he wanted nothing more than to sit on the squashy sofa with Grandad and watch their favourite old films on the dodgy DVD player.

Where had he been on Tuesday evening? Woody's life was uneventful so he'd probably kicked a ball around in the park and gone to the chippy. Looking at messages on his phone might jog his memory. He stood up, yawning.

I'm going to check my phone. There might be a website that tells you what the weather was on Tuesday. We need to get our stories straight and tell Mum to say the same before the police come back.' He paused as he reached the door. 'Why are you doing this for me, Grandad?'

'I don't want you to throw your life away for one mistake. I want you to learn from this and make amends.'

'I'll never steal again. I promise.'

Woody sat on his bed and waited for his phone to light up. It sparked into life and numerous messages popped up on WhatsApp. Six from Courtney and several from lads he knew from the park. His eyes widened and his mouth fell open. Roach had been arrested and Gus was dead. Shit. Dead? He couldn't believe it. And if Roach had been arrested what would happen to Woody now?

Chapter 54
6.30PM

Child missing - 33 hours 30 minutes

Tommy missing - 4 hours

DI Paton

As they drove back to Perth, Andy kept stealing sideways glances at Paton ,who ignored him and stared resolutely at the road ahead.

'Is there anything I can do to help, Boss?'

'Thanks for offering, but no. I need to deal with this myself.'

Silence lengthened in the car, then Andy said, 'Is it your wife?'

'What?' Paton couldn't find the words because his brain was in a complete fog. Surely this wasn't really happening. He'd wake up in a minute and laugh at how realistic the dream had been. Andy's voice brought him crashing back to the moment and Paton resented the intrusion.

'It's a family matter,' was all he could bring himself to say.

He turned his head to avoid scrutiny and stared out into the black night. Where was his precious son? Was Tommy scared or trying to convince himself to be brave?

When they finally reached the police station, Paton leapt from the car before it had fully stopped and ran to his own car. He drove home as fast as the speed limit would allow, then burst into the house. Kirsten rushed into the hallway, her hands on her cheeks and tears glistening in her eyes. Her mother came and stood next to her, ineffectually rubbing the small of her back.

'I'm sorry,' Kirsten said. 'I didn't know he'd gone out.'

Paton wanted to rail at her and ask her why she'd allowed him to be left alone for so long, but there was no point in throwing blame at her. It wouldn't bring Tommy back.

'My husband has gone to look for him down the shops,' Kirsten's mother said.

'I need to double-check he's not hiding here somewhere.'

Tommy had been known to go missing before. Paton had left him in the car once while he paid for petrol. When he got back in the car there was no sign of Tommy and Paton's heart had stopped with dread. Tommy then leapt out from a pile of coats in the footwell and laughed uproariously. Paton had been angry and told him off. Was Tommy playing the same trick again? Paton ran upstairs and searched Tommy's and the other bedrooms, then downstairs and in the shed. The cat appeared from behind a pile of wood and miaowed at him. Tommy must have pretended he needed a rest so he could sneak out to the shop. Devious little devil.

'It's all your bloody fault,' Paton told the cat.

He wanted to grab it and put it outside but Tommy would

never forgive him. He shut the shed door again as he left. He went back through the house and asked Kirsten if she could find something for the cat to eat, then dashed out to his car again. He drove slowly down the road, trying to visualise the white van he'd seen for any memorable features. Nothing came to mind. Paton parked near the shop then hurried through the doorway, almost bumping into someone leaving. It took a second or two for Paton to realise it was his neighbour, Michael, Kirsten's dad.

'Dave, have you found Tommy? He's not in here.'

'Have you asked the shop assistant if he's been here?' Paton looked over Michael's shoulder.

'I did but she's only been on duty since 6pm and—'

Paton didn't wait to hear more. He sidestepped Michael and headed straight to the counter. He took out his ID badge and showed it to the young girl.

'Who was on duty here this afternoon? Do you have CCTV?'

He looked wildly around the shop.

The girl stepped back and looked from side to side as though seeking help.

Paton took a deep breath.

'Sorry, I don't want to alarm you, but my son is missing. He has Down's Syndrome and wouldn't usually be wandering about in the dark on his own.'

The girl swept her long hair from her face and gave a weak smile. 'I haven't been here long but I'll call Janice for you. She was here from twelve till six working on the till.'

She turned to a cupboard behind her and took out a mobile phone. She called Janice, who answered promptly, then put the phone on the speaker setting. Paton asked Janice if she'd served a young man with Down's who was probably buying cat food.

'I remember him. He seemed really chuffed when he

counted his money out correctly, bless him. He bought cat food, then pointed to the picture on the box and told me he'd name it Oreo if he had a black and white cat like that.'

'That's him!' Paton remembered Tommy saying he would call a cat Oreo. 'What time was that?'

'It was around two-fifteen because Henry had just come on shift. He re-stocks the shelves.'

Paton's knees weakened and he held onto the counter for support: 2.15pm? That meant Tommy had been missing for over four hours. He would have gone straight home to feed the cat. He must have been taken. Paton needed to speak to Nigel. He ran from the shop and got back in his car, barely noticing he was doing 40mph in a 30 limit.

He drove in a daze of panic and confusion to the breaker's yard. Nigel would know how to reach the gang. He'd warned Paton this would happen. How could Paton have done anything differently, though? He couldn't ignore a crime because he'd received a threat. He should have told his DCI, confessed he'd taken Tommy to the breaker's yard. Would it have made any difference? He doubted it. The DCI would have rapped his knuckles and might even have taken the threat seriously. They were so short of officers, though, with all the cutbacks, that there wouldn't have been any protection available for Tommy.

If Tommy hadn't left the house alone, would they have burst in and taken him anyway? Paton doubted it. The gang had probably been watching the house, to find out his and Tommy's movements, and struck lucky.

Paton eventually reached the rutted lane and drove slowly to the closed gate. All was in darkness and a huge chain and padlock shone in the headlight beam. Paton didn't know where Nigel lived. He could ask Douglas to track down his address but Paton didn't want to ask. If he told the team Tommy had been snatched, he'd be pulled from the case, for sure, because he was convinced the car thefts, the gang and Gus were all linked. Getting him off the cases was probably the gang's intentions, but Paton needed to be part of the investigations if he was to stand any chance of finding his son. What if they harmed his boy? What if he never saw him again? Oh God. Oh God. A wave of fear and grief pulled Paton forward and he leaned his forehead on the steering wheel, screwed his eyes shut and opened his mouth wide to release the sobs that tore from his chest. All the pressures from his job, of trying to find Gus's killers and Louie, looking after Tommy, keeping his wife happy, were too much to bear. He'd failed at all of them. Could his life get any worse?

His phone rang.

Paton looked across to the other seat where his phone had lit up. Good grief, no. It was Wendy. He couldn't talk to her now. He couldn't tell her Tommy was missing.

Chapter 55
7.00PM

Child missing - 34 hours

Tommy missing - 4 hours 30 minutes

Tommy

The barn kept creaking and sounded like a ghost moaning. Or was it the wind? Or a real ghost! Tommy's stomach churned. He needed the toilet, but he couldn't go in that bucket. He did a wee in it earlier, which was quite good fun really, but nothing else. How would he even sit down?

Tommy sat in the car, with the furry blanket Spanner had handed him, but it was so small in there. He wanted to lie down but the baby seat was in the way, and he kept getting cramp in his leg. He climbed out again. He looked at his phone. Still blank. He tried the door again. Still locked.

He was so tired. His heart kept thumping too hard and missing beats. He tried to think of TV dramas where people had been kidnapped and then escaped, but he couldn't remember any. All he could see in his head were people being tied to chairs and tortured. His breath was too fast and his hands were sweating. Where was Dad? Did he know Tommy wasn't at home now? Tommy gulped at the tears that were stuck in his throat and sat on the big squares of straw. He was a man. He shouldn't cry like a baby. *Be brave,* he told himself. Dad was a good detective. He'd work out the clues and rescue Tommy.

A sudden scratching sounded in the corner. What was that? Another cat? Tommy hoped so. He wouldn't feel so lonely with a cat. Had Pringle been fed? Dad had probably found her by now. Tommy bet he was cross and hoped Dad hadn't put her outside. It was too cold at night, and she had a cosy bed in the shed. Tommy heard the scratching again and shone the small torch Spanner had given him into the corner. Red eyes flashed and a giant rat ran behind some old wood.

Tommy jumped to his feet, his heart hammering. Rats were evil. They leapt at your throat and bit through your blood tubes. He could picture a red spray splashing the barn walls and floor. He ran to the ladder. He'd have to sleep up in his den tonight. Rats couldn't climb ladders. Could they?

It was tricky carrying his blanket and torch so he draped the cover around his shoulders and put the torch in his mouth. He climbed the ladder carefully and stepped onto the top floor. It was a good job he'd practiced this earlier. He trod carefully around the edge of the barn then into his den. He wrapped the blanket around him, using a corner as a pillow, and lay down. He shone the torch around but it made too many creepy shadows, so he turned it off and shut his eyes. If he went to sleep, he would wake up and morning would be here quicker.

Chapter 56
7.30PM

Child missing - 34 hours 30 minutes

Tommy missing - 5 hours

DI Paton

Paton sat in his car and sent a brief text to Wendy, apologising for not answering the phone earlier. He said he was still working to find the missing boy, but lied saying Tommy was fine and they'd call later. He hated deceiving her, but knew how distraught she would be if she knew Tommy was missing, too.

As he drove home at breakneck speeds, Paton felt an overwhelming sense of panic. His life was spiralling out of his control. He should be able to find Tommy – after all, he had the resources at his fingertips – but he was totally out of his depth and helpless to save his son. He gripped the wheel tightly, leaned forward and yelled 'Aargh!'

Lights were on at home and his hopes rose. Was Tommy back? He rushed up the path and into the house then stood, paralysed with disappointment, when he realised it was just Kirsten and her parents in the lounge. They looked up expectantly at him then their expressions fell as they saw his face.

'No news?'

'Heard anything?' Paton and Michael spoke in unison.

Paton slumped into a chair and put his head in his hands. He took a lungful of air then looked up through sore eyes.

'I need to go to the station to organise a search. I think Kirsten needs to go home.'

He gave her a watery smile, then turned to her father. 'Michael, can you stay here in case Tommy comes back?'

'Sure.'

As Kirsten passed Paton, she whispered, 'I'm so desperately sorry, Mr. Paton. I hope you find Tommy soon.'

Paton gave a small nod and shut the door behind her and her mother. He collected a few things then hurried out into the night. As he passed the patch of shrubs in the middle of his lawn, he heard an urgent whisper.

'Mr. Paton!'

He turned sharply, his heart racing. A shadow emerged from the undergrowth and stood in front of him. It was a young woman. He leaned towards her and peered into her face in the half-light from the streetlamp.

'Becki?' He was shocked at her appearance. This morning when they'd visited the poodle owner together, she'd been immaculate. She must have been crying because her eyes were red and her cheeks blotchy. Her, usually neat, blonde ponytail was coming loose and strands of hair were sticking to her damp face. Her clothing was awry and there were patches of dirt where she'd been sitting on the ground. She was shivering. She reached out and clasped his forearm.

'I need to talk to you. It's urgent.'

'I can't talk right now,' Paton said. 'I've got an emergency to deal with.'

He pulled his arm free and carried on towards his car.

Becki scurried after him. 'It's about the gang. I know stuff and I'm scared they'll find me.'

Paton stopped abruptly and she bumped into him. He steadied her then opened his car door. 'Get in,' he said, glancing up and down the street. Maybe she could tell him something that would help find Tommy.

'Don't go to the station yet,' she said, as they drove away.

He changed direction then, after a few minutes, pulled into a parking space alongside the river, where lights reflected and danced on the water.

Paton turned to Becki.

'What's going on? Where have you been?'

'I know your son is missing and I want to help. You have to listen to everything I say, though, and I need your help in return.'

'Okay, but I won't jeopardise my career for you.'

As he said it, Paton realised he was already risking his job by not reporting Tommy's abduction and staying on the case. But it was worth it. He had to be on the inside. Sitting at home with a FLO and waiting for information, knowing how short-staffed the teams were, was not an option. He had to keep working.

Becki looked Paton full in the face. 'I just want to make it clear, before I tell you stuff, that I've always wanted to be a police officer and I'm an honest and good person,' she said. 'Sometimes events happen outside our control and even our best intentions go awry.'

Paton couldn't dispute that. Wasn't he in the same predicament?

'Go on,' he said, with a glance at his watch.

'I'll keep it short but you can ask for more detail if you need it. It started with my brother, Aaron. He's fifteen and a genius with computers. He's also got Asperger's, and finds it hard to make friends. He got in with the wrong people online and started working for them – designing websites selling car parts and used cars, and organising inventories of goods.'

Paton sat up straighter, his impatience forgotten. Car parts and used cars? He didn't interrupt as he was keen to hear more.

'Mum didn't realise what he was doing at first,' Becki continued. 'She was just pleased he'd made some online friends and he seemed happy. It was only when he said something about cars being taken to order, and she questioned him further, that she realised he was working for criminals. Aaron finds it difficult to be creative so doesn't tell lies. She told him it was wrong, so he tried to stop, but they threatened him. Said they knew where he lived. He was beside himself with worry and stopped eating. Mum was at her wits end so told me what he'd been doing and the mess he was in. I couldn't do much to help, and I couldn't tell the police for fear they'd arrest him, and it would put my career in question.

'We decided, instead, to move him to the Isle of Wight to live with Dad. Aaron's now changed schools and has removed himself from all the online groups and social media. We thought it was all over, but then the gang contacted me. They'd found out where I worked and wanted insider information on the investigations.'

Paton's blood ran cold. Becki was a bent cop. The lowest of the low.

'How much did you tell them?' he asked, his voice tight with disappointment and anger.

'At first I refused, but they threatened to find Aaron and beat him up. When I saw Gus's family at the hospital I freaked out. All I could see was me and Mum crying over Aaron instead. Next time the gang called I told them you were heading Gus's assault investigation as well as looking into stolen cars and the breaker's yard.'

'Murder.'

'What?' Becki's face was a mask of horror.

'Gus didn't make it. He died during surgery to relieve the pressure on his brain.'

Becki sat in silence while she absorbed the horrific news. 'That could have been Aaron. Now you can see why I had to speak to them.'

'Are they going to keep Tommy and blackmail me? Have they got Louie too?'

'I don't think they know about Louie. I said you were investigating a missing toddler and they said, "What missing toddler? Nothing to do with us." They said they needed to put a stop to your progress and you were getting too close for comfort.'

She picked incessantly at the skin around her finger. 'Nigel, at the breaker's yard, told them about Tommy and gave them your address, because they threatened his family too. They asked me if I knew where Tommy was this week, as the school was shut. I said he was at home but you were heading there. I thought it would stop them. I'm so sorry.'

Paton had had a gutful of young women saying they were sorry for Tommy's disappearance. He tried to keep a lid on his simmering anger.

'What do they plan to do next?' he asked her.

'They wanted you to be taken off the case while they shift all the goods and evidence. I'm to keep them informed about what happens. I think they'll let Tommy go after that. I heard them discussing him in the background. It sounded like Wiggy was having a go at someone else, about him needing a blanket and getting him a pizza, so I don't think they'll harm him.'

'Wiggy? Can you lead us to him?'

'I heard someone call him that, then he shushed them. They don't seem a very professional outfit. They call me on a withheld number – probably from a burner phone.'

'Do you know where their premises are?'

'Only Nigel's breaker's yard. You could search there first.'

Becki pulled at the same piece of skin on her finger then sucked it as a bead of blood appeared.

'Why have you decided to tell me all this now? You could have told me this morning, when we were alone in the car, that the gang was after information.'

'I so wanted to. I was trying to build up the courage but I'm terrified of what they could do to Aaron. They call the thugs who beat Gus "The Dogs". Did you know that? They said they'd "*set The Dogs*" on my mum as well, if I didn't co-operate, then they reeled off my address. It was horrifying.'

'Can your brother give you any more information?'

'He never met them or went to any of the premises. They just contacted him online.'

'Not even when he catalogued all their stolen parts?'

'They sent him random lists and he put them into Excel spreadsheets. I can call him though, just to be sure. What do I do now?'

Paton's head was whirring like a washing machine on its spin cycle. He needed a good old-fashioned pen and paper to try and make sense of it all.

'I daren't go home,' Becki added. 'Mum's on a night shift at the warehouse.'

Paton's mind began to steady itself.

'You need to call into work and say you had to go home suddenly. A migraine maybe. Say you've only just woken up and you should be in tomorrow. I'll take you back to mine and you can wait there in case Tommy comes back.' Paton suddenly remembered Michael. 'Tidy yourself up a bit. I'll have to send my neighbour home and tell him you're on duty. Here.' He reached into the glove box and drew out a packet of wet-wipes that he kept handy for Tommy. 'Clean the mascara from under your eyes and the mud off your trousers. Redo your ponytail.'

As they drove back, she did as he'd asked, then stood erect at the front door as Paton explained to Michael that a DC was going to sit in the house. If Michael found this a little odd he didn't say.

'I'll call later,' Paton said. 'Ring me straight away if you hear anything, but if the gang calls you, tell them I've reported Tommy missing and am off the case. Then say you're off duty until lunchtime tomorrow, so can't tell them anything else. The less they know the better.'

As Paton drove away, he wondered if he'd made a terrible mistake by not handing Becki in. It was too late now, though, and this way he had a conduit to the gang, albeit only in one direction at present. He headed towards the police station, uncomfortable in the knowledge that he'd already crossed the line.

Chapter 57
8PM

Child missing - 35 hours

Tommy missing - 5 hours 30 minutes

Mabel

They were late with the bedtime routine tonight, but what did that matter? Louie had slept on the sofa for a while so wasn't tired. Mabel didn't mind. She wanted to spend as much time with him as possible and create some special memories for herself and, hopefully, for Louie too. She'd decided to bake fairy cakes with him, something she'd always been keen to do with a small child, and was now being rewarded by his enthusiasm for the task. He knelt on a chair, neatly tucked in at the table, and scraped the wooden spoon around the mixing bowl. He lifted the messy spoon and licked it, not caring that more was spreading around his face and dropping down the front of his little sweatshirt than was going in his mouth.

Mabel watched, entranced, and took in every inch of him. His little pink tongue, his shining blue eyes framed in girlishly long lashes, his avid concentration as he tried to reach every last smear of cake mixture. He put the spoon down and picked the bowl up with both hands before holding it in front of his outstretched tongue.

Mabel laughed. 'You should be an anteater,' she said.

Louie put the bowl down and gave her a disdainful stare.

'Yuk! I not eat ants.'

'Let me show you.' Mabel opened her iPad and pulled up a picture of the long-tongued creature.

Louie stared in fascination. He clearly had a passion for animals, and Mabel physically ached with longing to keep him. She'd have a whole menagerie for him. They could even have a little goat. She showed him a few more wild creatures and he watched with rapt attention, until she noticed the time. Heavens, a quarter past eight! Less than twelve hours before Darren Woodrow would be here to accompany her to the park. Less than twelve hours before she lost her beautiful boy.

She scooped him up off the chair.

'Bath time!' she said, and blew a raspberry on his neck.

He giggled. He hadn't asked for Mummy or Daddy for the past two hours, and she wondered how long it would take for him to forget about his parents altogether. How many people could remember what their life was like before they were three years old? *Barely any,* she thought. She was probably four or five in her earliest memory.

Fresh, fragrant and no longer sticky, Louie snuggled up to Mabel as she read him his new, favourite tiger book. When his limbs softened and grew heavy, she eased herself off the bed and settled him onto his pillow. She leaned down and kissed his brow.

'I love you, little Louie,' she said, her voice thick with suppressed emotion.

He half-opened his eyes then wrapped his small arms around her neck and squeezed. Mabel's eyes filled with tears and her heart soared with pure joy.

She couldn't bear to be apart from him on their last night together so, ignoring the mess in the kitchen, she quickly brushed her teeth and put on her nightwear, then slipped into bed beside him. She held him gently in her arms as he snuffled softly in his sleep. She must have drifted off because she was jolted awake by Louie. His little body was rigid. Was he having a nightmare? He relaxed for a moment then went rigid again before his limbs began to spasm and thrash about.

Mabel jumped out of bed in panic. She put the light on and watched in horror as Louie, head thrown back, eyes shut and jaws clenched, writhed and flailed in his tangle of bedding. My God. He was having some sort of fit. Mabel stood, holding her breath, not knowing what to do. She'd never seen anyone have a seizure before. Should she call an ambulance? Her pulse raced as she considered the implications. Maybe he'd come out of it in a minute. Perhaps he'd got too hot with her lying next to him. She'd heard of children having... what were they called again? Febrile something. That was it. Febrile convulsions. She knelt down next to Louie and stroked the damp hair off his forehead.

'Louie, Louie, it's okay. I'm here. I'll look after you.'

The convulsions began to subside, and Louie lay quietly again. His breathing steadied, and he now appeared to be sleeping normally. Mabel let out a long breath and began to untangle the sheets to cover him over but then realised he'd wet the bed. The poor wee lamb. This might have been why he'd wet his bed last night, and why she'd heard the bed banging on the wall. He probably didn't need an ambulance. He'd recovered from that one and been fine all day, hadn't he?

She went to the airing cupboard and pulled out clean bedding. She rolled him gently from side to side, as she used to when caring for her mother, and managed to change the sheets without disturbing him. Mabel needed to understand more about Louie's condition so that she could decide what to do. She hurried downstairs and collected her iPad then returned to sit with Louie. She scrolled through websites and the more she read, the more certain she became. It was unlikely Louie was having febrile convulsions. All the evidence – the times when he went vacant on her, wetting the bed, the way his limbs had thrashed about – indicated epilepsy. Was Louie on medication for it? Was he on a special diet? If there was that much of a risk though, surely a small boy with life-threatening epilepsy would be on the news?

Thirty minutes later, after further research, she came to a decision. She fetched pen and paper and wrote a letter then set her alarm for 6.30am.

Chapter 58
8.30PM

Child missing - 35 hours 30 minutes

Tommy missing - 6 hours

Melanie

Leaning her elbows on the banister outside Noah's bedroom, Melanie listened to Simon murmuring goodnight and switching on the little car-shaped night light. He gently pulled the door to, then went and stood beside her. When she didn't straighten up, he put an arm around her shoulders and gently squeezed.

'Come on, love. Let's go downstairs. I'll make you a hot drink.'

She allowed herself to be led to the sofa where she sat, motionless and silent.

'Don't go to pieces on me now, Mel. I need you. Noah needs you.'

'This is all my fault,' she said. 'I don't deserve to be a mother. All those women in the world, desperate to have kids, who are better people than me, and I was blessed with Noah and Louie yet couldn't be trusted to keep them safe.'

'You can't blame yourself for the criminal actions of others. I'm sorry I was angry with you. I can see why you'd think Louie would be safe in the car, and you didn't mean to stay chatting so long.'

'I know!' Melanie wailed. 'Jemma kept talking and talking and I couldn't get a word in edgeways. I didn't want to be rude. How stupid am I?'

Simon sat down next to Melanie and rubbed her back.

'Don't beat yourself up, my love. You need to stay strong for Louie. He'll need you when he comes back.'

'But he may never come back!' Melanie's voice rose in pitch. 'You've seen the news, where kids go missing and their parents never see them again. If they do, it might be years later. What if I don't see him for twenty years and I don't recognise my own boy? Or what if he's being fed carbohydrates and his seizures worsen? He won't be getting his meds, and you know how his seizures worsened when he missed two doses through having a tummy bug. What if he dies in the night?' She was almost shouting now. 'Oh God, I can't bear this!'

'Sshhh, you'll wake Noah again.'

Melanie pictured Noah's face. How it had crumpled when he realised his little brother still wasn't home.

'You said he'd be back by teatime. You promised!' he'd yelled at Melanie, red in the face, then burst into tears. 'I wouldn't let him play with my tractor,' he sobbed.

'You can share your tractor with him when he comes back,' Simon had tried to reassure him.

'He'll be scared, won't he, Daddy?'

'He may not be. Whoever has him might be looking after

him very well until he comes home. Cheryl will be back here in the morning and she may have good news for us. They've caught the naughty teenager who stole Mummy's car so they should find Louie soon.'

It had taken both parents and several stories to calm Noah. The poor little love was shattered and, eventually, his eyes had grown heavy and he'd surrendered to sleep. Melanie was exhausted too. The nausea had been lingering all day. Melanie wasn't sure if it was caused by the trauma or her pregnancy.

'I can't keep this baby,' she said suddenly.

Simon pulled away from her and stared at her. 'I thought you wanted it.'

She stared at him. 'I'm not worthy of being a mother.' Her voice cracked. 'I'm not capable.' She buried her face in her hands and began to sob. 'I just want my Louie back.' Her words were muffled and snotty.

'Hey, hey.' Simon wrapped her in a tight embrace and rocked her gently. 'We'll get through this together. We'll have Louie home soon and in a few months' time he'll have a new little brother or sister.'

'You said you didn't want this baby.'

'I've come to realise how precious life is, how precious our children are. I'm sorry I ever suggested getting rid of it. I'm ashamed of myself.'

Melanie lifted her head and gazed at him. This Simon was new to her. He never admitted he was wrong and rarely showed any emotion.

'I can't believe I thought not having money for luxuries and holidays was so important,' he said. 'It's not things that matter, it's people. And family is the most important of all. 'Come on, dry your eyes and let's have a hot drink.'

Chapter 59
9PM

Child missing - 36 hours

Tommy missing - 6 hours 30 minutes

DI Paton

If the team were surprised to see Paton back at his desk, they didn't say so. They were all aware of Paton's family commitments and knew how difficult it was for him to work late into the evening. They probably assumed he'd got extra support in for Tommy, in light of the high-profile cases he was managing, so Paton kept his trauma to himself. He didn't want to lie to anyone but, if they asked, he'd say Tommy had gone to stay with his Auntie Ursula.

Paton switched on his computer, gratified to see that most of his team were still working despite the late hour – after all, many had been there since eight this morning. He knew that if he told them Tommy had been abducted, they'd probably stay all night too. Tommy had been a big hit with the team when he'd done his work experience in the staff canteen, and they always asked after him.

Paton was desperate to confide in someone, to share the burden of fear and guilt that was almost crippling him, but he couldn't take the risk of being suspended. Was he arrogant, thinking only he could solve these cases? He didn't think so. He was acutely aware of the shortages and cutbacks that were stifling the work they were doing. At times it felt as though they were fighting a forest fire with only a garden hosepipe. If he wasn't here to oversee the two teams, then who could step in? He was already covering for his DCI, while he attended vital training, and the other SIO whose wife was in labour. A brief stab of remorse pulled Paton's thoughts away from work, as he remembered that he hadn't returned Wendy's call. He'd pluck up the courage and talk to her tomorrow, to tell her Tommy was missing.

Paton had to concentrate. He read the recorded updates on the Police National Computer, then called his team together and stood at the front of the incident room.

'Hi everyone. Thanks for working this evening.' Paton tried hard to act normally, to not let the horror of the situation show on his face or in his behaviour. 'As you probably know, Andy and I went to arrest Darren Woodrow but it seems his grandfather is providing him with an alibi. We're not too happy with the validity of this so we'll visit again in the morning. Douglas, I need weather reports for this area for the past week, as the grandad said it had been raining heavily when Darren Woodrow arrived.

'Now, could we go around the room and share any progress we've made on Operation Oakwood, please? We need to keep it brief because I'm due to call Tony at the custody suite.

Roachford is losing his arrogant edge, and we're hoping he'll soon be babbling like a baby.'

'Once he realises the quality of guests in his B&B he'll do whatever he can to check out,' Colin quipped.

The team chuckled.

'Yeah, wait until the pubs and clubs turn out. There's nothing like the smell of sick to focus the mind,' Andy added.

Paton tapped his pen repeatedly on the palm of his hand. They were right but he didn't have time for this. His son could be in mortal danger and they were larking about.

'Ian and Kev, I see from the database that you found items of interest at Roachford's house. Can you tell us more?'

'We found the DO NOT SUBVERGE hoody, seen in the dashcam footage, and also a pair of jeans with a torn back pocket. They're with forensics. We sent a photo of them to the Murder Investigation Team handling the Gus Chambers case and they showed it, along with a few photos of known criminals, to Mrs Roberts, the seamstress who owns the red poodle. She picked Roachford out of the photos and recognised the jeans. The MIT have placed a vehicle outside her house, as she's extremely anxious the gang will come after her and her dog, now that she's a key witness.'

'That's excellent news, although the poor woman must be terrified.' Paton had no doubt this gang would take revenge. They might not be the brightest bunch but they'd shown they were capable of violence. They could be hurting Tommy right now. 'Colin—' Paton dropped his pen and scrabbled to pick it up again. Could anyone notice his hands shaking? 'Did you find out the name of Gus Chambers' sister?'

'Rachel,' he replied.

Paton nodded and did his utmost to focus and stay calm. 'That's interesting. Roach mentioned her. It seems he fantasises about her. And what about his mother, Ms. Eden? Does she have previous convictions?'

'Just the usual – theft of make-up from Woolworths at the age of fourteen, then claiming benefits when she wasn't entitled to them, as a young mother.'

'It's clear where Roachford gets his values from.' Paton knew her background wasn't too important to the current situation, but it gave him a fuller understanding of Roachford and called into question the honesty of any alibi she may provide in the future. He had a sudden thought. 'Colin, can you check out Woodrow's grandfather? Let's see how honest he is too. Ian and Kev, you haven't mentioned the Run Swift trainers. Did you find those?'

'Nowhere to be seen, boss,' Ian said. 'They must belong to the other youth in the footage.'

'The evidence is certainly stacking up against Roachford. I'm calling Tony now and I'll watch the next interview.' Paton was determined to do his best for his team and his son. He felt his mind clearing as he thought through what needed to be done. 'Douglas, please call the MIT and ask how the house-to-house enquiries are going and whether they've spoken to any kids in the park. Also, Tony is sending Roachford's phone across so we can check the contacts and history. I'd like you to examine it and get onto the phone company for records. Thanks everyone, we're making good progress.'

As the team dispersed, Paton called after Douglas. 'Could you also try to find out where Nigel, the owner of the breaker's yard in Crieff, lives? I'd like to pay him a visit soon.'

Paton returned to his desk with a huge sense of relief. He'd managed to hold it together in front of his team. Even so, Tommy filled his mind. Was the gang taking reasonable care of him? Would his heart be strong enough to cope with such a stressful situation? Was he distraught or did he see his situation as being in the middle of one of his favourite dramas? The latter thought gave Paton a tiny measure of reassurance. Knowing Tommy as he did, he was probably looking for clues so he could arrest the baddies. Paton hoped Tommy didn't anger the gang. He could inadvertently put himself in more danger. Paton had to get to him first.

Chapter 60
10PM

Child missing - 37 hours

Tommy missing - 7 hours 30 minutes

Woody

By his reckoning, Woody was probably nine or ten-years-old the last time he'd gone to bed at 9.30pm, but when Grandad had said he was dead beat and needed to turn in for the night, Woody had willingly gone himself. He felt like he'd been up for two days without sleep – spaced out, like the time he'd stayed at his mate Josh's house and they sneaked beer into his room, then sat up all night texting girls.

Perhaps he was knackered because he'd got up so early, or maybe it was because of everything he'd been through today – being shit scared of getting arrested, finding Louie, arguing with Mabel Grimstone and the guilt. Especially the guilt. He was being eaten away inside, thinking of all the awful things he'd done. Leaving Louie by the road, taking the mother's car, making Grandad lie to the police for him, even swearing at his mum yesterday because the milk was sour. What a little bastard he was. No wonder Dad had abandoned him.

There'd been one lucky break in his day though. He'd found a website that gave historical weather reports. His luck was heading in the right direction for once because the app said it had rained heavily on Tuesday. He remembered now. He'd sat on his bed and listened to it lashing on his window while he played football on his X-box, because the weather had been too bad to play the real thing.

Woody enjoyed playing football and he'd miss it now that he'd decided to avoid the park. But there was no way he could meet up with mates there after this. Without warning, Gus's face loomed up in Woody's mind, laughing at something Woody had just said or cheering at a goal he'd saved. Woody's spirits sank further as he realised he'd never see him again. What a hero Gus was, sacrificing himself to protect his sister Rachel. He made Woody feel even worse about himself. Woody didn't have a sister but, if he had, he wasn't sure he would have been brave enough to do the same.

Woody tossed and turned, trying to sleep, but his brain felt like it was wired up wrong and he was getting more and more uptight. What if the police came back tonight? What if they took him away, and the only time he got to see Mum or Grandad again was in court? He leaned out of the bed and plucked Fred Bear up off the floor. So what if he was sixteen? It wasn't as if anyone could see him. He'd had no practice at being a grown-up and the world was suddenly scaring him shitless.

An owl hooted in a nearby tree; a hollow, ghostly sound. Woody wasn't scared of owls, but tonight it made him feel horribly lonely. He swung his legs out of bed, clutched Fred

Bear to his chest and made his way to Grandad's room. He tiptoed around the bed and slipped under the covers. The sheets were chilly through his pyjamas, so he inched nearer to Grandad to steal some of his warmth. Grandad smelled lovely – of woodsmoke and earth.

Grandad grunted and turned onto his back. 'What are you doing in here, lad?' he asked.

'I'm cold.' What if the police hammered on the door in the middle of the night? It would freak Cassie out and give Grandad a heart attack.

'Come here,' Grandad said.

He lifted an arm and Woody snuggled his head onto Grandad's pyjama-clad shoulder.

'Still cuddling that old bear?' he chuckled. 'Never too old, eh?'

'It was raining on Tuesday,' Woody said, 'so we're okay. We just need to tell Mum.'

'We'll call her first thing in the morning. Now stop fretting and let me get some well-earned sleep.'

Within minutes, the sound of Grandad's snores bounced off the walls like a bear in a cave, and Woody, soothed by the vibrations through his cheek, soon drifted off to sleep.

Chapter 61
10.30PM

Child missing - 37 hours 30 minutes

Tommy missing - 8 hours

DI Paton

It was taking every ounce of will-power not to leave work, jump into his car, and drive around aimlessly, looking for Tommy. Good grief, he knew exactly why Simon Cameron had done it now. As Paton watched the live-streaming of Roachford's latest interview, he had to keep reminding himself that what he was doing was far more likely to result in Tommy's return.

After obtaining an extension to hold Roachford for another twelve hours he'd called Tony and they'd run through the next set of questions to ask, with two main aims.

'First and foremost,' Paton said, 'we need to know what he did with Louie Cameron but, secondly, we need to find out if this theft was part of a bigger operation. Who was the person with him? Was it Darren Woodrow? Who are they working for?'

Tony had scribbled down questions as they spoke and they'd then discussed a strategy for him and Mitchell. Tony sounded exhausted. It had been an extremely long day, but everyone was going the extra mile to find the vulnerable little boy with life-threatening health issues. They knew they could take a few hours off in lieu when the station was quiet but, for now, they were keen to work as many hours as was physically possible.

Roach was nowhere near as arrogant as he had been. He was leaning forward, with his shoulders hunched and arms wrapped around himself, constantly chewing on his bottom lip. He had dark circles under his eyes and, every now and again, he almost succumbed to rocking like an inmate of a Victorian asylum.

His mother had one elbow on the table, with her head resting on her hand, and was indulging in frequent jaw-cracking yawns. But if Ms. Eden looked tired, then the solicitor looked almost comatose. He sat with his hands hanging between his knees, and his chin on his chest, and Paton wondered if he'd nodded off. He looked as weary as Paton felt.

'You were seen walking on the outskirts of Burrelton towards the village at 8am. How did you get there?' Tony asked.

'No comment.'

Roachford's voice had all the energy of a dead battery.

'It was barely daylight then, so I can't imagine you'd walked all the way from Perth or Dundee along country lanes in the dark. Even Coupar Angus is nearly an hour's walk away, and we know you don't live there.'

'I might have a friend in Coupar Angus,' Roachford said.

'Do you?'

'No.'

A hint of the cocky grin was back.

Paton's teeth clamped together and he forced his jaw to relax. It wouldn't help if he brought on a headache.

'So, who dropped you off?'

'No comment.'

'What vehicle did you arrive in?'

'No comment.'

Roach folded his arms on the table and laid his head down on them. 'Can I go soon?' His voice was muffled through the sleeve of his sweatshirt.

'We've got a few more questions tonight, then you can have the eight hours rest you're entitled to before we start again at eight in the morning.'

Roach sat up and his mouth fell open. 'More? I'm bloody knackered.'

A sudden loud banging sounded in the background and Roach glanced nervously at the door. Paton could hear someone shouting and swearing from the corridor outside the interview room. The usual nightshift was starting.

'I won't be able to sleep with all this racket, and the bed is really hard.'

Ms. Eden wobbled her head in mockery and muttered, 'You should have bloody thought of that before you dragged us into this mess.' She looked at Tony, waiting for him to continue.

'And I'll be too tired to talk in the morning. Eight's too early.' Roachford sounded like a whinging toddler. 'Can't we start later?'

'What did you do with the car after you stole it?'

Roachford sat back in his chair and folded his arms, his mouth set in a tight line.

'No comment.'

'I'm surprised you chose to steal an ordinary little Fiesta. Weren't there any flashier cars around? Surely a Mercedes or an Audi would be more your standard.'

Paton saw Roachford give an almost imperceptible nod, despite trying to remain detached.

Mitchell clearly saw it too as he asked the next question. 'I bet there were some nice motors in a pretty village like Burrelton. Would you say you're a BMW or Porsche man?'

'No comparison.' Roach said. 'I'll have a Porsche one day.'

The solicitor's chin was still on his chest but now he shook his head.

'Good choice.' Mitchell smiled. 'So why only a Fiesta when there were better cars around? Didn't you know how to break into those?'

Roachford rolled his eyes. 'Duh! The keys were in it.' He pursed his lips, clearly realising too late that he'd said too much. He looked across at his solicitor who abruptly lifted his head to glare at him. 'Well, that's what someone told me.' He tried unsuccessfully to backtrack.

Paton's heart quickened. At last, they were getting somewhere. His thoughts returned to Tommy and he had to drag his focus back to Roachford's interview.

'Are you admitting to taking the Fiesta?'

Roachford remained silent and stared at his lap.

'It must have been a hell of a shock when you realised the child was in the back. Did you drop him off at that point or take him on somewhere?'

'No comment.'

At the mention of the child Ms. Eden angled her chair slightly away from Roachford as though she was trying to disassociate herself from him.

'This little boy isn't yet three-years-old and he has a

medical condition called epilepsy. He has seizures. Do you know what they are?' Mitchell asked. Roachford shrugged so Mitchell continued. 'If Louie doesn't get his medication, he could become seriously ill, suffer brain damage and even die. We need to find him quickly. Where did you take him?'

Roachford said nothing.

Mitchell leaned towards him.

'Do you want this on your conscience? Think what his parents are suffering.'

Roachford looked sideways at his own mother. Paton, watching the whole scene several miles away, shook his head at Mitchell's mistake. It'd seemed as if they were getting somewhere, but asking the teenager to empathise with the child's parents, given the relationship he had with his own, was the wrong approach.

'Was the child awake or asleep?' Tony cut in quickly.

'No comment.'

'My guess is the boy was asleep when you stole the car, which is why his mum had left him in there, but then he woke up. Did he cry?'

'No comment.'

'I bet it was loud in that little car.' Tony said.

'Yeah.' Roach bit his lip and sat back abruptly, clearly realising his error. 'I bet it was,' he added.

'Who did you steal the car for?'

'No comment.'

'Do you think it's fair that you're the one in here being questioned, while everyone else is still enjoying their freedom?'

Roachford shrugged.

'If you tell us who else is involved, then the jury might look more favourably on you. By co-operating, you'll show us that you're not so bad after all.'

Roachford replied but his voice was too faint to make out what he was saying. Paton leaned forward as though getting closer to the screen would help. Had he just mentioned 'The Dogs'?

'Please speak up for the recording,' Tony said.

'I'm scared of "The Dogs"!'

Roachford almost shouted the words and glared at Tony then Mitchell. His eyes reddened and watered. Was he about to cry?

'Since when have you been scared of dogs?' his mum asked. 'You used to love Auntie Jean's whippet. And what's that got to do with anything?'

Tony and Mitchell looked at each other in puzzlement but Paton knew what Roachford meant. After seeing the state of Gus's face following his beating, Paton would be scared of them too. He rang Tony to explain. Tony nodded then hung up.

'We can offer you protection if you tell us everything,' Tony said.

Roach looked up, his eyebrows raised in hope.

'We were talking about the child crying in the car and you agreed that it was loud. So, what did you do with him?'

Roachford sighed as though finally resigned to his fate. 'Woody put him on the grass by the road. He said someone would find him and hand him in.'

Paton groaned inwardly. They should have arrested Woodrow after all. He couldn't have ignored Kirsten's call but he could have sent someone back out there.

The solicitor leaned towards Roachford and murmured something.

They were so close now. Paton wished the solicitor would shut up and let Roachford talk.

'Whereabouts was this?' Tony asked.

'I dunno. In a country lane somewhere.'

Mitchell began typing on his laptop. He pulled up Google Maps then turned the screen towards Roachford.

'I'm showing Roachford a map of the area,' he said aloud for the sake of the recording.

Roachford studied it for what seemed like ages.

'I'm not sure,' he said. 'Anywhere between here and here.'

Tony and Mitchell studied the screen and wrote down the locations.

The solicitor picked up his pen and scribbled a few notes then laid it down with a clunk. He folded his arms and sat back with an exaggerated sigh. Paton half-expected him to roll his eyes like a teenager.

'I need to make another phone call,' Tony said. 'We'll take a ten-minute break.'

Paton picked up on the first ring. Mitchell was highlighting a screenshot of the map with the possible places Louie had been dumped and was sending it over.

Were they going to find Louie soon, and would Roachford lead them to the gang that was holding Tommy? Paton could barely keep the excitement out of his voice.

'I'll get Douglas to locate any houses in the area that Roachford specified and we'll find out where the nearest ANPR cameras are to that road, to see if we can spot the Fiesta. Either someone has taken Louie into their home nearby or someone has driven off with him.'

'Either way this isn't looking good, because they haven't contacted the authorities,' Tony said.

'Quite. I want you to find out more about the second person. Roachford said it's Woody again, but that boy has an alibi. Douglas has checked the weather for late Tuesday afternoon and it was raining, so Grandad could be telling the truth. I think we'll need to arrest Darren Woodrow, though. We'll then have authority to search his home and the grandad's house for the Run Swift trainers. I also want to obtain his phone to see if there was any communication between him and Roachford.'

Chapter 62
11PM

Child missing – 38 hours

Tommy missing – 10 hours 30 minutes

DI Paton

Writing lists on scraps of paper was an old-fashioned approach, but one that worked for Paton. Sitting at his desk late at night, with his head fit to burst trying to make sense of everything, and his heart heavy with dread over Tommy, it was the only way he could organise his thoughts. There was so much to be done the following morning that Paton didn't have enough officers on his own team. Now that he was convinced that the car theft, Louie's subsequent disappearance and Gus's murder were all linked, he'd called the MIT and explained his findings so far. If the teams all pulled together, they might manage to get to the bottom of this crime ring soon and arrest the key people. He was tempted again to tell everyone that Tommy was missing but what difference would that make? They wouldn't find him any quicker, and Paton would be unable to lead the search.

Instead, he had obtained a warrant for the breaker's yard and several officers would conduct a thorough search of the premises in the morning. With twisted metal and glass in precarious heaps, it was too dangerous a place to search at night, even with spotlights. Paton had also spoken to the fire brigade who had agreed to attend and give advice on unstable structures. Another action was to send two officers to arrest Darren Woodrow, then organise a search of his mother's and grandfather's houses.

Most vital of all to Paton, though, apart from finding his own son, was locating Louie. It seemed a huge coincidence that the road the stolen car had travelled along was just a couple of miles from the farm belonging to Darren Woodrow's grandad. There must be a reason for it. Only a handful of properties bordered the route identified by Roachford so Paton had suggested they widen the radius of the search to include adjacent lanes and houses. Douglas has listed them all and Paton had organised officers to visit these homes in the morning, to ask the owners if they'd seen the small boy. The officers would also be alert to any suspicious behaviours that might indicate the homeowners had Louie, and return with sniffer dogs if necessary. If they had no luck, they might drive Roachford to the area, to see if he could identify the exact place he'd abandoned the child.

Paton rested his head in his hands and took deep breaths. He was struggling to stay focused, and for the first time in his career, he seriously questioned why he was doing this job. For years he'd sacrificed quality time with his family and friends, had no time for hobbies or the fun things in life but, worst of all, he'd put his son in jeopardy. The worry was debilitating, lessened only a fraction by the comment Becki had made about Wiggy insisting Tommy had a blanket and pizza. Surely the gang didn't intend to harm him but when would they release him?

'Still here, boss?'

Paton looked up to see Cheryl's blurry form leaning on the door frame. He rubbed his eyes to clear them.

'Is everything okay? You look terrible,' Cheryl said.

Paton inhaled deeply and stood to stretch his back.

'There's just so much to do, but it's all coming together. At least I hope it is.'

Cheryl looked at him quizzically and waited for him to say more. Out of everyone on the team, she knew him best and she was an astute reader of body language. If anyone was going to pick up on his silent horror, then she would.

'I'm heading home very soon,' he said, to avoid her scrutiny. 'I need to get back for Tommy. What are you doing here at this time of night?'

'I was visiting my parents nearby, then just wanted to touch base with the team before I went home. I feel out on a limb being with Louie's family.'

Paton nodded slowly, with understanding, and asked how the family were coping, then updated her with the recent findings, promising to call her as soon as there was more news. Several people had gone home now, and Paton thought he'd better do the same. *Act normal*, he told himself. People were beginning to notice there was something wrong. He knew he wouldn't be able to sleep but he could check on Becki and see if she'd contacted her brother. He'd be back here at first light.

As Paton was leaving, Douglas beckoned him over. 'The MIT interviewed some more kids in the park and one of them called afterwards to say he'd filmed the attack on Gus Chambers. It's a great piece of evidence and puts Roachford at the scene along with two heavies the kid called "The Dogs". Apparently, everyone is shit scared of them but this kid decided, if he could provide evidence to get them prosecuted, without the gang knowing it had come from him, it would make the streets a safer place.'

'Brave kid,' Paton said.

'They're analysing the video now, to see which of them could have caused the injury that led to Gus's death.'

'Roachford can tell us more about "The Dogs". Tony is aware and is focusing on that now.' Paton looked at his watch. 'They'll be winding up soon, but I expect MIT will take over the questioning in the morning, now that they know Roach was part of the assault.'

'Just a couple more things,' Douglas added. 'Mr. Harcourt, Darren's Grandad, has a clean record, and I've found the address for Nigel Anderson, the breaker's yard owner, through Companies House.'

Paton felt a dart of excitement. As Douglas reeled it off, he consigned it to memory. He'd go there now and confront him. He didn't care that it was late at night. Nigel was part of the crime set-up. He'd know where their hiding places were. He probably knew where Tommy was.

Fifteen minutes later, Paton stood and hammered on the front door of Nigel's well-appointed bungalow. The house was in darkness but, at this hour, he and his family were probably in bed. He waited for a light to come on. *Please, anything to show there's life inside.* Nothing. He hammered again.

'Oi, shut that racket up!'

A bald head, atop a neck almost as wide, poked out of a window next door. Paton stepped back to get a better look at him.

'What do you think you're doing banging on people's doors at this time of night?'

The man gave Paton a belligerent stare.

Paton removed his warrant card from his pocket and waved it towards the man.

'Police,' he said.

'Working alone? How do I know that's a legitimate card? What's your name and rank?'

Paton could feel his temper fraying at the edges. Who was this man? Nigel's bodyguard?

'Do you know where Nigel Anderson is? I need to speak to him.'

'Who is it, Edgar? What's going on?' A thin voice drifted from the open window.

'Nothing, love, go back to sleep. I'll sort it.' He turned momentarily from the window but soon returned. 'Nigel's gone away,' he said in an urgent whisper. 'I saw him, his wife and two kids getting in a taxi with a ton of luggage. Probably gone to that house he owns in France.'

'Where in France? When did he leave?'

'Brittany somewhere and yesterday evening. Now leave us in peace. My wife's not well.'

Paton turned away, frustrated at being thwarted from interrogating Nigel, but also somewhat ashamed of disturbing the neighbours. He decided to head home.

Becki rushed to the hallway when she heard him enter.

'What's happening?' she asked.

Paton was tempted to snap that he wouldn't tell her anything, but his instilled good manners prevailed. How could he trust her with information when she was passing it to the gang? She'd said she wanted to help, but he only had her word for that, and he didn't know whether to believe her when she said she wasn't able to contact them. He should arrest her.

'Have you spoken to your brother?' he asked, ignoring her question.

'He doesn't have any of the gang's phone numbers or addresses,' Becki said. 'But he told me they go by the names of Eagle, Pilot and Razor. They're the top bosses. Next you have... hang on, I wrote it down.' She pulled a piece of paper from her pocket. 'Nigel who runs the yard, Spanner who organises the team, Wiggy and Ronnie who organise the goods and drive the thieves about, then the runners and thieves are Roughhouse, Spliff, Roach and Woody. There might be more but these are the only names my brother knew.' Becki looked at Paton expectantly, as though hoping she'd won his approval and trust.

Paton's stomach fizzed. He already knew of Roach and Woody, so this must be accurate information. Darren Woodrow's grandad must have been lying for him. Paton would get back to the station early to make sure the boy was arrested before dawn and, if necessary, he'd apply for another extension of Roachford's detention period. With so much to find out, and a young child in jeopardy, twenty-four hours weren't enough.

'Good work, Becki. Have the gang been in contact again?'

'They called to ask if you were off the case and I said yes. I told them I wasn't on duty until lunchtime tomorrow, so couldn't find out more without it looking suspicious.'

'Well done.'

'I'm sorry to ask, but is there anything to eat? I've only had a piece of toast this morning and, I hope you don't mind, I ate a couple of your biscuits.'

'Let's see what we've got.' Paton led the way through to the kitchen. 'There isn't much because I need to go shopping.'

A sudden memory of Tommy begging to go to the shops came to mind. The cat! It would be starving, too, and no doubt Tommy would be worrying about it. Paton opened the food cupboard and rummaged about.

'How about a tin of tomato soup?' He passed it to Becki

then moved tins around to find something a cat might eat. At the back, gathering dust, was an old tin of corned beef. Perfect.

He opened the door to the shed cautiously and flicked on the light. The kitten emerged, blinking in the bright light. It stopped at his feet, then looked up and let out a long, pitiful miaow. Paton lowered the saucer of chopped beef, and the cat scoffed it hungrily. As he watched it eat, he wondered what would have happened to the cat if Tommy hadn't taken it in. Would someone else have found it and taken it to a vet to check for a microchip, or would it have huddled, starving and cold, under a hedge? Tommy had been desperate for a cat, so even though he'd been wrong not to hand the kitten in, the improvised bed and litter tray showed that he'd tried to look after it well.

Paton's mind turned to Louie. Was he huddled under a hedge somewhere, shivering and crying, lost in the wide expanse of countryside, or had someone found him and taken him in like a stray kitten? If so, why hadn't they been in touch? Where had they taken him and what did they intend to do with him? Paton shuddered, then closed the door on both his thoughts and the shed before hurrying back indoors. It was far too cold to put the kitten out tonight. Was Tommy warm enough?

Chapter 63
7.30AM

Child missing - 46 hours 30 minutes

Tommy missing - 17 hours

Tommy

There were voices downstairs. Tommy stirred and, for a moment, he thought they had burglars. Good job his dad was a policeman. He listened hard, trying to work it out.

'Where is he?' That voice was familiar. 'Tommy?' it yelled.

Something was scratching his cheek. He lifted his hand to rub it and opened his eyes. Oh no. He wasn't in his bed. He wasn't even in his house. He was lying on prickly straw in the barn and it was still quite dark. He sat up and listened, his heart galloping like a horse.

'I can't see him anywhere down here, Spanner. Maybe he went up the ladder.'

It was Wiggy's voice.

'I'm surprised he went up there. I'll fetch him down. He can help shift the goods.'

Tommy didn't want to 'shift the goods'. He climbed off the square of hay as quietly as he could then crept behind the pile of bales.

He heard Spanner climb the ladder, moaning as he went.

'Where are you, you little bugger?' A torch flashed light around. 'Hey Wiggy, he's built himself a little den up here. Very cosy. He's even got a sodding picnic laid out on a plastic sheet. Show yourself, Tommy.' Spanner sounded cross.

Tommy stayed where he was and tried not to breathe too loudly.

He heard a plastic cup being kicked and it bounced past him. Then the rustle of the cake packet as Spanner pushed it with his toe. Tommy peeked out as Spanner lifted his foot and stamped hard on the biscuits. There was a loud crack, a splitting noise and, suddenly, Spanner and the picnic vanished through the floor, dragging the plastic sheet with them. Wow! It was like a magic trick. There one second, gone the next. Tommy heard a loud thump and a whoosh.

'Aaargh. Fuck! My leg. I've busted my leg. Help me!'

Tommy inched towards the edge of the broken floor and peered over. There were lights downstairs. Spanner must have landed on the car then fallen off, because there was a big dent in the roof and he was on the floor. His leg stuck out all wonky. Wiggy appeared and shone his torch up through the hole at Tommy.

'Bloody hell! Get yourself down here, boy, and help me get him in the van. We'll have to take him to hospital.'

'Call a fucking ambulance, you moron.' Spanner groaned in pain.

'Do you want them to find this place? We've got all this

gear spread about, and the motor is in here.' Wiggy waved towards the blue car.

Spanner didn't answer. It looked like he'd gone to sleep. Tommy went carefully around the edge of the barn until he reached the ladder then swung his leg over and climbed down, taking his time and holding on tight. He didn't want to fall and have to go to hospital. He reached the bottom and saw boxes and parcels everywhere. The doors were open to the grey morning, and Tommy wondered if he should run away. At least only Wiggy could chase him. The van was parked outside and the back doors were wide open ready for the boxes.

'Tommy, get over here.'

Wiggy was watching him and he could probably run faster than Tommy.

He stared at Wiggy who was trying to drag Spanner across the floor. Spanner's leg didn't look wonky now but he still had his eyes shut. Wiggy dumped Spanner down again, then swung his head about, looking for something. He hurried to a corner and dragged out a bit of old wood. Well, more like lots of bits of wood nailed together. He tried to move Spanner again.

'Help me... roll him... onto this,' he said. He was puffing hard. Spanner was bigger than their fridge-freezer at home and probably twice as heavy.

Tommy grabbed Spanner's jacket and pulled when Wiggy told him to. They rolled him over. Spanner let out a long moan then opened his eyes and looked straight at Tommy.

'You did that on purpose,' he gasped. 'You little bastard.'

Tommy stared back and said nothing. He'd only wanted to cover up the messy floor and make his den look nice. It wasn't his fault Spanner was so big and heavy and Tommy couldn't help grinning when he pictured Spanner stamping on the biscuits.

Spanner turned to Wiggy.

'He's not as—'

Wiggy was lifting Spanner's leg onto the wood.

'Waaagh!'

The roar was scary and Tommy backed away. He sounded like the football crowd when Dad had taken him to see St. Johnstone FC and they'd scored a goal. It had been too loud and Tommy had wanted to go home. He wanted to go home now, too.

Between them they pushed and dragged the wood across the barn and outside to the van. Wiggy took the head end and asked Tommy to take the feet but Spanner was just too heavy. In the end, Wiggy found some rope and poked it through a gap in the wood frame and tied Spanner on tight. He and Tommy both lifted the head end and rested the wood on the edge of the van, then both got the feet end and slid it onto the dirty van floor. Spanner moaned and swore and sometimes went to sleep.

They shut the van doors then Wiggy said, 'Get in the front.' He didn't wait to see what Tommy was doing. He got in the van and started the engine.

This was it. This was Tommy's chance to run away. He darted back and around the barn and hid behind a huge water butt.

'Tommy! Get back here.'

Tommy waited.

'Sod you, then.'

Wiggy must have decided he was too tired to drag Tommy about as well because the van drove away down the lane. Everywhere was quiet. Tommy crept out and looked about. He could smell the stinky fumes from the van but there was no sign of it.

He straightened his jacket and scarf, pulled on his gloves and set off down the lane. If the van came back, he'd squeeze through the hedge or hide in the ditch. When he reached the road, he tried to work out where to go. Which way had the van turned in yesterday? He couldn't remember. He turned right and started walking. He'd take it slowly and have a rest if he needed one.

Yay! At last, he heard a car. He watched it get nearer and nearer. It was a red one with a man in the front. Tommy put out his thumb, like he'd seen people do in old films, but the car went round him and drove past. Bother!

He walked on, glad it wasn't raining, until another car came along. This one was silver. He put out his thumb again and the car slowed down. The driver was a lady and, as she passed, she stared at his face. She looked surprised. She drove a bit further then stopped. He turned and hurried towards her. She leaned over and opened the passenger door. Tommy bent down. 'What are you doing out here this early on your own?'

'Can you take me to the police station? I need to see my dad. He's a detective.'

'Get in,' she said, moving her bag off the seat. Her face was round and smiley. She looked kind. 'Do you mean the station in Perth?'

'Yes.'

'In that case you were walking in the wrong direction.'

Chapter 64
8.00AM

Child missing - 47 hours

Tommy missing - 17 hours 30 minutes

DI Paton

It had been a long night and Paton hadn't slept at all, so when he returned to work and came face-to-face with the team again, he half-expected them to comment on his haggard appearance. He'd tried to rest at home, as he knew a lack of sleep would impair his thinking, but anxiety over Tommy and Louie had meant his brain wouldn't switch off. He'd offered to get Becki a taxi home when he returned from Nigel's, rather than drive to her place. He needed to stay at home in case Tommy came back.

'Can I stay here?' she'd asked. 'I'm too scared to be on my own. What if they come after me? If you don't catch them soon, I might have to move in with Mum for a bit.'

He didn't have the headspace to worry about her well-being and future right now. He'd given her a duvet and left her to sleep on the sofa, then lay on his bed, tossing and turning pointlessly for a couple of hours. Where was Tommy sleeping? How was Louie's body reacting to his lack of medication?

Paton had given up trying to sleep. He'd stumbled to the bathroom before dawn, shocked at his worn-down appearance in the mirror. His skin was the colour of old porridge and his eyes were so red they resembled something out of a horror film. He'd shaved, but his hands trembled so much he nicked his chin with the razor and a bead of blood appeared. He knew he was no Adonis, but he'd aged ten years overnight and he'd taken on the look of someone haunted by fear. How was he going to hide his distress from the team? He'd showered quickly, left Becki a note asking her to stay there for the day in case Tommy came home, and to call him immediately if she had news, then returned to work, dreading what the day might bring.

By 8.30am, several of the team had left for the search on the breaker's yard, another officer was heading to Nigel's home address to double-check whether he was there, and a team of officers was going door-to-door in the vicinity of the lane where the teenagers had supposedly dumped Louie. Having organised everyone else, Paton was preparing to leave with Colin to arrest Darren Woodrow. Lynn, the office manager, poked her head around the door.

'Sorry to disturb you, boss, but your son is here and asking for you.'

'Tommy's here?'

Paton's heart lurched with hope. Had he misheard her?

'Shall I say you're busy? I could tell him—'

He was here! Paton rushed past Lynn and into the corridor. He ran through to the reception area and had to choke back tears when he saw his beloved son. It really was him. His heart swelled with pure joy and he pulled him into a tight embrace. Tommy grunted in surprise.

'My lovely boy, Oh God, I'm so happy to see you.'

Paton pulled back to look into Tommy's face then hugged him again.

Tommy laughed. 'Dad, you're squashing me.'

'What happened? Where have you been?' Paton could see the woman on reception watching them, but he was too happy to care. Tommy was back and nothing else mattered.

'The baddies took me in their van.'

'Did they hurt you?'

'No. They got me pizza but I was very cold and the straw was prickly. I've got clues for you, Dad.' Tommy pulled a piece of paper from his pocket and presented it, a huge beam on his face. He pointed to a drawing of a big man with wonky teeth and a hairy mole. 'This is Spanner,' he said. 'I didn't like him. He stamped on my biscuits.'

Next, he pointed to a man with no hair, tiny ears and a bump on his nose.

'This is Wiggy. He's not so bad because he got me the pizza and a blanket and this is... this is...' Tommy's face fell. 'Doh! I can't remember.'

'I can see this last one has a... what's that? A shark's tooth necklace?'

'Yeah. And a black thumbnail.'

'Clever lad, you've done well. Do you know where these men are? How did you get away?'

'Spanner went through the floor. It's got a big hole in it now. He's gone to hospital to have his leg mended.'

'What floor?'

'In the barn.'

'Which hospital have they gone to? Do you know where the barn was? How did you get here?'

The questions crowded together in his head and jostled their way out of his mouth. Paton tried to hold back so that he wouldn't overwhelm Tommy.

'This nice lady brought me here.'

For the first time Paton noticed a woman seated a few yards away, watching him and Tommy. She stood and came over.

'Hi, I'm Tina Brooks. I was on my way to work and saw your son thumbing a lift so picked him up. He looked – how can I describe it? – vulnerable.'

She gave a weak smile as though apologising for the possible reference to Tommy's Down's syndrome.

Paton clasped her hands in his. 'Thank you, Tina, thank you.'

'Did I get you good clues, Dad?'

'You certainly did, son. Let's find somewhere quiet and you can both give me all the details.' Paton walked over to Lynn who was hovering nearby and listening to every word. 'Can you ask Andy to accompany Colin to the arrest, please? Andy knows where to go. I need to stay here. In the meantime, ask Douglas to check the nearest hospitals for any admissions of a man with a leg injury.' If Spanner did have a broken leg, they should be able to find him soon. He'd either be at the Perth Royal Infirmary or one of the hospitals in Dundee.

Lynn's mouth was agape. 'Was Tommy missing?'

'I can't talk about it now. Just do as I ask, please.' Lynn took a step back, her face a picture of shock at his unusual abruptness. Paton didn't want to acknowledge his son's kidnap right now. Plenty of time for that later. Would Lynn keep this to herself? At this moment he wasn't sure he cared. He was just so glad to see Tommy that everything else paled into insignificance.

He turned to Tommy and the kind woman who had brought him back, then led them to a side room where he could ask them questions in private. He realised too late that they'd need Tommy's clothing for forensic examination. Paton hoped he hadn't contaminated any evidence by hugging Tommy, but not even wild horses would have been able to drag him away from embracing his son.

Chapter 65
8.30AM

Child missing - 47 hours 30 minutes

Woody

Opening the window made all the difference and was worth the horribly cold air nipping at his skin. Now, Woody was able to see beyond the yard to the fields where Grandad was bent over, with Cassie at his side, fixing wire to fence posts. Good.

Woody pulled on his joggers, T-shirt and thick hoody, then hurried to the kitchen. He hadn't liked lying, and had felt terrible when Grandad had hobbled downstairs on his aching knee to fetch Woody a glass of water and some tiny squares of toast and Marmite.

'Try and eat something,' Grandad had said. 'It might settle your stomach. You probably feel sick because you're anxious. The police may not bother coming back, now that I've given you an alibi.'

'Have you spoken to Mum?'

At the thought of dragging Mum into this mess, Woody had started to feel sick for real. He knew he was a chicken for leaving the task of ringing her to Grandad, but he couldn't bring himself to do it.

'She wasn't happy, and I had to go through it a couple of times, but she said she could understand the need to protect your future. She's coming over after work. She wants to talk to you.'

Woody had lain back down in bed and curled up under his duvet. If only he could stay there until everything blew over. Instead, he had to get to Mabel's and sort out Louie. At least he could put something right. He'd realised it wouldn't be safe to leave the little boy completely on his own, so he was going to suggest to Mabel that he hide in bushes nearby, to keep an eye on him until a school mum found him. If the wrong sort of person took him, then Woody would run out of the bushes and say he's been having a wee and Louie was his brother. It was all a huge risk, but he couldn't think of a better plan.

The kitchen was empty without Cassie there. Woody loved it when she greeted him with an old sock or a teddy in her mouth, her bum wiggling in ecstasy at seeing him. He tugged on wellies and a waterproof jacket and wrapped a thick scarf around his neck. It was going to be freezing waiting, and for a moment, Woody wondered if his plan was crap. Would any mums bother taking their kids to the park in this cold weather?

Circling the farm so that Grandad wouldn't spot him, Woody trotted on to Mabel's place. He reached the kitchen and peered through the window. The room was empty. Panic twisted in his gut and he hurried around the cottage to the driveway. The car was gone. Fuck. He hammered on the front door, knowing it was useless, then made his way back to the kitchen. The back door was unlocked so he rushed in.

A note was propped up on the table with *Darren* written on the front. He snatched it up and tore it open.

Dear Darren,

I know we agreed to take the wee bairn to the park this morning to be 'found' but everything has changed. I can't bear to leave Louie alone in the big wide world. Louie deserves more than being abandoned again. He needs me to take care of him. He's not safe to be left so I've come up with a new plan.

Woody read through to the end and sat down hard on a kitchen chair. Bloody hell. The stupid woman! Where did this leave him now? He could keep his head down and hope Mabel kept him out of it when the police finally caught up with her, but what if the police didn't find her? He couldn't live with the guilt of knowing he was keeping the small boy from his parents. He looked around the room for any trace of Louie, but couldn't see anything. He went upstairs but the bed was neatly made, the books had gone and there was no sign that a child had ever been there. It was almost as though Woody had dreamt it. He walked slowly back downstairs. It was no good. He couldn't live with this any longer. He'd have to tell Grandad and face the consequences. If he told the police everything, and explained it wasn't him who put Louie on the verge, he might get away with fines and community payback. Surely the prisons were full to bursting?

Despite not wanting to hurry, it seemed he was back at the farm way too soon. He was desperate to slip upstairs and under the duvet again but that was a coward's way of dealing with things. He had to grow some balls – face up to this now and deal with it. Spare his family getting on the wrong side of the law. He'd make Grandad a cup of tea and take it out to him then tell him about the boy.

As the kettle began to rumble on the Aga, he heard Cassie bark and his heart turned over. Was that a car? He went into the hall and looked out of the dining room window. Oh no. Oh no. The police were back already. He had to stop Grandad lying for him.

He opened the front door before they even knocked. Grandad was coming from the side of the farmhouse.

'I did it,' he said immediately to the policemen.

They stared at him in astonishment and Woody guessed they didn't get many criminals admitting guilt so readily.

'I stole the car with Roach and he dumped the boy by the road. I tried to stop him and I went back to look for the kid but he wasn't there.'

Woody knew he probably wasn't making sense but he wanted to get his confession over with before he changed his mind.

'Are you Darren Woodrow?' one of the policemen asked.

'Yes.'

Grandad puffed along the path, a worried frown on his face.

'I've told them, Grandad. I've told them I took the car. I didn't know there was a boy in the back, I promise. I went to look for him afterwards.' Woody felt his resolve crumble and he grabbed the door frame for support. 'I'm so sorry, Grandad.' His breath stuck in his chest, his face twisted then, to his shame, he was crying like a toddler.

'Shall we go in out of the cold?' the taller policeman asked, turning to Grandad who was just standing there, a look of horror on his face. 'I'm DC Colin Dalton and this is DC Andy Carpenter.'

Grandad took Woody's arm and led him none-too-gently back indoors. They went through to the lounge, the two policemen filling the hallway behind them.

'Darren Woodrow, we're arresting you on suspicion of stealing a car and abducting a child.'

As the policeman talked on, Woody forgot to listen. All he could focus on was Grandad's face. The poor man looked suddenly very old and Woody felt fresh tears on his cheeks. 'I'm so sorry, Grandad,' he said again. The policeman was putting handcuffs on him now, but Woody felt strange, like he'd floated up to the ceiling and was looking down on everyone. It wasn't really him down there. This wasn't real. He was watching actors on Netflix or maybe he was having a bad dream.

It wasn't until the cold air hit his face, like a bucketful of water, that he came to his senses and his stomach churned ominously.

'I need the toilet,' he said.

The two policemen looked at each other and one shrugged.

'Please,' he pleaded. 'I promise I won't run away.'

With a policeman waiting outside the bathroom door after checking Woody couldn't escape out of the window, Woody sat on the loo, thinking it could be a long time before he had privacy again. He was such a fucking idiot. He deserved this. He washed his hands, then held out his wrists for the handcuffs to be put back on and walked quietly to the car. As it bumped and lurched down the uneven track Woody spoke up.

'I found Louie,' he said, 'but he's not there now.'

The car stopped abruptly, and both policemen swivelled to look at him.

'Where?' DC Carpenter asked.

'At Mabel Grimstone's cottage. It's near Grandad's farm.'

Chapter 66
9.00AM

Child missing - 49 hours

Paton

The incident room buzzed with the sounds of animated chatter, scraping chairs and tapping keyboards. Paton stood for a moment, watching and absorbing the energy in the room. While he waited for the last few officers to find a spot to sit or stand, he mulled over his conversation with the DCI.

Had he done the right thing in not reporting that Tommy had been abducted? Paton knew he could still be suspended for not following procedure and admitting to a personal involvement in the case. But Louie's family deserved the best the force had to offer and losing Paton as SIO at this stage could be disastrous. So, he'd kept quiet, understanding the consequences could be far worse later but prepared to take the risk for Louie's sake.

The DCI and Paton had decided between them that now it

would be necessary to initiate a Child Rescue Alert. From Woodrow's confession in the police car, it seemed likely the child was somewhere in the community with Mabel Grimstone, so might be spotted by members of the public. They could tell the press it was a possible abduction without having to explain that his own mother had left him alone in the car with the keys in the ignition. This way, she might avoid being slandered and hated by the public. To cope with the potential onslaught of calls, the DCI had taken time out of his training course to draft in resources from other areas. Paton was now able to set up a team to answer the phones and follow the leads.

Because of all this, the incident room was crowded with the new officers awaiting instructions. Some sat on the edges of desks, others perched on windowsills trying not to entangle themselves in the blinds. For the past hour, information had been flying in from all directions, and Paton was struggling to process everything. His brain was sluggish and his eyes felt raw from lack of sleep, but an energy drink, adrenaline, and excitement at getting so close to finding Louie, as well as breaking up the crime ring, was keeping him going.

At least Tommy no longer dominated his thoughts, and gratitude was making Paton even more determined to find Louie. He'd taken Tommy to Ursula's after briefly questioning both him and Tina Brooks, the woman who'd brought him to the station. Tommy's clothes had been taken for examination and, much to his delight, he'd been given joggers and a sweatshirt to wear from the spare clothing cupboard. Tommy had confessed about the cat and been desperate to see her, but Paton had assured him she was fine and he could spend time with her later.

Ursula had kindly agreed to book the morning off work to keep Tommy safe. She'd made him a bacon sandwich and a cup of tea, and Tommy was now tucked up in the spare bed, catching up on his sleep. Paton half-wished he could do the same but knew it would be some time before he could enjoy that luxury. Instead, it was his time to shine, to prove he could manage high-profile cases and pull everything together.

During the interview, Tina had explained to Paton where she'd found Tommy, and Paton, not wanting to admit to the abduction yet, had told Douglas that he'd heard a rumour about a barn in the area that was being used by the gang. Douglas had raised a quizzical eyebrow but hadn't questioned Paton, then managed to locate three barns in the vicinity. Officers had been dispatched to check them out and had quickly found a barn with a hole in the first-floor platform, along with a tonne of other evidence.

Paton walked to the front of the room where a huge Operation Oakwood banner sat atop numerous maps, photos and lists of suspects. He cleared his throat and a hush ensued as everyone gave him their full attention. He thanked them all for their time and commitment then launched into his prepared briefing.

'Our priority now is Operation Oakwood to find Louie Cameron. We're initiating a CRA today and I'm meeting the press at 1pm. We've a team here ready to take the calls and a number of officers to follow the leads.'

He waved a hand at a group of unfamiliar officers. They nodded and lifted hands in greeting to the rest of the room.

'We've located a barn used by a car theft gang. Inside, we found Louie's mother's car and a number of car parts ready for shipment, most likely from other stolen cars. We've been told by Jayson Roachford, the youth who stole Mrs. Cameron's car along with Darren Woodrow, that they didn't realise the boy was in the back, so left him by the roadside in the hope someone else would find him.'

'The poor wee bairn,' one officer said.

'He could have wandered into the road,' another pointed out.

'Shocking,' a third muttered. 'On such a cold day, too. I hope the judge bangs them up for years.'

Paton was inclined to agree but kept his opinions to himself.

'As you'd expect, we checked hospitals and doctors' surgeries, as a routine measure, when he first went missing and no injured or sick children fitting his description were seen. We've yet to find out who was responsible for abandoning the boy, as each suspect is blaming the other. The good news is there's been a recent sighting. Darren Woodrow tells us he saw the boy at a cottage belonging to a woman called Mabel Grimstone. It's located next to his grandfather's farm and is only two or three miles from where the boy was left.'

'That's a bit of a coincidence, isn't it?' A young officer asked. 'Near his grandad's farm?'

'Apparently, Darren was directing Roach along country lanes he knew from childhood, to avoid cameras.'

'How do we know he isn't lying? It wouldn't be the first time youths have murdered a small boy. Maybe they've buried him somewhere.'

A chill descended on the room and everyone looked at the large photo of Louie pinned to the wall, of his sunlit blond hair, clear blue eyes and mouth wide with laughter. A boy full of animation and the joy of life.

'He's provided some evidence and I'm inclined to believe him at this stage. Darren's told us that he met with Mabel Grimstone and the boy yesterday. He went back to the cottage early this morning but she's taken the child off somewhere. He's given us a letter that she wrote to him. I've authorised us to apply for a warrant so I need two officers to search her property immediately, along with the SOCO.'

Paton chose two DCs from the new team.

'We're looking for any sign that the child might have been there. CSI will meet you there to see if they can find any DNA, and we can check the fingerprints on the letter against prints around the house. Also, see if you can obtain any photographs of Ms. Grimstone. We can ask Darren's grandad to verify it's her. We can use them in the media to help locate her.'

A keen DC in a crisp outfit of white blouse and navy trousers, hair neatly braided and eyes alive with intelligence, raised her hand as though in a classroom.

'Why was Darren Woodrow going to the cottage, boss, and why did Mabel Grimstone write him a letter?'

'Sorry, I should have explained.' Paton wished he'd had a strong coffee before the briefing. 'Darren said he was going with Ms Grimstone to take the child to a play park and leave him there, in the hope he would be found by a school mum and returned to his family.'

'That would have been risky,' the young DC said.

'They didn't want to incriminate themselves and Darren later decided, after they agreed the plan, to watch from a distance to ensure the boy was safe. In the letter it appears Mabel changed her mind for some reason, and now we don't know where she's taken Louie.'

Paton tried to collect his thoughts but struggled to remember what came next. He looked down at his handwritten list.

'I need an officer to check the details of the vehicle Mabel Grimstone owns, then look at ANPR in the area surrounding her cottage and up to 100 miles beyond, I hope we can pick up a thread from there. Cameras are scarce on the B-roads, but hopefully she'll have got onto a main road. We need to put alerts out to patrol cars within a 200-mile radius as they could have gone some distance by now. Louie was wearing a blue coat and yellow wellingtons when he was abducted. We have no reason, at this stage, to believe he will be wearing anything else but, we can't rule it out.'

Everyone stared at the photo again, as though picturing the little boy in his bright outfit.

'I also need you, please, and you,' Paton selected two officers, 'to find out everything you can about this woman, Mabel Grimstone. Her age, who lives at the address with her, what she does for a living, her background, friends, family and so on. Does she have children of her own? Has she ever done anything like this before? Does she have a criminal record? The more we know about her, the more we'll be able to understand her motives and maybe get an idea of what she's likely to do next.'

As Paton spoke, a waft of sickly perfume, mingled with the smell of sweet pastries, drifted across the room and he felt suddenly queasy. Exhaustion always affected him like this. He was so desperately tired he could easily lie on the floor and fall asleep immediately. He needed a minute to compose himself.

'Douglas, can you please share what you've found?'

Paton picked up his paper cup and took a mouthful of water. He definitely should have opted for strong coffee. Perhaps he could sit in his car for a short break after this briefing and lean his head back. If he could lose consciousness for even five minutes, it would be enough to revive and sustain him for the rest of the day.

Douglas began speaking and Paton fought hard to concentrate.

'We've been told that one of the car gang fell through the floor of the barn. We contacted the hospitals and a man with a broken leg was admitted to Perth Royal Infirmary at 9am. He was taken there by a friend who immediately left.'

'If that's the quality of his friends, I'd hate to meet his enemies,' quipped Andy.

People around him murmured in agreement.

'He's had x-rays and is waiting for the nurse to plaster him up,' Douglas continued.

'I wouldn't mind getting plastered with a nurse.' Andy was on a roll now.

'Can we stick to the facts, please,' Paton said. 'We don't have time for jokes right now.'

Paton usually welcomed a dash of humour as much as the next officer, but today he couldn't tolerate it.

'Sorry, boss.' Andy sounded surprised at Paton's tone but sheepishly looked around the room. 'Sorry, everyone.'

Douglas shrugged and took up his report again.

'Before the injured man leaves hospital, the doctor has to assess he's fit for discharge. It could be several hours before he's seen as they're so busy.'

Paton spoke next. 'DCs Colin Dalton and Mark Edwards are currently at the hospital to arrest him and question him about the other gang members. We also have some information about the so-called friend's appearance, so I need another officer to go to the hospital to check the CCTV for the car park, as well as the interior of A&E. If you get a numberplate you'll need to check ANPR in the area to see where the van went. We need to be mindful that this is part of a car-theft ring, so the driver will probably go somewhere to change the plates at his earliest opportunity.'

The nausea was wearing off and Paton was feeling stronger again. It was a good job he wasn't going to the hospital to arrest Spanner. He might not be able to rein in his anger at Spanner kidnapping his son. The thought of his hands around the man's throat and shaking him was too appealing. It would be gratifying to see Nigel caught and punished as well.

'I should have the results of the search on the breaker's yard soon. We strongly suspect it was being used as a chop shop for the gang to break the stolen cars into saleable parts. I believe the larger parts, such as the engines, are being exported. Catalytic converters were also found in the barn, which goes some way to explaining the spate of thefts of those lately.

'We're also searching Woodrow's mother's house and his grandad's farm. We're particularly looking for the Run Swift trainers to place him at the scene of the crime. 'Douglas, any update regarding Roachford's phone?'

Douglas nodded.

'We're awaiting information from the network provider but, so far, it's clear he's been contacting Woodrow.'

'Woodrow is now under formal arrest and is at the custody centre. He'll be questioned very soon by DS Tony King and DC Mitchell Tomkins. We're hoping it will lead to further arrests, as this is clearly a large, organised group of criminals. We've got nick-names for those higher up the hierarchy, so we'll see if Woodrow and Roachford give us the same names. The MIT is trying to track down two thugs known as "The Dogs" in connection with Gus Chamber's murder. I think that's enough information to be going on with. Sorry if it's a bit jumbled. Does anyone have any urgent questions before we all get on with our actions?'

'Are you putting the parents in front of the press?' one DC asked.

'Not at this stage. I think they'd make mincemeat of his mother given that she inadvertently left the child in the car with the keys in the ignition. She's already suffering enough.'

The room fell silent as everyone contemplated this catastrophic lapse in parenting. A lapse made by parents in every town, every day, but, fortunately, not with the same outcome.

'Report back to Lynn with any findings and she'll update the system. See you all later.'

The room immediately became a hive of activity as people picked up phones, grabbed coats off the backs of chairs and called out to each other.

'Good luck everyone,' Paton said, but everyone was too busy to hear him.

Chapter 67
10.00AM

Child missing - 49 hours

Woody

It had taken every bit of self-control for Woody not to cry again when he saw Mum waiting at the police station. He clenched his stomach muscles, set his jaw and held his breath to hold in the sobs that threatened to burst from his chest. He'd already upset her enough, so losing the plot would make it worse. Her face was tight and upset, and she looked at him with such worry and confusion that he'd wanted to rush over to hug her and apologise over and over for being such a dick. Instead, he tried to be strong and did everything the custody officer asked of him, quietly and politely, to show how sorry he was for everything and not embarrass her further.

He told them he didn't want a solicitor and said he was keen to give a full confession. His mum had nodded in agreement. Somehow, not having a 'legal representative', as they called it, made everything seem a bit less scary. It was just him and mum and two policemen – he'd forgotten their names already – who were surprisingly friendly. Woody couldn't wait to tell them everything, to get all the guilt off his chest, and, as soon as the interview started, he explained from the beginning how bored and lonely he'd been since moving to Perth, how he'd made friends at the park who'd later got him to help them move stuff around. The money had been great, especially as Mum couldn't afford anything but the basics, and when he'd been told he could earn £300 in a couple of hours he hadn't asked any questions. It had been exciting, good for his street cred, and the freedom he got from having money had been amazing. He hadn't thought about the misery he was causing other people until now. He told the kind policemen about the moment Roach had dumped the little boy out on the roadside.

'I couldn't believe it,' he told them. 'The poor little sod wasn't much older than Ryan, my cousin's kid. I wanted to go back for him but Roach wouldn't. I was going to phone the police as soon as I got back, but then I saw Gus mashed up and I freaked out. If I dobbed Roach in they'd know it was me and it would be me, or Mum attacked next.'

He looked at Mum and her eyes filled with tears.

'Erica next door told me we had people banging on the door twice looking for you,' she said. 'They insisted she tell them where you were and they were very intimidating. She said you'd gone south to stay with your dad.'

The policemen looked at each other.

'We'll ask your neighbour to give a statement,' one told her. 'However, we can't allow you, as the appropriate adult, to dispute or corroborate anything your son says at this stage.'

'That's fine,' she said. 'I'll keep quiet. Sorry.'

'You're entitled to speak if you feel we're treating your son unfairly and not respecting his rights. That's why you're here.'

'I understand,' she said, and gave Woody a small smile.

His heart lifted a little knowing that she was on his side. His biggest fear in all this was that she'd be angry and disappointed in him. He carried on talking with renewed confidence.

'I went back on my bike to look for the boy, but he'd gone. Then I saw him the next day near Grandad's farm.'

'Are you sure it was the same boy?' the young policeman asked.

Woody explained how he'd visited the cottage to look for him and recognised the teddy blanket, then gone back twice more. The two policemen just nodded and wrote notes. They didn't need to say anything to make him talk. He couldn't stop if he wanted to.

He told them about his argument with Mabel, how she shouldn't keep Louie from his family and what he and Mabel had agreed to do.

'We were going to get him back to his Mum and Dad but we were scared of being caught. It was getting too dark to leave him anywhere, so we agreed to go the next morning. I was gutted when she wasn't there.'

'Do you have any idea where she might have taken him?' the older policeman said.

'I'm not sure but I reckon it would be somewhere nice. She was looking after him really well. The night before, she said she wanted to give him a bath and read him stories for the last time. He loved *The Tiger Who Came to Tea* and *Mog and the baby*. He loved animals, especially her big cat and the rabbit. I don't think she'd hurt him. You could tell she thought he was wonderful and wanted to keep him. Did you know she lost her own baby?'

The older policeman sat up straighter and looked excited. 'Did she tell you that?' he asked.

'It was really sad. Her dad pushed her down the stairs and it was born too early. It was a girl. Mabel was only fifteen. He wouldn't tell her where she was buried so she had a rosebush in her garden called Victoria Rose, same as the name she'd chosen.'

The younger policeman was slowly shaking his head from side-to-side and he looked proper sad. The older one was scribbling in his notebook.

'Did you know Louie has epilepsy?'

'What's that?'

'Did he have any convulsions – fits, shakes or twitches, maybe – or did he act in an unusual way?'

'He looked a bit spaced out at times. Mabel said he was tired but I wasn't sure.'

'Do you know what she was feeding him?'

'I didn't see but the house smelt lovely – of cakes or shortbread or something. I thought anyone living there was lucky.' The words left Woody's mouth before he'd thought about how this would make his mum feel. She reached across and squeezed his hand. He looked at her. 'I know you work hard and do your best, Mum. I'm sorry I've been so lazy.'

The older policeman cleared his throat.

'Did you see anyone else at the property?'

'Grandad said Mabel lives alone. I didn't see anyone else.' He swallowed hard but the question that had been buzzing in his head couldn't be batted away any longer.

'Will I go to prison?'

Chapter 68
10.30AM

Child missing - 50 hours

DI Paton

As Paton watched the interview with Darren Woodrow, he couldn't help marvelling at the contrast with Roachford. Darren was polite, helpful and contrite whereas Roachford was belligerent, cocky and obstructive. The mothers contrasted sharply too. Darren's mother showed her son warmth and affection, despite his wrong-doing, but Roachford's mother made it clear she was uninterested and inconvenienced.

It was difficult not to decide that Roachford was the one lying about who abandoned Louie by the road, but Paton had seen too many devious criminals acting a role to be totally sure. The one certain factor was that they were both guilty of stealing the car, so, whatever Woodrow did now, he would still be charged with theft.

The first part of the interview brought no real surprises. A disaffected youth, a lack of parenting and money, and the lure of criminals, keen to exploit the innocent. However, Paton's interest sharpened, and he watched the screen avidly, once Woodrow talked about his encounter with Louie. The fact that Woodrow had seen the boy previously, and recognised his teddy blanket – an item detailed by Melanie – made his witness statement all the more plausible and less likely to be a mistaken identity. *But wait*, Paton reminded himself, *there were no hard facts or evidence.* Apart from the letter, and they had yet to prove that Mabel had actually written it. The DC's comment about Woodrow possibly lying because he'd harmed the boy niggled away in the back of his mind.

It was only when Woodrow began talking in more detail about his visits to the cottage that Paton became convinced he was telling the truth. Woodrow painted a vivid scene – the cosy kitchen that smelled of cakes, the chickens, cat and rabbit, the children's books by the bed...

Paton's head was beginning to clear, his tiredness forgotten. He was able to envisage, and begin to understand, this lonely woman, desperate for a child then stumbling across an abandoned toddler in a quiet country lane. Louie must have seemed like a gift from God. Paton was reminded uncomfortably of his wife, Wendy, and her primordial urge to have another baby, which affected her every day. He thought of her building her hopes up every month, only to have them smashed against the rocks of disappointment when she discovered, yet again, that she wasn't pregnant. Time had all but run out for her, and it had certainly run out for Mabel Grimstone.

Paton knew he was being a coward, avoiding calls from Wendy and sending brief texts instead. He just didn't have the energy to cope with her today. If she hadn't started her period, she'd be deluding herself that they were going to have another child, and her excitement would be climbing. If she'd started menstruating, she'd be inconsolable for several days at least. He wondered how Wendy would cope this time, without him on hand to support her. She wouldn't be able to take to her bed if she was caring for her mum. Had he perpetuated her bouts of depression with his love and care? The thought that he might have enabled that situation was too difficult to consider.

Paton listened as Woodrow talked about Mabel losing her child, and not knowing where the baby was buried. It was tragic, but while finding Louie and caring for him in the short term would have been commendable, to keep a lost child from his parents was abhorrent. Paton wondered what a jury would make of it all.

He pulled up a scanned copy of Mabel's letter on his computer screen and read the second half again, trying to get inside the head of a woman tainted by a life of disappointment.

He needs me to take care of him. He's not safe to be left...

Did Mabel mean Louie was at risk from members of the public, or was it perhaps the cold weather? Or did she now know about his epilepsy?

...so I've come up with a new plan which I know Louie will love.

What would Louie love? Had she got to know him that well in the short time she'd had him in her care?

I've come to accept that there's no future for me...

Paton caught his breath. Was she contemplating suicide? Surely she wouldn't put the child through that. From what she'd written, it was clear she was very fond of the little boy.

Was she of stable mind though? What if she had a terminal illness?

...so I'll let events take their course and delight in every moment with him until we're found.

She expected to be found then. Was she going somewhere public? Paton looked at his watch. He needed to prepare for the press interview. The press officer had asked him to jot down the key points, so that she could write a statement for him to read out. It could wait another ten minutes. He wanted to analyse this letter further. He kept thinking something was staring him in the face and he was blind to it.

I hope you learn from your wrongdoing, Darren, and turn your life around. I don't condone what you've done but I have to thank you for bringing such joy into my life at a time when I'd given up hope of ever finding it.

I don't regret keeping him and what I'm planning to do next.

What? What was she planning to do next? Paton's whole body tensed with pent-up frustration. He read on.

Life has been unfair and cruel to me so I believe I deserve this last vestige of happiness.

By keeping someone else's child? What about Louie's mother? Did she deserve to lose her child?

Take care, Darren dear boy, and please behave yourself from now on,

Yours Sincerely,

Mabel Grimstone

Paton read the letter over and over, trying to fathom out what she meant. Where would she go? What was he missing? He watched a section of the interview again. Mabel had a cat, a rabbit and chickens. It didn't always fit, but Paton often found that people who cared well for animals and pets were often kinder-natured and more compassionate to others. He liked animals but he'd never have time for them in his busy life.

Dear God, the kitten! He had a sudden vision of it howling in the shed for food with no one to hear it. Paton knew Tommy would be asking about her when he woke up. Perhaps Paton should let Tommy enjoy one last day with her before he took it to the local rescue centre, given the trauma he'd been through. Paton read the letter again, his heart thumping. *A day of happiness... until we're found.* The clues were all there. Louie was to Mabel as the kitten was to Tommy.

Paton rushed through to the incident room.

'Has anyone here got small children?' he asked. A few faces turned to give him questioning looks. One young DC, Will Grantham, raised his hand.

'I've got a three-year-old and a five-year-old', Will said.

'Where would you go around here for a nice day out, given it's November and very cold.'

He frowned. 'It depends on what the kids want. My youngest wouldn't manage to sit through a film at the cinema, but they both like the soft-play centre. We sometimes go swimming or to a farm. My eldest is mad on pigs.'

'How long a journey can they cope with?'

'Hmm. They get bored quickly so no more than an hour, tops.'

'Thank you.' Paton almost wanted to shake his hand. 'Douglas!' he called across the office. 'Can you find me all of the children's activity places within a fifty-mile radius, especially farms and zoos with indoor areas? I want someone to call each one and see if an older woman has visited with a child wearing a blue coat and yellow wellies.'

Chapter 69
11AM

Child missing - 50 hours

Louie

If he had his car seat, Louie would be able to see out of the window better. The silly cushions kept moving. He dug his fingers into the car door and pulled himself up.

'Look!' He pointed at a big, big animal and slipped again, the seat belt tight on his neck. *Doh.*

Grandma turned around to watch him. 'Would you like to sit on my lap?' she said.

He nodded and she leaned through the gap and clicked his seat belt off. 'Can you climb over?'

He didn't need asking twice. He put one foot through, then pulled on the headrest and soon he was on her lap. He could see much better now.

'That's an elephant,' Grandma said.

'Does it eat ants?' he asked.

'I'm not sure what it eats,' she said. 'Plants, I think, and peanuts.'

'I want the aminal that eats ants.'

'Animal,' corrected Mabel. 'I'm not sure if they have those here. We've got the monkeys next. I think you'll like those. They can be very naughty.'

'Like Noah?'

Grandma laughed. 'Maybe,' she said. 'Let's see.'

She moved the stick and turned the wheel and the car went along the little road. This was fun. He put his hands on the wheel and laughed as it turned. He was driving the car. Wait until he told Noah.

'I see Noah soon? And Mummy and Daddy?' He wanted Grandma to say yes but he wanted to see the monkeys first. And the tigers. They were the bestest animal.

'You'll be back with everyone later today. We want to see all the animals first, don't we?'

'Yeeeesss!!!' Louie shouted so loud and laughed when Grandma jumped.

'You'll frighten the animals,' she said.

A big elephant stared at their car, then walked off, its funny long nose swinging side to side.

They went through a big gate with a big fence, then another gate, and soon there were monkeys everywhere. One jumped on the car and Louie gasped. It stared right through the window at him and Louie giggled.

'Will it be naughty now?' he asked.

The monkey had tiny hands. It pulled on the swishy window thing until it came away from the window, then the monkey bit the end. It had tiny, sharp teeth. It tore a long bit off the swisher then threw it on the ground.

'Nooo,' Mabel shouted. 'Don't ruin my wipers.'

She pulled a stick and the swisher went up and down. The monkey jumped off the car.

'Again,' Louie laughed.

'I'll have to get a new wiper now,' Grandma said. 'I just hope it doesn't rain on the way home. Unless the police manage to find us first. If they do, you'll be going home in a police car.'

'Police car? It go nee naw, nee naw?'

Grandma laughed.

'It might. But that's later. Look, there's the sign for the tigers.'

Chapter 70
11.30AM

Child missing - 50 hours 30 minutes

DI Paton

Appearing on television to discuss a serious case was something Paton had always aspired to, but, now that it was imminent, his nerves were getting the better of him. He'd drafted key points for the press officer, who'd written him a statement to recite. He now had to read it through and check it was accurate.

'Try not to stray from the script,' she told him. 'Those journalists will tie you in knots in no time and are highly skilled at extracting information. One slip and they'll be at you like piranhas on a bare ankle.'

Being in the public eye was daunting enough, but this, and the worry he might utter something that wasn't politically correct, was terrifying. He'd seen too many figures in the public eye ,lately, being decimated on social media for a slip of the tongue. He took deep breaths to calm himself, then read the statement aloud to get a feel for it.

'Very good, boss.'

Ian was standing in the doorway, a wide grin on his face.

Paton could sense the warmth building in his cheeks. He looked away and shuffled his papers. 'Find anything at Darren's or his Grandad's house?'

'We found the Run Swift trainers, boss. We'd almost given up, then Kev checked the shed and they were there in a box underneath other boots and shoes.'

'Excellent. If they match the footwear mark, we'll have evidence to place him at the scene, too.'

'Not only that, his fingerprints are on the Fanta bottle that Colin retrieved from the bus stop.'

Paton was impressed. 'I'll have to thank Colin for his quick thinking on collecting that too.'

Ian nodded over his shoulder. 'The team has just got back from the breaker's yard search and Nigel's house.'

Paton thanked him, then stood and went to find them.

'The house was empty, boss,' the DS who'd visited Nigel's home said.

Damn. Paton's face must have shown his disappointment because the officer quickly continued.

'But the neighbour came out and was very helpful. Said he thought we'd be back and had located the address of Nigel's holiday home in Brittany.'

'Wow. No love lost between those neighbours, then.' Paton couldn't help grinning at the thought of Nigel being caught.

He might have tried to warn Paton off but in the end, he'd given the gang Paton's address and put Tommy at risk. That was unforgivable.

'Apparently, the neighbour didn't like the company Nigel

was keeping. He said they were being disturbed at all hours and it upset his wife. She's unwell.'

Paton recalled the man's anger the night before and felt a tug of guilt. 'Refer it to Interpol immediately. I'm sure the French police will be keen to track Nigel down, especially if he's extended his business dealings there too.'

Paton approached the other officers with anticipation. Was this to be the big break he was hoping for?

'What did you find at the breaker's yard?' he asked.

'Quite a stash, boss.' The young officer couldn't keep the excitement from his voice. 'There were several chassis with the VINs ground off. We found three reported stolen cars, a pile of catalytic converters waiting to be cleaned up and packaged, and a box full of specialist keys and decoders. Quite an operation, I'd say. There's also a workshop around the back where we think damaged cars that have been bought at auction are repaired and sold on without proper safety checks or genuine MOTs. There were some in the workshop that had clearly been involved in accidents. I'm sure we'll find out more when we contact the auction houses. This is car theft on a huge scale.'

Paton couldn't help the feeling of pride at initiating such a successful haul. This was a significant achievement and he hoped this would go some way to appeasing the DCI, once he found out about Paton's deception. What was important now, though, was finding Louie and catching the criminals who ran the operation.

'Were there any people working, or did anyone turn up while you were there?' Paton asked.

'The place was like the *Marie Celeste*, boss. Not a soul in sight. They must have somehow got wind we were coming, or maybe Nigel laid them off the day before.'

'Possibly,' Paton said.

Had Becki tipped them off? With the day being so manic, he'd completely forgotten that she was in his house, waiting to see if Tommy came home. He'd better call her soon and tell her to go to her mother's place, or a hotel even. Anywhere, as long as she left his house. He didn't want to be associated with her. He was in it up to his neck as it was. He needed time to think everything though and decide what to do about her. Hopefully, she'd take his advice and speak to her supervisor and confess to sharing information with the gang, without the need for him to intervene.

'Have the officers returned from searching Mabel Grimstone's place?' Paton asked, looking around the incident room. He couldn't see them.

'They've just arrived, boss. I think they're on their way up.'

Paton hurried to meet them. He hoped they'd found evidence of Louie in the house. They needed to be sure about Mabel Grimstone before they announced publicly that she'd abducted him.

'We've taken several prints from around the cottage to match those on the letter written by Mabel Grimstone. We're fast-tracking them because of the urgency of this case, so you should have the results in twelve hours,' the SOCO said. 'We have good news too. We found the notepad she used and there is an imprint of the letter on the next page. We've also discovered prints we believe belong to a small child, so we've sent a SOCO to the family home to take prints from Louie's toys. It appears the child was in the cottage. The CSI team have found hair with follicles in the bed and, possibly, saliva on a wooden spoon that has had cake mix licked off it. We also found the story books that Darren Woodrow described. In fact, the whole place was as he described it.'

Paton felt a wash of relief lighten the burden on his shoulders. The child had been at the cottage, probably well cared for, as Darren Woodrow had said. Now they just had to find where Mabel might have taken him for the day.

'Did you find a photograph of her?' Paton asked.

'That wasn't so easy, I'm afraid,' another officer said. 'We only found some very old photographs of what must be her with her parents. I suppose when you live an isolated life there isn't anyone to take pictures of you, and you're hardly likely to get professional ones done.'

This was true, Paton thought. Even with family around he couldn't think of any photographs of himself that had been taken in recent years.

Douglas saw the group talking and left his desk to join them.

'We've been onto the DVLA and discovered that Mabel Grimstone owns a silver Nissan Micra,' he said, and read out a number plate. 'We've also found out she's sixty-two years old, lives alone and has lived at that address for forty-seven years. Prior to that she lived at the farm belonging to Darren Woodrow's grandfather. The DVLA have sent us her photo.'

'Have you checked ANPR for her vehicle?'

'Her car was recorded in Perth and then heading out on the A9. Unfortunately, she must have left the main road for smaller B roads, as we have no trace of her after that.'

'What about places to visit with children? Have you come up with a list of possible venues?'

Paton's heart was thumping. They were so close now.

'There are several options. If Mabel continued in that general direction, then she could be heading to Broadslap play barn and farm shop café, or the Auchingarrich Wildlife Centre, or Blair Drummond Safari Park, or even doubled back to Noah's soft play centre. There are several other venues in the area too.'

Paton rubbed the side of his face with the palm of his hand.

'Let's hope the public appeal leads to some sightings, once we publicise Mrs Grindstone's photograph. We can prioritise any leads we receive in this area first.'

He looked at his watch and his stomach fluttered with nerves. Less than an hour before he appeared before the media. He'd better call Becki and ask her to leave his house. Paton also needed to tell Ursula and Tommy to watch the news. Tommy would never forgive his dad if he missed it.

Chapter 71
1PM

Child missing - 52 hours

Tommy

All Tommy needed was a tub of popcorn and the kitten on his lap and his day would be complete. He sat on the edge of the sofa, his eyes glued to the screen, as Ursula turned up the volume.

'Dad's the best,' he said, unable to drag his eyes away to see if she was as excited as he was.

His dad was going to be on the telly! He couldn't wait to go back to school to see if his friends had watched it. They all knew about his dad because he'd been to their school and talked about catching the baddies. His friends had even been allowed to sit in a police car. They thought DI Paton was cool too.

'I'm going to be a detective one day,' he'd told them. 'I helped my dad solve a case.'

He had too, when he'd heard something at the bus stop. It was his proudest moment. He hoped his clues were going to help this time, as well.

Ooh, how exciting! There was Dad, walking into the room and sitting on a chair at the front. There were lots of lights flashing and Dad blinked. His eyes were very red and he looked like he did when he worked lots of days in a row. He had his best tie on, though. Tommy's chest swelled with pride and he couldn't help looking at Ursula. She smiled back at him and put up her thumb.

The lady next to Dad was young and pretty. She sat up straight and smiled.

'My name is Katie Lock and I'm the media liaison officer. I'd like to introduce DI Paton from the Perth and Kinross constabulary, Perth City North division. We are here today to appeal for witnesses to the abduction of a small child. DI Paton will give you the details, but I'm afraid there will be no opportunity for questions at this stage.'

She touched Dad's arm and he jumped.

He looked worried. Like when *24 Hours in A&E* came on the telly and they were showing an operation and loads of blood. Dad hated blood. It made him throw up. Tommy hoped Dad didn't throw up now.

Dad cleared his throat and looked at his papers, then he lifted his head and stared right at Tommy through the telly screen, as though Tommy was the only person that mattered in the whole wide world. Tommy bounced up and tucked his foot under his other leg. He lifted his arms up and down, unable to hold in his excitement.

'We're making this appeal for a missing boy aged almost three,' his dad said.

A picture of a little boy with blond hair, blue eyes and a laughing face came up. Then Dad carried on talking.

'His name is Louie and he was last seen with an older woman who we now think may have abducted him. We have reason to believe she is still in this area, but there is some possibility she could be slightly further afield. She's driving a silver Nissan Micra.' Dad read out a numberplate, then showed a picture of a grey-haired lady. 'Louie is likely to be wearing a blue coat and yellow wellington boots. If you see this woman and child, please do not approach them but call the incident room number or Crime Stoppers.'

Dad then read out two numbers and pointed to them on a big picture behind his table.

Dad had told Tommy that he was looking for a missing boy but what about the nasty men who had taken Tommy? Wasn't Dad going to talk about them too? Tommy was a bit disappointed. He thought Dad might mention the clues he'd given him. Still, his dad was on the telly doing his job of being an important policeman and that was all that mattered.

'I repeat, if anyone knows anything, please call the incident room or Crime—'

Before Dad had finished his sentence all the people in the room started shouting at him.

'DI Paton, where was the boy taken from and where was the mother at the time?'

'Do the family know this woman?'

'How long has Louie been missing?'

Tommy was shocked. Didn't these people know it was rude to all talk at once? Everyone was calling Dad's name and his head moved from side to side like he was watching tennis. He opened his mouth but nothing came out. He looked at the pretty woman next to him and she tipped her head towards the door as if to say, 'Let's get out of here.'

Dad picked up his papers and stood but people were still shouting.

'Wasn't there something on Facebook about a missing boy two days ago?'

The room went suddenly quiet then the shouting started again.

'DI Paton, if the boy went missing two days ago why haven't you asked the public for help before?'

'Are you up to this task, Paton?'

Chapter 72
1.30PM

Child missing - 52 hours 30 minutes

DI Paton

The questions were relentless and, as Paton crossed the room, his neck tightened, sending throbbing pain up and across his scalp. His mouth was dry and his heart was kicking in his chest. God knew what Tommy must be thinking, especially when the journalist questioned whether he was up to the job. Paton was beginning to wonder that himself. He needed to get out of this stuffy room fast and had been hugely grateful when Katie indicated that they should leave. As they rushed towards the door more questions were thrown at them.

'Hey, Paton, wait. Is it true the mother left him in the car alone with the keys in it?'

Paton froze momentarily then stepped around a chair, his eyes firmly fixed on the door.

'Is this a case of neglect? Are Social Services involved?'

'If you find Louie, will he be taken into care?'

'Is it a criminal act to leave your kid in a car with the engine running?'

Even closing the door behind them didn't stop the questions ringing out. Bloody hell. This was exactly why he hadn't wanted to call a press conference. He hoped Melanie wasn't watching. He needed to call Cheryl straight away and tell her what had happened. He had to stop the parents checking social media. Facebook, Twitter and Instagram would be going crazy now.

Had it been worth it? Would the public be on the lookout for little Louie, or would their attention be more focused on baying for Melanie's blood?

Cheryl answered within three rings.

'How did it go?' she asked.

'Did the parents see it?' Paton held his breath.

'I told them it was best not to and they agreed. Reluctantly. I had a quiet word with Simon and warned him the press could be unpleasant, so he backed me up.'

Paton let out his breath in relief and told Cheryl of the questions he'd been bombarded with.

'They're probably going to sniff out where the family live. It's been on Facebook, apparently, but until now it was just rumour, so I doubt people paid it too much attention. Keep the curtains closed and tell the parents to stay indoors, and under no circumstances answer their phones unless it's from their nearest and dearest. This could get nasty.'

'The SOCO was here earlier,' Cheryl said. 'That was upsetting for the parents but also gave them hope. The officer also took hairs from Louie's brush.'

'I've just heard the letter matched a notepad in Mabel Grimstone's cottage,' Paton said. 'We think Louie was there. You can tell the parents and say it appears he's been well looked after. Mabel is an older woman who, so we're told, was unable to have children of her own. We think she's taken him to a children's play centre or zoo. In fact, could you go and ask them where he'd most like to visit? Mabel has intimated in her letter that her plan is based around something Louie will love.'

'Hold on, I'm in the back garden.'

Paton heard the door click and muffled voices.

'He absolutely loves animals, they both said, so you'd be best off focusing on zoos and farms. They're excited by the progress you've made.'

Paton was excited too, but they didn't have Louie yet.

'You'll be the first to know if we find him.' He paused. 'I mean *when* we find him.'

As soon as he reached the station, Paton called his team together for an impromptu meeting in the incident room. He was desperate to know what they thought of the appeal, but didn't want to ask in case they thought he was fishing for compliments about his presentation. He needn't have worried. Judging by the comments that erupted as soon as he entered the room, the press conference was at the forefront of everyone's mind.

'I bet half of them have left their kids in the car for a few minutes.'

'How many parents get their kids out of the car when they pay for petrol?'

'Blood sucking leeches.'

Paton raised his hand and the room fell silent. He wanted to rant about the press too, but he had to lead by example. Being the SIO on a high-profile case was a lot tougher than he'd envisaged.

'We need to minimise the damage to the family now by cracking on with finding Louie. So far, we've ascertained that Mabel is a single woman with no known relatives. She doesn't have any previous and, so far, the house-to-house calls haven't led to anyone who knows her. The only person with any knowledge of her is Darren's grandad and he tells us she's always been desperate for kids of her own. We've reason to believe she's taken Louie to a farm or zoo, so I need officers on stand-by to follow any leads that may come in from the public appeal and our enquiries with local children's attractions. I want to be told straight away of any sightings in this region.

'Moving on to the suspect with the broken leg, who's currently awaiting hospital discharge.'

Paton nodded to a DC who had visited the hospital. The young officer took his cue and stood up, almost knocking his chair over. He grabbed the back of it and his face coloured.

'We've checked the hospital CCTV and a man, who we now believe is known as Wiggy, was seen approaching the A&E desk to report a friend outside with an injury. Apparently, he'd left Spanner – as the suspect with the broken leg is known – on a bench near the car park, then, when the porters went to fetch him, Wiggy ran off. We've checked CCTV in the car park and ANPR cameras locally. The vehicle was last recorded driving along Feus Road. We've visited several garages and workshops in the area and encountered another of the possible suspects. The one described as wearing a distinctive shark-tooth necklace and having a black thumb nail. He denied seeing a white van or changing numberplates, but we've brought him in for questioning.'

Paton nodded his approval, delighted that Tommy's information seemed reliable.

'Let's hope Shark-tooth's prints match those in the barn where the stolen parts were found.' Paton turned to Douglas. 'Any news from the telephone network on Roachford's contacts?'

'It seems the gang have been swapping their burner phones

around, but we've managed to ascertain that, over the previous days before his arrest, Roachford was in regular contact with Wiggy, Spanner and Darren Woodrow. We've got transcripts of texts and they show meeting arrangements. There's evidence of Wiggy saying he'll collect the lads and drive them to Burrelton.'

'According to Woodrow,' Paton added, 'the lads were dropped off somewhere with no money, so their only means of getting back was by stealing a car.'

The eager young DC raised her hand again, as she had done in the previous briefing.

'No need to put your hand up,' Paton smiled at her. 'We're not in school now.'

'Please, sir, may I go to the toilet?' an officer nearby teased her in a childlike voice. She turned and pulled a face at him, then laughed.

Paton was pleased to see she had a sense of humour as well as enthusiasm for the job.

'Have the MIT investigating the murder of Gus Chambers found any links to the car gang yet, boss?'

'Good question. All we have so far is a witness statement saying one of the attackers was wearing jeans with a ripped pocket similar to those Roach owns, but it's not enough yet. They're currently focusing on tracking down the thugs known as "The Dogs".'

Douglas looked up from his phone, something Paton wouldn't normally allow in a briefing, but Douglas was his IT guru so he knew it would be work-related.

'Have you seen social media, boss?'

'Not yet but I can hazard a guess at what's being said.'

'Everyone is blaming Melanie Cameron rather than the two scrotes who nicked the car. They're saying she's not fit to be a mother, and if Louie's found, he should be put into care.'

Paton sighed. This was what he'd been dreading and why a CRA may not have been the best course of action.

'What angle have the press taken?' he asked.

'They're saying the mother is a bad parent, the police aren't doing enough and crime rates are rising, meaning no one is safe these days.'

Paton felt his guts tighten in anger.

'Let's not waste any time on these people,' he said. 'I'll see what leads we have locally then we'll follow them up.'

Paton closed the briefing and went to the room set aside for the call handlers. He picked up the call sheets and scanned down them. Several caught his eye. A witness had called in to say she knew a woman called Mabel Grimstone who'd been to the farm shop, where she supplied her eggs, a couple of days ago. Mabel was with her cousin's granddaughter who was called Louise. The witness thought it was odd, as it was well-known locally that Mabel had no family.

Paton would send someone to question the witness straight away. She could help them identify Mabel. Another caller said he'd seen a child fitting Louie's description at the front of an HGV heading south down the M74 and another had seen him in London riding up front in a milk float, of all places. The phones were going crazy as people claimed to have spotted the boy all over the country. Some could be genuine, but some were clearly from people inventing stories just to be a part of the drama. *What sad lives they must lead*, thought Paton.

He stood next to a call handler and listened in.

'And what is the child wearing?' she asked.

'How old would you say the woman is, roughly?'

'Do you know what car she's driving?'

He watched as the call handler scribbled Silver Nissan Micra and Blair Drummond Safari Park on her notepad and turned it towards him. His heart hammered with excitement and he almost snatched the phone from her.

'DI Paton here. Can you tell me the exact time you last saw them? Are they still there? Don't approach them but keep a close eye on them. Send a photo if you can take it without the woman noticing. The call handler will give you a number to text it to. We're on our way.'

Chapter 73
3PM

Child missing - 54 hours

Mabel

Louie giggled as a meerkat climbed out of his lap and scrambled up his arm to perch on his head. It sat there quite happily making Louie grin. Another young meerkat ran past, pursued by its siblings who caught up with it and rolled around the floor in a play tussle. Louie followed them with his eyes but didn't move. Mabel wished she had her phone with her to take a photo, but she'd had to leave it behind in case the police tracked her down too soon. She'd taken B roads for the same reason.

This day had certainly been the happiest of Mabel's life, in spite of the constant threat of being stopped by someone. She knew Darren would have found the letter, and wondered if he'd had the guts to confess to what he'd done and hand the letter in. He seemed a nice enough lad but then he had stolen a car. She wished now that she'd taken a bit of time to get to know him better but her whole attention had been fixed on Louie, and Darren had been like a buzzing fly threatening to land on her prized cream cake.

If there were any alerts out for Louie, she might be spotted soon. This time she'd made no attempt to disguise his gender or change his clothes. She'd even called him Louie in front of the waitress when they'd sat in the café, as Louie tucked into smiley-faced potato shapes, beans and mini sausages. She almost wanted to be caught so that their time together could end on a happy note.

Mabel knew she couldn't keep Louie, especially now she was aware he had a medical condition. She was keeping a close eye on him and would call for help at the first sign of any seizure activity. He seemed well today and his thrill at being with the animals infused her with a deep happiness that would sustain her through the dark days ahead.

Unless people had experienced it for themselves, Mabel thought, no one would be able to understand the profound loneliness that infected every moment of every day. The isolation of her existence was gnawing at her guts like a starving rodent that could never be sated – until Louie burst into her life, like a firework on the darkest of nights. Such colour, such magnificence, such awe-inspiring wonder.

Louie was a seam of gold in the hard granite of her life. It had been worth shattering her world for this precious gift, however short-lived. Mabel knew she was heading for prison ,and all the horrors that may reside there, but she'd never be alone again. Her memories of Louie would be her closest companions. Her only concern now was for her animals. She hoped an animal rescue charity would find them loving homes before the plentiful supply of food and water she'd left them ran out.

The meerkat leapt off Louie's head, and he stood and brushed sand off his trousers.

'Can I have ice-cream?' he asked.

'You can have whatever you like, my sweet boy.'

Louie slipped his hand into Mabel's and they left the barn and went back to the café. Mabel studied his perfect features as he tucked into the bowl of pink and yellow ice-cream.

'Can we come back soon?' he asked between mouthfuls. 'Can Noah come too?'

Mabel would cut off her right arm if it meant she could bring Louie back here, but it could never happen. She couldn't risk another night with him being away from his family. Night times seemed to be when he had his seizures. If the police didn't find them by teatime, she'd have to hand Louie in.

As Louie scraped the last of the ice-cream up and licked his spoon she thought she heard a distant siren. Her stomach flipped over and her mouth went dry. This was it. They'd found her. She helped Louie off his chair and back into his blue coat then took him outside to an open green area. Better they do this where there was space and fewer witnesses.

She bent down and picked Louie up. He wrapped his arms around her neck and his legs around her waist and snuggled his face in. She breathed in the distinct smells of baby shampoo, meerkat and strawberries. The cars had turned off their sirens and were approaching silently across the grass.

'I a monkey,' he said, giggling.

'You are indeed,' Mabel said, her eyes filling with tears. She waited as the cars got nearer.

'Why you crying?' Louie asked, leaning back and peering into her face.

'I'm crying because I'm happy and I love you,' she said.

'Mabel Grimstone.' An older man with thinning hair had

climbed out of a police car and was walking towards her. 'Put the child down, please,' he said.

Mabel kissed Louie's forehead then lowered him to the floor. A policewoman stepped forward and took his hand, and he looked up in surprise as she led him away.

'I'm arresting you...'

Mabel didn't listen to his words. All her attention was focused on Louie ,who'd tugged his hand away and was running back to her. She hunkered down and reached for his tiny hands. The policeman paused as though allowing her this last goodbye.

Mabel took Louie's little fists, that had wrapped around her forefingers, and pressed them to her eyes to stop the tears.

'Don't forget me, Louie,' she said. 'Just remember that I love you and always wanted the best for you. You've given me more joy than I could ever have dreamed of.'

The policewoman returned and spoke to Louie. 'We're going to find Mummy and Daddy now.'

Louie gave Mabel a questioning look.

'Go with the nice lady,' she said. 'She'll look after you and take you to Mummy.'

Louie smiled at Mabel then touched her wet cheek before turning away. The policeman stepped forward again, and Mabel was surprised to hear a catch in his voice as he spoke.

'I'm arresting you on suspicion of abduction...'

Mabel stopped listening. She straightened up and stood to watch Louie getting into the car. She waited until it turned and drove away before she crumpled to her knees and allowed the sobs to wrench from her tight chest.

Chapter 74
LATER THAT EVENING

DI Paton

It was late by the time Paton turned the key in the front door and allowed Tommy to enter the hall in front of him. He was utterly exhausted, but hadn't been able to refuse Ursula's kind offer of a meal she'd just cooked for both him and Tommy. She'd really tried, bless her, and Tommy had helped her with the preparations, but the roast potatoes had been too hard, the vegetables too soft and the gravy like jelly. He supposed they had to be grateful the chicken was cooked through. God, he missed Wendy's cooking. He missed Wendy. So much so, that he could even smell her familiar perfume on the air.

'Mum! You're home,' Tommy cried as soon as he entered the lounge. 'Dad, Mum's back.'

Paton hurried in behind Tommy and was delighted to see his wife clambering up off the sofa. 'You're a sight for sore eyes,' he said, and took her into his arms. He held her to him and buried his face in her soft hair. 'God, I've missed you.'

She pulled away but held his forearms, then kissed him full on the lips.

'Ooh, get a room!' Tommy said, and they both broke into helpless giggles.

'Where have you heard that?' Paton gasped, wiping his eyes.

Tommy grinned. 'On the telly,' he said.

'Come here.' Wendy opened one arm and drew Tommy into a group embrace. He smiled happily.

'Anything much happen while I've been away?' she asked.

'Not much,' Tommy said.

Paton gave Tommy's arm an extra squeeze. *Good lad*, he thought. He'd told Tommy not to say anything and let his dad explain everything.

'Tommy, how about making us one of your lovely cups of tea each while I chat to your mum?'

As Tommy left the room, Paton perched on the sofa and pulled Wendy's hands to sit her down beside him.

'I don't quite know where to start,' he said.

'At the beginning?' Wendy said.

Paton quickly recounted Louie's abduction, the boys who'd stolen the car and the crime ring. He omitted Tommy's kidnap. He'd tell her that at the end. He described in detail how he'd found Mabel and the heart-rending scene where she'd handed Louie over. Wendy was silent throughout but Paton could tell she empathised with Mabel. He then went on to say how they'd apprehended the gang.

'The one called Spanner waited for the security guard to go to the toilet then tried to escape. He detached his hospital equipment but hadn't counted on the fact that he'd need crutches. Our officer was coming out of the lift with a coffee when Spanner saw him. Spanner tried to escape down the stairwell but lost his balance. He now has a broken arm, too, and has finally admitted defeat and squealed on those up the line in the gang.' Paton recalled the cheer that had gone up in the incident room at this news. 'We arrested them an hour ago and they're now in custody. The French police even picked up Nigel, the breaker's yard owner.' Paton had wanted to dance around the office at this point.

Tommy came in with the tea and set it on the table.

'Dad was on telly,' he said. 'Did you see him? He found the little boy. He's a hero.'

'I was on the train,' Mum said, 'so haven't seen any television. I had my head in a book the whole journey. You'll get a commendation for this,' she said, turning to Paton.

'I'm afraid not,' Paton said. 'I've been suspended pending investigation.'

'What? Why?'

'Wendy's face drained of colour as Paton told her how he'd taken Tommy to the breaker's yard with him and of Tommy's subsequent kidnap.

Her mouth hung open with shock.

'I can't believe you didn't tell me. No wonder you wouldn't answer your phone. I'd never have forgiven you if something had happened to Tommy. Promise me you'll never put him in danger again.' She reached across and took Tommy's hand. 'Or keep secrets from me.'

'I'm sorry, Wendy. I was frantically trying to track Tommy down and knew how you'd worry.'

He and Tommy would need to broach the subject of the kitten in the shed soon, or they'd be keeping more secrets from her.

'Dead right I would. You should still have told me anyway. What do you think will happen now?'

'There's a lorryload of mitigating circumstances around

why I didn't report Tommy missing, but it will be harder to defend the reasons why I took him to the breaker's yard.'

'But surely they won't dismiss you after all you've achieved.' Wendy pursed her lips and shook her head. 'We can't afford for you to lose your job, Dave, especially now.'

Chapter 75
TWO WEEKS LATER

DI Paton

'Sit down, Dave.' The DCI gave him a tight smile that didn't quite warm his eyes. 'As you've probably surmised, we've completed our investigation into your possible misconduct.'

Paton's stomach was twisted with tension. 'Before we go any further, sir, I've been doing a lot of thinking and there's something I'd like to say.'

'You can tell me when we've concluded this business,' the DCI said.

Before Paton could interrupt again the DCI went straight into what was clearly a practiced speech.

'You're a great detective, Dave. One of the most tenacious and resourceful I've had the pleasure of working with. Sadly, though, your judgements are sometimes impaired – largely due to your noteworthy commitment to your family. I understand it's difficult for you when you have a son with Down's, and a wife with bouts of depression, and I know they rely heavily on you. It's inexcusable though, for you to have taken your son to work with you, the day you visited the breaker's yard. You put him at great risk. Yes, you told him to wait in the car, and no, you didn't know at the time that Nigel was part of a much bigger crime ring, but the rules are there for a reason. I overlooked it when you brought Tommy to the station on that occasion last year, and I even went so far as to allow him to do his work experience in the canteen, but I'm afraid you seem to be somewhat of a loose cannon where Tommy is concerned.

'The other area of possible gross misconduct was continuing to run Operation Oakwood when your son had been snatched by suspects who were clearly linked to the case.'

Paton was beginning to feel nauseous. How could he face the team again? He opened his mouth to speak but the DCI held up his hand.

'Let me finish,' he said. 'Again, I acknowledge that you did it with the best of intentions, given the shortage of senior officers and the urgent need to find Louie and the gang members, but your decisions must have been influenced by events with your son and you weren't fit emotionally to run such a high-profile case.

'Aside from all this, you've done a bloody good job in apprehending this gang and we now have, we think, the entire sorry lot in custody. Your actions have significantly reduced the amount of car crimes in the area and made Perth a safer place to live and work.'

A wave of relief swept over Paton. 'If I could just say something, sir...'

'You'll get your turn in a minute, Dave. Be patient. With regards to finding little Louie, I'd just like to say your decision to delay the CRA was the right one. If you hadn't tracked Louie down so quickly after the press conference, I think the parents' lives would have been a living hell. The press were outside their house within half-an-hour. There are also some sick and sad people out there – keyboard warriors, I think they're called – who like nothing more than to stir up trouble for people, with their vicious and harmful comments. They'd already started posting skewed opinions on Facebook. However, you'll be pleased to know that Louie has settled nicely back in with his family and seems to have suffered no after-effects. His mother and brother Noah have some anxieties, but they're getting help with that.'

Paton was glad to hear Louie was doing well. Despite his desperate need to say something, and hear the final outcome of the investigation, Paton couldn't help asking, 'What's likely to become of the two lads and Mabel Grimstone?'

'I'd expect Darren Woodrow to get off with a spell of community payback, but Roach and the two lads known as "The Dogs" have been identified in the video that recorded the assault on Gus Chambers. They've been charged with murder. It's now for the experts to decide who gave Gus the fatal kick in the head.'

Paton winced. 'And Mabel Grimstone?'

'I'm not so sure about her. She cared for the boy well enough but, when all was said and done, it was what we call Plagium – or child stealing. It dates back to the Victorian era. Did you know that?' The DCI gave Paton a piercing look. 'She didn't return him when she should have done. Louie could so easily have had a major seizure leading to permanent disability or even death. I'm sure a jury will have some sympathy for her circumstances and history, but she may be facing a spell in prison.' He paused and frowned at the papers on his desk. 'Given her lack of previous convictions, the fact that she merely found the boy instead of taking him might make the sentence more lenient, but the case will be heard in the Sheriff and Jury Court. If she's lucky she'll just be admonished. At worst she'll get five years, but I very much doubt it will get to that.'

The DCI looked up abruptly.

'We're digressing, Dave.' He cleared his throat. ''Okay, the outcome.'

Paton could feel a pulse beating in his temple.

'After taking into consideration all the circumstances surrounding your work performance, the investigation determined there was neither misconduct nor gross misconduct. Therefore, given all you achieved in your role as SIO, we'd like to reinstate you as DI with immediate effect. However, I have been asked to implement improvement action.'

His good name was intact. What a relief.

'Thank you, sir. That's wonderful to hear. However, as I said earlier, there's something I need to tell you.' Paton cleared his throat and looked down. 'Wendy and I have been discussing our future. We haven't told anyone yet, but Wendy is now ten weeks pregnant.'

He glanced up to see the reaction to his news.

The DCI's face was a picture. He stared, open-mouthed at Paton.

'Forgive me for asking, Dave, but was this planned? I didn't realise you were trying for another.'

At your age, Paton added in his head.

'Wendy's eight years younger than me, sir, and she's wanted another child for years. I have to confess it was a surprise.'

He laughed self-consciously as he remembered how stunned he'd been at Wendy's news. His brain had rewound to the previous month as he'd tried to recall whether Wendy had been uptight or low in spirits. He couldn't recall anything and was surprised that it hadn't registered with him. He must have been so busy with work that he hadn't noticed the absence of the usual monthly upsets.

'I was nervous at first but now I feel quite excited. Tommy is beside himself at the idea of getting a brother or sister.'

Paton felt a warm glow as he remembered how Tommy had performed his happy dance around the room when they'd told him.

Paton watched the DCI and let him squirm for a moment. No doubt he was wondering how Paton would cope with even more family responsibilities, and was probably regretting Paton's exoneration from the allegations against him.

'So, is this what you wanted to say?' the DCI asked.

'Wendy and I have come to a decision. I'd like to take retirement, sir. I've just completed thirty years of service, so I think I qualify. We're planning to move back to Weymouth. Wendy's mother is getting frail and, rather than admit her to residential care, we're going to move into the family home and arrange home carers for her. The house needs a lot of work, but it's big enough for all of us and worth the investment. It'll be Wendy's one day anyway.'

The DCI stood and shook Paton's hand.

'Congratulations, Dave. We'll be sorry to lose you, but I can understand your decision. You'll certainly need more time with your family. In fact, you're the second person leaving to be with their family.'

'Really? Who else?'

'Becki has just handed in her notice after being on two weeks' holiday. She's moving to the Isle of Wight permanently, to live with her brother.'

'Still working for the police?' Paton held his breath, hoping Becki had taken his advice in exchange for not reporting her misconduct.

'She's taking a complete career change. Training to be a

social worker, apparently, because she wants to help people with autism and social disabilities.'

Paton felt his shoulders relax. It was highly likely Becki would have lost her job, so this way she could start afresh and do a job she still felt was worthwhile.

'Will you do anything with your time, Dave? I can't imagine a man with as active a brain as yours being at home all the time.'

'Oh, I've got big plans, sir. I'm going to open my own private Investigation business and Tommy is going to be my assistant.'

The DCI sat back down in surprise then slapped his knee and laughed.

'Well, I didn't see that coming! Good luck to you, Dave. I'm sure you'll both do well.'

Chapter 76
EIGHT MONTHS LATER

Dear Darren,

How's life on the farm and how's your grandad? I can't begin to tell you how much your letters brighten my days in this place. Your stories of little Tyler cherishing his plants and regular updates of how many eggs you've sold lift my heart. Thank you again for taking care of the animals. Little Louie loved Flump and Humbug so I'm really grateful to you for taking them in.

How's the community payback going? I'm so pleased they put you onto the ground maintenance scheme. I bet the roundabouts and parks of Perth are looking much finer for your tender loving care.

I had a meeting yesterday with the powers that be and they've said I may be released in the next four weeks due to my good behaviour. The time here has gone quite quickly considering I spend a lot of time in my cell. Thank goodness for books! I was wary of other prisoners at first but I've become something of a mother figure come agony aunt to the young women here. I've promised to keep in touch with some of them when I leave.

I've done a lot of thinking in my cell and I've come to realise that I was foolish to let one event take over my life. I've wasted so many years wallowing in bitterness and disappointment that I've missed many opportunities to find happiness. Being with Louie made me see that I could have so much to offer with the care of children but sadly my criminal record will prevent me doing any paid or voluntary childcare in future. I've decided instead, to offer my help to the local animal sanctuary. I've a lot of love to give and the animals there will be in dire need of it. My probation officer is helping me to get an interview with them.

I'm so pleased you've said we can be friends when I leave here and for seeing me as a good person. I can't wait to spend time with you, Tyler and your family and promise I'll keep you safe. We can do so many fun things together. You and Tyler will both love the safari park and I'll be able to tell you about the voluntary work I'll be doing.

Please give my regards to your grandad and thank him for taking care of the chickens. I bet he's relieved to have you helping on the farm. It must be a huge task for one person and it keeps you from mixing with the wrong sort.

I'll be in touch again when I have a release date.

Your friend,

Mabel Grimstone

Chapter 77
NINE MONTHS LATER

Dave Paton

'What do you think, son?'

Paton watched Tommy's face closely as he looked around the room. Dust motes, lit up like tiny fireflies, danced in the beams of sunlight that spread into warm, buttery slices across the rough wooden floor.

Tommy stepped further into the room and stroked the gritty old shelves lining the walls before going to the window and looking down onto the busy street. Paton went to stand next to him. Tommy remained silent.

'If you crane your neck to the left you can just see the sea from here,' Paton said, 'and the tall clock. I'll be able to check if you're late for work.'

Tommy turned to his dad.

'Will I have my own desk?'

'Of course. We can put it there or there. You choose.' Paton waved an expansive arm around the small room.

'Will we have a kettle?'

Paton pulled a wry grin at Tommy. 'As if you need to ask.'

Tommy's eyes filled with tears and Paton stepped back in alarm.

'Don't you like it?'

'I love it, Dad. I'm just so happy I might burst.'

Paton pulled him into a rough hug.

'I'm glad. I wanted you to see it first but now we need to get home. It's my turn to feed Flossie... and your turn to change your sister's nappy.'

Tommy grimaced then laughed.

'One more thing before we go, PI Tommy. We need to come up with a name for our new Private Investigation Company. Any ideas?'

'*The Sweeny?*'

'I think that's been done before and younger people might not know what it means.'

'I do.'

'That's because you watched my old box set constantly. Any other ideas?'

Before Tommy could answer a voice drifted into the room. 'Hello? Are you moving in?' A petite young woman with pixie hair and huge eyes peered around the door. 'I heard there were new tenants.' She put out a delicate hand, and Paton shook it carefully, afraid of hurting her.

'I'm Tiffany. PA to Duncan Broadfoot. He's the solicitor next door.'

'I'm Dave Paton and this is my son, Tommy.'

She held out a hand to Tommy, too, and he took it with a beaming grin.

'We're detectives,' he said, puffing his chest out. 'We're going to catch baddies and help find missing people for rewards. I got fifty pounds because I found a kitten. The owners said I looked after her really well.'

'Tommy was upset, when he had to give her up but the reward cheered him up,' Paton added.

'Tiffany's eyes widened as she looked from one to the other. 'You're detectives?'

'My dad was a very important policeman. He was on the telly. He's left now because I've got a baby sister. I'm going to be his left-hand man.'

Tiffany laughed. 'Don't you mean right-hand?'

'I'm left-handed,' Tommy replied, his face serious.

'Are you really detectives?' Tiffany asked, turning her attention to Paton.

'We will be soon. Tommy is my assistant.'

'In that case, I might be your first customer. I'm trying to track down my missing brother. Can you help?'

Tommy's eyes widened and Paton watched him carefully. He didn't want Tommy getting too excited and alarming Tiffany with his over-enthusiastic happy dance.

'Tommy, you know the coffee shop at the end of the street?'

Tommy nodded. 'Do you want a coffee, Dad? I'll get it.'

'Good lad. Perhaps you can get Tiffany one too while she tells me all about her brother.' Paton gave him a £10 note and Tommy headed for the stairs. 'Then when you get back, I'll tell you all about it. After all, a good assistant should always know what's going on.'

Tommy nodded, pausing on the top stair.

'Shall I call Mum and say we'll be late?'

'You're just trying to get out of the nappy changing,' Paton teased. 'Good idea though. We don't want her worrying.'

Tommy grinned. He took his phone from his pocket and tapped on his mum's photo as he walked downstairs.

'Watch where you're going,' Paton called after him. 'And don't forget we need a name for our agency. You can think about it while you're queuing for coffee.'

Acknowledgments

Writing can be a solitary experience, but over the years I've built up a network of great people who support, encourage, advise and inspire me.

Lesley Eames, you are the biggest influence in my writing career. From the early days as my tutor, then editor and now friend, you have motivated me, been brutally honest but constructive in telling me how to improve, praised me when I got it right and delighted in my successes. I wouldn't be the writer I am today without you.

Lynn, Alan, Graham and the real David Paton – thank you for reading my early drafts and giving your honest opinions. I will always listen to your sage advice.

Graham Bartlett, thank you for answering my random questions on police procedures and keeping me on the straight and narrow. I can hold my head high knowing we've got the facts straight and I can enjoy pointing out the flaws with the police dramas on TV to my husband, Keith.

Most importantly, I'd like to show my heartfelt gratitude to Rebecca Collins and Adrian Hobart of Hobeck Books. You have been, and continue to be, amazing publishers, and I'm hugely honoured to be one of the Hobeck family. Your commitment, hard work and dogged determination to succeed is inspiring and exciting. I hope we continue on this journey together for many years.

KERENA SWAN

About the Author

Kerena Swan (known as Kerry to friends and family) has spent her working life supporting children and adults with disabilities. With a social work degree and 25 years' experience working in Social Services, latterly in senior management, she left the safety net of her career to set up a care agency for children with disabilities. After receiving an 'outstanding' rating, nearly losing her eyesight and being diagnosed with cancer, she decided it was time for a fresh challenge and to tick 'getting a book published' off her 'yet to achieve' list. She signed up for a novel writing course and within a year had received an offer from a publisher for her first novel. Three books later Kerena was delighted to be offered the opportunity to write a series for Hobeck Books featuring the tenacious DI Paton and his engaging son, Tommy.

Here She Lies

Buried truth is hard to find ...

Here She Lies, a tale of family trauma and guilt, introduces DI Paton and his son, Tommy, the stars of the gripping crime series by Kerena Swan.

Harry

It is the middle of the night when Harry receives a shocking phone call from his estranged sister, Stacie. Despite being sworn to secrecy, terrified and haunted by what he's been told, Harry is compelled to tell the police.

DI Paton

DI Dave Paton has a hunch that all is not as it seems with Harry's story. But can he unravel the mystery?

To download your free copy please go to the Hobeck Books website **www.hobeck.net**.

Blood Loss

BLOOD LOSS
DI PATON INVESTIGATES: BOOK ONE

FAMILY TIES, FAMILY LIES
KERENA SWAN

DI Paton Investigates Book 1

WINNER OF THE CHILL WITH A BOOK PREMIER READERS' AWARD!

Sarah

With one eye on the rear view mirror and the other on the road ahead, Sarah is desperate to get as far away from the remote Scottish cabin as she can without attracting attention. But being inconspicuous isn't easy with a black eye and clothes soaked in blood...

... and now the fuel tank is empty.

DI Paton

When a body is discovered in a remote cabin in Scotland, DI Paton feels a pang of guilt as he wonders if this is the career break he has been waiting for. But the victim is unidentifiable and the killer has left few clues.

Jenna

With the death of her father and her mother's failing health, Jenna accepts her future plans must change but nothing can prepare her for the trauma yet to come.

Fleeing south to rebuild her life Sarah uncovers long-hidden family secrets. Determined to get back what she believes is rightfully hers, Sarah thinks her future looks brighter. But Paton is still pursuing her...

... and he's getting closer.

Praise for Blood Loss

'This is no doubt the first of a block-busting series.' Graham Bartlett, bestselling author of *Bad for Good*

'...in the same league as Ian Rankin and L J Ross...' Graham Rolph

'My arms broke out in goose-bumps! Wow!' Susan Hampson, *Books From Dust Till Dawn*

'Oh my word, *Blood Loss* was one hell of a start to what I am sure will be a fantastic series. I was drawn into the story from the very start.' GingerBookGeek

'This book had me hooked from the start.' Sarah Burbidge

'Blood Loss is a page-turner from the beginning, and the suspense never eases up.' Felicia Denise

Hobeck Books - the home of great stories

We hope you've enjoyed reading this novel by the brilliant Kerena Swan. To find out more about Kerena and her work please visit her website: **www.kerenaswan.com**.

This novel is the second of full-length DI Paton Investigates, of which there are many more to come. Kerena has also written a prequel novella to the DI Dave Paton investigates series *Here She Lies* which is free as an ebook to subscribers of Hobeck Books. To download your copy visit the Hobeck website.

Also please visit the Hobeck Books website for details of our other superb authors and their books, and if you would like to get in touch, we would love to hear from you.

Hobeck Books also presents a weekly podcast, the Hobcast, where founders Adrian Hobart and Rebecca Collins discuss all things book related, key issues from each week, including the ups and downs of running a creative business. Each episode includes an interview with one of the people who make Hobeck possible: the editors, the authors, the cover designers. These are the people who help Hobeck bring great stories to

Hobeck Books - the home of great stories

life. Without them, Hobeck wouldn't exist. The Hobcast can be listened to from all the usual platforms but it can also be found on the Hobeck website: **www.hobeck.net/hobcast**.

Finally, if you enjoyed this book, please also leave a review on the site you bought it from and spread the word. Reviews are hugely important to writers and they help other readers also.

Other Hobeck Books to Explore

Swindled

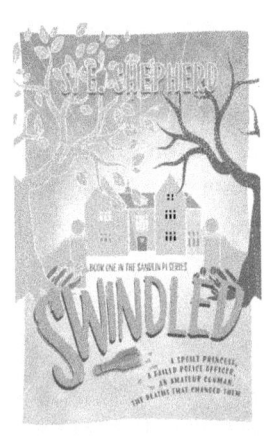

'A great debut mystery thriller with a touch of cozy.' Advance Reader

'...will definitely takes your breath away...an absolute stunner of a thriller...' Surjit's Book Blog

'He's out there somewhere. He's taken everything from me, and ... I hate him!'

Lottie
Beautiful, but a little spoilt, Lottie Thorogood leads a charmed life. Returning home from horse riding one day, she finds a stranger, drinking tea in the family drawing room – a stranger who will change her life, forever.

Hannah
After a bad decision cut short her police career, Hannah

Sandlin is desperate to make her mark as a private investigator. She knows she has the skills, but why won't anyone take her seriously? She's about to become embroiled in a mystery that will finally put those skills to the test and prove her doubters wrong. It will also bring her a friend for life.

Vincent

Vincent Rocchino has spent his life charming the ladies, fleecing them and fleeing when things turn sour. How long can he keep running before his past catches up with him?

Over Her Dead Body

A B MORGAN
OVER HER DEAD BODY

THE QUIRK FILES BOOK ONE

CAN GABBY'S DEATH CHANGE HER LIFE?

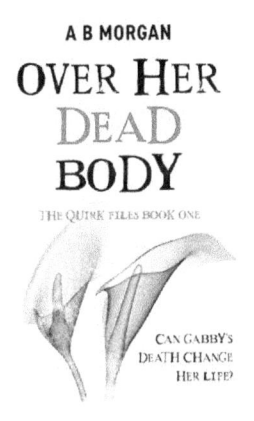

'OMG WHAT A PAGE TURNER!! ... I finally turned the last page at 2am.' Peggy

Gabby Dixon is dead. That's news to her...
Recently divorced and bereaved, Gabby Dixon is trying to start a new chapter in her life.

As her new life begins, it ends. On paper at least.
But Gabby is still very much alive. As a woman who likes to be in control, this situation is deeply unsettling.

She has two crucial questions: who would want her dead, and why?
Enter Peddyr and Connie Quirk. husband-and-wife private investigators. Gabby needs their help to find out who is behind her sudden death.

The truth is a lot more sinister than a simple case of stolen identity.

Hobeck Books – the home of great stories

Daria's Daughter

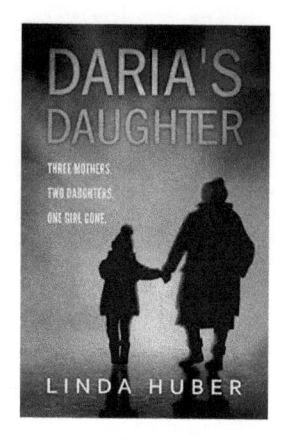

A mother and daughter torn apart
An explosive accident on the way to Glasgow airport leaves Daria hurt, bereaved and confused. Her daughter has vanished without a trace and nobody is telling her what happened. Evie's gone. That's all. Gone. What does Daria have left to live for?

A mother and daughter reunited
Margie can't believe it. Bridie is hurt. Bridie needs her. They manage to escape the smoke, the noise and the confusion. They are together, that's all that matters. Everything will be better in the morning, Margie tells Bridie. And it will.

The bonds that never break
Will Daria ever be able to put the pieces of her tattered life back together after the loss of her daughter? Is it possible that things aren't quite as they seem? Can the unimaginable turn out to be the truth?

Also by Kerena Swan

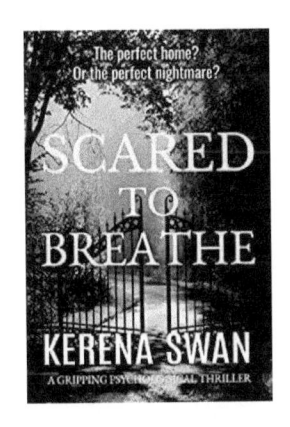

A COMPELLING SUSPENSE THRILLER
WHO'S THERE?
Friends can't always be trusted
KERENA SWAN